Praise for the novels of Renee Ryan

"*The Widows of Champagne* is a standout among its historical fiction peers. The struggles, betrayals and fear of war-torn France is a moving backdrop to a story whose heart is centered around the complicated love between mothers and daughters, and the sacrifices one makes for survival."
—Karen White, *New York Times* bestselling author

"*The Widows of Champagne* is a riveting novel of WWII France. I held my breath many times as the three generations of widows negotiated the treacherous landscape of war. Highly recommended."
—Robin Lee Hatcher, Christy Award–winning author of *Make You Feel My Love*

"With complex characters and a stunning setting, *The Widows of Champagne* will sweep you into a wartime story of love, greed, and how one should never underestimate the strength of the women left behind. I couldn't put it down. Fans of Kristin Hannah will love it!"
—Donna Alward, *New York Times* bestselling author

"Exquisitely crafted, masterful storytelling. Do not miss this book!"
—Heather Burch, bestselling author of *One Lavender Ribbon*

"A story of valiant women, detailed in its research, moving and tense."
—Natalie Meg Evans, author of *The Dress Thief*

Books by Renee Ryan

Love Inspired Historical

Charity House

The Marshal Takes a Bride
Hannah's Beau
Loving Bella
The Lawman Claims His Bride
Charity House Courtship
The Outlaw's Redemption
Finally a Bride
His Most Suitable Bride
The Marriage Agreement
Stand-In Rancher Daddy

Love Inspired

Thunder Ridge

Surprise Christmas Family
The Sheriff's Promise

Village Green

Claiming the Doctor's Heart
The Doctor's Christmas Wish

Visit the Author Profile page at Harlequin.com for more titles.

THE
WIDOWS *of*
CHAMPAGNE

RENEE RYAN

LOVE INSPIRED
INSPIRATIONAL ROMANCE

LOVE INSPIRED®
INSPIRATIONAL ROMANCE

Recycling programs
for this product may
not exist in your area.

ISBN-13: 978-1-335-42707-6

The Widows of Champagne

Copyright © 2021 by Renee Halverson

This edition published by arrangement with Harlequin Books S.A.

For questions and comments about the quality of this book, please contact us
at CustomerService@Harlequin.com.

Love Inspired
22 Adelaide St. West, 40th Floor
Toronto, Ontario M5H 4E3, Canada
www.Harlequin.com

Printed in U.S.A.

To Veuve Clicquot, Pommery, Laurent-Perrier and Bollinger,
the real widows of Champagne, who with their courage,
their business acumen and their trailblazing innovations
turned sparkling wine into the world-famous beverage it is today.

No weapon that is formed against thee shall prosper, and every tongue that shall rise against thee in judgment thou shalt condemn. This is the heritage of the servants of the Lord, and their righteousness is of me, saith the Lord.
—Isaiah 54:17

"Remember, gentlemen, it's not France we are fighting for, it's champagne."
—Winston Churchill

THE
WIDOWS *of*
CHAMPAGNE

Part One

Chapter One

GABRIELLE

Reims, France. 3 September 1939

Beneath the creaking bones of the ancient château, clocks chimed from room to room, speaking to one another in a secret language all their own. Gabrielle LeBlanc-Dupree moved quickly through the darkened corridors, counting off each peal as she went. Twelve in total.

Not enough time. It had to be enough. Evil lurked on the horizon, prowling like a hungry lion. Tonight, Gabrielle would prepare for the unthinkable. That she had to act alone only heightened her sense of urgency. And pushed her feet faster. Faster.

Wrapped inside the thick folds of her cloak, she exited the house as soundless as a wraith. She'd taken this path hundreds of times, thousands, down the twenty-one stone steps, through the vineyard, past the champagne house, and into the miles of limestone caves cut beneath the chalky earth.

The frigid wind blew over her face, carrying the scent of rain and decay, a stark reminder that the Lord had taken His hand off her family long ago. History haunted the LeBlanc vineyard like an uninvited ghost at a christening. *We are people marked by war,* her grandmother said. *The soil is drenched in blood and death.* More was coming.

Gabrielle kept moving, never faltering, never stopping to wail against the unfairness of two enemies bearing down on her. The rain let loose, waging its relentless war on the vines her family had tended for two hundred years. The weather was proving a more immediate threat than the evil lurking on the other side of the Maginot Line.

One bad harvest would not ruin them.

The other enemy very well could. Hitler and his ravenous henchmen showed no mercy. They conquered. They invaded. And then, they looted. If France fell into Nazi hands, they would not get the best of the LeBlanc treasures. Not if Gabrielle succeeded tonight.

All but running now, she unlocked the heavy door and plunged into the wine cellar cut into the stone beneath the vineyard. She hurried past the racks of upturned bottles maturing under the 24-volt lights. This young wine, not yet champagne, was her family's legacy. Their future.

The bottles at the back of the cellar represented their past. Gabrielle had personally selected the most valuable blends from the last two decades. She'd also chosen from the previous century. Most notably the single-vintage 1867, and the infamous 1811, rumored to be of remarkable quality because a comet had crossed over Champagne that year. Finally, and not without much internal debate, she'd added five hundred bottles of the celebrated 1928.

When she'd first come up with her plan, she'd considered confiding in her grandmother and perhaps, in that moment, she would have, if the rain hadn't started up again and pulled her attention to the vines. Now, she was glad for the interruption. What her grandmother didn't know, she couldn't worry over. Gabrielle alone would carry this secret, this burden.

Twenty thousand bottles were a mere drop in their stock, but enough to start over if the worst happened and the Nazis—

She did not let her mind finish the thought.

She went to work instead, constructing one horizontal row of stone at a time, bottom to top. Last week she'd instructed her vineyard manager to place the stones in this part of the cellar. He'd given her no argument. His loyalty had encouraged her to confess her intent. But he'd stopped her, hand on her arm, and said, "What is left unspoken can never be repeated."

Pierre was not wrong, but Gabrielle could have used his help tonight. Her unschooled methods proved full of error. And wasted precious time. Beads of sweat trickled into her eyes. She wiped at her face with her sleeve, hardly noticing how the dirt coated her hands and dug under her cracked fingernails.

Her muscles cried out from fatigue.

One hour turned into two, two into three. Then, she stepped back and her stomach swooped from satisfaction to despair in an instant. Her construction was faulty at best.

Someone will notice the wall. Only if she let them in this part of the cellar.

She kept building. Until one gruesome task remained. Teeth gritted, she retrieved the jar she'd left hidden in a nearby wine barrel. Dozens of spiders crawled over their fellow prisoners, each attempt at escape a miserable failure. Gabrielle could not feel sorry for their plight. She hated spiders. Nevertheless, they would serve their purpose.

Hands shaking, she released the little devils. They scattered across the wall, invading their new home with focused, frightening precision. The creatures would spin their webs. They would capture their prey, eventually creating an archaic façade over the freshly laid stone.

Feeling as old as the champagne house, Gabrielle exited the cave and stepped into the dark nothingness before dawn. A moment of utter aloneness laid siege on her tired brain. She nearly stumbled under the weight of it but managed to keep moving toward shelter, toward home. The rain still fell, slow and steady, stippling the puddles at her feet.

Back in her room, she tossed her clothing in the basket with the other muddied garments she'd worn in the vineyard the previous day and the one before that.

Promising herself she would take a short rest—a few minutes, nothing more—Gabrielle collapsed atop her bed. She fell into a fitful sleep, dreaming of crumbling walls and giant spiders. The grotesque bodies marched across a bloodred field, their eight legs becoming four then morphing into Nazi swastikas. They circled around her, round and round, spinning, spinning until her arms and legs were trapped and she could no longer move. No longer breathe.

She woke gasping for air, her heart battering against her ribs. Only a dream, she told herself, not real. She blinked into the predawn light, again and again.

But the terrifying images of spiders remained.

From that day forward, the eight-legged little monsters would remind Gabrielle of war.

Chapter Two

JOSEPHINE

In the still moments before dawn, Josephine Fouché-LeBlanc wandered among the sodden vines she'd tended the past sixty years, first with her husband, then with her son, and now with her beloved granddaughter whose name she couldn't quite recall. It was there, just on the edges of her cluttered mind. If she concentrated hard enough. Just a little harder...

Gabrielle. Yes, Gabrielle. The younger woman was the heart of the vineyard now, as Josephine had once been. Her granddaughter would usher Château Fouché-LeBlanc into the second half of the century, not Josephine.

The end of her struggle drew near. The Lord wanted her home. She could hear Him calling her to Glory. Antoine would join her there. Or would she join him? The latter, of course. Her husband had been gone for many years.

Her mind wanted to play tricks on her this morning, the battle stronger than usual. She was ready to succumb. Once the harvest was complete. Then, only then, would she submit to the irresistible whispers swirling in her head. The dark, seductive lure was always there, like a breath in a stillroom inviting her to simply let go.

So very tempting.

A light drizzle accompanied her as she slogged along a path her feet remembered, even if her mind did not. The world was eerily quiet, neither dark nor light but a blur of muted grays. The solitude helped her think, to sort through the creeping chaos in her mind.

Josephine treasured these moments alone with her darling vines, as precious as children. She knew each vine intimately. The sense of recognition was a physical ache in her chest.

She paused, looked around until she had a better sense of where she was. On a clear day, standing in this very spot, she could see across the sweeping hills peppered with Fouché-LeBlanc vines and their immature grapes. The vineyard stretched to a point beyond where the eye could see, all the way to the very edges of the world. It was a whimsical thought, and Josephine was anything but a woman prone to whimsy. Those days had died with Antoine, then been permanently sealed in their son's coffin.

A bird cried in the distance, jerking Josephine out of her painful memories.

She'd lost track of time.

Much had to be done before she welcomed Champagne's finest citizens into her home. The party celebrating Château Fouché-LeBlanc's two-hundred-year anniversary would be her last. Josephine was too old for parties. Nevertheless, this one would be spectacular. For the sake of the ones she'd lost too soon.

She began retracing her steps.

The château rose in the distance, three stories high, the

ivy-covered marble hidden within the morning shadows. The windows appeared menacing as they stared down at her, like black, hollow eyes in a condemning face. A trick of the light. Still, she shivered.

The air hung heavy, bloated with the earthy scent of the rain-soaked soil. Josephine shivered again. Would today be full of sunshine and optimism? Or would the sky continue its watery attack? She wanted to cry over the invasion of such an unpredictable enemy. She usually disliked submitting to emotion, but, today, she allowed the tears to come. The drizzle chose that moment to turn into rain, sliding down her cheeks. A silent collaborator, as if knowing she wanted her tears camouflaged, even from herself.

Lord, call me home. I am ready. But that wasn't true. Too much left undone.

Josephine paused midstep and wiped at her cheeks. She felt a pang of déjà vu so strong her mind leaped over forgotten decades, the individual years immaterial in the bittersweet journey.

Past folded over present, stopping at a single moment. The first time she'd met these vines she'd wept as she did now, but in awe and wonder.

Antoine had taken her hand and leaned in close. "Tell me, *ma chère*, what do you think of your new home?"

Hopelessly naïve, Josephine had shifted from one foot to the other. Behind the tangle of blushes and schoolgirl innocence, she'd been desperate to impress her husband of a few hours. She'd wanted him to think of her as a woman, not the wide-eyed ingénue he'd married to merge his champagne house with her father's. And yet, she'd answered with the truth spilling from her heart. "It is where I belong."

The sense of homecoming was as real now as it had been

that fateful day, when she'd been an untested bride to a man much older than her seventeen years.

"Yes," he'd agreed, looking pleased, the smile lines deepening at the corner of his eyes. "This is where you belong."

Their union had been a business arrangement between two powerful families, but their marriage had turned into a grand love affair for them both.

"We will make many babies, you and I."

She'd managed to give him only one, a boy.

"They will tend the vines with us and grow to love the land with the heart of a true *Champenois*."

In that, their son had not disappointed.

"Our life, it will be good for us both."

She'd blushed then, caught up in the picture he'd painted of their future. Later that night, he'd made the promise again, but with a very different meaning. "It will be good for us both."

Antoine had been a compassionate man, and a patient tutor both as a husband and a *vigneron*. He'd taught Josephine how to let the vines set the rhythm of their lives, to tend the grapes, to sample the *vin clairs*, and then, with uncanny accuracy, to predict how the base wines would mix together to make something truly magnificent. The Great Transformation, he'd called the process.

Josephine loved her small corner of the world, the rolling hills, the vines that had replaced the children she'd miscarried. The subsoil made up of fragile shells from ancient marine animals held a special place in her heart. She could hear the chalky earth whispering forgotten secrets from a time when dinosaurs roamed these hills.

The siren's song had her stooping to the ground and scooping up a handful of dirt. She stared at the wet clump, the grizzled hand not that of her younger self but of the seventy-seven-year-old woman she was today.

She blinked again and again, and then, at last, she no longer held wet earth. She saw only the dry soil of decades before leaking through her seventeen-year-old fingers. She reveled in the warm feel of that ancient dirt sifting through a hand unscarred by time and toil. The sensation was as vivid as it was real, the experience an almost mystical connection to God's creation.

Josephine knew her mind was playing another cruel game, tricks upon tricks. But this time, she wanted to disappear into the lie. She wanted to escape from the harsh realities of dismal weather and looming war. She was tired of death robbing her of loved ones. Would it be so terrible to spend a moment in a time before her life had been touched by tragedy?

The chalky soil warmed her palm.

Was this real, or just a memory?

She didn't know.

Momentarily caught between past and present, she breathed in slowly, hoping to find her way. But where did she want to go? Back to when life was bright and easy? So tempting.

She breathed in again. The foul scent made her recoil, a touch of death to the nose, and that was it. She was once again standing in the present. The wet, decayed soil was unbearably cold in her hand, yet she dropped the clump as if it were a ball of white-hot fire.

Rain continued falling from the dreary sky, sliding beneath her collar. The grapes would be decimated by rot and mold. Gabrielle and her workers would prune, check for fungi or disease, and tie back shoots that came loose. Day after day, week after week, month after month, they had waged their war valiantly. They would still fail.

The enemy was too strong.

The enemy was crafty and cruel.

The enemy was…

Her feet were cold.

Josephine looked down. She was standing in mud that wanted to claim the top of her boots. How long had she been frozen in this moment to have sunk so far into the earth? A few minutes? An hour? The sky with its deceptive cloud cover gave her few clues.

Go home.

Josephine hurried back to the house. It was a fifteen-minute walk, enough time to gather her thoughts into some semblance of order. Back in the kitchen, routine took over. She stripped off her coat, then climbed out of her muddy boots to pull on thick, dry socks. She made a pot of strong coffee, then moved to the scarred table, cupping the steaming mug between her palms.

Her thoughts grew fuzzy again. Luring her, always so enticing. Her mind wanted to drift back across time, back to happier days full of nothing but brightness. She would not allow such frailty of spirit. *Still so much to do for the party tonight.*

Tonight? Was the party tonight? She thought maybe yes.

How had she missed the passage of two whole days?

She stood on shaky legs, glancing around at her surroundings. She'd come to the kitchen for a reason. Brushing the wet strands of hair off her face, she paced a bit until she remembered. The list. The one she'd begun the night before. Remembering now, she snatched it out from beneath a stack of other papers on her writing desk. Placing her mug on the table, she sat and studied the empty page.

Empty page? Her list had somehow vanished in the journey from desk to table.

No matter. She would start again.

Pencil poised over the paper, she forced herself to concentrate on the party. The champagne would flow freely, that much Josephine promised herself. They would serve only the best. Definitely the 1928. She wrote it down. The '37, possibly the '26. She made another series of notations. Once started, the ideas poured quickly from brain to hand to list.

Preparing for the anniversary party made Josephine proud of the past and gave her hope for the future. Perhaps all was not lost. Château Fouché-LeBlanc had survived tragedy before. Bad harvests had given way to better ones. Economic crises had forced them to move into international markets. Even untimely death had taught those left behind to fend for themselves.

There was much to celebrate.

A fragment of paper, torn from somewhere—she couldn't remember where—slipped from tabletop to floor. Josephine reached for it. Words blurred as she laid the ragged page gently back on the table. She ran her fingertips over the looping text. Her handwriting. That was her handwriting.

When had she made this list? Today? Yesterday?

Unearthly silence settled over her. Darkness beckoned, seductive and full of false promises. Shutting her eyes, she confronted the familiar battle with her legendary iron will. One day, she would lose this fight, but not today.

No, she vowed. Not today.

Chapter Three

GABRIELLE

Church bells rang from the Cathédrale Notre-Dame de Reims. The high-pitched peals rolled through the village, across the vineyards, summoning children to their breakfast, families to worship and, inside the room on the top floor of the château on the hill, they pulled Gabrielle gasping out of her terrifying dreams of spiders and war.

Staring up at the ceiling, she silently traced a thin crack in the plaster from one corner to the other. Her heart carried a similar scar, no longer a gaping wound, but there. Always there.

She stretched, trying to relieve the ache in her arms. Her palm met the sterile, empty spot in the bed beside her. Her life wasn't supposed to be like this. She wasn't supposed to be alone. Squeezing her eyes shut, she searched for a peace that always seemed just out of reach. For the strength she needed to carry on another day. Nearly five years had come and gone, and she still hadn't gotten used to facing life without the man who'd been her best friend first, then her companion and confidant and, for too brief a time, her husband.

Forcing open her eyes, Gabrielle considered the hours upon hours that lay ahead. Hours of battling the elements with only one goal in mind. Save the grapes.

A nearly impossible feat at this point in the growing season.

Nevertheless, she would contend with the weather, for her family. The ones lost and the ones still alive. It was enough. That's what she told herself when she slid out of bed and began the process of dressing for a long, punishing day among the vines. Most of Reims would attend Mass today. There would be no Sabbath for Gabrielle.

The sound of the tolling bells faded, but the ringing remained in her ears, a constant reminder that Reims was a city of cathedrals. From her earliest memories the church bells had marked off every important event in her life. They told her when to wake, when to work, when to break for meals. They called her to worship, to celebrate a marriage, a birth, and to mourn. Gabrielle had attended too many funerals in her twenty-seven years.

There would be more. As certain as this year's harvest was ruined, war was coming, death its eager companion. God had forgotten France. Nothing would stop what was coming now. Not even the celebrated French army.

She attempted to stretch away the stiffness in her back. Every muscle protested, her arms especially. With effort, she tied the tangle of dark, sleep-mussed hair off her face, then moved to the small, circular window that overlooked the vineyard. The sun spread tentative fingers through a seam in the clouds, as if trapped in a moment of uncertainty. Unfortunately, the decision was already made. A band of thunderclouds boiled over the northern skies, moving quickly toward the vineyard.

It was moments like these when she missed Benoit most. Her husband had taught her to love the process of growing grapes. Even now, as she stared out over the sodden vines, his favorite phrase came to mind. "August makes the must." The must—juice from the grapes—was the first and most important step to making champagne.

A dry hot August was always better than a cold wet one.

She exited her bedroom on a sigh and hurried toward the back stairwell that emptied into the château's kitchen. Marta, the family's housekeeper, would already be on her way to town. A devout woman, she honored the Sabbath with as much dedication as she served Gabrielle's family. One more person Gabrielle must protect now that the men in her family were gone and her grandmother was succumbing to old age.

Hesitating outside her sister's room, she debated a moment, then, as quietly as possible, pushed open the door and smiled at the sleeping form. Paulette would turn seventeen next month. The girl hadn't a care in the world, beyond what dress to wear or which boy to flirt with next.

So unlike Gabrielle.

Paulette had arrived after their father returned from the Great War, the child that would save their parents' failing marriage. She'd been born out of false hope. Étienne LeBlanc had come home too damaged by his experience, while his wife had remained too unchanged by hers. Hélène hadn't really tried to make the transition smooth for either of them, favoring her baby over the empty shell of a man her husband had become.

Étienne's wounds hadn't shown on the outside. The mercurial temper, the inability to enjoy life, these were only a few of the demons that had tortured him. He'd died a wretched man.

Gabrielle's husband had suffered similarly, though Benoit's illness hadn't been caused by war.

A pang of grief whispered through her, dark and consuming. And she was wasting precious time. With a noiseless click, she shut her sister's door. By the time she reached the kitchen, Gabrielle felt weary and worn to the bone, the sort of exhaustion that would take a thousand years to sleep off.

She stepped into the scent of coffee. And froze.

Her heart took an extra hard beat. Her grandmother sat alone at the scarred table in the center of the room, head bent over a single sheet of paper. In the gray morning light, Josephine Fouché-LeBlanc looked somehow smaller, frailer and every bit of her seventy-seven years.

The need to protect came abrupt and fierce. Widowed at thirty, Josephine had dedicated her life to turning Château Fouché-LeBlanc into one of the premier champagne houses in the world. She claimed her success was due to the rosé recipe she'd created by blending pinot noir wine with white champagne instead of the usual elderberry juice.

Gabrielle knew better. Château Fouché-LeBlanc thrived because of Josephine's dedication to preserving her husband's legacy. The two had been united in their collective vision until the day Antoine died unexpectedly from a ruptured appendix.

It seemed the LeBlanc women were destined for heartbreak, all of them widowed too young. God had spoken, leaving them to face the world without their husbands. For her part, Gabrielle would not feel sorry for herself. She would accept her lot in life and follow in her grandmother's footsteps. She, too, would dedicate the rest of her life to the champagne house.

It was not so terrible a fate. Remarkable, actually. A noble duty, but also a labor of love.

Josephine made a notation on the paper. The slight shake in

the older woman's hand was new, as was the soft mumbling. Josephine never mumbled to herself—until recently.

Gabrielle cleared her throat.

Her grandmother didn't look up, which increased her worry a hundredfold. Josephine's hearing loss was a stark reminder of the older woman's mortality. *I am not ready to lose her.*

When that day came, she would be alone, truly alone, despite the others living in the château.

It was a dismal thought best not explored. "What are you working on, *Grandmère*?"

Faded blue eyes rolled up to meet hers, confusion swirling in their depths. It appeared the older woman didn't immediately recognize her own granddaughter. Then she blinked. Once, twice, a third time. Finally, the clouds in her gaze disappeared. "Ah, *ma chère*, come. Sit. We have much to do before the celebration this evening."

"The party isn't for another two days."

Silence met her remark.

"Grandmère, did you hear what I said?"

Several more blinks, a slight shake of the head, and then Josephine scowled in her familiar way. The matriarch of the family had returned. "I know when the party is. I set the date myself. Now, stop frowning at me. I misspoke, Gabrielle, that is all."

"You have a lot on your mind." She pushed the words past the lump in her throat. This wasn't the first time her grandmother had shown signs of confusion. For months now, Josephine randomly referred to dead family members as though they were still alive and asked after workers long gone from their employ.

Eyes burning, Gabrielle sat down at the table and studied her grandmother's beloved face. Josephine was still an attractive woman. The lines of time and a life spent outdoors only added to her beauty. And yet she appeared overly tired this morning. Age was catching up to the iron will.

The older woman returned her attention to the paper.

Gabrielle lowered her own gaze. *No.* Her stomach took a slow, painful dip. *No, no, no.* "Are those the champagnes you wish to serve at the party?"

Years came and went before her grandmother spoke. "They are." The older woman struck out two, added three more in their place. "I am determined to serve only the best we have to offer."

Panic sliced through the fabric of Gabrielle's calm. "May I see the list?"

"It's not yet complete."

"Maybe I can help refine your choices."

After a brief pause, Josephine pushed the jagged piece of paper across the table.

Gabrielle read in horrified silence, her breath coming fast and hard in her lungs. She made it halfway down the page before she lost the ability to breathe at all. She should have prepared for this.

It was true that Château Fouché-LeBlanc was known for serving superior champagnes. This uncompromising dedication to quality was the hallmark of every gathering they hosted. But they always—*always*—reserved the truly remarkable for private family celebrations.

Gabrielle had counted on her grandmother following her usual pattern. And that was where she'd gone wrong. She'd assumed Josephine would treat this party like any other, when it was anything but.

"Grandmère." She spoke in an even cadence, while her heart pounded like wild wind. "Perhaps we should rethink some of your selections and serve the…" *Think, Gabrielle.*

Think. "…1924. It's what we always serve for parties as large as this one."

The '24 was a lovely, robust, single-vintage champagne. Not nearly as fine as the '28 or the '37, or any of the other wines her grandmother had selected for the party. But every bottle sat in its original place among the racks on the right side of Gabrielle's makeshift wall. A party, even as large as this one, would not deplete the massive stock of the champagnes she now suggested, at least not enough to draw suspicion.

"Gabrielle, *ma chère*, now is not the time for economy. The anniversary celebration will mark two hundred years of champagne making in this family. We must serve the very best from our cellars. We must honor the past."

Yesterday, she would have agreed with her grandmother. This morning, Josephine's words struck like a fist. Was she to be found out so soon?

"I beg to differ." Her voice held a desperate note. "Now is precisely the time to practice caution." *More than you realize, Grandmère.* "We cannot deplete our most valuable stock when there is no knowing what is to come from the harvest."

They would normally pick the grapes at the end of September. But due to the unprecedented moisture levels, Gabrielle predicted a late harvest, perhaps mid–October, or earlier if the sun came out from behind the clouds and stayed put.

Please, Lord…

She let the words trail off in her mind. Prayer was fruitless when spoken to a silent God. As if to prove her point, the threat of rain announced itself in a clap of distant thunder. They turned simultaneously to the window overlooking the vineyard and shared a collective shudder.

Josephine recovered first. "We have survived rainy seasons before." She plucked the list from Gabrielle's hand. "The Lord will provide again, as He has in the past."

Frustrated with her grandmother's unshakable faith, Gabrielle lowered her head. The Lord provided, it was true, but He also took. The searing pain of grief, the pent-up sorrow that came from too much loss, it was all so…unavoidable.

"Rain is only one of our enemies, Grandmère." Ignoring the fear churning in her stomach, she dropped steel into her voice. "The Nazis have invaded Czechoslovakia and now Poland. France *will* respond. War is coming. We must be prepared."

The older woman waved off her worries with a flick of her wrist. "While France is at peace, we will celebrate. It is the *Champenois* way."

Though Josephine spoke boldly, the older woman looked scared. She should be scared. The "war to end all wars" had come at great cost to France. No family in Reims had been left untouched by the slaughter.

Gabrielle started to argue her point further but was cut off by the delicate click of feminine heels. She glanced toward the doorway just as her mother entered the kitchen, the scent of May rose and jasmine following in her wake. A beautiful woman in her early fifties, Hélène wore a draping green silk dress that tied around her narrow waist, a bright, unexpected splash of color against the gray light. As out of place as the day Étienne had brought his young bride home. Despite years of living on the vineyard, Paris still clung to her, wafting around her trim body like the cloud of expensive perfume she wore.

"I am in agreement with Josephine." Hélène's silver-blue eyes slid past Gabrielle, brushed over her mother-in-law, then returned to her daughter. "In dark times such as these, we must take joy where we can. We will provide our neighbors with a spectacular party. They will be grateful for the respite."

Gabrielle had no ready response. If the unthinkable happened, and the Germans invaded France as they had other parts of Europe, they would come seeking spoils. There could be no cause for them to suspect bottles of Château Fouché-LeBlanc's finest champagnes were missing.

Perhaps it was time to confess what she'd done. Perhaps sharing this burden was the right thing to do. The ringing telephone prevented her from saying the words. Gabrielle stood, but her mother moved faster and reached for the receiver first. After issuing a short greeting, she said nothing more.

As the one-sided conversation continued, Hélène's face drained of color. She eventually thanked the caller, and then, with startling calm, set the telephone receiver back in its cradle.

One look at her mother's face and Gabrielle's first thought was of death. *"Maman?"*

"France has declared war on Germany."

Chapter Four

HÉLÈNE

With the horrible news lingering in the air, Hélène attempted to pull herself together. She stood quietly clutching her hands at her waist, tighter, tighter, until each knuckle turned white as bone. A movement from somewhere in the distance had her glancing out the window that overlooked the kitchen gardens.

Rain silvered the glass, obstructing Hélène's view beyond her own watery image. There was something chilling in that distorted reflection with the red lacquered lips and kohl-black eyelashes. Like looking into a lie. Not far from the truth. The line between her true self and the veneer she carefully constructed each morning was practically invisible now. The expensive makeup was a tool in her ongoing charade, as was the couture clothing she traveled weekly to Paris to purchase.

But now, the identity Hélène had so carefully built threatened to crumble at her feet. And the stakes were much higher. France was at war with the same enemy that had killed her husband. No, not the same enemy. Not Germany. The Third Reich.

And so, it continued. More secrets. More lies. The rewriting of histories all over again.

Hélène allowed herself a single moment of despair before smoothing a steady hand over her neatly coiffed head. No one could know of her inner turmoil, especially not the other two women in the room. She could feel their eyes trained on her.

Ignoring them—she was very good at ignoring them—she continued staring at her indistinct features in the glass. The blackness surrounding the faint image reflected the blackness creeping into her heart. Hélène knew what came next. Heartache and death, the blind waste of bright young men. The bloodletting would leave no family untouched. As before, France would become a nation of old men, abandoned women, hollow-eyed children and invalids.

Outside, the rain pattered on in a steady, endless stream. The harvest was ruined. It seemed the peasants' legend about war and wine was more than a cautionary tale. To announce the coming of battle, they claimed the Lord sent a bad crop. Hélène wished she didn't know what was coming. She desperately wanted to escape to Paris and lunch with friends who'd known her before Étienne.

Dear God…

The prayer remained unformed in her mind. As so many before it. Where was her faith when she needed it most? Not dead, surely. Merely dormant. She would resurrect it. For Paulette's sake. And possibly for her own. Hélène would not be defeated by war a second time.

Unfortunately, the politicians conspired against her. Cocooned in their smoke-filled rooms, with their expensive brandies in one hand and cigars in the other, they'd made the decision to go to war. Could they not have found another way to stop the Nazi bullies?

She felt the familiar fear rising, swamping her composure until her hands wanted to shake. She would not let them. Nor would she give in to the urge to crawl into a dark, lonely burrow and wait for the worst of her terror to pass.

That weakness was for another day.

Wrapping her signature calm around her like trusted armor, she turned her back on her image in the weeping window. "Monsieur Chardon will arrive within the hour. He and I will finalize the menu today." The caterer was the best in Reims. They had been wise to secure his services well in advance of the anniversary party. "Do either of you have requests I should convey on your behalf?"

This earned her identical blank stares. Both women seemed frozen in perpetual immobility. Hélène could not allow herself to sympathize with their numbness. The declaration of war was not something meant to be taken lightly, but she would not allow it to interfere with her plans.

She could hardly look at her daughter. Even in stunned silence, Gabrielle's face was too much like Étienne's. The feminine version of the perfectly shaped oval, the smooth, unblemished skin that refused to age. The finely sculpted cheekbones, the full lips and, most heartbreaking of all, the serious gray-green eyes. "Truly, Maman?" Gabrielle asked, once she recovered her voice. "The...menu?"

"Yes, Gabrielle. The menu." Hélène added a confident, breezy air to her words. "For the anniversary party."

The manner in which she spoke must have betrayed more than she'd intended, for Gabrielle became contemplative in a way Hélène had not seen in recent years, maybe ever.

"There are several details left undone." She punctuated her tone with finality.

"You cannot think we will have the par—"

Hélène cut off her daughter's objection with a shake of her head. "Oh, but we will. There will be many days for anguish and despair in the coming weeks." Perhaps even years, but not yet. *Not yet.* "We must carry on as usual."

"But, Maman, we should be putting our efforts into preparing for the enemy. We must—"

Again, Hélène spoke over her daughter. "The menu is nearly complete." Her voice sounded as cold as the blood rushing in her veins. She softened her tone, but only a little. This was no time for fragility. "There are choices Monsieur Chardon and I are in disagreement over. I will prevail. Nothing will prevent us from serving an exquisite selection of French cuisine."

"Hélène." Josephine surveyed her with equal parts frustration and resolve. "We are at war now. We cannot proceed as before. You understand, *non*?"

Hélène blinked at the forceful way in which Josephine spoke. How quickly her mother-in-law had switched sides. Gabrielle and Josephine, with their identical scowls, were once again a united front. Two against one. Their joining forces wasn't wholly unexpected, nor was it the first time Hélène had combated these particular odds.

Such familiar ground, she thought, with her looking in from the outside, never quite belonging in this family. Yet also an integral part. Without her, Gabrielle did not exist. No, Hélène would not be dismissed. Her voice would not be ignored. "Have you finalized the list of champagnes you wish to serve our guests?"

The question seemed to throw the other two off their guard. With wary expressions, both women glanced at the paper sitting on the table between them. They looked up simultaneously, then shared a moment of uncertainty. Ah, well, then.

Excellent. Their movements had been synchronized, but their alliance was still on unsteady ground. They had yet to decide which of them would take up the gauntlet against their common opponent.

Hélène took advantage of their temporary indecision.

She strode to the table, the click of her heels like hammers to nails, and picked up the scrap of paper. A quick scan told her all she needed to know. Josephine had selected the best of their champagnes, mostly single vintages, with a few unparalleled blends from the previous decade to round out the collection.

"I approve." She purposely returned the list to its place on the table, turning it slightly until it rested at the same awkward angle as before. "Our guests will be treated to a once-in-a-lifetime experience."

"This. Maman, *this*..." Gabrielle paused, visibly shuddered, then tried again. "This is not the time for celebration."

Oh, but it was. Hélène knew this better than most. She would not be swayed by Gabrielle's protests, which seemed overly intense, even for her serious daughter. "We must continue with our lives. To do otherwise is to let the enemy win before a single shot is fired."

"We are at war with Germany. You must understand what that means."

Hélène shook her head in disappointment. This daughter of hers, the one she so rarely understood, actually believed she didn't comprehend the magnitude of what was to come? Who better than she to know the harsh realities that lay in wait for the French people?

Pictures from the previous war lived in her mind, as did memories of the subsequent battles after the weapons had been laid down. She'd greeted her husband's return with such hope. Except, Étienne hadn't returned. Not really. He'd come home a walking invalid, his lungs burned from mustard gas, his mind shattered from the horrors he'd witnessed.

Étienne had taught Hélène a valuable lesson about war. It was only after the fighting that a soldier's wounds were revealed. For five agonizing years, her husband had battled his demons. Peace had only arrived in death.

Hélène had wanted to die with him. Who would miss her? Gabrielle had been working in both the vineyard and the champagne house with her grandmother by then, the two more mother and daughter than she and Gabrielle had ever been. Her oldest daughter had also had Benoit, her best friend at the time, a budding romance not far off. But Hélène had another child. Paulette had been little more than a baby at the time of her father's death. The child had needed a mother.

And so, in her youngest daughter, Hélène had found a reason to live.

Mon Dieu, the Nazis would not steal her purpose.

"We cannot allow the Germans to win before the fighting has even begun. Nothing has changed." *Everything has changed.* "We will hold the party as planned."

"Hélène." Josephine's soft voice came from what seemed a great distance, as if she was speaking through water. The older woman touched a light hand to Hélène's shoulder, making her start. When had Josephine moved to stand beside her? "I know what is in your thoughts. You lost your husband, and I lost my only son. We share that pain."

Hélène wanted to tell the woman she didn't need coddling. She didn't want her sudden, unexpected show of solidarity. And yet, she couldn't stop herself from saying, "Étienne was the best of us all."

"Yes, he was." The grief swimming in Josephine's rheumy eyes matched the emotion threatening to consume Hélène.

In that moment, they were allies, united in their loss of the man they had both loved. Hélène was aware of Josephine's unmasked pain. How could she not be moved by the raw sorrow in the other woman? This was the first time in years she'd spoken of her son. The circumstances surrounding his death were not a topic allowed in the LeBlanc home. Even the mention of his name was forbidden.

But now, less than an hour after France declared war on Germany, Josephine had a point to make. When the matriarch of the family had a point to make, it was always wise to listen.

"The French army is powerful," the older woman reminded her. "You mustn't worry. This war will not be the same as before."

"No," she agreed. "It won't be the same." *It will be worse.*

The Nazis were strong and clever, and very, very deadly. They operated without conscience. While Josephine returned to sit beside Gabrielle, their heads bent in whispered conversation, Hélène's mind conjured up images of this new and terrible enemy.

She'd seen the pictures. She'd watched the newsreels, horrified, as the marching masses of uniformed men saluted their leader, swastikas clinging to their outstretched arms. These modern German soldiers—so many of them—had hard, ruthless eyes. They were younger, rougher and more brutal than the men of the previous war. They had anger and hate in their hearts. Hate for people they deemed inferior. People like her father. Like her.

Hélène should have listened to her father, now living and working in New York with his brother in their family's bank. He'd foreseen this day. After he'd read Hitler's memoir *Mein Kampf,* he'd known what was coming. Hitler himself had warned the world what he planned. She should have moved her daughters from this home—this country—as her father had begged.

It is not too late.

Oh, but it was. Gabrielle would never leave Château Fouché-LeBlanc. She was too devoted to the vines and her grandmother. Paulette would be just as hard to lure away. She was a happy, popular girl among her friends. And she adored Paris. Hélène had made sure of that. *How did I not see this coming?*

"We will cancel the party." Josephine's voice was firm, her word final.

"We cannot cancel." She hated the lack of resolve in her voice.

Josephine held her stare. Hélène remained perfectly still, outwardly calm, her stony silence the final weapon in her arsenal. The tactic seemed to work.

"You are determined?" Josephine asked.

Hélène nodded, knowing not to ruin her argument with more speeches.

"Very well." The older woman glanced at Gabrielle, a silent warning in the look cast upward. "We will not cancel. We will postpone." Josephine swept her gaze back to Hélène. "We will hold the celebration after the harvest."

The matriarch had spoken.

Gabrielle did not argue.

Nor did Hélène, though it required great effort on her part. She wanted to remind her mother-in-law that waiting until after the harvest, although but a handful of weeks away, could prove too late. The battles could have already begun by then. But perhaps not on Champagne soil. The Maginot Line would provide the necessary fortification against the enemy. She refused to believe otherwise.

The thought ignited a spark of hope, and enabled Hélène to maintain her silence. She'd won this round. Not a great victory, but a victory she would claim for herself. Torn between triumph and new resentments, she lifted her chin at a proud angle. "I will inform Monsieur Chardon his services will not be required until after the harvest."

With nothing more to say, she turned to go.

"Maman?"

That whispered, almost cautious tone, so unlike her oldest daughter, had her glancing over her shoulder. The shattered look on Gabrielle's face made her heart ache. The young woman carried too much of the burden for their family. And did so without complaint. Hélène vowed to shoulder more of her share in the coming months.

She opened her mouth to make the promise, but Gabrielle was speaking again. "Do you think Paulette will be very disappointed we are postponing the party?"

"Yes. Very." And now Hélène's heart ached for her other daughter.

"How will you explain?"

Hélène fought back a surge of annoyance. Did Gabrielle know nothing of her own mother? Hélène indulged Paulette. There was no argument to be made there. And perhaps she pampered her youngest daughter beyond what was sensible. However, she rarely lied to the girl. There were omissions, evasions certainly. Sixteen was, after all, still so very young.

But, in this, no, Hélène would not shelter Paulette. "I will tell her the truth."

Then, she would pray. Oh, how she would pray, for her family, for her country, for the brave young men they would lose. And, of course, she would pray that the Maginot Line proved as strong as the government claimed, strong enough to hold back the Nazi animals.

Chapter Five

GABRIELLE

The LeBlanc women held their collective breaths in the weeks that followed. Each dreading, for her own reasons, the infestation of Nazis on French soil. Other than light skirmishes near the border town of Saarbrücken, it was as if France had never declared war on Germany. The fighting would begin eventually, no one disputed this. But as Hitler forced his will on the rest of Europe, the upcoming harvest took priority.

The rain continued pounding Champagne. Gabrielle battled the weather with the few workers she had left now that all able-bodied men had been conscripted into the French army. As she walked the vines, she thought of her husband. She tasted the grapes as Benoit had taught her—the only way to know if they were ripe—and checked for mold among the leaves. She cut away impending death with the razor-sharp clippers that had once belonged to him. She sampled, studied, snipped.

At last, on a cold day in mid-October, the wait was over.

"It's time to pick the grapes," she declared to her vineyard manager, a grizzled veteran of the previous war whose loyalty was without question. "We'll begin tomorrow at first light."

To his credit, Pierre did not argue her decision. Nor did he point out that the harvest was nearly three weeks behind schedule. He did, however, say, "We're woefully short of workers."

"We'll make do," she assured him. What choice did they have?

The following morning Gabrielle awoke to the familiar peals of church bells echoing in the gray light of dawn. The tolls did nothing to ease the heaviness in her heart, or the loneliness of orchestrating another harvest without Benoit. The day, she knew, would bring more despair than joy. Still, her purpose was clear. For the next two weeks, she would lose herself in the picking of grapes, her hands working by rote, every part of her swallowed up in the process.

Dressed in clothing to combat the cooler temperatures, she exited her room. The sound of the housekeeper's voice had her pausing on the threshold of the kitchen. Gabrielle didn't often eavesdrop, but something warned her to stay put awhile longer. Pressed against the hallway wall, she squeezed her eyes closed.

"You will eat every bite," Marta instructed the other occupant in the room, proving herself a prime example of French fortitude against a formidable opponent. "You will do this, or I will tell your granddaughter you are too frail to join her in the vineyard."

Holding back a gasp, Gabrielle peeked around the corner. Grandmère glowered at the massive pile of ham, goat cheese and freshly baked croissants. "It is too much."

Gabrielle winced at her grandmother's fractious tone. Marta was not so impressed. The short, sturdy woman had served the LeBlanc family since Josephine was a young bride. She had her role to play. And she did so with the conviction of a seasoned mother hen.

"You listen to me, Josephine Fouché-LeBlanc." Marta's voice held steel, and very little else. "The day will be long. You *must* fortify yourself."

Josephine subjected the housekeeper to her own brand of steel. She, too, had her role to play. She, too, did so with conviction. "This is not my first harvest. I know what is required."

"We waste time with this arguing. Eat." Marta nodded to the untouched food. "Or I will prevent your exit from this house."

It was no empty threat.

The fork found its way into Josephine's hand. And then, she took her first bite. She chewed slowly, and with very little enthusiasm. In that moment, as Gabrielle watched her grandmother struggle with this common task of feeding herself, grief exploded inside her heart, fueled by helplessness and bone-deep sorrow at the irrefutable fact that Grandmère was becoming too old to work the vines.

But she was not there yet. Her iron will was still very much alive. She would do her part this year, if slower and with difficulty. Even if Gabrielle didn't need the extra pair of hands, she wouldn't take that away from her grandmother.

She stepped into the kitchen. *"Bonjour à tous."*

"Ah, Gabrielle, *ma chère*." Grandmère smiled, her eyes tired but clear of confusion. That alone was a triumph. "There you are."

"Here I am." She took her place at the table.

Marta set a plate in front of her, followed by a mug of coffee. The liquid was hot and dark as petrol, exactly as Gabrielle preferred. The housekeeper moved to stand beside Josephine, a fist parked on one generous hip. "You eat like a bird."

"I am not much bigger than one."

The two women glared at one another. But there was soft-
ness in their manner now, a deep affection born from years
of proximity and routine. Suddenly, Gabrielle felt as if she
were on the outside looking in, an observer only, separate
and wholly apart. It shouldn't matter. But it did. It shouldn't
hurt. But, oh, it did.

"There was a day..." Marta let the rest trail away, perhaps
deciding it best not to remark on Josephine's recent weight
loss. At an age when most women fattened up, Grandmère
had grown too thin. More signs of what was to come.

The housekeeper shuffled to the sink, filled it with water,
then went to work scrubbing a dirty pan. Like Josephine, age
was catching up to Marta. She moved slower these days. The
passing years showed in her stooped shoulders and the lines
around her eyes and lips. A road map for her anguish. The previous war had taken her only son in the first wave of battles.

Too much death in this home, Gabrielle thought. Too much
loss. She sipped her coffee and turned her attention to her
grandmother. "Pierre and I are in agreement. We'll start on
the north end of the vineyard. And work our way south as
the picking progresses."

After a moment of strained silence, Josephine set down her
fork. "Do we... Is that..." She seemed to search for the words.
"Is it usual for us to begin so far away from the presses?"

The question cut deep. Gabrielle glanced away, unable to
bear the light of confusion staring back at her. "The grapes
suffered less rot atop the hills," she said softly, dropping her
words onto her own untouched food. "We'll focus on the best,
before we deal with the worst."

Silence met her explanation.

She dared a glance across the table. Josephine had gone
unnaturally still. Thinking, or possibly trying to grasp what
Gabrielle had just explained. "I understand, yes. Yes, I see."

But did she?

Abandoning her post at the sink, Marta went to Josephine and placed her hand on one of the bony shoulders. "Come, *mon amie*. Let's get you dressed for a day with your vines."

Josephine put her hand on the table and, with Marta's help, hoisted herself to her feet. "I will need my boots, I think."

"*Oui*. And your coat. The air is cold this morning." Marta shared a troubled glance with Gabrielle, then guided Josephine out of the kitchen.

We won't have many more harvests together. Despite its futility, she prayed for five more seasons with her grandmother. No, ten. And still, it wouldn't be enough.

Before her grief could spiral into something darker, the sound of her mother's heels clicking on the stone floor heralded her arrival. Hélène's perfume entered the kitchen first, the woman two beats later. Dressed smartly in a belted, two-piece suit with a tightly fitted jacket and slim-cut skirt, she looked fashionably chic. She carried white gloves in her hand, as if she planned to take tea with her friends at the Ritz.

"Maman, you cannot think to travel to Paris this morning."

"It is Wednesday." She spoke as if that explained all. And perhaps, in her mind, it did.

Gabrielle's heart twisted in her chest, this time with frustration. How she wished for her mother to be, somehow, a different woman. *Any* other woman but this perfectly groomed creature with such a careless attitude toward recent events. The thought was a betrayal of the worst kind, Gabrielle knew this, hated herself for thinking it. Hélène was her mother. There'd been a time when that meant soft hugs and comforting words. Now, she didn't know what to think of the woman who had given her birth. "You do recall we're at war?"

Her words came out harsher than she'd planned.

Hélène didn't seem to notice. "It's been six weeks and the Germans have left us alone. Today will be no different."

"You can't know that for sure." Gabrielle tried to keep the judgment from her voice, the fear. She failed at both. "It's safer to stay in Reims."

But that wasn't entirely true. During the previous war the trenches of the Western Front had cut through the heart of Champagne. Constant, heavy shelling had uprooted countless rows of chardonnay and pinot noir vines. Gabrielle still remembered being herded into the wine cellars with the others, unsure what they would find when they returned above ground. She'd clutched her mother's hand and had found comfort from the assurances whispered in her ear.

As if she could read her daughter's mind, for a moment, Hélène seemed to visibly soften. She touched Gabrielle's hair, kissed her cheek, leaving behind a trail of perfume as she stepped away. "Do not trouble yourself, *ma chère*. The Maginot Line will hold the Nazis to the other side of the border. That's what it is there for."

"Concrete and barbed wire will not stop a German panzer."

"Then the French army will."

This wasn't the first time they'd had this argument. *Same song, new verse.* "We shouldn't be so complacent as to—"

"The Maginot Line will hold." Her mother's tone held no room for further discussion.

Gabrielle attempted a different approach. "The harvest begins today."

She could use an extra pair of hands in the vineyard, though perhaps not her mother's. Hélène was not one to dig around in the dirt.

"Then it is better I make myself scarce." With the elegance of a born Parisian, Hélène straightened her suit jacket with quiet precision. "I will take Paulette with me."

Of course her sister would accompany their mother to Paris. Gabrielle had expected nothing else. Hélène was teaching her youngest daughter to move through the world as she did herself. Paulette had no interest in the vineyard, or the champagne house, and their mother seemed to encourage the girl's indifference.

Gabrielle despaired of ever changing her sister's mind. Who, then, would take over when she followed in Josephine's footsteps? When it was Gabrielle's turn to succumb to old age, who would carry on the LeBlanc legacy?

"I'm not late, Maman," came a voice from the doorway. "I'm merely running a few minutes behind schedule."

Paulette wandered into the kitchen at an unhurried pace, one shoe on her foot, the other dangling from her fingertips. She wore a fashionable blue day dress that accentuated her slender frame, small waist and narrow hips. Even her manner was reminiscent of Hélène's confident air.

"Do not trouble yourself, *ma chère*." The same words Hélène had said to Gabrielle, although spoken with far more affection. "We're in no hurry this morning."

Paulette returned her mother's serene smile, then turned a bland stare in Gabrielle's direction. "*Bonjour*, sister."

"*Bonjour*."

And that was the end of their conversation, no different from most days. How could they share the same mother and father and yet be so different? Gabrielle had no interest in art or fashion. Paulette thought of little else, except maybe flirtations with local boys. She also showed an artistic talent that went beyond the ordinary, as evidenced in the countless drawings she created in her mother's studio while Hélène painted her landscapes.

"I'm nearly ready to leave, Maman. As soon as I put on my— Oh, are those fresh croissants?" Without waiting for an answer, Paulette plucked a pastry from Gabrielle's plate with her free hand, the shoe still dangling from the other. The move, seemingly small and insignificant, revealed the young woman's ever-increasing thoughtlessness. If a croissant lay in front of her, it was hers for the taking. No matter that it was meant for another.

"By all means, Paulette, help yourself."

Not a student of subtlety, the young woman nibbled the croissant without acknowledging Gabrielle's remark. She took another dainty bite and turned to her mother expectantly. "Where shall we shop first?"

"I think Mademoiselle Ballard's atelier." The shop was a favorite of both women, and the designer, unlike Coco Chanel, had continued selling her clothes despite the declaration of war.

Hélène sat beside her youngest daughter. The two leaned in close, their heads nearly touching as they set their plans for the day. A wave of longing crashed over Gabrielle. What would it be like to have her mother as a confidante? Josephine had once filled that role in her life. And some days—most days—she still did. But not as often as before.

Gabrielle would be alone soon, more even than when Benoit had died. She already mourned the loss of her grandmother. But now. This moment. The vineyard called to her. There was only one thing to do.

Answer.

Chapter Six

JOSEPHINE

Josephine lost track of the day. Her sense of time and place had disappeared. The harvest was underway, but she couldn't remember when the picking had begun. Possibly last week. Maybe only yesterday. She should have marked the date in her journal. Now, the memory was only a smudge of its former self, a mere blur in her mind, like so many before it.

She looked down at her hands, as if the answer lay in the shriveled skin and crooked joints. When had she acquired that series of scratches across her knuckles? This morning? Yesterday, perhaps?

It was hard to think when she was so tired.

Every muscle in her body ached as she reentered the château. She could hear her own breathing, labored, filled with exertion. Today, it had been harder to hide the ravages of time. All morning, she'd struggled to keep the limp out of her steps and the creak out of her bones. Gabrielle had noticed anyway. And had sent Josephine back to the house to "rest."

Her pride had wanted to argue, but the look of pity and fear on her granddaughter's face had been too much to bear. An insult that left her feeling ashamed and exposed. Josephine had been unable to spend another minute stripped of her dignity by her own flesh and blood. For the first time in her life, she had left the work unfinished. Tomorrow would be a better day.

"That scowl will scare the mold right off the grapes."

"Oh." Josephine gave a little start. "Marta...you..." She swiveled to face the housekeeper, the move costing her precious energy. "You startled me."

"Forgive me, *mon amie*." The other woman flashed an apologetic grimace as she exited the pantry, her arms full of flour and eggs, sugar and butter. "That wasn't my intention."

"Of course not."

Marta dumped her load onto the chopping block, her eyebrows pulled together. "You should not be back so early. What happened to chase you indoors?"

"Nothing has happened." Josephine snapped out the words as unwanted emotions rose to the surface before she could tamp them down. Fury, humiliation. She hated how well Marta could read her, as if Josephine were a book the other woman had read many times over.

"You are especially tired today. More than usual."

For a moment, Josephine could only stare at the other woman, mortified by her uncanny ability to voice what she would never openly admit. "I'm cold." When she saw the skepticism on Marta's face, she added, somewhat defensively, "The thermoses are empty. I came for coffee."

"You will have to pour it yourself." Marta hitched her chin toward the empty mugs sitting near the sink. "Then you will tell me why your granddaughter sent you home. And why you are acting as surly as a scolded child."

"Gabrielle did not—" She closed her mouth, thought over her response, attempted another try. "I am not—"

"Lie to yourself, Josephine," Marta said, relentless as only she could be. "Do not lie to me."

"You—you know nothing."

"I know enough." Marta's expression softened. "Now, get your coffee and sit down before your legs give way."

Josephine poured the hot liquid. She did not sit. Her pride was too great. She leaned against the counter and watched Marta sprinkle flour into a bowl. Butter came next. Milk, eggs. Then, the kneading. The finished pastry would become something greater than the individual ingredients. The process was not unlike the LeBlancs' technique for making the finest champagnes in the world. The *methode champenoise* was a careful, artful blending of juices from several harvests, three at least, but as many as five.

Marta's hands paused. "I know what you are thinking."

"You have begun reading minds in your spare time?"

Shaking her head, Marta's hands resumed molding the dough. "You are thinking of war."

"*Non.* I am thinking of champagne."

Marta gave Josephine one of her penetrating stares. "You carry too much worry in your head and too much burden in your heart. It's unhealthy."

"I fear what is to come." She set down the untouched coffee. "Our family may not survive this one."

"Now you are thinking of war." Marta sighed. "And it's my fault."

"War is always in my mind." LeBlanc history was a tale of blood and death. Their home was at the center of Europe, with no mountain barrier, nothing to protect the land, putting this region—the LeBlanc lands—in the path of invading armies. The Goths, the Visigoths, and others had marched through Champagne. Yet of all those wars, the last one had been the worst, a festival of slaughter.

Why could she remember so much about the long-ago past and so little of the first day of harvest? "This new war will be harder than the last," she said in a whisper.

Marta laid her hand on the table, no longer working the dough, but paused in a moment of rest. Like Josephine, the gnarled fingers, now covered in flour, carried the signs of age and daily toil. "Many young lives will be lost."

Face tight with emotion, Marta joined Josephine at the sink. In shared silence, they studied the vineyard beyond the terrace with its centuries-old balustrade.

"They are my old friends." Josephine didn't need to expand her meaning. Marta knew she spoke of the vines. "And yet, these days, they have become strangers."

"You are looking at them with the eyes of the past."

Marta was only half-right. "I am looking at them with the eyes of an old woman."

Her vision wasn't what it once was, and perhaps that explained why everything looked wrong in the vineyard today. Or perhaps it was simpler than that. Perhaps it was the dark, ominous clouds rolling in from the north and casting a pall over the vines. They seemed to strain against the wires that held their trunks steady, fighting their confinement like souls trapped between this world and the next.

"We will survive this harvest," Marta said.

"Yes, we will." The vines had an uncanny ability to wither one season and thrive the next. War, however, left its horrors on the land and its people for generations.

Signs of past battles were everywhere. If Josephine craned her neck to the left, her eyes would fall on the Monument to the Heroes of the Black Army of Reims. The five bronze figures represented a group of French and African soldiers united in their defense of the city in 1918.

There had been great heroism in the midst of brutality. She closed her eyes, lifted up a prayer for…what? She didn't know what to pray for anymore. A fine harvest? A quick end to a war that had yet to begin? So many uncertainties.

One thing was clear, Josephine must find a new brand of courage. Now, today, before she lost her will, she must safeguard her family's future as she'd done during a previous war.

She could not do it alone.

She turned to her companion, purpose filling her. "Marta, I require your assistance."

Later that night, the two women left the house in the veil of darkness, the moon their only light. The buzz of a German plane sounded overhead. Josephine's hand reached out to grip Marta's. Frozen in place, they looked to the sky. Marta crossed herself as the plane flew dangerously low, skimming across the sky almost lazily. It was alone. Although not the first to take this circuitous route from Germany to Paris and back across the border again.

The random flybys were meant to intimidate. The tactic often worked. The people of Reims would fall into a stupor, lulled by Germany's silence. But then a lone plane would appear in the sky, and everyone would snap to attention. For a time. Eventually, they fell back into their flimsy sense of complacency. Until the next roaring dot appeared in the heavens.

Josephine continued watching the plane. Marta stood quiet and unmoving by her side. Only once it was swallowed up by the dark western sky did the housekeeper break her silence. "It's gone."

"Let's continue." Josephine led the way.

She and Marta each carried a heavy cloth bag laden with jewelry, statuettes and other small valuables plucked from Josephine's private collections. In total, the pieces were worth a small fortune. There were larger items that would have to be hidden. But not yet. Not until the fighting began. Any sooner and she would draw attention to what she was doing. With suspicion came questions she wasn't prepared to answer.

"I don't understand why we must do this." Marta kept her voice low, as if someone might be listening.

Josephine frowned into the night. She would have preferred not to include the other woman in her scheme. But she could no longer trust herself to keep things straight in her mind. "We have been over this, Marta. You are to be my memory if mine fails."

A heavy sigh met her explanation. "I meant, why must we do this at night?"

"No one can know where we are hiding these treasures."

"You do not trust your own family?"

"It's not a matter of trust." With secrets came lies. With lies came the weight of guilt, the burden often too heavy to carry alone. Josephine had done it once before. To protect a single member of her family. She would harbor this new secret to protect all the others.

Marta's voice sliced through the still night air. "The Nazis may not come."

"They will come. And they will rob us." Josephine had a sick, queasy feeling at the thought. "Or they will stand by while others steal what belongs to my family."

As they'd done in Germany nearly a year ago. The authorities had looked on as mobs ransacked and looted homes and businesses. Though called *Kristallnacht*, the Night of the Broken Glass, the violence had lasted for days. Lives had been lost. Irreplaceable treasures had fallen into the hands of thieves and charlatans. If the Nazis allowed such horrors on their own streets, how much worse would it be for France?

Josephine surfaced at Marta's voice. The woman had been talking while she'd been thinking of injustice. "You are missing one rather significant point about that terrible night."

"And that is?"

"The violence was targeted solely on Jewish homes and businesses." Marta's eyes glimmered like sparkling black diamonds under the bright moonlight. "No one in your family is Jewish."

Marta was wrong. One of them was, in fact, by Germany's definition, a Jew. But that was a secret Josephine would never reveal. Not to Marta.

Not to anyone.

Chapter Seven

GABRIELLE

Her mother insisted they reschedule the anniversary party to coincide with the last day of harvest. Gabrielle protested the timing. "It's too soon."

"Nonsense." Hélène punctuated the word with her distinctive flick of a wrist. "There is no better time to celebrate two hundred years of champagne making than the end of harvest."

"Maman, the vines will need tending once we've stripped them of their fruit. And the infant wine always requires a close watch through the course of its first fermentation." She gave other reasons, but Gabrielle didn't mention war. What would be the point? Her mother would only toss out one of her platitudes about seeking joy while the battles remained outside France.

"Gabrielle, *ma fille*, even you cannot work both day and night. There must be moments of rest. Is that not the reason the Lord made the Sabbath?"

Bringing God into the conversation was a bold move, even for Hélène. But it worked to her advantage. Josephine immediately sided with her daughter-in-law. "The last day of harvest it shall be."

Which explained why Gabrielle now stood on the edge of the party, the scent of the vineyard washed from her skin, and dressed in a sleek evening gown her mother had loaned her from her own wardrobe. She'd wondered aloud why it mattered what she wore. Hélène had been clear. "You will represent this family properly."

Another battle lost. Nevertheless, Gabrielle could admit her mother had been right about one thing. Their neighbors wanted this party.

They arrived in their finery like stylish waves rolling along the still night air. The women in their shimmering dresses, the men in their pristine white jackets and ties. Their smiles seemed strained, their laughter a little too loud, and Gabrielle sighed at the forced merriment. The thin coating of cheerfulness was as flimsy as a house built from cardboard and paste.

But perhaps, for some, the pretense was as real as it would ever get. They smoked their cigarettes—Gabrielle had never understood the fascination—and ate Monsieur Chardon's exquisite food. They drank the champagne Gabrielle had selected without her grandmother's knowledge. Devious, perhaps. But necessary. If questioned, she would cover her decision with an inspired response. "The 1919, 1920 and 1921 single vintages represent the only time in our history we've been blessed with exquisite harvests three years in a row."

So far, no one had questioned her selections.

A high-pitched, girlish giggle sounded from the other side of the room, drawing Gabrielle's attention to her sister. Draped in a gown designed by Mademoiselle Chanel before she'd closed her atelier, Paulette was at her most beautiful. She happily entertained a group of young men and women.

The sliver of love slicing through Gabrielle caught her off guard, more powerful for its unexpected arrival. Most days, she felt disconnected from her sister and she worried the silly teenager would turn into a silly woman. Now, in this moment, she saw only the little girl who'd loved her dolls and make-believe tea parties.

Gabrielle took the pleasant image with her out onto the terrace. Standing in the fresh air, away from the sickly-sweet aroma of clashing perfumes and cigarette smoke, she was able to breathe easier. As she stared up at the full moon, she breathed in again, this time holding the smell inside her. *I will remember this scent long past tonight. It will always remind me of my mother's determination to have a party, my sister's desire to be the center of attention, my grandmother's failing memory and my own desperation to protect the women I love.*

And, oh, how she loved them, with the fullness of a heart that couldn't bear another loss. It was nights like these Gabrielle felt the most alone, when laughter rang from others' lips and not her own. Never her own, not since Benoit's death.

The familiar pang of grief struck as a glittering couple strolled past. Gabrielle watched the woman slip her arm through the man's and whisper something in his ear. He laughed from deep in his throat. And then, they eased away to a darker portion of the terrace.

Gabrielle understood the desire to enjoy a private moment away from the crowds. She and Benoit would have done the same. She sighed, feeling his absence deeply tonight, as painful as losing a limb. Ironic, since a lost limb had hastened his death. The memory of his suffering brought an ache in her chest that nearly stole her breath. Biting her bottom lip, she looked down at her work-chafed hands. Her mother's expensive lotions had done little to hide the consequences of her time among the vines.

Benoit would have considered the collection of blisters and cracked nails a badge of honor. Though she wished for his presence, his strength, his smiles and laughter, she was glad he wasn't here to see the results of this year's harvest. So much waste, with too many grapes deemed unworthy of anything but a shallow burial at the roots of their vines.

The smell of someone's cigarette intruded on her solitude. She knew that scent. Her mother's unique brand imported from America. Gabrielle turned her head and found Hélène leaning against the stone wall next to the terrace doors. Partially cloaked in shadow, her mother's eyes were closed. A lit cigarette dangled from her fingertips.

She did not look herself.

No, that expression of hopelessness did not belong to her mother. Hélène's outward calm rarely slipped. Until this moment, Gabrielle hadn't realized how much she relied on her mother's unflappable confidence in herself, in her place in the world, in the Maginot Line to hold back the Nazi monsters. "Maman?" She tempered her voice to hide the thread of panic slipping down her spine. "Are you unwell?"

Nothing else explained the wretchedness shimmering off her like a fragrance gone bad before its time.

Hélène turned her head slowly. She blinked, as if only just noticing Gabrielle stood by her side. "I am well." Hélène's shattered expression told a different story. "The champagne, however, is running low."

"Let me see to the problem for you," Gabrielle offered.

"We have hired Monsieur Chardon to deal with such matters."

True. They had not, however, hired him to rummage around in their wine cellar. "Then I'll inform monsieur of the situation."

Without looking at her, Hélène lifted the cigarette to her lips. "Thank you, Gabrielle. That would be a great help."

She opened her mouth to respond, but her mother was already spinning on her heel and returning to the party. Sighing, Gabrielle located the caterer in the kitchen. He was a squat, balding man with a vile temper and a doughy face currently pink and shiny from exertion. "Monsieur Chardon, may I have a word?"

He regarded her with a distracted half glance, half glare. "What is it you need, Madame?"

"I understand the champagne is running low."

"We have plenty of the '19 and '20." With a jerk of his chin, he indicated the uncorked bottles lined up in neat rows along the counter. "But the 1921 has been depleted. I will need a key to get into the cellar to secure more."

"*Non*, I'll get the champagne myself. You will want...ten bottles?"

"Twenty."

That seemed excessive, considering there were plenty of the other two vintages waiting to be uncorked. She kept silent on the matter, because Monsieur Chardon's request served her own purposes, as did the party itself. Now that it was in her mind, Gabrielle would use this opportunity to address an important, potentially ruinous detail she'd neglected when she'd executed her plan to hide the champagne.

She prayed she hadn't waited too long.

In this, timing was on her side. François's duties currently kept him busy among the wine racks at the front of the cellar. He had no reason to venture to the spot where she'd built her makeshift wall. That didn't mean he hadn't done so.

She located him speaking with her grandmother in the main salon near the fireplace. A small, thin-faced, bearded man in his early seventies, he'd been with her family since the previous century. He was clearly uncomfortable attending tonight's formal event. The way he continually tugged at his collar gave him away. He would welcome an excuse to exit the party.

"Ah, Gabrielle," her grandmother said, spotting her approach. "This is such a lovely celebration, *oui*?" Josephine gazed over the crowd with the smile of a benevolent monarch approving of her loyal subjects. "The people of Reims seem very cheerful."

"Very."

"This is the first of many more happy days to come." Josephine's black eyes shone with an unfocused light that tore at Gabrielle's very core. "You will see, *chère*. The worst of the war is over. We can rebuild now."

The words were from another party, at the end of another war. Gabrielle remembered her grandmother saying this the night they'd received news that her father was returning from the trenches. She prayed she was mistaken. But no. Josephine's unfocused gaze showed the condition of her mind. The older woman was lost in another time.

Should Gabrielle attempt to pull her grandmother back into the present? Or let her enjoy this moment in the past? She ventured a neutral approach. "Grandmère, I've come to steal your companion for a bit."

Josephine turned her smile onto the man standing uncomfortably beside her. Had Gabrielle not been watching her grandmother closely, she might have missed the confusion that lived in the fast-blinking eyes. But then her gaze cleared, and she patted François's arm with affection. "Thank you, my trusted friend, for humoring an old woman and her memories."

Relief nearly brought Gabrielle to her knees. As quickly as she'd disappeared, Josephine had returned to the here and now.

"It was no hardship, I assure you." François took Josephine's tiny hand between his work-roughened paws. "We carry many of the same memories in our hearts, *non*?"

"We do, indeed."

They shared a brief smile. And then François turned his attention to Gabrielle. "I am at your service, Madame."

She had a moment of nerves. Was this the right night, the right time? Should she simply let well enough alone? She quickly discarded her indecision. There would never be a perfect time to test her wall, or the person most likely to discover what she'd done. "Come with me, François."

He obeyed without argument. She'd expected nothing less. His loyalty to her grandmother extended to her. He'd never married, never even ventured beyond Champagne. His life— his entire world—began and ended with Château Fouché-LeBlanc. The thought was a balm to her nerves as she led him along the same route she'd taken six weeks before.

This night, the moon guided them across the terrace, down the stone steps, along the barren rows of vines, naked and at rest now. At the cave's entrance, Gabrielle had to pause and take a steadying breath. The monumental consequences of what she was about to do played out in her mind. This would be the wall's first test.

Giving nothing away, she unlocked the door and shouldered into the cave first. François joined her under the soft glow of the 24-volt lights. As he stood comfortably in his personal domain, Gabrielle realized again the risk she'd put him in without his knowledge.

There was still time to protect him. "Monsieur Chardon requested twenty bottles of the 1921," she said breezily, trying— and failing—to hide her worry inside the mild tone.

"Josephine specifically told me you were serving the 1928 tonight."

François's even tone gave Gabrielle pause. He seemed to be

waiting for her to say something more. Was *he* now testing *her*? She searched his face for the answer. His expression never changed. He simply stood in the low light, waiting, letting her look. "We cannot serve the 1928," she said. "Not tonight, or any other night for many days to come."

He nodded. "It would not be wise, I think. Perhaps, even dangerous."

Gabrielle's breath caught in her throat.

She was still trying to work out how much he knew, when he said, "There is something you need to see. Come with me and I will show you what I mean."

He directed her down the long corridors with their low ceilings and inadequate light. They journeyed in silence past the wine racks holding bottles of champagne in their second fermentation, their necks positioned at a precise thirty-five-degree angle for the sediment to collect at their corks. Part of François's duties was to oversee this process. He alone gave the bottles their fractional turns at precise, predetermined intervals until the wine was clear and ready for the next phase in becoming champagne.

They rounded the first corner in silence, descended a tiny flight of steps cut into the limestone and then moved through yet another series of corridors that housed the oak barrels and more champagne. Finally, they came to the very end of the cellar. He placed his hand on the fake wall and turned to look at her, saying nothing.

Gabrielle's entire body went cold, but she held his stare.

He'd said he wanted to show her something, so she moved in next to him and looked. Shoulder to shoulder, they surveyed the stones together.

The first thing Gabrielle noticed was that the spiders had done their job. As if they'd known their purpose, they'd spun their webs at strategic, seemingly random points. Her second thought was that François wasn't voicing his opinion about the wall, its location, the spiders. Nothing. He had something to say. She could see the truth of it in the way he rubbed at his beard, the sign he was thinking.

"You understand what I've done?" she asked.

He made a sound in the back of his throat that could have been agreement, or possibly a warning, Gabrielle could not say which. "You have protected your family's future in a very clever way."

"And now, by the very nature of this conversation, I've put you at risk as well." The moment the words left her mouth, she felt the magnitude of what she'd done. She'd brought this man into her confidence without giving him a choice in the matter. As surely as the spiders had captured their unsuspecting prey, Gabrielle had woven François into her web of lies. "If the burden is too much, I will find you another situation. Perhaps in my father-in-law's vineyard."

"You will do nothing of the sort." He patted her arm in a paternal gesture that brought a sting to her eyes. "Your grandmother was wise to put you in charge of this project."

"She doesn't know. She cannot know." Her voice cracked with the urgency she felt in her heart. "François, please, she must never know. This stays between us."

"You are asking me to lie to your grandmother?"

"It would be a lie of omission. But yes, that is what I am asking."

"Very well." He turned to look at her. "During the last war, Josephine and I buried the bottles beneath the vines. This, I believe, is a better solution. Now. Look. Some of the stones have shifted. You see? There." He indicated a spot on their right, then pointed to another position three feet lower. "And there."

There were other places of concern, large enough to expose her faulty construction if someone looked closely enough. François had. Others would, too.

Dismayed, Gabrielle tugged in a hard pull of air. Mistake upon mistake. Lies upon lies. She'd acted in haste, and now the stones themselves exposed her recklessness.

"The wall has to be stabilized," he said. "I will do it now, while the party distracts your grandmother."

How easy it would be to let him take care of her mess. How cowardly. "I've already involved you more than I should. I can't allow you to—"

"You can and you will. It is settled. You will let me do this for your family."

"We'll fix the wall together," she countered. "After the party. For now, we have champagne to deliver to a fussy, over-paid chef who is enamored with his own brilliance."

Chapter Eight

HÉLÈNE

Hélène had made a very large mistake. She'd allowed Gabrielle to see past her mask of restraint and self-possession. She would not let it happen again. She *could* not let it happen again. There were reasons, of course. Reasons she would take to her grave.

At least the party was a success. Hélène's personal touches were everywhere. In the hothouse flowers she'd ordered and then placed strategically throughout the château. In the delicate crystal glasses filled with their finest champagnes. She'd even handpicked the local boys serving as waiters now weaving through the crowd with their trays of Monsieur Chardon's delicacies. The evening was progressing exactly as planned. And yet, Hélène fought to keep the smile on her face.

It was the party itself. The gaiety made her nostalgic. It had been a long time since they'd invited so many people into this home. She remembered Étienne's words from the early days of their marriage. "The *Champenois* like to celebrate," he'd said, laughing a little as he added, "Especially with Fouché-LeBlanc champagne in their glasses. Each sip is a small taste of eternity, or so my mother says to anyone who will listen."

Étienne's passion for his family's business had been contagious. Hélène had been half in love with him long before she'd discovered he was no common vintner, but one of the grand French champagne masters of his day. He'd been marked for greatness. Then the war had come and stolen everything.

"You're frowning, Maman."

Hélène sighed. Now both of her daughters had witnessed an unforgivable slip in her composure. Rearranging her features, Hélène lifted a jeweled hand to smooth across her daughter's shiny dark hair. "I was thinking of your father. He would have enjoyed this party."

Not a complete lie. The man Étienne had been before the war would have lifted his glass in a sentimental toast to his beloved mother. His words would have been heartfelt and inspiring. He would have toasted his deceased father next, and all the family members that had come before them. His daughters would be next. Then, he would have said something kind, and most assuredly loving, about his wife.

Hélène breathed past her sorrow and forced herself to speak evenly. "You are enjoying yourself, Paulette, are you not?"

"I'm having a lovely time. This is one of the best nights of my life."

Her daughter's enthusiasm brought a genuine smile to Hélène's lips, no need to pretend.

"I'm glad." Her words came out strained, which had not been her intent. This party was supposed to be her shining moment. There would be no more after tonight, not until the war was over. The war, she thought bitterly, that had yet to begin. But would destroy many.

Seemingly unaware of her mother's mood, Paulette continued chattering about the party and how admired she was among her friends. "Jean-Claude and Lucien are fighting over me."

As Paulette continued happily discussing all the ways each boy worked to gain her favor, Hélène thought, *to be sixteen again.* Or perhaps, not. She hadn't been as lighthearted as her daughter, or as beloved by her friends. The girls at school had whispered behind her back about her own mother's poor choice of husbands. A common banker, they called him. Never mind that her father's financial advice and support had kept their families afloat during hard times.

Abraham Hirsch-Jobert, son of Isaac Hirsch-Jobert, would never be worthy of them. He did not belong to the old French nobility. He attended the local synagogue and sometimes brought his daughter with him. He was an outsider, a usurer...a Jew.

As if to make up for the subtle cruelty of her peers, her father had encouraged his wife to raise Hélène in her church. Beyond that, he'd denied his daughter nothing. What she wished for, she received. There'd been no criticism, no reining her in when she went too far. Even at nineteen, when she'd begun frequenting the salons of notorious artists, poets, philosophers and American ex-patriots, her father had given her no warnings, no insistence for moderation.

The first inkling that he may have disapproved of her lifestyle came when she'd met Étienne and brought him home for dinner with her parents, something that had surprised all of them. Étienne was not her usual fare. After he'd left, her father had taken her hand and, with pride shining in his eyes, had asked, "You like this man, this maker of fine champagne?"

"I like him very much."

Her father had nodded. "I like him as well. A superb choice, indeed."

From that night forward, Hélène had begun to see herself and her sparkling, sophisticated crowd through a different lens. She grew to recognize the cynicism in their manner, and hers. The way they accepted all, and yet cared for none.

Even as she'd come to see the callousness, the blatant self-interest, she'd also come to understand why she'd gravitated to them in the first place. It was more than like recognizing like, though that had been part of the fascination. They'd never asked about the origin of her father's last name, or where *his people* came from. She had simply been witty, beautiful Hélène Hirsch-Jobert with an unrivaled talent for watercolors.

But then Hélène Hirsch-Jobert had become Hélène Jobert-LeBlanc. With a name change, and the love of a good man, came the rest of her transformation. The clothes she wore, the books she read, even the church she attended, all had become part of the complicated, layered lie and—

"Maman, did you not hear me?"

Hélène flinched at her daughter's voice. Paulette had asked her a question. She had to think a minute to bring the words back into her mind. One of her daughter's friends had been to the Ritz for lunch, and now Paulette wanted to go. Hélène rarely said no to the girl. This time, she would. She must. The hotel restaurant, even in the afternoon, was no place for a sixteen-year-old girl with nothing but fashion, parties and boys on her mind. Too many temptations. "We will discuss it tomorrow."

"Why not now?"

Hélène sighed, unwilling to explain herself. The words would not be right. Her own bitter disillusionment over past mistakes was too strong tonight, too close to the surface. "Because the party requires my attention, and your admirers require yours."

"They do, don't they?" The prospect of winning two hearts at once catapulted Paulette across the room.

With a sense of foreboding, Hélène watched her daughter rejoin her friends, then concentrate solely on the two young men battling for her affection. Paulette would toy with them, Hélène knew. The girl would charm and captivate and make each boy think he was her favorite. Until she lost interest in them both and moved on to another.

That was how Paulette maneuvered through life. She was careless with people, her admirers especially, never fully satisfied with a conquest, always looking for the next triumph.

Hélène had a moment of suffocating insight into her greatest mistake as a mother. By requiring so little of her daughter, she'd created a replica of her former self. She'd raised Paulette to accept all, and care for none.

Mon Dieu, *what have I done?*

Part Two

Chapter Nine

GABRIELLE

19 May 1940

The months dragged on. 1939 rolled seamlessly into 1940, and then winter dissolved into spring, and the war remained on the other side of the Maginot Line. Hitler seemed too preoccupied with the rest of Europe to bother with France. There was no predicting how long his indifference would last, and the business of champagne making couldn't be ignored.

Gabrielle left the château as she did every morning—with the sound of church bells ringing in her ears. Her feet moved swiftly through the present, while her mind refused to relinquish the past. She'd been a child during the previous war, and her memories still informed her decisions now, adding a sense of gravity to her work. And always, tangled in her thoughts, was the knowledge of what terrible things were to come because of what she'd experienced before.

Today, she skirted the vineyard in favor of the champagne house. The vines had been pruned, their shoots lifted off the ground, and the soil at their roots replenished. Pierre, in his role as vineyard manager, was one of Gabrielle's most trusted employees, his loyalty equal to François's. Now that the harvest was complete, she left him in charge of the day-to-day tending of the vines, which freed her to focus on the *vin clairs*.

She conducted continuous tastings of the base wines, exploring different combinations in her search for the perfect marriage between aroma and taste. Grandmère had taught her how to use her nose and palate to produce their signature blends. It wasn't chemistry. Not art, either. But a combination of the two that required as much trial and error as meticulous planning.

Her mind on the first blend of the day, Gabrielle climbed the wide stone steps that curved around the exterior of the building. She imagined the taste. Crisp, smooth, beautifully elegant, with a hint of pears, or maybe apricots, perhaps a bit of both, the result a pleasant, toasty finish. The champagne would be a lovely addition to other Château Fouché-LeBlanc wines, an exquisite, pure, effervescent chardonnay, refreshing but not too sweet.

Inside her workroom, she surveyed her tiny domain. This was her most cherished refuge when she wasn't in the vineyard, where she became an artisan-blender of award-winning champagnes. Focusing on the process had helped her through the worst of her grief after Benoit's death. She'd mourned in this room, and had learned to live without him, slowly, one day at a time. One perfectly blended champagne at a time.

She ran her fingertip along the edges of the worktable, across the beakers, the measuring cups, the stacks of ledgers where she wrote down her formulas, whether success or failure.

She liked to think of herself as practical, but the French

blood in her could not be denied. She tried to contain the more passionate side of her nature to small indulgences: a vial of Chanel No. 5, a tube of red lipstick, the little black dress designed by Mademoiselle Chanel herself. Sometimes, though, when Gabrielle was alone with her thoughts, and melancholy tried to creep in, she admitted she wasn't fully satisfied with her life. In those moments she couldn't help feeling wholly, completely alone, wanting something that had died with her husband. A legacy beyond herself. A family of her own. A child.

Agitated now, she organized her space and went to work creating a wine whose whole would be greater than its parts. She measured, tasted, considered, chose.

Her first attempt was wretched, the second not much better. But at least her mind was on her work. Mostly. A vague feeling of dissatisfaction hung over each of her attempts, and she knew why. Josephine had thought today was the first day of harvest and had become angry when Gabrielle attempted to correct her. It had taken Marta's intervention to calm Grandmère.

Do not sigh, she told herself.

She sighed.

With unsteady fingers, she reached for three more *vin clairs* and began to blend, to build.

She took a sip, letting the wine sit on her tongue. Her heart lifted. The crisp notes of apricot and buttery pastry were there. The blend was extremely fresh, with a lively, appealing finish full of candied lemons, but also—she gave in to that sigh a second time—a bit steely.

"Another failure," she mumbled.

"You are too hard on yourself."

Gabrielle drew a sudden breath. Her mother rarely came into the champagne house, and never during working hours.

"The blend isn't right," she said, staring at the wine, grateful she had someone to listen. "Something's missing."

"You'll figure it out. You always do."

Her mother's confidence, so rare, so unexpected, should have filled Gabrielle with light and stars. But the tone was all wrong, flat and full of suppressed emotion. She looked up and drew another involuntary breath at the sight of her mother's bloodless features. "Maman? What is it? What's happened?"

"The Germans—they have invaded France."

Gabrielle's throat seized on a breath. Her voice, when it came, was hoarse and full of horror. *"Mon Dieu."* The German war machine had made its move at last. She'd known this day would come. "Tell me what you heard."

"There isn't much to tell." Her mother took her hand. "Come, we'll turn on the wireless and discover the details together."

Half running, half stumbling, Gabrielle returned to the château with her mother.

Josephine and Marta stood in the kitchen, arms linked, eyes wide. There was no sign of Paulette. She must have already left for school.

"Grandmère?"

Her voice gave her grandmother a jolt. "Marta," she said in a barely there whisper. "Tell Gabrielle what you heard at the *boulangerie*."

The housekeeper relayed the information in a dull, even tone. "German panzers crossed the Ardennes early this morning."

That couldn't be right. "General Pétain declared the forest impenetrable."

"He was wrong. Our defenses have crumbled at the first show of German might."

Gabrielle swallowed the bile rising in her throat. The Maginot Line had not held back the monsters. The Germans had crept through the back door, sweeping in like angels of death.

It took barely four weeks for France to fall. The army had been strong on paper only.

Many mornings, Gabrielle sat in the southeast parlor with the rest of her family, silent and miserable as they listened to the wireless. Paulette rarely joined them. Her excuses ranged from the reasonable—schoolwork—to the flippant—a desire to practice a new coiffure. There were glimpses of her fear, too. Not often, and never for long, but enough to leave Gabrielle hopeful her sister was beginning to understand the gravity of their situation.

The disembodied voice reported the latest development. "The French government has fled to the spa town of Vichy."

Gabrielle shook her head. Marshal Pétain had run from the consequences of his bad choices. Like so many politicians favoring appeasement, he'd tried to spare effort and, instead, had brought disaster on the French people.

Her mother took this news with stoic cynicism. Josephine's grief was not so subtle. With tears sliding down her face, she choked out, "Not a fight. Not one show of resistance. The Germans invaded and no one stopped them."

"Marshal Pétain is a coward," Marta snarled under her breath. Perhaps she thought no one heard her. They did, of course. Her words were a summary of what they were all thinking.

"Perhaps he may surprise us yet," Hélène suggested, though her words were wistful rather than convincing.

The news only got worse.

With Paris under siege, the residents fled the city in packs. They left in buses and private cars. Others piled their belongings in carts and mule-drawn wagons. When the incendiary strikes began, more terrified residents left on foot. The roads became congested.

France surrendered at the end of June. Government officials signed an armistice with Germany that cut the country in half. The occupied zone in the north—where the Germans would exercise the rights of an occupying power—and the free zone in the south, run by the puppet French government.

Like Paris, the entire region of Champagne fell into the *zone occupée.*

Gabrielle could no longer listen to such dreadful news. She stepped out onto the terrace and down the stone steps where Pierre stood at the edge of the vineyard. Sunlight danced off the vines. The sky above their heads was a hard, crisp blue unmarred by a single cloud. Except...

There, in the distance, coming from the very heart of Reims. One black smudge spiraled toward the heavens, a shocking stain on the otherwise pristine blue. At first glance, Gabrielle thought the unusual-looking plume was a thundercloud and she nearly said, "Rain's coming," but there was something not quite right about the dark cloud swirling upward, dense and black.

She took an involuntary step forward. "Do you see that?" she asked Pierre.

Shock jumped in the man's eyes. "Smoke. *Fire.*"

In unison, they said, "It must be quenched." Before the flames spread to the vines. The spring had been especially dry, something they'd agreed was a turn of fortune after last year's rains. Now...

If fire spread to the vineyards...

Pierre took off in the direction of the smoke. Gabrielle allowed herself one crumbling instance of weakness to grieve for what would be devoured by the flames, then raced into the house. Her mother was in the kitchen, staring into a half-full cup of coffee. "Maman, I need your car."

"Why? What's happened now?"

With cold, concise precision, Gabrielle explained about the fire. In the distance, the wail of a siren shattered the June air.

Hélène abandoned her cup on the kitchen table. "I'll drive."

They traveled the short distance in strained silence. Tension showed in her mother's pinched expression as she navigated the streets of Reims, the flames her guide.

The noise hit Gabrielle first, a loud earsplitting roar. Thick, menacing flames speared up into the sky. Others curled backward, into the bakery, licking at the structure with greedy, destructive tongues. Smoke rolled within the fire, pluming upward, rising, rising. The stench seared her nose. The whirling dance of flames burned her eyes.

If the wind shifted, it would carry sparks to other buildings. The vines. The LeBlanc château. The fire must be stopped.

The moment her mother pulled the car to a halt, Gabrielle jumped out. She was immediately swallowed up in the crowd and lost sight of Hélène within seconds. She tried to push through the dense humanity, thinking only of joining the fight, but she made little progress. Too many people surrounded her, crying, shouting, tugging at her, and then shoving her away.

The chaos was nothing like she'd ever experienced. She couldn't seem to find a single coherent thread in the complicated mess of her thoughts.

German soldiers were everywhere, gleefully laying claim to the fire. They ignored the chaos they'd started and became like uniformed ants swarming in and out of buildings. With cold-eyed stares, they filled their arms and then their vehicles with treasures that did not belong to them.

A little boy watched the destruction with wide, terrified

eyes. "Make them stop," he wailed. "Please, Maman. Make them stop."

The woman pulled the child against her, tears filling her eyes, her words of comfort lost in the confusion. Her curses on the Germans came through much clearer. The fire was loud, and it was hot, and Gabrielle could not get close enough to help. All she could do was watch the sparks fly from a distance and feel the oppressive heat on her face.

She wanted to pray. The words would not come. In her heart, she knew the Lord had already made His decision against her country, her city, her home. Her family.

They would suffer hunger, fear and loss. They'd felt the fangs of all three before. They'd survived and would do so again. That's what Gabrielle told herself. That's what she believed, what she *had* to believe. But then the soldiers began stacking crates of champagne along the base of the Fontaine Jean-Godinot, and she knew this war would be different than before, worse. The enemy would act without honor this time.

They would not get what belonged to her family. Not without a fight. She wiped the ash off her face and took off for the château at a dead run.

Chapter Ten

JOSEPHINE

Josephine refused to hide in the wine cellar. No amount of badgering by Marta could change her mind. "This is my home. I will not surrender it to German marauders."

Marta squeezed her hand. "This is your pride speaking. Pride will not protect you from the savagery of these men."

It was not a matter of pride. It was the memory of another war. Forced underground, huddled with her neighbors among the racks of fermenting wine, quaking in terror. This time, this war, Josephine would not be sent to cower in fear when the rest of her family was...

Where was the rest of her family?

In the moments she'd spent arguing with Marta she'd lost them. This was not the time for her mind to play its tricks. She took in her surroundings in an attempt to gather her wits. How had she ended up in the parlor, the one Hélène consid-

ered her own personal sanctuary, as sacred to her as the cathedral was to other Frenchwomen?

The wireless, perhaps? Yes, yes. Josephine remembered now.
She'd come to listen for news of her beloved France. "Why
am I, and you," she added when her eyes landed on Marta,
"the only ones in this room? Where are the others?"

"I do not know."

Josephine had other questions. Why could she not make her
mind form the thoughts she needed to speak? The harder she
tried to shape the words into sentences, the stronger the ache
pounded behind her eyes. It was as if she'd sipped too much
champagne and had come away with a sore head. "Where is
Gabrielle? Hélène? And…" There was another in the home.
A girl. Her name… "Paulette?"

Marta shrugged.

That girl, always disappearing, doing what she wished,
when she wished it. Hélène should not encourage such rebellion. To be a mother meant not always making the easy
choices. Josephine understood why her daughter-in-law hid
certain secrets from Paulette, but that didn't mean the girl
should be allowed to run free.

Static from the wireless cleared, and the voice of a French-
man reported the news with uneasy desperation. "The Germans have overtaken Paris completely. Nazi flags drape our
buildings. Soldiers swarm like insects to every part of the city.
They have spread to the outskirts, setting fires to buildings.
They loot, and now they—"

"We waste time with things we cannot change." Marta
turned a knob on the wireless and the room went silent. "Come,
Josephine. The Germans are invading. We will hide—"

"We will not hide," she said, cutting the other woman off.
"We will stand strong."

Bold words, and yet…

For a paralyzing moment, Josephine had no idea what to do next. She looked down at her hands, clenching and unclenching at her waist. She was suddenly very cold. Reaching up, she rubbed at her arms to warm herself. The clamor in her head had taken on a frantic spinning of voices upon voices. She would not let the whispers win.

With a tug on her hand, Marta attempted to pull her out of the room. Josephine allowed the housekeeper brief success. One step, another, then she dug in her heels at the sound of the brass knocker slapping at the front door.

"The Germans." Marta made a strangled noise deep in her throat. "They have come."

A chill ran down Josephine's spine. *I will not surrender. I will not willingly give what belongs to me and mine. They will have to take it, but I will not give.*

Slowly, as though she might disturb her own fragile hold on restraint, she looked to Marta. The housekeeper's gaze chased around the room, landing nowhere. Another woman grappling for control.

The knocking turned more insistent. "We must answer the door," Josephine said, thinking of her family first, praying they were somewhere safe.

Why could she not remember where they had gone?

Marta drew herself up. "I will do it."

"Non." Josephine set a steadying hand on the other woman's arm. "I must be the one to face the wolves at my door. You will stay out of the way."

Marta did not argue, but she did not obey fully. She followed Josephine, only stopping when they reached the edge of the foyer. Josephine continued on her own. With her chin lifted at a haughty angle, she braved the journey with purposeful strides. Each step restored her strength, even as time seemed to bend and shift in her mind, taking her back to another war when the Germans had shown up on her doorstep.

She pulled open the door and flinched. The light of the stark, afternoon sun shone too brightly. Her hand immediately went to cover her eyes.

"Madame Fouché-LeBlanc." The masculine voice spoke her name in perfectly accented French. Not a native speaker, but close.

Josephine lowered her hand, only to press it to her throat as she experienced a viselike tightening of her breath. That face. She knew it. The sight brought both shock and fury. Not because of the hard angles and sharp planes, but because of its familiarity. This man was no stranger to her. He had roots in Reims. A German wine importer she'd invited into her champagne house, now draped in the uniform of the enemy.

He wasn't alone. He'd brought along two hard-eyed soldiers to add to his look of importance.

"I know you," she said. His hair was lighter. Threads of silver now glinted in the pale blond strands that were shorn shorter than when she'd last stood in his presence.

"I'm pleased you remember me."

"It would be hard to forget a man such as you." Josephine had never liked Helmut von Schmidt. Her aversion had started from their first meeting nearly a decade ago. It was his eyes. There was no light in them. Pale, icy, not quite blue, not quite gray, they'd always made Josephine uneasy, especially when he looked straight at her. As he was doing now. She felt the chill of his stare, like a breath of frost on her face.

Her stomach roiled. Then her mind cleared, becoming so free of confusion that she could remember each of their encounters in stark relief.

She wished for the fog to return.

His eyes went to the interior of the house behind her, a

quick, thorough inventory that brought a hint of satisfaction to his bearing. "You are alone, Madame?"

"Non." She did not expand.

He spent another moment considering her. Then, he stuck out his hand but must have seen something in her face and let it fall away. "You know why I am here?"

"You have come for my champagne."

"Oui, but perhaps not in the way you assume."

Something there, in his eyes. An ugly greed she'd noted in the past, when he was a younger man not quite able to reach the heights in his career he thought he deserved. In a flash of memory, she recalled the way he signed off on a number of cases, while writing on the bill-of-sale a different one that benefited his own pocket. Her insides shook a little. "I trust you will enlighten me, Herr von Schmidt."

"It is *Hauptmann* von Schmidt," he corrected, snapping to attention and clicking his heels smartly for emphasis. "I have been given the rank of captain in the Wehrmacht."

She said nothing, not even when he shot out his arm and expressed his allegiance to his führer. Heil *Hitler, indeed.* The vile autocrat did not deserve such loyalty, not even from a man with his own questionable character.

"I have been commissioned into a special corps of the Wehrmacht to oversee the purchase of champagne for the Third Reich."

Purchase. That was what the Nazis were calling their theft? Josephine stared at von Schmidt hard, daring him to continue along this ridiculous vein of lies. "Go on. Finish what it is you have come to say."

"I have been assigned to Champagne because of my connections to the region. I serve second only to Otto Klaebisch."

Another German with connections to Champagne. Both men were once wine merchants, now turned soldiers meant to *purchase* champagne for their führer. The Nazis had thought to organize their pillaging. She had not expected such forethought. Or that Hitler would be so smart as to assign men familiar with the region to do his dirty work. "You have come to tell me of your new career, or is there another reason for your arrival on my doorstep?"

"This, I'm afraid, is not an attempt to reignite our friendship."

At last, they were getting to the purpose of his visit. No matter how pleasant his manner, this man—this German—had come to rob her. How much of her champagne would he take? Whatever the amount, it would be too much. The stony-faced, broad-backed soldiers flanking von Schmidt were proof enough of that.

She would not make it easy for them to steal from her.

Josephine held her enemy's stare. It was time to form a defense. Her mind worked quickly, quicker than it had in months. And that reminder of her frailty was the strategy she would take. "I am an old woman. My mind is not what it once was. These pleasantries only make me confused. Please, Herr—" She paused. "Herr Hauptmann von Schmidt, I beg you to speak plainly. How much of my champagne do you want?"

With an apologetic incline of his head, he said, "Your champagne is safe. For now."

For now. Two words that took every ounce of control out of her hands and placed it firmly into his. She understood this game he played. He would toy with her, until he tired of the theatrics. Then, he would loot her wine cellar down to the limestone blocks.

Von Schmidt appeared to be waiting for her to respond to his remark. Did he expect gratitude from her? Of course he did. "Thank you."

"You are most welcome."

He would leave now. He should be leaving. Why was he not leaving? "If you have something else to say, Herr Hauptmann," she prompted once again, "please say it."

"Very well. I am requisitioning your home for my lodgings while I am in the region. Here is the paperwork." He made a flicking gesture with his fingers and one of the soldiers pressed a document into her hand.

Josephine blinked at the paper stamped with the official seal of the Third Reich. Her mouth would not work. Her throat had compressed to the size of a pipe stem.

"I see I have shocked you."

Of course he had shocked her. He was *stealing* her home.

She attempted to tamp down her panic, even as she watched his gaze take in the elaborate foyer behind her again, lust and greed filling his eyes. "I will, of course, allow you and your family to remain in your home for as long as you choose to cooperate."

She nearly laughed at the threat uttered within that seemingly magnanimous offer. What was she to say to such conceit?

"You will thank me now."

"Thank you." She had to force the words past her clenched jaw.

Von Schmidt didn't seem to notice her difficulty. Speaking in hard, rapid-fire German, he gave the soldiers their orders. Josephine didn't understand most of what he said, but she caught enough to know that he was the highest-ranking soldier. And he enjoyed the privilege of ordering his subordinates around.

This was not wholly unexpected.

Taking it as a given his demands would be obeyed, he turned on his heel and gave Josephine his full attention once more. "You will move aside and let me in now."

He removed his hat, secured it under his arm, then stepped across the threshold. Once inside the château, all signs of pleasantness vanished. He wore the face of a conqueror.

Josephine was quivering now, with a mix of fear and rage. She could not set aside the messy stew of her thoughts to move, to speak. To react at all. Where was her resolve to fight?

"You may begin my tour of the property."

The way he said the words...

Josephine didn't remember offering to show him around. Another slip within her mind? Or was this man—this German—issuing her orders as he had the soldiers, as though her obedience was a given? She thought maybe the latter.

She felt herself drawing away from reality, as if she dwelled under a glass dome and couldn't quite reach the world beyond her isolated bubble. The sensation was really quite lovely. And so very tempting. A seductive call she desperately wished to answer.

Her eyes fluttered shut, then snapped open again when someone touched her arm. "Grandmère."

Gabrielle stood by her side, breathing hard, her presence wrenching Josephine out of her confusion. Her granddaughter smelled of smoke and French outrage. Her eyes narrowed over von Schmidt, contempt dripping from her every pore. "What is the meaning of this intrusion?"

Chapter Eleven

GABRIELLE

Gabrielle held the soldier's stare, refusing to recoil under the severe slice of cheekbones and rigid set of his jaw. He seemed very German. But also, somehow, familiar. They'd met before, though she couldn't quite place the face.

She was too agitated to make more than a cursory attempt to recall their past connection. The images from Reims were still fresh in her mind, the smoke still in her nose, the feel of her neighbors' fear still humming in her blood.

Now, the horror stood in her home, wearing an immaculately pressed officer's uniform. She disliked him and his proprietary manner and, she feared, her derision had sounded in her voice. All of a sudden, she realized her mistake. She'd made demands of her oppressor. That had not been wise.

"Gabrielle." Her grandmother touched her arm, waited for her to glance in her direction before performing the necessary

introductions. "This is Herr Helmut von Schmidt, or rather…
Hauptmann von Schmidt."

Von Schmidt. The name did not bring up a memory.

"Herr Hauptmann, this is my granddaughter Gabrielle Le-
Blanc Dupree."

"A pleasure, Madame Dupree."

Gabrielle did not offer a response. She gave him no hand
to clasp, only a slight frown to convey her mood. She dared
not show more defiance. She wasn't supposed to be facing the
enemy with only her grandmother. If Benoit were alive—

He would be fighting in the French army. And Gabrielle
would still be confronting this soldier without him. For some
reason, that made her all the more furious over his intrusion.

Von Schmidt didn't seem to notice her hostility. Or perhaps, he simply didn't care what she thought of him. For a
long moment, he did not speak. He simply held her stare
with an arrogant one of his own. She wanted to shout at him
to get out of her home. To get out of her country. He didn't
belong. But that wasn't true anymore. France had fallen into
German hands. The government had rolled over and shown
its jugular to the dogs.

The truth of that still hadn't fully settled.

Gabrielle glanced at her grandmother. Josephine's shoulders were hunched and most of her color had left her skin. It
was as if she were shriveling away right before her very eyes.

Von Schmidt broke his silence at last, and Gabrielle was
struck by the faultless French accent. "I have long desired to
meet you, Madame Dupree." His eyes gave a contradictory
message. "My business was always with your grandmother in
the champagne house while, as I understood it, you tended
the vines."

A wine merchant, yes. She remembered now. Helmut von
Schmidt worked for an import company from the Rhineland.

Her grandmother had not enjoyed their association, but he'd been employed by one of her most important accounts.

Now, he was a soldier. An officer. Standing in their home. A ten-minute walk away from the wine cellar. He'd come for the champagne. Would he see the wall? Would he know it was fake?

And now, she couldn't get enough air in her lungs. Fear wanted to overwhelm her. She thrust the useless emotion aside. The images of the looting she'd just witnessed were not so easily dismissed. The soldiers' faces were the same as the one staring at her now. Hard, indomitable, full of arrogance and entitlement.

The comparison only made her dislike this man more.

What was he doing in her home? And why this pretense of civility? Gabrielle turned to her grandmother for answers, putting all her questions into a single word. "Grandmère?"

"Herr Hauptmann has requisitioned our home for the duration of his stay in the region."

Gabrielle's entire world crumbled at her feet. She opened her mouth to resist such an impossibility, but the man himself transferred the paper in Josephine's hand to Gabrielle's. "As this document explains, you will not be put out on the streets, if that is your concern."

It was one of many concerns. She wanted to ask about the champagne. She knew not to give him ideas.

"Now that the introductions have been made, you will continue showing me around your home." He spoke directly to Josephine, and she flinched under the brutality in his tone.

Gabrielle opened her mouth to scold him for his insolence. How dare he speak to Josephine Fouché-LeBlanc in such a manner? She chose a less combative tactic. "I will finish the tour of our home. Marta, come here, please." She motioned to the housekeeper lurking in the shadows like a frightened mouse. "Grandmère has grown tired from all the excitement of the day. She needs to rest. You will take her to her room."

Josephine put up a half-hearted argument that seemed to drain her of what little energy she had left, which only proved Gabrielle had been right to take over. She put her grandmother in Marta's capable hands, then directed von Schmidt to follow her. "We'll start in the parlor."

The room looked as though it had been abandoned in haste. A half-filled coffee cup sat on the small table near the window. Newspapers lay spread on the seat around the window recess. At least someone had thought to turn off the wireless. She did not want to hear details of the German invasion with one of them standing beside her.

Jaw set, she guided von Schmidt to another room. He became engrossed with the contents and studied one of the paintings very closely, a Renoir, then went on to the next, a Degas, and the next, a Monet. Gabrielle half expected him to pull out a notebook so he could keep a tally.

She led him to another room. Again, he took his time inspecting the contents. As she watched him taking his mental inventory, her fear began peeling off, exposing the fury beneath. This was her home. This man's very presence was an insult, an outrage. A LeBlanc had lived within these walls for two hundred years. Von Schmidt had walked on these floors for less than an hour and was already treating the contents as if they belonged to him.

His conceit was too much.

"A word of advice, Madame Dupree." Von Schmidt's exquisite French broke into her internal tirade. "Your dislike means nothing to me."

It would be unwise to respond. She would not speak well for herself, or for her family. They were her top concern. She must maintain her composure for them.

Von Schmidt seemed to approve of her silence for he gave her a small nod. "I can be of great service to your family."

"Oh?"

"I can protect you from certain...*realities* of occupation." He let this hang between them for several seconds. "I can be your friend or your adversary. The decision rests with you."

How simple he made it seem. Even he must know that having a choice was not the same as having control. "And if I choose wrongly?"

He slid his gaze over her face. "I think you would not wish for a misfortune to befall your grandmother."

Her breath clogged in her throat. In that moment, she knew, with unavoidable certainty, that this man's control over her and her family was absolute. Her fury didn't vanish under the weight of the revelation, nothing so sudden. It dissipated like a fragile mirage fading from view. "I will keep your advice in mind."

"See that you do."

She led him into the main salon with its white-and-gold Louis XIV decorations. He ran his fingertip along the edge of the mahogany table once used by Napoléon during his Elba exile. As it had in the previous room, his interest moved to the paintings on the walls. One in particular caught his eye, an equestrian scene by Delacroix. Gabrielle attempted to take in the room from his perspective. All she could see was lost hope and renewed despair.

The tour of the first floor came to an end. She felt sick that she must show him the upper levels where her family slept. Once he chose a room for himself, the invasion of their privacy would be complete. For a terrifying moment, she could not continue. Her legs felt boneless. She had to reach out to the nearest wall to steady herself.

Von Schmidt's eyes went to her hand and she saw the look

of pleasure in his gaze. He knew what this "tour" was costing her. Her hatred for him became a burning rage so profound she hardly recognized herself. Despite her distance from God, this was a disturbing turn for a woman raised in the Christian faith. She was supposed to love her enemies.

Not this one.

"Are you unwell, Madame Dupree?" The question sounded like a taunt.

Gabrielle would not allow herself to react. "It's nothing. I lost my footing for a moment, that is all." She feigned a carelessness she didn't feel. "The bedrooms are on the second floor. I assume you would like to see them now, perhaps pick the best for yourself?"

If von Schmidt noticed her disdain, he did not remark on it. He mounted the stairs ahead of her, passing so closely that she smelled the tang of his cologne. Another scent she would never forget. It would always remind her of her own capacity for hate.

A whiff of brimstone would not have been so foul.

Something her father said during one of his lucid moments came to mind. *Courage is not a single act, Gabrielle, but a mindset that, like the vines, requires constant tending.*

"We will start with my sister's room." She gave a cursory knock before opening the door. To her relief, the room was empty.

"Your sister could use a lesson in discipline."

Gabrielle saw no reason to respond. Paulette's disregard for order showed in the pile of discarded garments on the floor, the bed, everywhere but the hamper.

She led von Schmidt back into the hallway. Without commentary, she showed him her mother's room, then her own, both of which were larger and tidier than Paulette's. He took his time among her belongings. She endured the indignity in fuming silence. When he picked up the framed photograph from her wedding day, she moved swiftly, snatching the picture away and setting it back on her dresser. "My grandmother's suite of rooms is at the end of the hallway."

With a hitch of her chin, she indicated he take the lead.

He remained unmoving, his eyes hard and very German beneath the neatly trimmed silver-threaded blond hair. "Madame Dupree. Whether it is out of rebellion or ignorance, you seem not to understand the magnitude of the gift I have given you and your family."

Her stomach clenched, but she managed to make her mouth curve. "What gift is that, Herr Hauptmann?"

"I have saved your champagne from the looters." He leaned in close and assaulted her with his nauseating scent again. "Is that not a grand gesture on my part? Is that not a show of faith that I mean to be an easy guest?"

Of all the insults he'd thrown at her today, this false show of kindness was the hardest to swallow. "What payment, I wonder, will you require for this...gift?"

To his credit, he didn't pretend to misunderstand her meaning. "I ask only that you provide me with fine cuisine and your best champagne from your private stock to wash it down. Not so terrible, you see?"

She saw his intent very clearly.

He took a slow, assessing turn around her room then gave a sharp nod of satisfaction. "This one will do nicely. You will have it prepared for me at once."

He turned to leave.

She made to follow him out of the room.

He stopped her with a hand in the air, palm facing out. "I will finish my inspection of the château without your assistance, Madame."

There was nothing more she could do but watch him go,

her thoughts as heavy as the despair weighing in her heart. Only an hour earlier, she'd witnessed the barbarity of German soldiers ravaging her city. Rabid wolves, all of them, without a single ounce of conscience. Now, one of them would be living in her home. Taking liberties as he pleased.

After all she'd done to protect the champagne, it was secondary to another, more insistent worry. If Reims was not safe from the enemy, if her own home was not safe, what of her family? Her mother, her sister...*Grandmère*. What would become of them?

You will keep them safe, she told herself, thinking of the women she loved. Not herself. Her family, only them.

You will do whatever it takes.

No matter the cost.

Chapter Twelve

HÉLÈNE

Hours after witnessing German thuggery firsthand, Hélène stepped out of Paulette's room and drew the door closed with a furious snap. She stared hard at it, wondering if she'd gone too far. Or perhaps, she hadn't gone far enough. She'd been harsh with her daughter, and there had been real shock in the girl, even a glimmer of fear. But only for a moment, wiped away by a willful refusal to understand the dire circumstances they now faced.

Reims was under siege. German soldiers looted businesses. They confiscated champagne from wine cellars. It was only a matter of time before they made their way to Château Fouché-LeBlanc. Yet all her daughter understood was that there would be no trips to Paris this week.

"It is more complicated than a canceled shopping excursion." Hélène had tried to explain the situation without bringing in her personal reasons for taking greater precautions now that the Germans had invaded Champagne.

Again, she regretted not listening to her father's warnings. He'd been worried ever since Hitler took power in 1933 and had kept her informed as a steady stream of Jews poured into France from Germany seeking refuge. He'd left for New York soon after the onslaught began.

Hélène hadn't understood his insistence that she and her daughters join him in America. She'd thought he was being unnecessarily cautious. Now, she realized her mistake. With the German invasion came the hardest of questions: How long would French Jews be safe? "We are an occupied nation," she'd said to her daughter. "Our government has given Champagne to the Germans. They are our rulers now."

Paulette had shoved away her concern in a gesture reminiscent of her own dismissive hand flick. "What do I know of politics?"

Not enough. Which was Hélène's fault. And so, she'd given it one final try. "Adolf Hitler has an agenda to rid the world of anyone who disagrees with him. His list grows longer by the day, Paulette. For now, he targets social democrats, Marxists." She swallowed. "And Jews."

Paulette's response was to look away, her eyes troubled, but her voice was as stubborn as before. "We are none of those things, Maman."

Hélène had not contradicted her. She'd chosen to let her daughter enjoy her ignorance a little longer and hope that with time Paulette would come to understand the reality of war. For now, Hélène stood in the hallway, feeling desperate and defeated. She considered reentering her daughter's bedroom. Then decided to give the girl a few moments to think through their conversation.

Frustrated with herself, with Paulette—with them both—

she went in search of more news of the German invasion. As she made her way toward the winding stairs, her heart was full of grief for the man she'd lost. Étienne may have been able to get through to their daughter. Hélène felt the same draining energy she did every time her husband filled her thoughts. The sensation always left shadows on her soul. She'd seen what war did to good men. She knew what Herr Hitler wanted to do to people like her and, by association, possibly, if he changed his brutish laws, her daughters.

"You are in quite a hurry, Madame LeBlanc," said a low voice at her back.

Startled, Hélène swerved around and nearly lost her balance. A hand reached out to keep her from toppling down the stairs. She fought against the hold, and tried to regain her balance on her own, which proved difficult as she found herself facing a broad chest covered in a German field uniform. What was such a man doing in her home?

Confused, and a little exasperated, she tilted her head and confronted a pair of piercing blue eyes. The man was stunningly handsome, she noticed that right away, also quite tall. His pale hair and angular cheekbones reminded her of every German she had ever met. Her fear was immediate.

Reims had only just been overrun this morning by the enemy and already she had one of them lurking in the halls of her home. Again, she wondered why such a man roamed unaccompanied on the floor where her family slept? The possibilities were few, each one more terrifying than the last. "You seem to know who I am," she said, held captive by the icy stare. "But I am at a loss as to how we are acquainted."

She could have met him any number of ways. But, really, what did it matter? It was unimportant how they met. Peripheral. This man was one of the invaders. And he was looking at her with a sense of ownership no man had ever dared, not even Étienne. *Especially* not Étienne.

The German took a step closer, saying in perfect French, "Allow me to introduce myself. I am Hauptmann von Schmidt. You may remember me as Helmut von Schmidt when I worked with the Becker and Shultz Import Company."

The phrasing and his manner did nothing to dispel her disquiet. Nor did the fact that he was a wine merchant with ties to the region. He watched her closely as she shifted away from the stairs, and then—finally—his grip on her arm. It was that calculating look that brought another image to mind.

In a sudden rush of memory, she saw this man in a navy-blue suit with a swath of silk peeking from his pocket that matched his bloodred tie. He'd been leaving the champagne house as she'd been about to enter with a question for Josephine about...

Hélène couldn't remember what.

She and this German had exchanged a few words. She did recall that. Their interaction had been nothing more than a nod and a cursory greeting, but she'd been left with a sense of never wanting to repeat the experience. When she'd asked Josephine about him, her mother-in-law had said: *This man is not someone you want to be associated with.*

"We met outside the champagne house last year," she said. "Or possibly the year before."

"The year before." He was smiling at her from his great height, with something not altogether pleasant in his eyes. It was the same look he'd leveled on her that long-ago afternoon. A smile that hit bone and chilled her to the marrow.

This man is not someone you want to be associated with.

Her fear became a living, breathing thing. Without betraying her reaction, she ventured in a perfectly reasonable voice, "May I ask after your business here today?"

She kept the question vague. It was a clumsy attempt at getting him to reveal his intentions and he saw through it. She could see the knowledge dancing in his eyes. "Madame Fouché-LeBlanc has been kind enough to offer me lodgings while I am in the area."

Hélène repressed a gasp. Josephine would never have *offered* this man lodgings. Her low opinion had been formed before he'd dressed himself in a German uniform. "Are we to find separate accommodations for ourselves?"

"I wouldn't think of banishing you from the château, Madame LeBlanc."

Such a polite way to indicate they were to be prisoners in their own home. It was unconscionable. It was the reality of occupation. "And will we be able to come and go as we please? Or will you dictate our schedules?"

The question brought an amused twist to his lips, as if he relished his newfound power in a house full of lonely widows. "Your behavior will decide how you are to be treated. Your future, Madame, is completely in your hands."

Not true. The future was up to the whims of a wine merchant turned soldier.

"As I will be holding small, intimate dinners and the occasional party, I will require an impeccable female hostess to represent my interests. You, Madame LeBlanc, will perform this duty for me."

What he requested was unthinkable. Her reputation would be in tatters before the first course was served at one of his small, intimate dinners. He might as well have put a stamp on her forehead that marked her as his property.

Hélène saw the future in her mind, the months ahead, possibly even years of protecting her secret—and the people she loved—with tiny little evasions and insignificant half-truths to hide the biggest lie of all. There would be constant watching what she said, how she said it, praying she never made a mistake, all the while performing her *duties* as this man's hostess.

So much more to lose besides your pride, she reminded herself. A cold comfort.

"I am sure my mother-in-law extended you the courtesy that is your due. Let me add mine as well. Welcome to our humble home, Herr Hauptmann von Schmidt." Could he tell that her heart was in her throat? Could he hear her words were slightly strangled? "Let me know if there is anything I can do to make your stay as comfortable as possible."

With a long, slow smile, he took her hand in his, placed a kiss on her knuckles. "I see you understand the situation perfectly."

Oh, she understood. She had a brief thought of relinquishing the château to this German. It wasn't hers to give. She had another thought of leaving anyway, of stealing away in the night and taking the women she loved with her. They would never go.

So, then, neither would she.

"You and your family will dine with me tonight in celebration of our new alliance." He issued the invitation as a command. "You will dress for the occasion."

"Of course."

"I expect the first course to be served at precisely eight o'clock, sharp."

"I will see to the details myself."

Before she could say more, a door opened and shut from down the hallway. Seconds later, Paulette breezed into view, a magazine in her hand. "Maman, I want to show you— Oh!" She froze at the sight of von Schmidt. A sliver of uncertainty pulled her brows together. Then it was gone. "Well, hello."

Hélène did not like the way Paulette recovered from her

shock so quickly. Nor did she like the way von Schmidt bounced his attention from her to her daughter and back again.

A sly smile curled at his lips. She had to press her knuckles against her stomach to still the churning. "And who is this stunning creature?"

"This is my daughter Paulette." Hélène made the introductions through gritted teeth. "Paulette, this is Hauptmann von Schmidt. He is to be our guest for the foreseeable future."

His smile grew slimy. "You are very beautiful, Mademoiselle. I see the echo of your mother in you."

Paulette seemed very pleased with the German's compliment. "What a lovely thing to say. Maman is one of the most beautiful women I know."

Von Schmidt took a step closer to the girl and Hélène's heart went stone-cold. The instinct of a mother had her moving quickly and without thought to consequences as she pushed herself between the two.

"Herr Hauptmann was just leaving," she managed to say. It took tremendous concentration not to go for the man's throat. "And you, Paulette, have unfinished schoolwork."

Von Schmidt's mouth thinned to a flat line, sharp as a blade. Hélène held her ground. "Go on, *ma fille*. I will check on your progress once I see our guest to the door."

To her astonishment, her daughter obeyed without argument.

Surprisingly, von Schmidt did not watch the girl leave. He seemed only to have eyes for Hélène, as if her show of maternal protection had intrigued him. She saw him thinking, calculating. And then, something ugly came into his eyes. Something she knew to be masculine interest. "You will now walk me out, Madame LeBlanc."

His tone was like a slap. She wanted to slap back. She was not that foolish. She sensed great cruelty in this man and that worried her as much for her family's future as her own. "Yes, Herr Hauptmann. I would be delighted."

At the door, he stood motionless, a pool of silence swimming between them. Hélène scoured her mind for something to say. She came away empty save for a bright, blank smile.

Her inability to find her voice seemed to bring him pleasure. Gaze locked with hers, he swung open the door, revealing the last threads of sunlight shining brightly in the courtyard.

The sun should not be shining. The sky should be weeping over the fate of the French people.

"You will personally select the champagne for tonight's meal. I require a special blend that represents the best from Château Fouché-LeBlanc's cellars. Do not disappointment me."

With those unsettling words, he left her gaping after him.

Chapter Thirteen

GABRIELLE

Gabrielle deposited the last of her belongings atop the bed in her new room above the kitchen. She'd chosen this one, out of the three on this side of the château, specifically for its view. Ignoring the piles of clothing, shoes, toiletries and other assorted sundries, she moved to the window that overlooked the wine cellar's entrance. Closer to the house stood the stucco-walled garden where Marta cared for her herbs with the same affection Pierre tended the grapes.

The sight made Gabrielle wistful. Within the stone barrier lay a dozen nooks and crannies where she and Benoit had played as children, innocent games that had become not-so-innocent as they grew older. She'd lost more than her husband the night of his death. She'd lost her closest confidant. Her best friend.

But most of all, she'd lost the future they'd dreamed of sharing with their children. They'd had such plans. Even as she reached for the photograph from her wedding, she knew dwelling on her grief was an indulgence she could not afford. An intruder had infested her home and had demanded the entire family join him for an elegant dinner. It was to be a formal affair, no half measures for the German, oh, no.

She dressed quickly and left the room to navigate the maze of corridors and stairwells down to the first floor. The house had all the identifiable features of a French château that had begun its life as a medieval castle. The exterior boasted the requisite round tower on the southwest corner. The roofline featured tall chimneys, seven in total, and multiple dormers. The arched entryway and a balustraded terrace completed the picture. With contributions from previous generations, the interior was equally grand. In some cases, the rooms were tastefully decorated, in others...*non*. Every inch of the walls contained paintings done by the masters. Rembrandts and other portraits shared space with Monet landscapes and Degas ballerinas. There were even a few of the American Impressionists' works, including one of Gabrielle's favorites by Theodore Robinson.

The Lord had blessed her family with many beautiful things. Then He'd taken away the people that mattered more than priceless trinkets and renowned artwork. The emptiness that constantly plagued her dug deeper, and not only because she'd been banished from her room by a German dog. The burdens she carried were never supposed to be hers to shoulder alone. A solitary life had never been in the plan. She didn't even have a child to nurture.

Delightful scents drew her into the kitchen. "It smells wonderful," she told Marta.

Focused on preparing a luscious-smelling soup, the housekeeper accepted the compliment with a nod. "And you, Gabrielle," the housekeeper said, eyeing her from over her shoulder. "You look very lovely this evening. *Très chic.*"

She accepted the compliment with her own small nod. She'd selected the austere black dress she'd worn at her father's funeral, and again at her husband's, to make a statement. The color of mourning fit the situation perfectly. She'd added no jewelry, no makeup, and had pulled her hair into a severe style better suited for a convent than a formal dinner.

"The others have already gathered at the table."

"Très bon." She was nearly out of the kitchen when the row of champagne bottles caught her eye. She counted five in total, an excessive amount. The panic was instant, crackling and hissing like static on the wireless. It took every ounce of self-control to keep her voice even. "Marta, do you know who chose the champagne for tonight?"

The housekeeper went quiet for a moment, then gave another nod. "Your mother. At the German's insistence, she took the bottles from your family's private stock."

Not from the main cellar. Good. The floor steadied beneath her feet.

Aiming for an air of boredom, she stepped into the dining room. The scent of German cigarettes filled her nose. One glance told her von Schmidt had already exerted his control over her family. He sat at the head of the table, smoking casually, almost idly, already comfortable in his role as lord of the manor. Her mother sat on his right. Josephine, his left, Paulette next to her.

He did not rise upon Gabrielle's entrance. Unsurprised at his rudeness, she chose the empty seat beside her mother. "Good evening," she said to the room in general.

Von Schmidt leaned back in his chair and took a slow drag from his cigarette. "You're late."

A harsh response slid to the edge of her tongue. She swallowed the words. There was something in the German's eyes that made her skin prickle in warning. "I apologize. The time got away from me."

"You will want to watch the clock more closely in the future."

He looked about to say more, but Hélène drew his attention. Gabrielle could not decipher what her mother said, but it put a wry smile on the German's face. He took another pull on the cigarette before stubbing it in the ashtray next to his hand. "Now that we are all in attendance—" he gave Gabrielle a look as a silent reprimand for her tardiness "—let us toast to new friends and a happy living situation for us all."

The series of choked gasps were immediate. The women's collective response seemed not to bother the man. He simply lifted his glass and waited for them to do the same.

Gabrielle could not do it. Her mother must have sensed her mood, because she leaned close enough to whisper in her ear. "This is not the time for petty rebellions." She straightened, lifted her glass and parroted von Schmidt's toast. "To new friends."

They drank in silence. Hélène first. Paulette next. Then Josephine. And finally, Gabrielle. The champagne turned bitter on her tongue. Another loss among so many. There were few champagnes in a woman's lifetime that surpassed mere excellence and struck the sublime. The 1928 was one of those wines and Gabrielle could not enjoy even a small taste.

Pressing his advantage, von Schmidt made a second toast. "To Germany's rapid victory."

This time, only Hélène drank. He watched her mother closely, too closely, and Gabrielle wondered what he was plotting. He reminded her of a cobra hypnotizing a small woodland creature into submission. The man had nerve.

As if sensing her furious gaze on him, he gave Gabrielle an arch look. She felt the heat drain from her cheeks. This man would sleep in her bed. He would eat her family's food and drink the best of their champagne. And he would do it all as though it was his right.

"I have always believed," he said, twirling the crystal stem between his thumb and forefinger, "no one makes wine like the French."

And no one cheapens champagne like a beer-swilling German. Again, Hélène leaned in to whisper in Gabrielle's ear. "Whatever it is you are thinking...don't."

She gave her mother a long, measuring look, skimmed a glance over von Schmidt, then whispered back. "I will give you the same warning, Maman. Don't."

Marta served the first course. A beautiful onion soup as only a Frenchwoman could make. Von Schmidt controlled the conversation for the entirety of the meal. Tall and self-important in his dress uniform, he required only the faintest of responses, all given by Hélène.

Even Paulette grew subdued as the night wore on. Gabrielle gained her sister's attention with a soft smile. She tried to communicate what was in her thoughts. *He is only a man, a bully that will be gone soon enough.*

It was a lie, of course. There was no telling how long he would be living in their home. Von Schmidt was like the snake she'd compared him to earlier in her mind. An opportunistic hunter, slithering through their house until he was ready to strike. Gabrielle would be wise to keep a close eye on him.

Marta served the next course, an airy spinach soufflé and her signature coq au vin. Von Schmidt refilled his glass with the 1928. He seemed to have an endless desire for the vintage. Hélène continued to entertain him with her customary wit and charm. He appeared riveted, and perhaps that was her mother's intent. To keep his notice away from the other women in the house. It was a risky approach, all the more dangerous for the way he ran his gaze over her face with a proprietary air that made Gabrielle sick to her stomach.

Over dessert—a rich chocolate mousse—von Schmidt switched his focus to Josephine. "Tomorrow you will show me around the rest of the property. We will start in the champagne house then move on to the vineyard and wine cellar from there."

How harmless the request sounded, how ordinary, if one didn't notice the sly look in his eyes. Gabrielle's own eyes blazed, she knew, and she attempted to smooth out her expression. She could not allow this man—or her grandmother—in the wine cellar without her.

As she'd done earlier in the day, Gabrielle offered up herself in service. "I will be happy to give you the tour, Herr Hauptmann. We can begin at eight o'clock in the morning, if that suits."

He turned his sharp gaze onto her. They stared at one another for a long, long time. Then he glanced at her grandmother, lifted a brow. Josephine lowered her gaze. He pondered her bent head a moment, then turned back to Gabrielle. She expected him to dismiss her suggestion. He surprised her by giving a nod of approval. "Eight o'clock. We will meet in the foyer."

Chapter Fourteen

JOSEPHINE

After von Schmidt released them from the dinner table, Josephine gave her promise to Gabrielle that she would head to bed shortly. First, she wanted a moment alone in the house that had been her home for over half a century. She wandered through the darkened château and thought of the countless generations that had come before her. The women especially, who, like her, had raised their children within these walls.

Exhaustion was heavy in her limbs tonight. It had been a long day. France had fallen within a month of the German mobilization. Josephine couldn't quite understand how it had happened so quickly. A month, just thirty days and all was lost. Or had it taken longer for her country to submit to the invaders? Was this yet another trick of her mind?

She didn't think so.

Josephine's mind and body suffered from the endless sitting at the table with a man she'd never trusted. *Join me for dinner,* he'd demanded. *Dress appropriately,* he'd insisted. *Supply me with your best champagne.* And then, the *coup de grâce. Give me a tour of everything you hold dear so I can steal what is most precious to you.*

Her feet ground to a halt and she looked around. This room, it was not known to her. She'd lost her way in her own home. A little circling would bring her back to the familiar.

The endless ticking of the clocks accompanied her from room to room, down one hallway into another. The rhythmic sound dragged her through time, back to when the end of a long day meant a well-earned rest and a chance to sleep beside her beloved Antoine.

Such a simple world she'd shared with her husband.

Was it any wonder her mind constantly wanted to return to that easier time?

Josephine entered a large entrance hall and stopped on the marble floor. Staring at the ornate door, she tried to recall when she'd first opened it to the German and his soldiers. Had it only been this morning? It seemed a lifetime ago.

She and her family rarely used this part of the château. Despite two hundred years of creating some of the world's premier champagnes, Josephine and her husband had been farmers at the core. Their visitors and business associates were not always so humble. They expected to see displays of wealth from the owners of Château Fouché-LeBlanc. So here, in this grand foyer, and the adjacent rooms, the LeBlanc family presented the expected trappings of success.

She'd seen the lust in the German's eyes when he'd stepped across the threshold. He wasn't the first to covet what belonged to her family. Over the years, Josephine had welcomed dignitaries from three continents, including a prince regent who ultimately became a king. The many faces of those visitors were a series of blurred, bobbing buoys on the sea of her memory.

Why am I here?

Josephine spun in a slow circle, trying to find her bearings.

This was an impressive space, gilded, wallpapered and dressed to impress the most discerning connoisseur of fine architecture. Lit only by the thinning moonlight seeping through the paned windows, the ceilings rose three stories high. It hurt her neck to look to the top. Ah, yes, she knew where she was now.

Why had she come into the foyer?

That, she still couldn't recall.

There was no sound but a silent, deafening hush. Then, the rustle of feathered wings had her searching for the phantom bird. Round and round she spun, until she nearly lost her footing and her vision clouded. She sat on the bottom step in an effort to regain her equilibrium. Her head throbbed. Her body ached. She wanted to go to bed.

Above her, the gabled windows bared their teeth. They glared at her, as if to say, *I know your secret. I know your mind is failing.*

She shivered.

The smell of mildew and something faintly rotten assaulted her senses. She tore at the pins in her hair, only managing to free a few. They sifted through her splayed fingers, landing on the marble at her feet with a series of quiet pings. The noise jolted her. She was in the entryway. Sitting on the bottom step, her knees pulled up against her chest.

What are you doing here, Josephine?

She didn't know.

She looked down at her feet. They hurt. Her feet always hurt, but now they ached. No wonder. Those shoes with the thin black leather strap across the top. They were the ones she wore to church. Why had she gone to church at night?

She hadn't.

She would pray anyway and speak to her God as she did whenever the darkness closed in around her. She let the Holy

Spirit provide the words when they refused to form properly in her head. She begged for peace, for the eradication of evil in her home, for her family's future, for…the ticking in her ears distracted her. "Marta?"

Her first call wasn't answered, nor was her second. But her third, louder and a little more desperate, brought the sound of footsteps. From the corner of her eye, a shadow moved across the marble. It elongated, then morphed into a stooped form. The woman was small and slight, and almost familiar. The white hair cut short, grayed and curled at the ends wasn't right.

"Josephine, *mon Dieu*, what are you doing all alone in the foyer?"

She had no answer. No outrage. No bluster. The fight had left her body. It was just…gone. Only bone-deep weariness remained. "I am tired, Marta."

"Of course you're tired. It's been an eventful day."

What had happened to warrant that look of devastation on her friend's face? Josephine insisted her mind call up the memory. She couldn't quite put the pieces together. "Has it been eventful?"

"Very." The careful patience was unexpected. "We do not host marauders very often."

The German at her table.

Josephine remembered now. The wine merchant, helping himself to her home. Her food. Her finest champagne flowing freely down his German throat. This could not continue. Josephine needed to settle some things with their guest. Not tonight, tomorrow. After she slept.

"I wish to go to bed now." She tucked her legs under her and, leaning heavily on Marta, managed to stand without a single bobble. Rather proud of herself, she stood tall and issued a command in the voice of the family matriarch. "We will go up this way."

Marta nodded. But before they mounted the stairs, Josephine shifted around to glance about the space again. Her gaze landed on the large, heavily lacquered door. Marta had asked why she'd come here. Had she answered the other woman?

Confusion fought with her fatigue, the two sensations twining together to form a new emotion that felt like panic. A silent taunt from the voices in her head. Why did they speak in German and not her native French?

Josephine pressed a trembling hand to her cheeks. "I was moving through the house, looking for..." Had she been looking for something? Someone? "I came in here to..."

Nothing.

Her mind simply had no answer to explain how she'd ended up sitting on the stairs in a part of the house she rarely visited without a reason.

"Never mind, *chère*." In the other woman's eyes, Josephine saw the worry she'd filtered out of her voice. "You do not have to explain yourself to me."

Josephine hated this new frailty of hers. It was infuriating, never knowing when the shadows would sneak up on her and steal a thought.

She looked anxiously around, searching for her husband. It was easy to picture Antoine in his evening clothes, pacing across the marble floor, then pausing, turning toward her. His hand reaching out for hers, beckoning her to join him before their guests arrived.

She moved in his direction but was pulled up short by a hand on her shoulder.

"This way." Marta threaded her arm through Josephine's, guiding her up the stairs, up and up. Josephine paused at the second-floor landing. Thought a moment, then turned right.

She must have chosen well. Marta did not correct her.

By the time they navigated the gloomy hallway, Josephine's

head was pounding again. She entered the room first, Marta a step behind. A narrow band of light winked from the slit in the drawn curtains. Josephine heard her own soft intake of breath and desperately tried to focus on that single sliver of light.

Marta flipped the light switch. The room was suddenly flooded with harsh, unnatural light. Her body immediately drained of heat. "I am cold."

"We'll get you warmed right up. A bath is what you need."

The suggestion made her brutally aware of how their roles had switched somewhere between the foyer and this room. "I want to sleep in my own bed."

"And you will." A single sweeping gaze from Marta's brown eyes gently scolded Josephine. "Once you have had your bath."

Josephine hesitated, wanting to argue, unsure if she should. Such moments between her and Marta were new, forged from the shift in their stations. Where once Josephine was in charge, she now took orders.

The voices had been right. Her secret was not so secret, after all.

"Come. Let us get you out of this dress."

Again, she wanted to argue. The words disappeared as a frightening blankness rose in her mind. Something terrible had happened today. She mustn't forget what it was. She reached for her journal even as Marta guided her into a luxurious bathroom of marble and tile and drew her a hot bath in the claw-footed tub.

Later, when she emerged from the scented water, it was with mild relief. The exertions of the day were still there, but sufficiently muted.

"You will sleep now." As Marta wrapped her in a thick blanket, a new reality took hold. This was to be her life. Relying on another for her most basic needs at the end of a day when fatigue of mind, body and soul overwhelmed her.

Still, it was not without gratitude that Josephine allowed Marta to tuck her into bed.

Warm… Josephine was finally warm.

"Do you need anything else before I take myself off to bed?"

"You may go."

Marta touched her arm. An intimacy Josephine would have never allowed in the past. Tonight, she let the housekeeper's touch bring her comfort. "Sleep well, Josephine."

"You too, Marta."

At last, the other woman left her alone.

Despite her fatigue, sleep eluded her. She stared up at the ceiling, feeling alone, abandoned, with only the empty hours between yesterday and tomorrow for company. The weight of her failing mind brought tears to her eyes. She needed to keep her wits, but dejection crept across her thoughts like a reproachful ghost.

The whispers began again, calling her home to Glory. Josephine could not give in. The Nazis were coming. No, they were already here. In her house. The German with a taste for vintage champagne and a boastful air that could prove useful over time.

An idea began to form in her scattered brain, clearing away much of the mustiness. She would fight her oppressor. To remain passive was to invite extinction. There were things she could do, things only a woman dismissed as feeble of mind and body could accomplish. Her frailty could work in her favor. Or against her.

She must prepare for both eventualities.

Yes, she would prepare. She'd experienced war and its tragedy before. And had found a way to fight back. She would do her part again. While the enemy slept, she would begin. There was much to be done before the sun rose.

Josephine climbed out of bed and went to work.

Chapter Fifteen

GABRIELLE

The next morning, Gabrielle woke gasping for air and tangled in unfamiliar bed linens. The nightmare had been similar to the others, yet different. The spiders were more organized and now worked in teams of two. Sometimes four. They marched into the vineyard with the precision of well-trained soldiers and systematically spun their webs around the grapes, then carted them off. The vicious little fiends shared one face— that of Hauptmann von Schmidt.

The usurper had spent one night in the château, and already he haunted her dreams.

Gabrielle shoved aside the covers and crawled out of bed. There were tears on her cheeks she didn't recall shedding. It came as no surprise. The nightmare had felt so real, and the pounding of her heart had yet to subside. She wiped at her face with a furious sweep of her fingertips. Then, reaching for the picture from her wedding, studied Benoit's smiling expression, a carbon copy of her own. Would she ever be that happy again?

Not while her country was at war.

Remembering the tour with von Schmidt, she returned the picture to its place beside her bedside and dressed herself in clothes appropriate for a day with the enemy.

An impatient Josephine all but pounced on her the moment she entered the kitchen. "Gabrielle. Hurry. I must speak with you at once."

Although her grandmother's eyes were bruised from lack of sleep—something they shared—her gaze was sharp and filled with purpose. "What's on your mind, Grandmère?"

"Not here." She took Gabrielle's arm and tugged her out into the morning air, away from the house, past Marta's garden, and farther yet, nearly to the edge of the terrace. And still, she kept moving around the perimeter of the château.

Along the eastern horizon, the sun emerged from a bank of reddening clouds and coated the vineyard with a rosy glow that seemed both ethereal and eerie. Solitary church bells made their claim on the hour. Gabrielle counted the tolls, putting a number to each strike. Six, then seven. She had an hour before she had to meet von Schmidt. "Where are we going?"

"Away from prying German eyes and ears."

She meant, of course, von Schmidt's prying eyes and ears.

Finally, Josephine drew to a stop beside the loggia beneath Gabrielle's new room on the opposite side of the house from the rest of the family. They were alone. "What is it you wish to say that couldn't wait until after I had my coffee?"

Josephine seemed to consider her words very carefully, or perhaps she was trying to capture a roving thought. "I think, no…I *want* you to assume control of the champagne house."

A denial came to her tongue, quick and instinctive. "I have

already taken over most of the operations. But that doesn't mean I don't value your guidance."

The echo of a smile crossed the older woman's lips. "You misunderstand my request."

"Then perhaps you would like to explain it to me?"

Again, Josephine seemed to struggle with her words. "It occurred to me," she said, eyes squinting, "that our houseguest does not understand the way of things in this home. He still thinks I am in charge of Château Fouché-LeBlanc."

Gabrielle knew this to be true. Both times he'd demanded tours of their property, he'd made the request of Josephine. And had only settled on Gabrielle upon her insistence. She thought back to the look of approval he'd given her at the dinner table. One interloper to another. "I meant no disrespect yesterday, Grandmère."

"*Non*, again you misunderstand. I am not upset over the change in our roles. He, however, only thinks in terms of the past. He does not consider that I may have allowed you to take my place willingly."

Willingly. Gabrielle's mind caught on the word and rolled it around. It appalled her that von Schmidt had misinterpreted her behavior as something brazen and impertinent. Naturally, he would think such a thing. That was how his ugly brain worked. He would only know how to assign motives that made sense to him.

"Grandmère. I'm sorry. I—" She broke off at the look on her grandmother's face. It belonged to the matriarch of the family, the incomparable Josephine Fouché-LeBlanc, widow to Antoine LeBlanc, the woman who'd guided their champagne house for nearly half a century. "You are pleased von Schmidt misread my intentions."

Another smile flashed and was gone almost immediately, replaced with a shrewd twist of her lips. Their gazes locked, and held, and Gabrielle couldn't look away from that unyielding stare. "Think what this could mean for our immediate future."

"I am trying."

"You are not trying hard enough. Listen to me, Gabrielle. *Non.*" Josephine touched her hand. "No sighing, no interrupting. Listen. I am not always in my right mind, I know this, I have much confusion. But not now. My thoughts are clear. You must let me speak before I lose them."

Gabrielle nodded, though it hurt not to come to her grandmother's defense, even in this.

"It is to our advantage this German believes we are engaged in a struggle for control."

"To what end?"

"He will see me as weak and you as an opportunist like himself. Rather brilliant, wouldn't you say?"

Brilliant? They had two very different definitions of the word. "Grandmère, if he thinks you are weak, he will dismiss you. He will see you as nothing but a waste of his time. He will— Oh!" Understanding dawned and with it came a level of panic like she'd never before experienced. "No. It's too dangerous."

"The danger is minimal."

It was tremendous. "Men like Helmut von Schmidt should not be underestimated."

"Men like Helmut von Schmidt should not underestimate women like us. But that is his nature. He will assume you and I are too distracted with our own battles to pay attention to his trickery. We are smarter than that. We will watch him. We will hear things. We will see things."

"And what will we do with these things that we hear and see?"

"We will find ways to pass on what we discover. There are always ways, Gabrielle."

It frightened her to see her grandmother's eyes clear and penetrating as she spoke about this reckless plan. If Josephine was lost in one of her moments of confusion, Gabrielle could pretend to go along, then never bring up the topic again.

But such was not the case. Her grandmother was determined. She would not let this go. "I won't allow you to put yourself at risk."

"The Lord will protect me. He will protect us both."

Bitterness raged in her mind and flowed freely through her words, the same she'd thought on more than one occasion. "The Lord took His hand off this family years ago."

"And now we are at odds." Josephine's eyes crinkled with satisfaction. "This is a very good start, don't you agree?"

It was a terrible beginning. Gabrielle inhaled a breath that tasted like chalk and her own rising fear. Defeat was a short breath away.

"It is better we keep this between us," Josephine said. "We will not tell your mother of our plan. I have something else in mind for her."

Who was this scheming, reckless woman? Not the grandmother Gabrielle had known the past few months. Suddenly, her throat burned, and she couldn't think past the danger Josephine planned for herself, for Gabrielle. And, so it would seem, for her mother. "I don't like this. There are too many ways for it to go wrong."

"Gabrielle, *ma chérie*, we—you, me, Hélène—we are the last of the LeBlanc women. The future of our people rests with us. It is our duty to fight for those who came before us and for those who will take over after we are gone."

"There is another LeBlanc in this home."

"Paulette is a child. This battle can only be waged by women. We cannot—we *will* not—stay passive in this new and treacherous war. We will fight in our way, on our terms."

Gabrielle agreed, in principle. But when she considered the risks, she could not say the words that would align herself with her grandmother. Not this time.

"We will set our plan in motion this very morning. You will play the ambitious, grasping young woman who is fast losing patience with her senile grandmother."

"You are not senile." It wasn't true. It couldn't be true. Gabrielle would not *let* it be true. "I won't tell that fiction."

"It doesn't matter what you say, or even what you think, only what von Schmidt believes. Now, obey me and go." She made a shooing motion with her fingers. "He will be ready for his tour. You cannot afford to offend him by being late."

We are the last of the LeBlanc women. The future of our people rests with us.

The words sounded in her ears like an ancient war cry. The stakes were high, the danger great. She wanted to resist. But inaction carried risks, too. *It is our duty to fight.* Fight, or remain passive? The choice was easy, especially when she thought of Benoit, and what he would do in the same situation. Gabrielle threw back her shoulders and hurried into the house.

The first thing she noticed when she entered the foyer was that von Schmidt wore his uniform again, the hardware gleaming from a recent polishing. She wondered who'd done the polishing. Certainly not him. He had the manicured fingernails of a man who rarely dirtied his hands.

"Ah, Madame Dupree, you are right on time. And dressed for our outing, I see."

She hated his perfect French and the way his eyes ran from the top of her head to the tips of her boots. *We are the last of the LeBlanc women… It is our duty to fight…*

This wine merchant who thought himself a soldier would not take what belonged to her family. She would not give him the chance. "My grandmother suggested I show you the champagne house first." She paused. Then, with a note of superiority, put Josephine's scheme into motion. "We will start in the vineyard instead, before the heat of the day chases us indoors."

His oily smirk came fast, easy, conspiratorial. "Whatever you think is best."

"This way."

The moment they stepped into the vineyard, von Schmidt's eyes sparked with greedy interest. "How much land belongs to your family?"

"Two hundred hectares."

The spark flamed into liquid fire. "I had not realized the vastness of your operation."

"The boundary begins over there." She pointed to her left. "And continues all the way to there." She indicated the northern hills.

He nodded, looking very satisfied. "You keep the vineyard well tended. I am pleased."

The ownership in his voice brought a stream of denials to the tip of her tongue. Did he assume that by seizing their home he had also acquired the vineyard and champagne house? The entire contents of the wine cellar?

Gabrielle had spent a handful of hours in this German's company and already she knew him to be no better than a carnival showman playing a corrupt shell game.

He would learn the LeBlanc widows were no easy mark.

She led him onto the dirt road that spread through the middle of the vineyard. The route took them through freshly dug ruts. Open scars left by the wheels of German-made vehicles.

Gabrielle had heard them in the night and had known there was nothing she could do while they roared down each row. She'd watched them from her window, heart pounding, relief buckling her knees when they drove away. Not a single vine had been harmed. It seemed the Germans had no use for the grapes. They only wanted the wine.

She could not find it in her heart to be grateful.

"Tell me where we are in the growing season."

We. Already, von Schmidt laid claim on what did not belong to him. "My vineyard manager will continue tending the vines through the summer months. It's important to restrict excessive vegetative growth, but it is up to the grapes to ripen under the heat of the sun."

"I would think you want as many grapes as possible."

That he said this exposed his ignorance. "More is not always better. The sugars need to be evenly transferred from the vine to the fruit. This often requires human intervention."

"I see."

She doubted that he did. Holding silent, she took him down one row, up another, pointing out the trellises and wires that kept the grapes off the ground.

"I was surprised you offered to show me around." He gazed at her from the corner of his eye. "But now I believe I understand why."

Gabrielle kept her expression bland. "What is it you think you understand?"

"Your grandmother, she is not as sharp as she once was. Age has taken its toll, no?"

The need to defend Josephine came fast and hard. *Play your role, Gabrielle.* "If she were here, she would disagree."

"Ah, but she isn't here, is she?" He reached out and picked a grape free from its bunch and studied the pale green skin. "And we both know that is of your making."

Play your role. "Grandmère tires easily. The days are hard on her body. And her mind."

"You are very careful with your words, Madame Dupree." He gave her a long, slow appraisal. "You are not so daft as most women. I will have to keep an eye on you."

Better her than Josephine. "You will want to see the champagne house now."

Von Schmidt held his silence until they were standing

among the vats of fermenting wine. Here, he proved more knowledgeable.

"You know wine better than you know the grapes," she said.

"You speak your thoughts very freely."

"What can I say?" She put ice in her voice. "We French are an opinionated breed."

"You would do well to curb this part of your nature."

She had gone too far. If she wished to win this war, she knew she must lose this battle. *Play your role.* "I will be more restrained with my comments in the future."

"A word of advice, Madame Dupree." He leaned in close, so close she could see his pupils expanding. "One day this war will be over, and Germany will be the victor. When that day comes, you will want to be on the right side of my favor."

So he kept telling her. *Play your role.* "I understand, Herr Hauptmann."

She showed him the outbuildings next, taking her time, allowing him to ask his questions and make his inventory. When she pointed out the shed that housed several bicycles, he held up a hand. "Enough. You will show me your wine cellar now."

"Of course." With each step, her pulse roared in her ears. This was it. The moment of truth. She could stall no longer. He would discover the fake wall, or he would not.

"Hold."

Her feet ground to a halt. She glanced at von Schmidt, but he wasn't looking at her. His gaze tracked a black Mercedes cresting over the hill, moving as slowly as a funeral procession. "We will finish our tour another time."

"Whatever you wish, Herr Hauptmann." But she realized she was speaking to his back.

Go away, she thought. By all means, go away. Go far, far away.

Chapter Sixteen

HÉLÈNE

From her perch at the attic window, Hélène watched von Schmidt approach the black Mercedes pulling into the drive. The car's canvas top had been secured in place, thereby concealing the identity of the man inside. The Nazi flags flapping next to the front headlights declared the occupant's allegiance to the Third Reich, as did von Schmidt's deference.

Hélène pressed her lips together. *This cannot be good.* More Germans in her home. More Nazis. The sun chose that moment to disappear behind a bank of fast-moving clouds, turning the sky a dingy gray similar to the contents of her heart.

Through a slit in the blackened car window, von Schmidt began a conversation with the person sitting in the back seat of the Mercedes. His manner was almost submissive, the conversation brief before he removed his hat, tucked it under his arm and climbed into the car.

He closed the door with just enough force to betray his

mood. He didn't like his superior very much. Hélène filed that piece of information away and turned from the window.

A rare moment of peace settled over her. She let it come, let it spread light into her limbs, and then into her troubled soul. This space was hers, a natural extension of the artistic nature she kept hidden behind the mask of an elegant Parisian.

She'd filled the studio with the things she needed to create—graphite pencils and easels. Watercolors, oils. Palettes and brushes. She'd intentionally left the attic unfinished and the windows untrimmed so as to avoid distracting her from creativity. During the summer months, she gathered armfuls of flowers that grew just steps away from the château and arranged them into romantic bouquets. During the winter, she purchased hothouse flowers in Reims.

Roses were her favorite subject matter, their scent adding freshness to the stuffy studio air. Trite, perhaps. Her former friends would have called her work cliché. She'd long given up desiring their approval even before she'd married Étienne. She painted only for herself.

In this space above the château, she disappeared into her art.

Back when Paulette had been growing inside her, she'd needed an escape from her husband's mercurial moods. Étienne had found refuge in his vines, but she had struggled in the aftermath of his tantrums. The final years of his life had been fraught with turmoil. Hélène had loved him through it all. Even at his worst, Étienne LeBlanc was better than any man she'd ever known. But there had been very bad days that left both of them hurting.

Étienne had been the one to come up with the solution for Hélène's need for solitude.

When he'd first brought her to this dusty attic, she'd looked past the broken furniture, the boxes and the trunks, the layers of dirt, and had fallen in love with the space. She'd cleaned for weeks, and then moved in easels, paints and the rest of her tools.

A year ago, Paulette had requested a portion of the studio to create her own drawings. Flowers were of no interest to the girl. But she had a fine eye for fashion. Hélène had welcomed her daughter, clearing off a desk in the corner for the girl to sketch and to dream.

Sighing, Hélène moved to the paned windows on the west side of the studio. She looked past the meticulous rows of vines, to the Cathédrale Notre-Dame de Reims, and felt God's presence in her soul. She rested in the sensation, her mind lighter, her eyes on the stunning gothic structure with its immense stained-glass windows. There stood history and tradition. The cathedral had been the coronation site of every French king since the thirteenth century.

Hélène reached for the cross at her neck and wondered. Would the church survive this war as it had all the others before? Only God knew the answer.

She stepped to the easel with its unfinished painting. She could not find the enthusiasm to apply additional brushstrokes. A full twenty minutes later she was still staring at the canvas, despairing. If she could not create, she would not survive. The Germans had taken her country. They had taken her home. They could not have her soul.

Mouth set, she picked up her paintbrush and poised it at the ready. Her hand shook. She steadied it with a sheer force of will. She must paint, even if what she produced was drivel. And so, she painted. She knew not how long. A minute, an hour. A knock on the doorjamb had her dropping the brush with a start and whirling around to face the intruder.

Expecting to see von Schmidt, it took her a moment to realize Josephine stood in the doorway, breathing hard from having climbed the three flights of stairs. Her mother-in-law wore a pair of nondescript men's trousers and a work shirt that could have come from her husband's closet.

Something was wrong. Josephine never came to the attic. Hélène rushed forward. She took her mother-in-law's arm and guided her to a chair. "Sit, Josephine. Catch your breath. Then you can tell me what has brought you to my studio."

The older woman lowered herself onto the seat Hélène indicated.

"Let me get you some water." She returned with a glass she'd filled from the pitcher she kept for herself when the day turned hot.

Josephine pushed her hand away. "Don't hover, Hélène. It embarrasses us both."

"I suppose it does." She spoke more sharply than she'd intended and winced. Nothing seemed right anymore. Not her words. Her tone. The world had tilted sideways, and Hélène couldn't seem to find her footing. Even this unexpected visit left her off-balance.

Frowning, Josephine glanced around the large space, looking a little lost. "It smells of paint and dust and day-old flowers." She wrinkled her nose. "It is an odd combination."

"Is it?" Hélène hardly noticed. To her, the scent belonged to this room, as much a part of her creative process as the blank canvases and her brushes. "I rather like the smell."

The older woman muttered something under her breath Hélène didn't quite catch. She left it alone. "You don't often make the trip up so many stairs. I can only assume something of grave importance has urged you to do so now."

"Our house has been seized by the enemy. Matters rarely get much graver than that."

Hélène could think of many that did. She'd kept herself informed of the unconscionable horrors occurring in other parts of Europe. Jewish businesses seized, neighbors telling on neighbors, Jews being deported, many arrested without warning. "We have been allowed to remain in our home," she countered. "Others have not been so fortunate."

"This is true." Josephine momentarily pressed her lips together and glanced around as if reminding herself where she was. "And yet, our home has become the nest for a viper."

"*Oui*, it has." While Hélène waited for her mother-in-law to continue, she noted the changes in the older woman. Josephine was not the force she'd once been. She was slower of mind and body.

This morning there was nothing slow or measured in the way she hoisted herself to her feet. Or in the focused gaze she leveled onto Hélène. "I have come to ask for your help."

Hélène could not hide her surprise. Her mother-in-law rarely asked anything of her. "What is it you need?"

"Our houseguest has provided us a list of his requirements for his stay. Here, see for yourself." Josephine reached inside the pocket of her trousers, pulled out a slip of paper and handed it to Hélène.

She gave the bold, masculine script a cursory study, then looked up at Josephine, her eyebrows raised. "He has gone into excessive detail."

"Apparently, he doesn't trust us to see to his wishes without his heavy-handed guidance."

That much was clear.

Hélène returned her attention to the page. The list was full of von Schmidt's demands. None were wholly unexpected. He wanted someone to see that his clothes were properly cleaned and pressed. He also wanted someone to maintain his social calendar, prepare and review his correspondence, assist with social functions, plan and implement special dinners, meet and host visitors. The list went on and on. "Are these not the duties of an aide-de-camp?"

"This German is not a complicated man, Hélène. It doesn't take great effort to understand what is in his head. Even when my mind is muddled, I see him for what he is. Yes, he could assign a soldier to perform these duties. Instead, he uses this opportunity to exercise his control over us. He thinks we will fall in line. We will be one step ahead of him. You understand?"

Hélène understood perfectly. Her mouth went dry and she thought vaguely of running from the attic, from this house. "You are asking *me* to serve as von Schmidt's social secretary."

"He has an affection for you."

Josephine had noticed that, had she? How could she not? Even, as she'd put it, when her mind was muddled. Von Schmidt had not been especially subtle at the dinner table last night. Hélène had been too relieved that he no longer looked at Paulette with a leering eye, to think what his interest in her would mean. "What if he begins nosing around into my background? What if he has questions I cannot answer without lying?"

"Better that he asks them of you, rather than our neighbors."

She vehemently disagreed. "Our neighbors only know me as Hélène Jobert-LeBlanc."

"Are you absolutely certain of this? Are you willing to take that chance?" Josephine came to stand in front of her. She took her hand and looked at her with a transparency that had been missing for months. "Our country has fallen into the hands of a man who considers genocide a form of careful breeding. None of us are safe anymore. You, most of all, are at risk. As are your daughters because they share your blood."

"Are you saying I have tainted Gabrielle and Paulette with my Jewish blood?" She couldn't keep the bitterness out of her voice.

"I am saying nothing of the kind. We must be one step ahead of von Schmidt. It would not take much digging on his part to discover your truth."

"My mother was a Christian. She raised me in her faith."

"That will not matter to our invaders. The Nazis will bring their anti-Semitic policies with them. We live in the *zone occupée*, under the same roof as a soldier."

"He is a wine merchant." The words were barely a whisper.

"He is a man who takes pride in wearing the uniform of the Third Reich. Think, Hélène. Think what that means for you. Do not be naïve."

She grabbed her cross at her neck, clutched it in her palm. "I am not a Jew."

"You have two Jewish grandparents. By definition, that makes you a Jew. Hitler and his Nazi thugs want to wipe you—*you*, Hélène—off the face of this earth."

Shock bled through her calm, leaving her feeling weak and unsteady on her feet. "Must you speak so plainly?"

"I will speak plainly, while I still can, before the thoughts leave me." Josephine took Hélène's other hand. "You and I have not always gotten along. We have not tried hard enough to understand each other. But, you are the daughter of my heart, if not my blood."

She stared at her mother-in-law, shocked and pleased all at once. Warmth rushed through her veins, chasing away the coldness in her heart. She closed her eyes a moment, the cross heating her skin, and gathered up the image of her daughters. Gabrielle with her fierce, warrior beauty and Paulette, a near copy of herself. She thought of Josephine next, the ferocious matriarch of their family. She loved them all.

If her secret was discovered, they would be in danger. Gabrielle and Paulette because they were her daughters. Josephine because she harbored a Jew. "I will leave this home at once."

This morning. This very minute. It was the only way to protect her family.

"*Non*. You will not abandon this family. And we will not abandon you."

"I...I don't know what to do."

"Yes, Hélène, you do."

She felt the icicle forming in the back of her throat, sliding past her heart, into her stomach. "You want me to insert myself into von Schmidt's life, first as his secretary, then what? As his—" She couldn't say the words. "Josephine, it... it's too much."

"I'm not asking you to compromise yourself. Never that. I am only suggesting you make yourself indispensable to this German who thinks he owns us."

Which of them was being naïve now? Von Schmidt would want more than her company. How long would she be able to satisfy such a man with only her smiles?

"It will require great courage on your part."

Courage, yes. More than she had on her own. She called on her God and thought of the words she'd read this morning in the privacy of her room. *I send you forth as sheep in the midst of wolves*... "I have never been brave," she whispered.

"You stood by my son through his darkest hours, and never once thought of giving up on him. That, Hélène, is the very definition of bravery."

Her chest rose and fell on a sigh. She hadn't been brave. She'd been a wife. "I loved Étienne."

She loved him still. His death had stripped her of any hope for a happy future. What, then, did she really have to lose? "I will approach von Schmidt this afternoon and offer up my services as his secretary."

"You are a good girl, Hélène."

If only her mother-in-law knew the truth. To borrow Josephine's own phrase, she was nothing of the kind.

Chapter Seventeen

GABRIELLE

It came as no surprise that von Schmidt failed to keep his word. In the span of a few weeks, he confiscated over 30,000 bottles of champagne from the Château Fouché-LeBlanc cellars, then sent them to his superiors back in Berlin. The action had earned him approval, and a written commendation, but not the promotion he so clearly sought.

The only good that came from his duplicity, to Gabrielle's relief, was that her counterfeit wall had withstood the comings and goings of his soldiers. Von Schmidt's men had been so focused on stealing her family's champagne they'd paid little heed to the cave itself.

Unfortunately, Gabrielle's neighbors suffered even greater losses. In total, German soldiers stole more than two million bottles from the *Champenois*. Something had to be done to protect the wine. She was not the only producer to come to this conclusion. When she contacted her father-in-law, Maximillian Dupree invited her to his home to discuss the problem.

Gabrielle told no one about the meeting, not even her grandmother, and left the château under the cover of the black moonless sky. She chose a bicycle for her mode of transportation, which allowed her to keep to the vineyards and off the main roads.

The closer she pedaled toward her father-in-law's property, the more her mind pulled away from confiscated champagne and German occupation and turned to her deceased husband.

Benoit's death had been so unfair. So unnecessary. A wagon wheel had fallen on his leg, trapping him for hours before one of their workers found him. He'd downplayed the injury, hiding his pain until gangrene set in. It had been too late to save the leg. Or, as it turned out, his life. He'd sought morphine to dull his pain and died in a drug-induced stupor. Gabrielle had prayed while he suffered, and again during his final hours. God's response had been silence.

She'd learned her lesson, and now relied only on herself. Although there were times she felt lonely, it was better that way. Simpler. Also, better, simpler, to set aside her grief and consider what she would say when she arrived at her father-in-law's château. She would not speak of Benoit. That much, she promised herself.

Max himself opened the door. Gabrielle felt a pang in her chest. It hurt to see the echo of her husband in the face of his father.

Shifting uncomfortably, she shoved her hands in her pockets. In the next instant, she found herself pulled into his muscled, *vigneron* arms. She hesitated, almost recoiling in pain, then hugged him back. "I have missed you," she whispered.

"And I you, *ma chérie*."

Gabrielle wanted to cling to him. It had been too long since she'd seen Max. The last time had been at the anniversary party. Their conversation had been brief and stilted. Now, feeling that same awkwardness, she stepped back and studied the man who'd once been both friend and surrogate father.

He'd aged, and gone paunchy around the middle, but Maximillian Dupree was still a very handsome man. Dark hair with threads of silver at the temples, a lean poet's face and soulful, impassioned eyes.

This is how Benoit would have looked had he survived into middle age. The thought brought a bittersweet smile to her lips. Max returned the gesture, and again she had to swallow back a wave of emotion. He had the same look around the mouth as his son.

"You are the last to arrive," he said.

"I… Oh." She hadn't known there would be others.

"Come, Gabrielle, time is of the essence. We must be quick. We're meeting in the library." He led her through the cavernous hallways, the same ones she and Benoit had roamed as children. She could close her eyes and know the way. Each twist and turn was as familiar as any in her own home.

Max paused outside the room and indicated she enter ahead of him.

The space was full of men she knew on sight. Most sat, some stood, one leaned against the bookshelf. She counted half a dozen grape growers and twice that number of champagne producers. All were at least twenty years her senior, some contemporaries of her grandmother.

One in particular caught her eye, the head of Moët & Chandon. Count Robert-Jean de Vogüe was well respected among the *Champenois*, a natural leader. It was rumored he had connections to the Vatican and was related to most of Europe's royal families. His brother, Bertrand, the powerful head of Veuve Clicquot-Ponsardin, was, Gabrielle noticed, missing.

"I trust you know everyone."

She nodded, then went through the ritual of greeting each of the occupants of the room, saving de Vogüe for last. He was a striking man in his late fifties, his coloring almost swarthy, his green eyes deep-set and solemn. Like several other men in the room, he'd been a close friend of her father's. And had great respect for her grandmother.

De Vogüe was also in charge of this meeting. He waited for Gabrielle to take a seat beside her father-in-law to begin. "I cannot stress enough the importance of secrecy. Whatever is said tonight must not be repeated. Do I have your word?"

Every head bobbed in agreement.

"Excellent. Now, as you are aware, the German authorities have appointed Otto Klaebisch to serve as *weinführer* over our region. He will oversee champagne purchases for the Third Reich." De Vogüe paused, made eye contact with several people in the room, including Gabrielle. "Originally, this selection seemed a good one. Klaebisch is a connoisseur and understands how we do business."

The man on Gabrielle's immediate left raised a fist. "Better to be shoved around by a winemaker than by a beer-drinking Nazi."

"As many of us thought," de Vogüe acknowledged. "However, Klaebisch enjoys the trappings of military life and appreciates the power that comes from his new position."

De Vogüe could be describing Helmut von Schmidt as well.

"The *weinführer* has requisitioned my brother's château." De Vogüe's gaze held steady on Gabrielle. "He threw Bertrand and his family out onto the streets with no worry where they would go."

Gabrielle gasped. She had not heard this news, but now understood the man's absence.

With de Vogüe's gaze still on her, several heads turned in

her direction. She could easily decipher their unasked questions, the speculation as to why her home had been requisitioned and yet, unlike de Vogüe's brother, the LeBlanc women had been allowed to stay.

She confronted their suspicion directly. "I believe," she began, eyes only on de Vogüe, "von Schmidt has treated us differently because we are a houseful of women." Though she hated saying the words, she could not dismiss the truth behind them. "He does not consider us a threat. He repeatedly says our gender is weak."

The room fell silent as each man considered what she'd stated without inflection or emotion. Many, she knew, agreed with von Schmidt's estimation, although none said so now.

As if this settled the matter, de Vogüe continued the meeting. "My main purpose for calling us together is to discuss what German occupation means for our immediate future. I met with Klaebisch this afternoon and I am afraid the news is not good."

A low rumble spread throughout the room.

Lifting a hand, de Vogüe went on to explain. "We will only be allowed to sell our champagne to the Third Reich and its military. Also, German-controlled restaurants, hotels and nightclubs, and a few of Germany's friends such as the Italian ambassador to France and Marshal Pétain at Vichy. The marshal, I am told, enjoys large quantities of our special *cuvées*."

The room erupted in angry expletives, while Gabrielle's heart sank. Her hope soon followed. There could be no more doubt that the self-proclaimed leader of the French people had allied himself with the enemy. This was the final blow to any hope that the government would grow a backbone.

"What price are we to expect for this *privilege* of supplying our enemies with France's greatest treasure?" someone taunted from the back of the room.

De Vogüe quoted a number that was tantamount to robbery. "We either sell to the Germans at this dismal price," he added, "or we go out of business. Those are our only choices. And I'm afraid there is still more unsettling news. We are to supply the Third Reich with two million bottles of our champagnes every month, distributed among our houses in whatever quantities we decide."

Shocked silence met this additional revelation.

It was an impossible number. Angry curses shattered the library's already dismal mood. "This will ruin us," one of the producers claimed.

While others agreed, Gabrielle looked to her father-in-law. He returned her stare with the eyes of a man who'd survived bad harvests, the loss of his wife, then his only son. He did not appear beaten. His expression was fierce, as if to say: *We will not crumble. We will fight.*

De Vogüe answered questions, then brought the meeting to an end with one final proclamation. "If we are to survive German occupation, we must band together formally."

He laid out his plan. Answered more questions. Then set the date for their next meeting.

As the room emptied, Gabrielle hung back at her father-in-law's request. She knew that expression. It was the look of a concerned parent to a favorite child. "I don't like you living under the same roof as a German soldier."

In that, at least, she could alleviate his worry. "Helmut von Schmidt is an overreaching wine merchant who wears a soldier's uniform. It is not the same."

"You argue semantics when you should be thinking in terms of caution." His hand rested briefly on her cheek, then dropped away. "That uniform he wears makes von Schmidt a dangerous man."

"What would you have me do, Papa?" She used the name

she'd called him when she was still a girl. "Would you have me surrender the house that has been in my family for two hundred years because others have been forced to do the same?"

"I would have you be smart."

"I am not a reckless woman," she responded firmly, so he could not fail to understand her meaning. "You know this, Papa."

"What I know is that you will take excessive risks. It is in your nature. You have too much of your grandmother in you."

He was wrong. Gabrielle didn't have enough of Josephine in her.

"And yet, I will still make my request."

As if he'd been waiting for his cue, de Vogüe returned to the room and took over the conversation. "You, Madame Dupree, are in an interesting position to serve your country."

She did not know how to respond.

"I trust you heard General de Gaulle's broadcast from London?"

She nodded. "He urged the people of France to resist the Germans."

It had been a call to action. Opportunity within opposition. But then the Germans had come to Reims. And they had looted. Burned down buildings. Requisitioned her home. During it all, Gabrielle had thought only of her family and their champagne house. Now, de Vogüe was asking her to think of her country. It was not hard to understand what he wanted her to do. "You want me to spy on von Schmidt."

"It would be a simple matter for you to track his comings and goings. Perhaps monitor his correspondence when possible. Who does he invite to his table, and what is said when he thinks no one but his friends are listening?"

Grandmère would call this God's providence. And maybe, Gabrielle thought, she would be right. Maybe this was God's will for her life, a purpose that went beyond herself. Odd, that her mind would accept this, when her heart could not. She wanted to do her part for France, she did. But not at the risk of her family.

Your family is already at risk.

And Gabrielle had already set a plan in motion that would harmonize with de Vogüe's request. The sooner the enemy was vanquished, and von Schmidt was expelled from their home, the better. "How would I get this information to you?"

"You and I will never meet," de Vogüe said. "You will report directly to Max."

"You are comfortable with this arrangement?" she asked her father-in-law.

He nodded. "For the good of France."

It could be done, she knew. But not without risk.

Max touched her hand. "Gabrielle, I know we ask much of you. But not as much as we ask of ourselves."

"How would I get the information to you?"

"We would set a regular meeting time and place. Somewhere in public that would not draw suspicion." Max thought a moment. "Perhaps on Sundays. We could linger in the church, a concerned father-in-law checking in on his daughter-in-law."

The suggestion—*linger in the church*—made her stomach twist in nausea. Max knew what he asked of her. He'd been standing beside her at Benoit's funeral when the priest had served up his platitudes, then walked away when she'd asked the difficult questions about good men dying too young and God's random cruelty.

No, not the church. She would find another way. "What if I discover something that can't wait until Sunday?"

"Then we'll meet in the vineyard. At a spot we both know

well." Max's smile turned sad. "Three rows east of my family's chapel, halfway between the first and second hill."

Of course she knew the place well. It was the site of Benoit's fatal accident.

Not there, Max. Anywhere but there.

Her father-in-law took her hand, tears in his eyes. "Is it not fitting? We will join forces to save lives on the very spot where we lost the one life we couldn't save."

There were so many ways Gabrielle could respond. She could snatch her hand away. She could rail. She could simply walk out of the library. Or she could point out that Benoit hadn't actually died in the vineyard. He'd hung on for months, in pain and misery. None of those things would bring her husband back. "How will we know what time to rendezvous?"

It helped to focus on specifics. In times of uncertainty, taking action mattered. That's what she told herself, what she tried to believe.

Max explained a seemingly uncomplicated code they would use via the telephone. "After each exchange, we will reset the code."

A good precaution, she thought. "It appears you've thought of everything."

His smile was genuine, but still held hints of sorrow. "All that's left is your agreement."

She gave it, for the good of France. "I'll begin tomorrow."

Chapter Eighteen

~❧~

JOSEPHINE

At seventy-seven, nearly seventy-eight, Josephine was not the woman she'd once been, neither physically nor mentally. Old age was not the only factor in her decline. Perhaps not even the most significant. That revelation came as both a shock and a sorrow. She carried too many sad memories in her head. What had once been the occasional trespasser was now a living, breathing presence. Always there, dark and sinister, laying claim on her sanity.

Sometimes the images were so real they pulled tears from her eyes. Sometimes they were nothing more than gray, lifeless shadows within a watery haze.

Forgetfulness was an easy defense that protected her from the harder work of remembering the loss of loved ones, the bad decisions she'd made in her youth, even the betrayals she'd endured from trusted friends and colleagues.

Oh, yes, absentmindedness had its appeal. How else was she

to survive from one moment to the next? By being stronger than she'd ever been before, that's how.

The battle grew harder each day. Each hour.

Even now, her mind lured her into blessed oblivion. Josephine fought the invitation to rest in the comfort of darkness. She resisted not for herself, but for her family. She'd done what she could to prepare Gabrielle and Hélène for combat within the walls of their home.

Her own contribution had been minimal. She would be bolder this afternoon, fearless and unafraid. Course set, she made her way through the château in the clothes she'd donned for the vineyard, though she'd never made it outside. Too tired. Marta had fitted the men's trousers and baggy shirt to accommodate Josephine's shrinking frame. She would have to change for dinner with the German. Always, he demanded the family's presence at his table.

Always, they answered his summons without complaint. He thought this made them submissive, and that he had them sufficiently cowed. He was too arrogant to consider he might be wrong.

There was no honor in such a man, no character, no compassion or sense of fairness. Von Schmidt was the same as his führer. Greedy and selfish. Like Hitler, he knew how to break things, and how to tear down. He did not know how to create. But his greatest flaw was his lack of respect for women. Josephine knew how to fight this war. She'd been doing so since the untimely death of her husband fifty years ago.

She hurried her steps, knowing her time was limited. When she reached the top of the staircase, she listened to the chiming of the clocks. The six strikes told her she had two hours to complete her mission and still dress for dinner. The silence in the hallways broadcasted a similar message.

Allowing herself a small smile of triumph, she took the

staircase to the first floor and continued to the west wing of the château, her slippered feet soundless on the tiled floors. She practically floated. A few minutes, that's all it took, and Josephine found herself in a darkened corridor, unsure how she'd ended up in this particular hallway. She'd lost her way.

Focus, she told herself.

She thought for a moment. And remembered. She'd given herself a task. *Finish it.*

Bolstered, she moved wraithlike to the library, where von Schmidt had set up his private office. The door stood halfway open, beckoning Josephine to take this risk. She paused, listening for voices, the rustle of papers, anything to tell her someone worked in the room her husband had loved most of all. She heard nothing. Von Schmidt must be elsewhere in the house.

He could come back at any moment.

Josephine had a plan for that.

She peered around the black lacquered door into the empty room. This was her chance. She stepped inside, straight into the smell of leather-bound books, parchment paper—the scents belonging to her husband—and...German cigarettes.

That smell, it confused her. Why did this room reek of foreign cigarettes? Antoine smoked cigars. Her thoughts twisted, turned, battled with the whispers for her mind. She would not let the darkness win. There was important work left to be done.

If caught? She would pretend confusion—no great stretch— or perhaps she would try a more daring approach. Either way, she wasted precious time lost in her head. She picked her way across the patterned rug to the rolltop desk. Neat stacks of papers shared space with embossed stationery, pens, letter openers. Such obedience to the German's preference for order. Hélène had found her calling.

But again, Josephine wasted time allowing her mind to drift.

Breathe, she told herself. *Finish it.*

With quick fingers, she rifled through the documents, careful not to upset their position, then turned her attention to the drawers. She found tickets to the theater, stubs for train rides to Épernay, one to Paris, stamps, a host of official-looking documents and invoices. Within this cluster, she found a piece of buried treasure. An order for an outrageous sum of champagne. Its destination, North Africa.

Josephine held up the paper and read. She wasn't as well versed in the German language as she would like, but she knew enough to understand a large portion of the words, the markings, the numbers. She continued reading and, again, told herself: *breathe.*

She read and she breathed.

When she was confident she understood what she'd found, she replaced the document in the drawer and closed it with a noiseless click. Slowly, she stepped back and breathed. She took another step. Eyes still on the desk, she swallowed a smile, sensing—*knowing*—she had come across a significant piece of information. Where the champagne goes, so goes the German army.

Someone must be told. Someone she trusted. Someone—

"What are you doing in my office? You do not have permission to be in this room."

Stifling a gasp, Josephine whipped around and met von Schmidt's angry stare. She allowed herself one instant of panic. Then remembered she had planned for this.

Her voice, when it came, was hard and unforgiving, bordering on shrewish. "I will ask the same of you. What is the meaning of this, Antoine?" Letting her eyes go a little wild, she picked up a random stack of papers, waved them in the air, slammed them back on the desk. "You conduct business in a foreign language now, one I do not understand? Why is this? Why hide these transactions from me? Me? Your wife of nearly ten years."

Shocked at how authoritative she sounded, when inside her head the voices wailed, she watched von Schmidt hover in the doorway. His face contorted. Uncertainty coated over his obvious distaste, as if he wasn't entirely sure how to deal with this madwoman in his office. "Madame LeBlanc, I think you are confus—"

"Madame LeBlanc? *Non*, you will not address me as though I am a stranger to you. I am your wife."

"Madame. LeBlanc." Through gritted teeth, von Schmidt enunciated her name with furious precision. "You clearly have me mistaken for—"

Josephine spoke over him again. "You will *not* speak to your wife in that tone. I won't have it." She slid her gaze away from von Schmidt, looked frantically around the room, allowing a bit more paranoia to show in her eyes. "I have done nothing to deserve such treatment. When I think how I have cared for you, and now you—"

"Grandmère!" Gabrielle rushed into the room, all but shoving von Schmidt aside in her haste. "We were supposed to meet in the parlor. The parlor," she repeated. "Not the library."

Josephine turned her head slowly, taking her time, forcing herself not to rush, though she wanted to. Her granddaughter should not be here. This was not part of the plan. Gabrielle must have heard the shouting. And now Josephine would have to adjust, when all she wanted to do was escape this room before she forgot what she'd discovered. The shipment. To North Africa. *Do not forget.*

She managed a weak smile, added a vacant look in her eyes. The shipment. To…

Where? For a moment, she was overwhelmed by how tenuous her hold on the information had become, how rash she had been to snoop among von Schmidt's things when she hadn't known where he was in the house.

Had she known he was in the house?

The shipment. North Africa. Yes—that was where it was going. North Africa.

"Gabrielle?" She folded her lips into an expression of bafflement. "You have… You are…" She chased her gaze around the room, then flapped a hand in front of her own face. "I don't remember why I came into the library."

Gabrielle put a tense but protective hand on her shoulder. "To get a book, perhaps?"

More glancing around the room. Then she looked inside her mind, and saw the darkness creeping in from the edges. "I…perhaps I did come for a book." She made a grand show of pulling her eyebrows together. "Oui, *perhaps*."

"Do you recall which one?" Gabrielle asked the question gently, while also putting herself between Josephine and the German. The shipment. To North Africa. *Do not forget.*

Josephine shook her head. The appearance of her granddaughter brought a sort of cold comfort. She'd momentarily lost herself in the fiction she'd created. For just a moment, she'd thought von Schmidt was her beloved Antoine and that he had betrayed her. "I forgot."

"I'll help you remember."

Out of the corner of her eye, she saw the exact moment von Schmidt's patience came to an end. "Out. Both of you. Now. You will have this ridiculous conversation anywhere but in my presence."

"Of course, Herr Hauptmann." Gabrielle linked her arm through Josephine's. "We will not bother you a moment longer."

Grateful for the support, Josephine allowed her granddaughter to lead her across the rug, onto the hardwood floor. They made it nearly to the doorway.

"Halt." Stepping into their path, von Schmidt gripped Josephine's arm. Hard. His gaze was savage as it ran across her face. She nearly buckled under his rage, but somehow forced her knees to hold herself up. "I will allow you this one mistake. Next time I will not be so lenient. Do I make myself clear, Madame?"

"Very."

"*Gut.*" He let go of her arm. "You will leave now, before I change my mind."

She hurried out of the room, practically dragging her granddaughter with her. The moment they stepped into the hallway, von Schmidt slammed the door behind them. Gabrielle winced. Josephine hardly heard the terrible sound. Shipment. North Africa. "Take me to my room. Hurry, before I forget."

"You found something."

"*Oui.*" She would wait to explain until they were inside the safety of her room. Once there, she said, "Close the door. Quickly now. I must record what I discovered."

"Grandmère." Fear covered Gabrielle's voice. "You cannot take such risks as you did today and, *mon Dieu*, you cannot record anything you discovered on paper."

Josephine waved away the warnings. Shipment. North Africa. Her journal.

Where had she put it? She moved to her bedside table. Not there. Somewhere close. Hidden in the wall. Behind the baseboard.

"Tell me what you found, Grandmère." Gabrielle touched her hand. "I will pass it on, as we discussed."

Josephine hesitated, calculated the consequences of bringing her granddaughter into her confidence, then remembered their agreement. "I found an invoice for a large shipment of champagne."

"How large?"

The details rolled from her lips as quickly as she could think them. The destination, the number of bottles to be shipped, the date the train would depart Reims, even the houses that would be required to supply the enormous quantity.

"This is excellent information." The young woman looked prepared to say more, perhaps give her another warning.

Josephine was not in the mood. "I'm tired, Gabrielle. I wish to rest now."

"I'll leave you alone." She came close and kissed her on the cheek. Then, at the door, said over her shoulder, "We aren't finished with this conversation. I will have my say and you will do me the honor of listening."

Josephine knew she deserved a lecture. She'd been reckless today. She'd also been successful. She'd done her part for the war. For the good of France. The shadows could have her mind now.

At least, until she had to dress for dinner.

Chapter Nineteen

GABRIELLE

Hours after racing into the library, Gabrielle's insides still shook. What had her grandmother been thinking? Sneaking into von Schmidt's private office had been wildly unwise. There were so many ways he could have punished her if he hadn't been taken off guard by her outlandish accusations and shouting. It had been a masterful strategy on Josephine's part, but one that could never be repeated. Von Schmidt was not a stupid man. He would not be fooled twice.

When Gabrielle cornered her grandmother after dinner she told her this, and more. She'd added that under no circumstances was she to take such a risk again. It had taken considerable convincing, but eventually Josephine had agreed to stay out of von Schmidt's private office.

Only then did Gabrielle leave her grandmother in Marta's care to make the telephone call to her father-in-law. She'd used the code they'd agreed upon. And now waited for the rest of the house to go silent before venturing beyond her room.

Peering out into the hallway, she paused and listened. All was quiet. She slipped into the shadows and hastened down the back stairwell, carrying her shoes to keep her footsteps muffled. At the time she'd been tossed out of her own room, she'd chosen her new *accommodations* for the view and with the added purpose of getting far away from von Schmidt.

Now, as she exited the château, dressed from head to toe in black, she realized how fortuitous her choice had been. Von Schmidt was so concerned with his own position in the household that he'd failed to see the danger of putting Gabrielle so far away from him. He should keep a closer eye on his enemies.

She left the terrace and slipped on her shoes. Then, finally, she could run. How she needed to run. She let her mind stop and was simply inside her body, her legs pumping. Her feet, her arms, every part of her moved in a single coordinated effort. The wind whipped her hair around her face. Clouds swollen with rain hung low over her head.

A crack of thunder shook the air.

The journey from château to shed was short, but long enough to revive Gabrielle's spirit, and clear her mind. For this first clandestine meeting with her father-in-law, she'd alerted Max with the preset code he'd laid out in his library. Two rings of the telephone followed by a hang-up. Then, another phone call, and another hang-up to indicate the time of their rendezvous. One ring, midnight. Two rings, one o'clock in the morning.

Tonight, on the second call, she'd let the phone ring twice before hanging up.

It was raining by the time she mounted her bicycle and took off in the watery gloom. Her breath puffed, and her movements were full of intent as she made the trip through the blackened vineyard.

This year, unlike last, the rain came too late and entirely too infrequently. Where too much moisture had been her enemy a year ago, drought was the adversary now. The water-stressed vines had created a feeding frenzy for the grape moth and harvest worm. Advanced ripening, scorched leaves, and another harvest was ruined. They hadn't even attempted to pick the grapes. They'd buried the shriveled carcasses beneath their water-starved roots.

Gabrielle wanted to rage against a God that had allowed two bad harvests in a row. It would be a wasted effort. God didn't care about her, or her anger. His attention was elsewhere.

She pedaled faster, harder, head down, her memory guiding her along the rows as she lost herself in the rhythm of the spinning wheels. Now she was flying across the vineyard, up a rise, down another, her breath raw and painful in her lungs. Something caught her eye, a swish of stark white fabric, and she turned her head, expecting to see her father-in-law, but he wasn't there. Nothing was there but the withered vines. She came to a stop, set her feet on the ground and looked around, struggling to catch her breath, her bearings, under the hard drizzle of rain.

The movement came in the corner of her eye again. She straightened and swiped at her forehead, half thinking that her hair had been the culprit, though the movement had been much larger and lighter in color than the dark, rain-soaked strands.

Gabrielle closed her eyes and listened for something, anything, beyond the patter of rain forming puddles at her feet. She thought she heard the sound of labored breathing. Her own?

No, more sporadic.

A moan followed. Yes, that was definitely a moan coming from her left, a snippet of sound barely above the breeze. She kept her eyes on the row of vines bending under the rain. Her own breathing picked up again. Then, she heard her father-in-law whistle through his teeth, indicating his position three rows over from where they were supposed to meet.

She climbed on the bike again. Her legs took over, moving faster than before. She thought of the danger of being out in the vines when German soldiers were billeted only a few miles away. Had one of them come across Max? Was he hurt? Alone and writhing in pain?

There, in the distance, she saw him. She was nearly there. One row over, Max stood, beckoning her closer, his hand raised high in the air, his weight shifting from one foot to the other. She squinted past the rain. She could hardly make out more than his shape. She clambered off her bike, let it fall to the ground and started jogging in his direction. Her heart sped up as she saw the black lump at his feet. A person?

That couldn't be right.

Gabrielle stopped cold, pushed the water away from her eyes, but no. She wasn't mistaken. Her father-in-law stood over a slumped body. The moan came again, a pitiful sound.

The figure rolled up inside itself. It was a man, dressed in clothes she'd never seen before. Goggles covered his eyes and there was a sort of tube hanging from his odd head covering. A helmet? Flight gear, perhaps? There were markings on the side of the goggles. She looked closer, narrowing her eyes to see through the dark and the rain, but couldn't make out the writing. "A German pilot?" she asked Max.

He shook his head. "An airman, yes. A German, no. A foreigner."

The lump launched into a series of mumbled, incomprehensible words that projected his confusion and pain and very little else. Nevertheless, Max was right. The language was not German. Rather English. The accent was definitely British. At Grandmère's insistence, Gabrielle had spent a summer in England before she married Benoit. Her time had been spent learning the difficult language and meeting with wine merchants.

Where had this man come from? She hadn't heard a truck, or even a plane. Or any of the sounds she remembered from the previous war. "How did he get here?"

"Parachute." Her father-in-law indicated the pile of material, dingy and gray from the mud. "It either failed, or the wind blew him off course. He somehow managed to untangle himself from the contraption before I quite literally stumbled over him."

The swish of cloth she'd seen earlier. The gut-wrenching moans. Both had been real. "How long has he been here?"

"I don't know. He's hurt and, I think, delirious. His words make no sense. He could be speaking any number of languages, possibly more than one."

"I think he's British."

Max considered this. "Possibly. I don't speak English. Whoever he is, he needs our help."

It was the Christian thing to do. It was also the decent, human thing to do. And still, Gabrielle wanted to run away. She didn't want to be here. She wanted never to have left her bed. She looked away from the injured man, and from Max's earnest expression, and searched for her courage. The sky seemed to lower over her, creating a terrifying intimacy as she considered the ramifications of helping this man. Then, she considered what it would mean *not* to help him.

She faced her father-in-law once more. He'd lowered to kneel beside the limp body. She dropped her gaze. The injured man's eyes met hers. Even through the goggles she saw his silent plea, his pain. His fear. She went utterly still, then approached him, consciously making her decision. She would help him, whoever he was, however he'd come to be here. Whatever nation he'd sworn his allegiance to.

It didn't matter that she was as scared as he was, or that she was soaking wet and cold. "We need to get him out of the rain," she said to Max, who was already drawing to his feet.

"I'll fetch a cart. You stay with him."

She knelt beside the man and carefully removed the goggles from his face. He was shockingly young, possibly only a year or two older than Paulette. He attempted to speak. Gabrielle stopped him with a finger pressed to his lips. "You want to conserve your energy."

He blinked.

She lifted her hand. He immediately tried to speak again. Again, she placed her finger over his mouth and said, *"Non."*

This time, he nodded. Beneath the gesture his fear boiled in his unfocused eyes. She wanted to tell him he had nothing to fear. She wanted to tell him he was safe now. That would be a lie. She would help this man, but she would not lie to him.

The wind picked up, whipping a wet strand of her hair across her vision. She shoved it aside and, thinking it better not to know his name, said in French, "Where are you hurt?"

He blinked again. His confusion was evident in the blank, dazed expression. She asked the question again, but in English. It had been years since she'd spoken the language and the words came out heavily accented. "My leg," he croaked. "I think my leg is broken."

The words nearly unbalanced her. She had to fight to keep from falling backward. Her mind brought up the image of another injured man, lying prone like this, only a few rows over, pinned under a wagon's wheel, uttering the same words but in French. *I think my leg is broken.*

Max returned with the promised cart. He was out of breath, clearly flustered, his dark hair plastered to his head by the rain that continued its assault on their miserable little trio. Gabrielle glanced at him over her shoulder. "His leg is broken."

A grim sigh met the remark. And now her father-in-law was as dejected as she. She wanted to say something to alleviate the pain of their mutual loss. "Max, I...I'm sorr—"

"Shh," he said, his voice a harsh reprimand. "This is not the time to speak of him."

It took her a moment to process who he meant. By the time she did, Max was already leaning over the injured man and Gabrielle knew her father-in-law was right. Now was not the time to speak of Benoit.

"We must be quick. Someone may have seen him fall from the sky." Max took her arm and tugged her gently to her feet.

"We're going to move you now," she told the injured man from her standing position. "It will probably cause you pain. You will want to be as quiet as possible."

He was bigger and heavier than his crumpled form suggested. It took both Gabrielle and Max to load him onto the cart. Other than a nearly imperceptible hiss of pain, the airman remained silent. He even managed to provide a small amount of assistance, hoisting himself with his arms while they took care of his lower half.

The parachute was not so helpful, made awkward and heavy by the rain.

Gabrielle and Max agreed it would be best to hide the airman in the Dupree wine cellar because, as he stated, "I do not have a German living in my home." When they reached the muddy entrance, he tried to send her home. "You have done your duty. It is safer for you to walk away now."

She couldn't leave. She wouldn't abandon her father-in-law to take on this burden alone. Heart pounding, she glanced at the injured Brit. In the light from the cellar she could see that his skin had taken on a sickly tinge of green. She'd seen that color once before on another man's face. "You'll need my help setting the bone."

"I can do it myself."

It would be difficult, made harder because her father-in-law didn't speak English. And the injured man didn't speak French. "Let's get him out of the rain," she said.

Giving Max no chance to argue, she reached for the wounded man. There was no sound as they entered the wine cellar, nothing but a peaceful hush and the rasp of the man's strained breathing. Once they had him settled, and they'd cleared a space to work, Max ripped away the material and examined the injured leg.

Gabrielle leaned forward and let out a breath of relief. It was a clean break, no broken skin. They agreed on a plan of action, Max on the left, Gabrielle on the right.

"This will hurt," she told their patient. "Bite on this." She handed him a strap of leather she'd found in the cart. He still cried out, the sound that of a wounded animal rather than a man. His eyes rolled back in his head and then, nothing. No sound. No movement. Was he dead?

She checked his pulse, relieved to discover a thready beat. "He's alive. He just passed out."

"It's for the best," Max said, so calm, so certain.

They finished setting the leg, then dealt with the parachute. And that was that. Gabrielle had done what she could. The injured man was no longer her concern. Still, she asked, "What will happen to him?"

"De Vogüe will make that decision." Of course their de facto leader must be involved.

Outside, the rain had turned into a cold drizzle. She em-

braced the slap of cold on her cheeks. It helped clear her head.
She went to retrieve her bike. Max said her name.

She glanced back. "Yes?"

He scanned her face, looking for...something. "You have
information for me?"

In all the commotion, she'd forgotten the reason she'd asked
him to meet her in the first place. Quickly, succinctly, she
told him everything she knew about the massive champagne
shipment to North Africa. He smiled for the first time since
she'd come upon him in the vineyard. "Well done, Gabrielle. This is good."

"Is it?"

"The Germans reward their soldiers with our champagne.
They must be sending many troops to Africa."

They decided upon the date and time of their next meeting, assuming no surprises arose beforehand. Gabrielle also
walked Max through the steps needed to care for his unexpected guest should infection or fever set in. When there was
nothing more to say, they nodded to each other, and then Gabrielle was pedaling through the rows. The rain provided excellent cover. But then the church bells rang above the gloom.
Five strikes. A clear warning that dawn would soon be upon
her, though the sky was still dark as pitch.

She was careful to place the bike where she'd found it. To
hide the signs of her nocturnal adventure, she retrieved a rag
and began wiping. Mud had found curious places to settle. The
rain stopped before she was through, and gray light threaded
through a heavy fog.

Grateful for the concealment, she stepped into the murki-
ness. Closer to home, she kept to the shadows cast by the château's high walls. Near the terrace, a fine mist descended over
her, snaking around her feet. She swallowed back a wave of

unease. If someone saw her, she would claim worry over the vines had driven her out of doors.

Explaining her choice of clothing would be harder. The best solution was not to be caught. The morning chill followed her inside the house, and put an edge to her mood, but the hallway was empty, as was the back stairwell. She pushed into her room and quietly shut the door behind her. Her shoulders heaved. Then she sagged, her eyes closing on a sigh.

She'd made it. No one had seen her. She was safe.

She hoped Max and the injured airman found the same success.

Chapter Twenty

HÉLÈNE

Hélène's heart beat wildly in her throat. Something had brought her to the window, an impulse she couldn't explain. She caught a movement—there, in the distance—and looked closer. There it was again, a silhouette moving within the fog. Pressing her hand to the cool glass, she leaned forward for a better view.

The figure was gone.

She stepped away from the window and pressed her lips tightly together, wondering if what she'd seen had been real or simply a flicker of shadows. She knew, of course, and now she must make herself forget that figure sneaking around in the morning fog, for the safety of her daughter. For the safety of them all.

Please, Lord, clear this from my mind.

The prayer resounded in her head, over and over, with no

happy resolution. She'd seen what she'd seen and could never forget.

She looked out the window again, down into the damp garden, and there. She saw it again. The shape of a woman, clad in head-to-toe black, moving with quiet stealth.

Hélène recognized the owner of the silhouette. With that recognition, fear for her daughter's safety fell over her like a thick, wet blanket.

She had a sudden, uncanny conviction that Gabrielle was working with the resistance movement. The mother in her was terrified. But as she watched her daughter slink into the house through a door hidden within the ivy, Hélène could not help but feel secretly awed. She'd raised a strong woman. How could that not bring pride to her heart?

When the time came for her to make her own sacrifice, she prayed she would be as brave as Gabrielle. It would be soon. She'd laid the groundwork. All that was left was for her to take the final, fatal step.

There is no other way. That's what she told herself. That's what she knew to be her truth. Von Schmidt wanted complete control over her, mind and body. If she didn't give, he would take. Their alliance would either be on his terms, or hers.

It must be hers, or else she would break. She could not let that happen. There would be repercussions if the tide of war shifted. Hélène wouldn't think about that now. She would only think about protecting her daughters from the consequences of her Jewish blood.

Head high, she went into the kitchen to retrieve the tray of coffee and pastries von Schmidt demanded she bring him every morning. After a short, cursory knock, she entered the library and found him sorting through a stack of papers. He stood with his back to her, dressed in the field-gray uniform he preferred over the navy-blue suit he wore occasionally and only when he dealt with other German businessmen.

Hélène cleared her throat. When he glanced over his shoulder she caught the glimmer of calculation in his eyes. She did not like that look. It meant nothing good. "Ah, Hélène. Come in."

As she crossed the threshold, he turned around fully, the stack of papers still clasped in his hand. The sun streamed in through the window and washed over him, bringing out the pale blue of his eyes, and highlighting the dark gold of his hair. A handsome man, aging as splendidly as a well-blended champagne.

And yet, the sight of him brought only revulsion to her stomach. Perhaps because he was the enemy. Or perhaps because she knew he would strip her of every last shred of dignity before he was through with her. A shiver of terror joined the revulsion. She hid both behind a serene smile and readjusted the tray she carried.

"I see you are already hard at work, Helmut." They'd long dispensed with proper names and titles. He preferred she call him by his first name, an intimacy that she detested as much as that look in his eyes.

"I have received news I wish for you to explain." Barely controlled fury coated his voice, as if it took him much willpower to keep from lashing out at her—his favorite target for his rage.

This foul mood of his was as familiar as the ugly look in his eyes.

Tread carefully, she told herself. *He is spoiling for a fight.* What she didn't know was why. And then, fear grabbed her by the throat and squeezed the breath out of her. Had he seen Gabrielle sneaking into the château? *"Bien sûr,"* she said. "Of course. I will do my best."

With her heart cantering away from her, she set the breakfast tray on the table near the window that overlooked the main entrance to the champagne house. He preferred this view while he feasted on Marta's pastries made to his personal specifications, which always seemed to change. *More fruit. Not so much fruit. More cream and butter. Less salt. I said no fruit.*

The man was never satisfied. He enjoyed finding fault and pointing out her mistakes. If there were none to be found, he manufactured them. And then, his temper roared.

Hélène sat on the edge of a chair facing him, folded her hands in her lap and waited for him to take his usual seat. He remained standing, looming over her. A common strategy to make himself appear larger than he was, and more intimidating.

What had she done? What had she *not* done?

"How well do you know your neighbors?" he asked her in a low, even tone that to an outsider would have seemed reasonable. To her, it was a snare.

"I know some better than others."

He held her stare longer than was his usual practice. This cold, frigid calm was unusual and far more unsettling than any display of anger. "Would you say you know them well enough to tell me which of them would openly work against the Third Reich?"

So many words, she thought, with only one purpose. To confuse her into informing on her neighbors. "You are speaking of resistance?"

"I am speaking of sabotage."

Her mind went to the image of her daughter sneaking into the house and she made an involuntary sound in her throat. "I know no one who would dare such a thing."

But, of course, that was a lie. She knew several in this home alone. She had to lower her head to hide the truth that possibly showed in her eyes.

"Last night," he continued. "There was an incident at the railyard."

She lifted her head, careful to keep her expression neutral. "What sort of incident?"

He leaned over her. He was so close she could have slapped his face with very little effort. How satisfying it would be to see the mark of her hand on that clean-shaven cheek.

Before she could surrender to the impulse, he straightened to his full height. She was forced to crane her neck to continue looking into his eyes. "Someone," he said, his gaze boring into hers, "cut through the fence last night and emptied the wine from hundreds of barrels awaiting transfer to Berlin."

"Mon Dieu." It was such a bold act of rebellion against a merciless enemy. People disappeared from their homes for less.

Hélène turned blindly away from von Schmidt's searching glare, even as her mind went straight to Gabrielle. Had her daughter been part of this brave group of conspirators?

Von Schmidt must have read something in her face, because he yanked her to her feet and gripped her arms so hard bruises would appear within the hour. "You know something. What do you know, Hélène?"

Her denial should have been immediate. It should have already come, before he'd finished his accusation. She needed to be submissive, pliable, at the very least show her confusion. But in that instant, caution was the last thing on her mind. Her anxiety for her daughter pushed her to ask questions in the place of giving answers. "Did they leave clues to their identities?"

"The rain washed away any footsteps." His grip turned brutal, sending sharp pain down into her fingertips, up into her shoulders. "It's as if they were never there."

Louange Dieu. Praise God.

Gabrielle was safe. For now.

As if sensing her mind had wandered, von Schmidt shook her hard and his hands closed tighter, tighter still, until she cried out. "What do you know, Hélène?"

"Nothing, I swear it."

"Give me a name, anyone you suspect."

Her lungs burned with panic, and a sob burst from her lips. "I don't know anyone who could do such a thing. I don't," she added when he gave her another shake.

He tried to stare the lie out of her. She lifted her chin and let him see her fear. The fear, she hoped, of the wrongfully accused.

"You will tell me what you know. Or I will be forced to interrogate the rest of your household." Another threat delivered smoothly, in that low, even cadence. "I will start with your youngest daughter."

Her heart gave a quick stutter. The toxic mix of fear and panic, coupled with the screaming pain from his ruthless hold, made her momentarily light-headed. *Think*, Hélène. *Think.* "Perhaps it was local boys playing a prank."

"This was not the work of children. It was a coordinated act of treason." Von Schmidt's face went hard. And still, he held on to her arms. "The shipment was earmarked for top Nazi officials. Germany will not allow this to stand. We will find those responsible."

"What will you do to them?" The words were out before she thought them.

His grin was pure evil. "They will be executed for treason."

Hélène went perfectly still. Pinned under von Schmidt's cold glare, she couldn't think what to say to remove his suspicion. After so much preparation, so much careful planning and calculating, she feared she'd made an unforgivable misstep. Why had she gone to the window this morning? "I cannot think who did this, Helmut."

The use of his given name was intentional, as was the plea she placed in her voice. He studied her closely. Then nodded.

"I regret that I have upset you. That was not my intent." He held up a hand and used it to cup her face. She hadn't realized he'd let go of her arms. The pain still throbbed in her flesh. "Tell me, Hélène, and do not lie. I will know if you lie. Are you sympathetic to these saboteurs? Is that why you refuse to inform on them?"

This was it, then. The moment when she sacrificed herself to protect her family. "I am not with them. I am with you, Helmut. Only you."

There. It was done. The words were said. Something fragile fractured inside her, the thinnest of shells that left her exposed fully for this dog to pick at her bones. She'd given him her allegiance and had signed over her soul, the death knell to all she believed holy and sacred. *Forgive me, Lord.*

It was over. She would never be herself again.

A smile emerged on von Schmidt's face, a boyish grin that nearly had her believing he wasn't such a terrible man. She hated herself for thinking it even for a moment. His eyes crinkled around the edges, evoking reminders of the gentle man she'd lost. *Oh, Étienne, I am sorry.*

Von Schmidt reached up to run a finger along her jawline. Her hate for herself was nothing compared to the loathing she felt for this man who would claim her body. But he would never have her heart.

Forgive me, Lord.

"There is other news from Berlin I think you will find interesting."

So quick to cool the rabid temper, she thought, and realized how truly dangerous this man was, more than any of them had initially thought.

His hand idly played in her hair. This intimacy, it was too much. She stood stiffly under his loathsome touch. He didn't seem to notice her lack of response. Or perhaps, he didn't care. "All Jewish people in the occupied zone are now required to register at the police stations or *sous-préfectures* of their towns and cities. They will no longer be allowed to own or engage in business."

A scream of protest rose in her throat. She'd known this was coming, and still the news hit her like an iron fist to the gut. "Why are you telling me this?"

Nose inches from hers, von Schmidt brushed his hand down her arm, shoulder to wrist. Pain shot through her as his fingers grazed over her bruised bicep. Revulsion came next. "I believe," he said, "that you will want to share this news with the rest of your family, your oldest daughter in particular."

Hélène gritted her teeth, using her confusion as a reason to step away from his roving hand. "Why would this news matter to Gabrielle?"

"These new laws could benefit your family's champagne business." With those unsettling words, he revealed how well she'd hidden her identity. To him, she was Hélène LeBlanc—blonde, French, Christian.

"What are you suggesting?" she asked, appalled at the direction of their conversation.

"Now is the time to consider expanding your business. Tell your daughter to make plans. Once the Jews are swept clean from this country, there will be opportunities for the taking. She will want to be ready."

The horror of what he suggested made her tremble uncontrollably. She had to lean against the bookshelf to calm herself. She wanted nothing more than to escape into a dark hole and never come out, as she'd done after Étienne's death, when the world became too much to bear. Those days of self-indulgence were over.

"You know your neighbors, their names, the churches they attend. If they go to synagogue. You know who owns all the local businesses, and how well they do financially."

"Most of this information is common knowledge."

"Then you will have no problem making me a list of every Jew in the area. I expect you to include where they work, where they live, the names of their children. Everything you think important."

What he asked of her, it was unconscionable. With this list, Hélène LeBlanc would become the vilest of creatures. A collaborator. A traitor to her own kind. She would be sending her own people—men, women, *children*—to their deaths. But if she didn't do this, what would happen to her own daughters?

She could refuse this request and sign all of their death warrants.

Be smart, she told herself. *Be brave.*

There were many forms of courage, she reminded herself. Many ways to fight a monster. She'd already started down a path. Now there was no turning back.

She left the safety of the bookshelf and approached him, obvious intent in her gaze, her swaying hips making silent promises. He understood. Of course he did. He was a man. The smile curling across his lips only confirmed what she already knew.

With each step, she tapped into the woman she'd been before Étienne had come into her life. There was a great distance to be covered to return to her former self, to the woman who'd frequented salons, who'd rubbed shoulders with a life of decadence. It was oddly comforting, really, to fall back into her old ways. Or maybe that was another rationalization to get her through the monumental journey she had to make.

She leaned into her quarry and had a moment of regret for the self-respect she would lose once she sealed this offensive deal. Another inch, just a little closer.

The ringing of the telephone gave her a valid excuse to pull back. It took enormous effort to move away slowly. To reach for the telephone, to greet the caller in a cool, confident, breezy tone. She listened to the German on the other end of the line, her mind locking on the one word that mattered, then held out the receiver. "It's Berlin. For you."

He took the phone, but not before he gave her a thorough once-over. She had to look away to keep from revealing her hatred of him.

"This is Hauptmann von Schmidt," he said in German. He didn't speak for several seconds, just listened. Then, he ended the call, *"Danke,"* and hung up the phone with a bang.

Hélène immediately noticed the ridge between his eyes. Never a good sign, that ridge.

"The saboteurs have brought trouble on us all."

"How...how do you mean?"

His gaze, already hard, became razor-sharp as he glanced past her to a distant spot outside the window. "Berlin is sending a Gestapo agent to deal with the local rebellion."

Part Three

Chapter Twenty-One

❧

GABRIELLE

19 February 1941

With the fragile morning light of the winter sunrise illuminating her way, Gabrielle crested the hilltop in her mother's motorcar. Despite the thick gloves she wore, her hands shook from the cold and her breath froze on the still air. She'd never experienced such constant, bone-chilling temperatures. Following the worst harvest in her lifetime, Champagne had been hit with one of the most severe winters on record.

Fuel shortages of every kind made enduring the harsh weather a lesson in torture within the walls of the château. Except, in the rooms von Schmidt had chosen for his own personal use. The rest of the household suffered, while he enjoyed much comfort.

Gabrielle wanted to close her eyes, to find a prayer, but she needed to stay alert and keep her gaze fastened on the road.

She steered around a patch of ice, up and over another hill and, finally, closing in on her destination, maneuvered along the main street that ran through the center of Reims.

The sight of so many cathedral spires brought a moment of peace. Then she saw it. The gigantic Nazi flag hanging over the entire front façade of the mayor's office building. And then, she saw another one, equally massive, equally offensive, secured to the roofline of a hotel that had previously belonged to a Jewish family. There were more. She quit counting at five.

The message couldn't be clearer. Reims belonged to the Third Reich. If the Americans didn't join the war soon, all of Europe would fall. Even the mighty Great Britain.

There were other, equally upsetting signs of German occupation. Even at this early hour, soldiers from the newly arrived Waffen-SS unit roamed the streets, looking for trouble, finding it often. Dispatched to assist the Gestapo agent in quelling the acts of sabotage, these black-uniformed soldiers were harder and meaner than their Wehrmacht predecessors. Few in town had met their leader. But these soldiers, the Gestapo agent's personal henchmen, were young, none older than Gabrielle, and frighteningly, brutally handsome. They'd been in town less than a week, but already spread terror wherever they went as they banded together in packs like feral dogs. They were not above exerting their authority in cruel and petty ways.

All of Reims trembled in their presence.

Waiting for them to pass to the next block, Gabrielle then parked outside the *boulangerie* and scrambled into the frigid morning air. The queue outside the bread bakery was already long, stretching around the building and down the next block. Hunched inside her coat, she took her place at the end of the line.

She'd volunteered for this errand to ease the increased workload von Schmidt had heaped on Marta this morning.

He'd decided, without warning, to throw an impromptu dinner party tonight and, as was his custom, insisted on an impressive, seven-course meal. The menu was to include several rationed items that were nearly impossible to acquire without a special permit and endless hours of standing in lines. Hours Marta would need to prepare the various courses.

When she'd mentioned this dilemma to von Schmidt, he'd made it evident the details were not his concern. "You will figure this out on your own."

Such arrogance. Gabrielle had offered her assistance to the frazzled housekeeper. "I will go to the shops in your place."

"You have work to do in the champagne house. *Non.*" Marta shook her head. "I cannot ask this of you."

"You didn't ask, I offered. The work will be here when I return. Now, make your list and I will see about filling it." And so, here she now stood, in the unforgiving cold, at the end of an impossibly long line, her back purposefully turned to the swastikas defacing her city.

A burst of frosty air swept over the streets and alleyways, cutting through the hardiest of winter coats. Gabrielle drew her hat lower over her head, then edged closer to the bakery's entrance. Ahead of her, two shivering forms huddled together. They held hands, one much larger than the other, a silent show of support between a mother and her young daughter.

She thought of her own mother. Hélène had distanced herself from the rest of the family more than usual, rarely interacting with them, not even Paulette. Gabrielle thought she knew what triggered the change. She was too afraid of her mother's explanation to broach the subject.

A hard shove from behind pushed her forward. The line had moved without her. She muttered an apology and reclaimed her place behind the mother and daughter. Directly across the street was the police station where the Gestapo agent had set up his office a week ago.

Gabrielle hadn't seen *Kriminalkommissar* Wolfgang Mueller yet, not in the flesh. She wasn't sure anyone had. But his reputation preceded him. It was said that the people he arrested were never seen or heard from again. An involuntary shiver slinked along the base of her spine.

Finally it was her turn in the bakery.

She made her purchases and then stood in line at the butcher's. The grocer was next, then the *pâtisserie*. It took most of the day, but she exited the last of the shops with everything on Marta's list. Arms full, she made her way back to the car. There would be just enough time for her to deliver the items to the housekeeper, check on matters at the champagne house and then dress for von Schmidt's dinner party. She would rather skip the event, but Herr Hauptmann liked showing off the LeBlanc women as if they were his own personal property.

Shoulders hunched against the terrible wind, she neared the Cathédrale Notre-Dame de Reims. The towering monument to God was an emblem to the French people's faith and hope. Gabrielle had lost both long ago. The thought brought anguish rather than anger.

She was nearly at her mother's motorcar, a single block away, when a uniformed man exited the police station and headed in her direction. There was only time for impressions as he closed the distance between them with ground-eating strides.

He was tall, with broad shoulders and a powerful torso that tapered to a narrow waist. He walked with the authority of a man in charge and didn't seem bothered by the cold. He wore all black—black jacket, black jodhpurs, shiny black boots. His collar bore the SS runes and the red armband around his left bicep displayed the Nazi swastika. Most disturbing of all was the handgun strapped to his belt.

So, this was the dreaded Gestapo agent sent from Berlin to restore order in Reims. And he was heading straight for her. A moment of sheer panic passed over Gabrielle. She tried to shift out of the man's path. In her haste, she nearly stumbled over her own two feet. Her clumsiness drew his notice and he quickened his pace.

He was nearly upon her. She couldn't see his eyes beneath his peaked hat, but she sensed his gaze on her. He moved with feline grace. The boneless, liquid strides reminded her of a large jungle cat. Gabrielle was suddenly mesmerized by her own terror. She made another attempt to avoid him. This time, she did trip and her packages slipped out of her hands.

She automatically dropped to her knees.

He joined her there an instant later, his crouch far less awkward than hers. She could see his features now, a shockingly beautiful face with a hard, cruel edge.

"Mademoiselle. You would do well to watch your step." Even his voice held a low, predatory purr. "Let me help you."

It was the last thing she wanted. "I can manage on my own."

She wasted her breath. His hands were already gathering up her packages. The long, elegant fingers belonged to an artist, not one of Hitler's assassins. Too late, she realized he'd seized her bags and now stood, waiting for her to do the same. She rose and found herself staring at a row of polished silver buttons that cut a vertical line down his chest. His height was even more impressive up close. He had the build of an ancient Germanic warrior.

She lifted her head a fraction higher and confronted the face of the Gestapo. It was not what she expected from an instrument of tyranny. The chiseled angles and smooth planes were too...human. There was something not quite right here. Confusion overtook her fear.

The face was younger than she would have expected from a high-ranking police detective, only a few years older than her own twenty-eight years. The features themselves were shockingly beautiful, but also very, very masculine. The personification of Aryan racial purity.

Gabrielle couldn't look away, even knowing he'd come to Reims to seek out people who resisted their occupiers. People like her. This was why Berlin had sent him, no doubt. This hypnotic effect.

His eyes dropped to the packages he now held. There was obvious intent in the gesture, and also what she thought was disdain. "You are a French woman?"

"*Oui*, I am French."

Frowning, he searched the contents of her bags. "Are there not rations in place?"

"There are."

He lifted his head. Later, when she thought back on this moment, Gabrielle would remember the look in his eyes. Sharp and full of blue fire. He'd made up his mind about her in a single glance and she'd been found wanting. "You should not have been allowed so many purchases in a single day."

No, she should not. "I shop for the German stationed in my home."

His eyes narrowed at this explanation, two identical slits of hard, Nazi suspicion. "Who is this soldier requiring so much food during a time of shortage?"

She answered without hesitation. "Hauptmann von Schmidt. He is hosting a dinner party this evening and I was sent to acquire the necessary ingredients for the meal."

"I see."

She wondered about the conclusions he'd drawn.

"Your papers, please." She noticed his accent then. She hadn't thought it so thick before. But now, he spoke in stilted

French, with the guttural accent that belonged to a man used to speaking only German.

Her throat clenched on a squeak. "My papers?"

He watched her with the lazy patience of a cat. "This is not a complicated request, Mademoiselle. You either have your identification papers with you, or you do not."

"I have them." She lowered her head. Her face, surely, would show something she did not want him to see. Hands shaking, she fiddled with the clasp on her handbag. It took her two tries to release the latch.

Finally, she pulled out the German-issued identity card every French citizen in the occupied zone was required to carry and handed it to the man towering over her. He dropped her bags to the ground. And then, shoving several aside with his foot, snatched the document.

He took his time reading over her credentials. Gabrielle waited, pulse pounding in her ears. Behind him stood the gothic cathedral where French kings had been coronated. The way the late-afternoon light shone over him, it was as if he were an extension of the building itself, as if he'd recently ascended from one of the stained-glass windows. A fallen angel shed of his black wings, morphed into human form, contempt for mankind woven into his very fiber.

With each passing second her control vanished. She felt loose and shaky inside, and realized she was going to be sick. She couldn't give in to the urge, not here. He would suspect she had something to hide. *You do have something to hide.*

She'd thought herself so clever as she'd executed her small acts of treason against a bully regime. She thought her nocturnal adventures were easy enough to explain away if anyone caught her wandering the vineyard at night. How wrong she'd been. How foolish. And now Berlin had sent this man who made people disappear. A man who had yet to share his name or rank with her.

Resentment occupied every fiber of her being.

She would not crumple. She was a LeBlanc. Étienne's daughter. Benoit's widow. All she had to do was find her courage. And not be sick. She modulated her breathing, forcing down the bile that wanted to rise in her throat. She breathed in shallow, rhythmic puffs of air. Better. The nausea slipped away, leaving her feeling hollow, but also in control. A spurt of patriotism replaced her fear. The Free French would triumph.

They were gaining in strength, becoming more coordinated.

She was not alone in her fight for France. She was, however, alone in this moment.

Looking around, she noticed how deserted their section of the sidewalk had become. The citizens of Reims gave them a wide berth. None looked at Gabrielle. Did they think avoiding eye contact would keep them from suffering similar scrutiny?

"You are registered with two surnames, LeBlanc and Dupree." He snapped his gaze to hers. "Which of the two is real, and which one is fake?"

Her mind filled with absolute darkness. "I… Both are real." She lifted her chin, calling upon the noble blood of her ancestors, on the memory of the man she'd married. "I was born a LeBlanc. My husband, a Dupree."

His eyes went to her left hand. "You do not wear a wedding band."

She detested the way he mangled her language. "My husband is dead."

"Ah, you are a widow."

Her heart thudded in her chest. Was her loyalty to two families a crime? If this man carted her off to jail, would the people pretending not to watch them come to her aid?

No, they would not. They cared only for their own safety, like so many in the occupied zone. If the French didn't fight for each other, none of them were safe.

Despair washed over her. She could hardly keep it off her face.

He returned her identity card. She took it without looking directly into his eyes. They disturbed her. There was something not quite right in that pure, pale blue. Something she couldn't identify. His manner also troubled her. The relaxed stance didn't seem to match with the menace of his black uniform. And yet, somehow, fit all too well.

This man was not what he seemed.

"Mademoiselle—"

"Madame," she corrected.

He sketched a brief bow. She hadn't known such a large man could have so much control over his body. "The address you listed on your identity papers indicates that you live in the château connected with your birth family. Is this correct?"

Gabrielle felt her eyebrows pull together. "That's correct."

"And the man billeting in your home is from the corps of wine merchants."

She nodded, again surprised he knew so much about her.

A car backfired in the distance, a loud, shocking noise that made her jump. The Gestapo agent showed no signs of hearing the sound. Although, of course, he heard it. How could he not? Cool and composed, his eyes remained on her face. The air grew frigid around them, their breaths puffing inside miniature clouds around their heads. And still, he watched her. His scrutiny, she realized, was more speculation than censure.

Monsters hid behind such looks.

This was a dangerous man. And he knew where she lived. "May I go?"

"You may go." He waited for her to pick up her bags, without a single offer of assistance, then stepped aside to let her pass.

She glanced back only once. In that instant, the sun dipped behind the cathedral and the building's shadows swallowed him whole. But not before Gabrielle saw his lips curve in a slow, satisfied smile.

Chapter Twenty-Two

JOSEPHINE

Josephine forgot what it meant to be warm. This winter was harsher than most, though perhaps not the harshest she'd ever experienced. Surely, there had been worse. At least once in her childhood. She remembered being very small and trying to climb into the crackling fire, desperate for its heat. Her father had caught her up against his chest and held her close, softly admonishing her in a gentle voice. "This is not the way to escape the cold, *mon chou*."

His strong arms had been enough to warm her. She wished for them now.

Per Marta's instructions, she dressed in multiple layers and stayed that way for hours. Or possibly minutes, sometimes the passage of time was an unsolved mystery. She knew this additional clothing was supposed to help combat the cold. It did not. The extra garments only managed to weigh her down and made even the simplest of movements difficult.

Enough. She shed the top layer and left her room.

In the kitchen, Marta looked at her, eyebrows raised, as if she'd committed some unforgivable act of rebellion. "What?" she asked.

"You're shivering."

This was not news to her. "I'm cold."

"Then you should wear more clothing." Marta's tone contained the scold that had been absent from her father's voice.

Josephine shrugged and looked out the window. The vines slept under a thick layer of frost and the sun had traveled deep across the sky to a point far past the halfway mark. Another day vanishing too quickly. Behind her, Marta moved around the kitchen in a frantic rush. Josephine remembered von Schmidt had decided to throw another one of his pompous parties.

With her right hand, she reached out to clasp her friend's arm. Marta came to an abrupt stop. "Tell me," Josephine began. "What can I do to ease this burden he has put on you?"

The question seemed to surprise the other woman. Her mouth strained for a response. "You have done it already. You remember, *non*? You hired the Trevon sisters to assist with the last-minute preparations and the serving. They are to arrive within the hour."

Although Josephine wanted to ask for more details about these unknown sisters, she did not want to reveal the depth of her forgetfulness. *"Très bien."*

She left the kitchen, knowing that once again she had lost entire hours of a day and the events that had occurred within them. Tense and resigned, she walked through the château, without any kind of aim, and when she came to one of her favorite rooms she paused. She felt a rush of cold air and thought of her father's warm arms, which brought to mind the painting he'd given her on her wedding day.

She went into the room.

The interior was dark and empty and fragrant with the peculiar scent of lemon oil mixed with decades of mold hidden inside the walls. Sitting on a wooden bench beneath a row of paintings, she waited for her eyes to adjust to the poor light.

Minutes passed, perhaps more than a few. She didn't know how long she stayed. She may have dozed off, because she jolted upright. Moved by an impulse, she looked to her left, then to her right, then straight ahead. Time had escaped its formal structure. Josephine remembered very little of her journey through the château to get here, just that she had kept to the outer rooms, never penetrating the interior ones, and had stopped briefly in the kitchen to speak with Marta.

Maybe, deep inside her brain, she had planned to come here all along, where the Renoir hung. The Renoir. It was missing. She gasped, then jumped to her feet. Her stiffened leg muscles nearly gave way beneath her. She shook herself free of the discomfort and rushed to stand before the empty space. She stared, without moving. The Renoir—*her* Renoir—it was gone.

At first Josephine was too shocked to move. She just stood there staring, her eyes tracing the rectangular spot where the painting had once been. The plaster within the rectangle was several shades darker than the wall surrounding it, a sure sign her memory was clear on this point. The painting had been there once. And now was gone.

Had she done this?

Marta would know.

Josephine hurried to find her friend, taking the most expedient route. Marta was not alone. Two dark-haired teenage girls dressed in identical black dresses and white aprons worked alongside her. They were both unfamiliar to Josephine, but she thought she should know them.

This was not the moment for awkward introductions.

"Marta," she huffed, her breathing raspy from exertion. "I need you to come with me."

The housekeeper brushed the back of her wrist across her forehead. "Now?"

"Immediately."

"But I'm busy. I…" She must have seen something of the worry in Josephine's eyes, because she made a small nod and set down the spoon in her hand. "All right, yes." Out in the hallway, she asked, "Where are we going?"

"You'll see." Josephine maneuvered around Marta and took the lead. At the vacant spot where the Renoir had always hung, she asked, "Did we do this? Did we hide it from the Germans?"

Marta sighed a little. "*Non*. We did not hide the Renoir."

"You are certain?"

"*Absolument.*" There was a sad lilt to her voice. "We argued. I wanted to include it with the others. You thought the absence of such a well-known masterpiece would be too conspicuous."

She remembered saying that now, remembered arguing, remembered making the decision despite Marta's protests. She pointed to another spot farther down the wall where an unfamiliar painting now hung. "What about the Degas that used to be there?"

"That one, we took."

As they toured the room, Josephine's heart beat strong and wild in her chest. She and Marta had hidden many treasures, including several valuable paintings. But they had not taken all that were currently missing from the château.

Someone else in the household, then. Not Hélène, she would not be so bold. Gabrielle, perhaps? Possible, quite possible. But, *non*. There was a flaw in this thinking. Von Schmidt would have noticed the absent masterpiece. Hadn't he commented on the Renoir on more than one occasion? Hadn't he shown it off to his friends and colleagues? He would have demanded an explanation for its disappearance.

He had not.

There was but one explanation. The German was stealing from them.

Marta must have come to the same conclusion. "What can we do to stop his thieving?"

They could do nothing until after the war. In the meantime...

"I will make a list of everything missing." In her journal. Josephine would keep the record in her journal. "You will place a mark next to what we hid ourselves, and then we will know what he has stolen."

The list was long and took her nearly two hours plus several passes through the house to complete. When she was through, she had a single thought. *No one steals from Josephine Fouché-LeBlanc, not even a greedy, arrogant German dog with his teeth clasped on her neck.*

Chapter Twenty-Three

GABRIELLE

Gabrielle delivered the provisions to an exasperated Marta.

"He has added another person to his guest list," the house-keeper muttered, shaking her head in disgust. "A very important man. This is what he emphasizes over and over. Very important, he says. The food is to be perfect. I am not to disappoint him. He will have no excuses from me. The German..." She slapped at the pile of dough beneath her hands. "He is a tyrant."

Gabrielle agreed.

"The very worst of his kind."

This, Gabrielle could not agree with. After her trip into Reims she knew there were worse men than von Schmidt. Men whose gazes missed nothing and who were very clever with their questions. Men who knew her name and where she lived. She shut her eyes and tried to shed her unease. "Did von Schmidt make any special requests for champagne?"

Marta paused in her kneading. "Aside from a rosé, he wants

to serve the 1928, no less than ten bottles. Ten! He is a greedy man."

The LeBlancs' personal stock had been depleted weeks ago. Gabrielle would have to go into the caves to fulfill this demand. She did a quick mental calculation. She'd left more than enough of the 1928 on the right side of her fake wall to accommodate von Schmidt's insatiable desire for several months, perhaps even a year. There were many cases left, cases that should have been sent to Berlin per order of the *weinführer*. Somehow, von Schmidt had managed to circumvent this request. And, if caught, he would somehow lay the blame at Gabrielle's feet.

It was a worry for another day. "I'll pull the bottles myself."

"I have already sent François."

This was an acceptable alternative and so she let the matter drop. "Thank you, Marta."

"Gabrielle, before you go. I was told to remind you to dress appropriately for dinner, no men's trousers or bulky sweaters."

"Von Schmidt said this?" Of course he had. Nothing was more certain to rouse Gabrielle's ire than for von Schmidt to suggest she didn't know how to dress like a woman.

"Do not scowl at me," Marta warned. "I am only the messenger."

Although she considered several small ways to aggravate von Schmidt, in the end Gabrielle dressed appropriately for dinner. She even took a few moments to twist her hair into an elegant chignon and swipe a modicum of makeup on her face. Satisfied she looked acceptable, she went in search of her grandmother. The night always went better when the two of them presented a united front.

She found Josephine in her room, already dressed for dinner, sitting in a chair by the window, a leather-bound book in her lap, her head bent over the pages. Gabrielle had to breathe through a wave of great affection for this woman. If anything happened to her...

Gabrielle would lay down her life before she allowed any harm to come to her grandmother. On that note, she should warn her about the Gestapo agent. "Grandmère, I have something I want to share with you before we head downstairs."

Josephine placed a hand on the open book, then looked up. She blinked several times, as if focusing through a haze. "Is it that time, already?"

"Nearly." Gabrielle moved deeper into the room. The toe of her shoe caught on a loose floorboard and she nearly tripped. She looked down, gasping at the sight beneath her foot.

So, this was where Josephine kept her secret journal. It was good to know, but also troubling. If von Schmidt had been the one to seek out her grandmother, if he had taken the same route and hooked his toe on the floorboard...

What would he have found?

Gabrielle dropped to her knees and dug around with her fingertips. With very little effort, she freed the loose slab of wood. The shallow hole was empty. Her relief was short-lived because Josephine flashed a shrewd smile. "It's not in there."

"Where is it?"

She patted the book in her lap.

The emotion that swept through Gabrielle was like an afternoon summer thunderstorm. Quick, violent, startling in its ferocity. "Grandmère, you must be more careful. If von Schmidt had been the one to come into your room, he could have—"

"He never comes into my room."

Gabrielle put a hand to her forehead, pressed hard for several seconds. "What you mean to say," she corrected, lowering her hand, "is that von Schmidt hasn't come into your room *yet*."

"This is not a concern." She waved her hand. "Your mother keeps him occupied."

Gabrielle couldn't bring herself to respond. It was just too awful to have her own suspicions confirmed. Frowning, she fit the wooden slat back into place, stood, then stomped down to make sure it was securely set. "It would take only a small hint of suspicion for von Schmidt to come searching for the secrets you write in that book."

She understood why her grandmother kept the journal. The pages were her memory. And possibly could get her grandmother killed if the book fell into German hands.

"Gabrielle, *chérie*." Josephine set aside the book in her lap. "This is not my first war. I know what I am doing."

Her own hands clenched into fists. "You keep your journal under a loose floorboard."

For several seconds, she held Gabrielle's stare, saying not a word. Then, "Do I?"

Had her grandmother's mind slipped behind a curtain of confusion? It was hard to tell in the dim light. "It's the most obvious of places."

Josephine's answer was to tap her fingers on the book she'd set on the table beside her chair. "What did you find when you pulled away a piece of the floor?"

"I found an empty hole," she replied. "I assumed you'd retrieved your journal before I arrived and had failed to secure the floorboard properly."

"You also thought you'd come upon me reading it by the lingering afternoon light."

That was exactly what she'd thought.

Josephine offered her the book. Gabrielle took it, read the title on the spine, shook her head in sudden relief. *Prometheus* by Goethe. She opened to a random page. Not in its original German but translated into French. Well, well, her grandmother's mind was still sharp. Even her choice of reading material was selected with purpose.

There were times when Josephine's confusion was real, but maybe not as often as she pretended. What other chances did the older woman take, besides recording her secrets in a single, leather-bound book? And who knew what else, things that could incriminate others in the house. Gabrielle thought, *I must do something.* She had to do something, before her grandmother made a false step that would get them all killed. "Where do you keep your journal?"

"It is better you don't know."

She felt the lump rise in her throat and pushed it down with a hard, silent swallow. "What if you forget where you put it?"

"I have a plan for that."

"Grandmère—"

"You have your secrets, Gabrielle. And I have mine." She went to the mirror, smoothed a perfectly steady hand over her hair. "Our system." She turned away from her reflection. "It works. When I discover something that I think is important, I tell you. You relay it to your father-in-law. He takes it to the next person in the chain."

She made it sound so simple. But she'd missed a very key component to the process. "You also write the information down in your journal."

"I write many things in my journal."

And if that single, leather-bound book was discovered? In a flash, Gabrielle saw the face of the man she'd met in Reims this afternoon. She heard his demand to see her papers, remembered his careful questioning of her name, her place of residence. The encounter had left her confused and off-balance. Von Schmidt was a common, ill-bred, grasping individual. He looked to others to feed his own sense of importance. And still, he'd stolen into the LeBlanc home and caught them by surprise.

Now, an even more dangerous opponent had moved into Reims. With far greater power than their houseguest. "Matters have changed, Grandmère. I met the Gestapo agent Berlin sent and he is..." She flung her hands in the air, unable to come up with a description. "He is..."

Where were the words to describe this new enemy? *What* were the words? Clever. Cunning. Cruel. He was all of those things, and more. All-knowing, all-seeing. He seemed to know more about the LeBlanc household than he should. But what really scared Gabrielle was her inability to read him, to know what was inside his mind, to unpack his agenda. She could usually look past even the most carefully constructed masks and see the true character of a person beneath. It was one of her gifts, and perfectly useless with him. "I believe," she said, her hands trembling, "that he is the most dangerous German we have come across in this war."

"You are afraid of this man."

There were, Gabrielle knew, many ways to respond. She could ease her grandmother's apprehension. She could tell a pretty lie. Or she could speak a small half-truth. But nothing would change the fact that she believed, deep in her soul, that Wolfgang Mueller was the worst thing that had happened to her family.

"No, Grandmère, I'm not afraid of him. I'm terrified."

Chapter Twenty-Four

HÉLÈNE

Hélène sat at her dressing table and invested precisely ten minutes in front of the mirror perfecting her makeup. She kohled her eyes, rouged her cheeks, painted her lips a bold red—von Schmidt's favorite color on her—then completed the transformation by pressing powder over her skin to give it a matte finish.

She would have liked to dawdle over this ritual, her favorite before a party. She did not deserve the joy. She groomed herself for von Schmidt, not for her own pleasure, not anymore. The woman she'd become was foreign to her, and she felt more isolated than she had in years.

Your own doing.

Encouraging von Schmidt's affections necessitated pulling away from the people she loved. She'd always kept a certain distance, even from Paulette. But now Hélène added additional coats of aloofness that no one seemed to notice. That was, perhaps, the root of this new brand of loneliness. It was as if the women in her family didn't miss her because they had never really known her.

Your own doing, she reminded herself, borne from years—decades—of hiding her true self behind a carefully painted mask. Anti-Semitism in France had existed long before Nazi occupation. But, oh, how tired she was of feeding the charade she'd started when she was still a girl. Fabrications, evasions, carefully placed lies, all to protect herself from judgment. The stakes were higher now, and her nerves were constantly on edge. She was afraid of making a mistake, of pushing too hard, of not pushing hard enough.

They received news of the war from von Schmidt and the wireless, all of it censored by the German propaganda machine. It was impossible to know what was really happening outside of France. The Nazis monitored the postal service, the telephones. Some claimed even the walls had German ears.

So, she continued living her lie, biding her time and fighting her own war, in her own way. The relationship she cultivated with her enemy was vile to her. *He* was vile to her. She knew he would use her for his own pleasure. And when he tired of her, he would toss her away like yesterday's garbage.

That day could not come soon enough and, when it came, it would be too late.

She was already labeled a collaborator. She'd heard the whispers herself. *She grooms herself for him.* Wasn't she doing so now? *He clicks his heels, and she does his bidding.* Either that, Hélène had learned the hard way, or suffer the back of his hand.

The worst of the comments, the very worst, had come from a woman she'd thought her friend. *It appears taking a Nazi lover is all the rage these days.*

Hélène's reputation was sufficiently ruined.

There was nothing she could do now but endure the humiliation.

The door creaked on its hinges, pulling her attention away from her own scowling reflection to her youngest daughter's devastated face. She was on her feet in an instant. "Paulette, what's wrong?"

The girl collapsed into her arms, sobbing.

"Here, now." She held her daughter close and smoothed a hand over her quaking back. "What's all this about?"

"Oh, Maman, it's just so awful. Lucien…" Her voice broke on another sob. "He…he's been arrested."

"Arrested?"

"By the…the Gestapo."

This is not the way I wanted my daughter to understand the realities of war.

Hélène attempted to recall the boy. So many came and went in Paulette's life, too many to remember them all. She gave up and asked, "Lucien is…?"

"A boy from school." Still clinging, the girl took a shuddering breath. "He's really quite wonderful. He is always telling me how much he loves me."

"You feel the same for him?"

The question went unanswered. Paulette was too preoccupied with pulling back and placing a hand to her heart. "I don't know what I'll do without him. Lucien is the only reason I get up in the morning."

Hélène remembered the boy now. But she had to search her memory to bring up his image. Average height, a bit on the lanky side. Dark eyes, nearly black. He'd been one of the boys vying for Paulette's attention at the anniversary party. Dark hair tousled about his face. Very French. His family grew grapes on a small vineyard. Lucien had a mother and two younger siblings living at home, twin girls. His father

Renee Ryan   199

had been conscripted into the French army, which meant the boy was the man of the house. "What are the charges against your friend?"

"I don't know, something to do with passing out pamphlets for the Free French. It's all so terribly unfair." Paulette threw herself into Hélène's arms again. "I'll die without him, Maman. You have to do something."

What could she do? She had no power in this world.

"Please, you have to help Lucien." Paulette's voice was muffled against Hélène's shoulder. "You are the only person who can."

Confused by this statement, she pushed her daughter out of her arms. Paulette's nose was pink, and her eyes were swollen, and yet she was beautiful. Tragic and gorgeous in her misery. The girl was eighteen, no longer a child and already wielding the tools of a woman. It was a startling revelation, made more frightening because Hélène sensed Paulette knew the influence of her tears. "What is it you think I can do?"

"Isn't it obvious? You can go to *Capitaine* von Schmidt and ask him to put in a good word for Lucien. I've seen the way you bend him to your will. He'll do anything you ask."

Hélène gaped at her daughter. Paulette had caught the undertones between her and von Schmidt, and yet had completely misread their meaning. The despair she felt, she couldn't describe it. Cold and paralyzing. "I do *not* have that kind of relationship with the man. While I wish I could help, I can't do what you ask. It isn't possible."

"You think I don't understand the situation? Oh, I understand, believe me. I do. A lot more than you think." Her expression was so angry, and her voice was so bitter, that again Hélène hardly recognized her own child. She experienced a moment of utter hopelessness. Some of the emotion edged over into irritation. She started to speak, to correct this terrible mistake, but she paused and looked away, too sick over the example she'd set to bring up the right words.

"Well?" Paulette pushed. "Will you do it? Will you speak to *Capitaine* von Schmidt?"

"Even if I had that kind of sway with him, which I assure you, I don't, there is no guarantee he will be able to influence the Gestapo on behalf of your friend. He is not SS."

"Why would that matter?" Paulette looked genuinely surprised. "Germans are Germans."

"That is not true, not true at all. Some Germans are worse than others."

"Be that as it may…" Impatience glowed in the girl's eyes. "The *capitaine* likes you, Maman. He will do whatever you ask. I know it, even if you do not. What harm could it be to ask him to help Lucien?"

What harm, indeed. She started to explain. But then an image of the boy came into her mind and Hélène thought of his mother, his sisters. Could she take this risk?

Her father's words came to her in a rush. *What we do for ourselves, Hélène, dies with us. What we do for others, remains forever.*

She must be brave, for the sake of this boy and his mother.

Her hands reached for each other, twisted at her waist, fell back to her sides. "I will bring up the matter with von Schmidt. But I must warn you, Paulette. It is not a simple thing you ask of me. To do this I will have to—"

"Oh, Maman. I knew you would agree."

And just like that, the matter was settled in her daughter's mind. Paulette, tears quickly drying, took herself to Hélène's dressing table and proceeded to paw through the jars. Humming an American tune made popular by one of those swing bands, she dipped a brush into a small pot and, without fuss or hesitation, swiped the red dye across her lips. "I think this color suits me." The girl's impossibly long lashes fluttered expectantly. "Don't you agree?"

Desperation tried to get the better of her. She battled it back. "It's very lovely." Hélène rubbed at her tired eyes and, again, attempted to explain the situation to her daughter. "Paulette, I want you to understand why I make myself available to our…houseguest. This is important, so I need you to listen to what I tell you."

"Hmm," was all she said, her attention buried in a jar of face cream. The girl's complete disinterest teased Hélène's guilt to the surface. She'd allowed Paulette to believe their house was a safe haven, when it was anything but.

"France is at war," she began. "And we are at von Schmidt's mercy. I do not cultivate a relationship with him for my own pleasure. I do so for our family, for you. I…" The rest of the words slid down her throat. This time, she'd lost Paulette's interest to an atomizer of perfume. "We will speak of this another time."

When I have your full attention.

Hélène moved to the window. The pruning had already begun in the vineyard. Another year, another hope. Despite the cold, her hands began to sweat because she knew what she would have to do to save Paulette's friend. It shamed her, but not enough to turn from this path.

She should do it now, before she lost her nerve. Von Schmidt would be in the library, watching the drive, already dressed for dinner, debating with himself whether to have another cigarette. He would have it, of course. He denied himself nothing.

She left the window and stood before the full-length mirror. The air scratched in her lungs as she studied her dress, her face, the elegant hair. Tomorrow, there would be a different woman in the glass. More jaded, humiliated and stripped of what little pride she had left.

It had to be done. She could put it off no longer.

Hélène bid her reflection a silent farewell and, after smoothing down a stray hair, left the room. Outside the library, her stomach became a nest of writhing snakes.

Remember, Hélène, a boy's life is at stake. The words in her head were spoken in Étienne's voice. They pushed her through the door.

Von Schmidt was sitting calmly at his desk, smoking a cigarette. "Helmut." She said his name in a husky whisper. "Do you have a moment?"

"For you?" He smiled with just the hint of the predator in his eyes. "I have several."

For the boy, she reminded herself. *For his family. And for yours.*

It was time to meet her fate. And still, she hesitated.

Before von Schmidt had moved into her home, Hélène had done a good deal of entertaining. In the role of hostess her duties had required her to be solicitous and charming, a woman who listened to a guest—a man—and made him feel noticed, admired. Heard. She would use those same skills to take this next—and final—step in her own personal war.

She moved slowly, with obvious intent, her eyes locked with von Schmidt's. His smile deepened and she felt strangely emboldened. She reached down and put her hand on his knee, squeezed softly.

He reached to her. She skirted away. *Not yet.* She slinked to the bookshelf, ran her fingertips along a random spine. She didn't look back to see if von Schmidt watched her. She knew he did. The sun slipped below the horizon, casting the room in a pink-tinged glow. She heard him leave his seat. When he came up behind her, she turned, her back against the books.

Both of his hands came up, landing on the shelving, one on either side of her head, sufficiently trapping her in place. His gaze dropped to her lips.

She would not prevent his kiss. She would not encourage it, either.

He moved a step closer, his smile spreading. A smile to others, a trap for her. She allowed him to press her against the shelves, to brush his fingers across her cheek, then along her jawline. She focused on a spot above his right eye, pretending it didn't matter that he was taking outrageous liberties without the benefit of a locked door to afford them privacy. Anyone could walk in on them. Anyone could hear what they said.

His head lowered to hers.

Bile rose into her throat. She closed her eyes so he wouldn't see her revulsion. He took what he wanted, not gently, but with ruthless greed. She hadn't expected anything else. She figuratively gritted her teeth through every ugly minute of his assault. When he stepped back, her skin burned with humiliation. And hate. He saw neither emotion in her eyes. She gave him submission and nothing else. There were only so many lies she could tell.

"You will come to my room tonight," he said, hand gripping her throat. "After our guests have left for the evening."

It was not a request, but she knew he expected a response. She gave him a terse nod. It was all she could manage under the weight of her shame.

He returned to his chair and sat, stretching out his long legs in a languid manner. The satisfaction on his face nearly had her running for the door. Then she thought of Paulette's friend locked in a cage and leaned over von Schmidt, closing the distance, until her mouth hovered mere inches above his. She noticed, in some distant part of her brain, that the clocks in the hallway chimed the top of the hour, and that the room had turned an ashen, gloomy gray. Or perhaps that was only the color left in her heart. "If I come to you tonight," she whispered in the same husky tone she'd adopted since entering the library, "I will require something in return."

This seemed to amuse him. "Naturally."

"I want to know what is to become of young Lucien Trevon."

Recognition showed in von Schmidt's eyes. His slippery smile widened. "He was arrested by the Gestapo for an act of treason. I assume the punishment will fit the crime."

She shivered at the glee she saw in him and pulled slightly away. She needed distance for this next part. "I know this boy. He's just a misguided youth in need of a bit of discipline, nothing grand. A small reprimand. Perhaps you could put in a good word for him with the police?"

"You ask much of me, *Liebling*."

"Your influence is strong, Helmut." She knew such a statement played to his ego. "Surely, a word from you will have much weight."

"If I do this for you…"

"I would reward you dearly."

"Well, then. Consider it done."

"Thank you." She attempted to draw back.

He pulled her closer still. "You will show me your appreciation now."

Afterward, Hélène made an excuse about needing to retouch her makeup and retreated to the privacy of her room.

Once she was alone, she collapsed to her knees, covered her face with her hands and prayed for God's forgiveness. She prayed and she prayed. Then, she wept.

When there were no more tears left, she stood, raised her chin at a proud angle and made a solemn vow to herself.

Never again would she shed a tear because of Helmut von Schmidt.

Chapter Twenty-Five

GABRIELLE

Her mother had gone too far. Even knowing why Hélène tempted the enemy, Gabrielle had a moment of wretched despair. Von Schmidt was a devious man. He operated by his own set of rules. None of them really knew how deep his cruelty went.

This was not the way to find out.

She contemplated waiting until after the party to confront her mother, then remembered the words she'd overheard only moments before. *You will come to my room tonight.*

She'd nearly entered the library then, thinking to prevent another disaster much as she'd done with Josephine, but something had held her back. A sense that von Schmidt would question her interference.

He would assume she was spying on him.

Which, of course, she was. Though she hadn't meant to do so tonight.

She'd been in the process of escorting Josephine into the parlor, to a chair near the blazing fire, when Gabrielle had seen her mother rush past, her head high, chin firm, looking like an aristocrat heading to the guillotine. She'd called out, but Hélène kept going. Compelled, she'd followed her to the library, and instantly regretted it. She'd heard too much.

Now, after checking on Josephine and finding her reading, Gabrielle went upstairs and entered her mother's bedroom. She did not knock. She did not waste time with a polite greeting. "You must stop this flirtation with von Schmidt," she blurted out. "Before it goes any further."

Her mother turned away from the window, her makeup flawless, her eyes hollow. "You should not interfere in matters you don't understand."

She understood, all too well.

"I know what he demands of you." Gabrielle wished that she didn't. She wished she didn't comprehend why her mother had chosen to wear a formfitting gown that hugged her curves suggestively. "You're courting discovery."

They never spoke about Hélène's Jewish blood, but Gabrielle knew the need for secrecy and didn't bring it up directly.

"A young boy's life is at stake."

She wanted to be proud of this reasoning. Possibly she would have been, if her mother was telling the truth. "You've been planning this liaison for some time. Do not try to convince me otherwise."

"I do what I must to protect our family."

"You will be labeled a collaborator."

A slight, self-deprecating smile touched her mother's lips. "I already carry that name."

"Maman—"

"No, Gabrielle. *Ma fille*, you must not interfere. We each have a line we are willing to cross." With remarkable calm,

Hélène went to the mirror, pressed powder to her forehead, her cheek, her chin. "This is mine."

"This is a line you should never cross. It's too dangerous."

"*You* speak to *me* of danger?" Her mother set down the puff, her hand shaking now. "When you take your own risks while the rest of us sleep safely in our beds?"

Gabrielle felt a sudden terrible shock. "You…you know?"

"I know." Instead of judgment, her voice held pride. Then, she did something that surprised them both. She pulled Gabrielle into her arms. "Your secret is safe with me," she whispered. "As I know mine is with you."

Stepping back, she regarded her mother's shining eyes. Hélène was in agony. And now so was Gabrielle. A hole in her heart started opening, expanding. "There has to be a better way."

"The Nazis slaughter my kind without conscience. Hate lives in their hearts. Hate for people like my father. People like me. And, with the stroke of a pen or the change of a single law, people like you and Paulette."

It was the first time they'd spoken openly about Hélène's Jewish heritage. And, also, the first time Gabrielle understood what motivated her mother—maternal love. She liked the situation even less with this new understanding. "You must be careful around von Schmidt. He can't know your secret. Do you hear what I'm saying?"

"I hear you. Now you hear me. If the Nazis come for me, they could also come for you. No, don't interrupt. Listen. I will do my part to protect our family in the only way I know how and with the skills the Lord has provided. I will do this, Gabrielle. And you will let me."

Gabrielle felt the blood rush from her face. "Please, Maman, at least think this through."

"I already have. I know what I am doing."

Josephine had said the same. It was too much. Gabrielle was losing control over the people she loved, the only family she had left. First her grandmother, with her reckless snooping and dangerous journal-keeping, and now her mother, making this terrible sacrifice. Would Paulette be next?

"Make no mistake, Gabrielle. Survival in war is an ugly business."

"*Oui*, Maman, it is very ugly."

"Shall we go down to dinner now?"

"We might as well." They passed by Paulette's room without stopping. The girl had not been invited to attend the party. That, at least, brought some semblance of relief.

They found Josephine where Gabrielle had left her, in the parlor, asleep now and softly snoring. Von Schmidt was in the room as well, along with three other men, none of them familiar to Gabrielle. All four were dressed in Wehrmacht uniforms, with the patches and hardware similar to von Schmidt's.

The men spoke in German, with von Schmidt controlling the majority of the conversation. They were so caught up in whatever they were discussing they didn't notice the women's arrival. In silent agreement, Gabrielle and her mother separated. Hélène joined the group of men. Gabrielle went to stand by Josephine and tried not to cringe at the proprietary way von Schmidt draped his arm around her mother's waist.

Von Schmidt continued to rant, there was no other word for it, and let go of Hélène so he could pace. The more involved he became, the faster his steps were. Gabrielle had never seen him this agitated. He seemed barely able to contain the explosion of nervous energy that kept him moving through the room. Something had put him on edge.

"He is late." Von Schmidt muttered this in both German and French. He did not elucidate *who* was late in either language. Clearly, it was someone important, someone with considerable power and probably higher up in the political hierarchy.

The doorbell brought von Schmidt to an abrupt halt and Josephine startled awake. "Oh!"

He gave the older woman a single, dismissive glare, then turned to face the entryway. It took a moment before someone answered the door, probably Marta. Then, footsteps approached the parlor. Clipped, purposeful, with the kind of innate confidence that belonged to a man who knew his own worth.

Hand on Josephine's shoulder, Gabrielle had a terrible premonition. The footsteps grew louder, closer, Nazi entitlement reverberating in each strike of heel to marble. Nerves tried to rise, to blunt her edge, to make her panic. No. She would not panic. Panic was her enemy. A hush fell over their small crowd. And then...

He walked into the room.

Gabrielle's chest rose and fell in a sudden spasm. Of course, she knew him at once. The black uniform was the same one he'd worn earlier that afternoon. Hovering in the doorway, his face unreadable, he took a slow, careful sweep of the room. His gaze landed on Gabrielle. There was something in the way he looked at her that brought matters to a very basic level.

She was not the only one uneasy. Tension vibrated in the air, thick enough to cut with a blade. She wanted to run, this very minute. *You're panicking*, she thought, and lifted her chin to a haughty angle. This was her home. She belonged here. He did not. He looked about to say something, but von Schmidt was on the move, speaking in rapid German.

"Welcome to my home, *Kriminalkommissar* Mueller." Von Schmidt rapped his heels smartly together and extended his right arm, held out straight, palm facing the Gestapo agent. "Heil Hitler!"

"Heil Hitler," Mueller answered, shooting his own arm out in response. The rest of the men joined in the anthem to their leader.

"Herr Detective—"

"You will refer to me as Detective Commissioner, or Detective Mueller."

Von Schmidt stiffened, then nodded and made the introductions. The men, then the women, almost as an afterthought. In contrast, Mueller went to Gabrielle first. She couldn't speak, but she managed to make her hand do what it needed to do when he reached out to her. He went through the process with Josephine, Hélène, then the rest of the occupants in the room.

Gabrielle watched, revolted, as each of the German soldiers groveled before him. Mueller seemed thoroughly unimpressed with their adulation and subsequent flattery. His disdain was not hard to read. Nor did it come as a surprise. The Gestapo trusted no one outside their elite ranks, not even their fellow Germans.

There was a combined sigh of relief when Marta announced dinner.

As was his custom, von Schmidt took his place at the head of the table, resplendent in his self-appointed position as lord of the manor. He placed Mueller at his immediate right, Hélène on his left, Gabrielle next to her mother. Josephine sat at the other end of the table. The first course was served, along with an exquisite rosé her mother had chosen.

What Gabrielle noticed almost immediately was the strange dynamics between von Schmidt and Detective Mueller. While von Schmidt did most of the talking, Mueller was the one actually directing the conversation. He seemed to be laying some sort of trap for the other man, perhaps testing von Schmidt's loyalty.

How did the sycophant not see this? Perhaps he was too

much in awe of the Detective Commissioner to notice the other man's dislike.

Trying not to show her reaction, Gabrielle lowered her head and let the music of cutlery fill her ears. Then, suddenly, shrilly, the telephone rang. Two jarring rings. Then nothing. *No*, she thought. *Not now, Max. Please, not now.* The telephone rang again. Only once this time. Max wanted to meet at midnight. The code had seemed so simple that they'd decided not to change it.

Had that been a mistake? Did anyone suspect? Did Mueller? She risked a glance from beneath the fringes of her eyelashes. To her relief, the detective's gaze was still riveted on von Schmidt. Neither man mentioned the telephone.

Von Schmidt ordered Hélène to pour the next champagne. "You are in for a treat," he informed Mueller, waiting for all glasses to be filled before lifting his own. "A toast. To the Third Reich."

"The Third Reich," came a chorus of voices.

The room went momentarily silent as everyone took a sip of the champagne. Mueller's compliment was the first of several. "Excellent."

As if he'd had a personal hand in making the wine himself, von Schmidt took credit for the selection.

Mueller smiled. It was a smile that sent chills down Gabrielle's spine. He took another sip, then pulled the glass down and studied the bubbling liquid. "I have tasted this before."

Gabrielle's blood turned cold.

"You are drinking one of Château Fouché-LeBlanc's finest *cuvées*," von Schmidt explained with no small amount of pride. "A single vintage from the 1928 harvest."

Eyes flat, Mueller set down his glass with noticeable care. "All bottles of the 1928 were supposed to be shipped to Berlin immediately following the signing of the armistice."

The room went dead silent.

Von Schmidt actually squirmed under Mueller's glare, his own brow creasing into a vertical line. He looked worried. He should be worried. He had been caught saving the best champagne for himself.

Unfortunately, Mueller's wrath was not for him alone. He smiled again, smaller this time, and turned to Gabrielle. "What do you have to say about this, Madame Dupree?"

It was as if the light had been sucked from the room. All she could see was black. Somehow the detective knew she had hidden hundreds of bottles of the 1928 behind her fake wall. But that couldn't be. He was only testing her. That glint in his eyes, the one she couldn't quite define, it was goading her to lie. Daring her to play this dreadful game with him.

"There is an easy explanation," she began, doing her best to look at the man without actually looking at him. "We served several single vintages at the party we held to celebrate our two hundred years of champagne making. This, of course, depleted much of our reserves." It was an evasion, if not a complete lie.

"When was this party?"

Gabrielle breathed in, breathed out. "In 1939. On the final night of the grape harvest."

He said nothing. She said nothing.

Josephine stepped into the silence and launched into her favorite story behind her rosé blend that had become an international sensation. "It was almost a lark," she added, laughing fondly over the memory. "I decided to blend a chardonnay with the juice from the pinot grape instead of elderberries. The result was nothing short of—"

"Magical," Mueller finished for her, his eyes still on Gabrielle, his voice heavy with ice. "So you have said, Madame. Twice in the past half hour."

"I… Did I already tell you this?"

He looked at her. His mouth moved as if to smile but it was more of a twitch, almost a frown. "You did."

Visibly shrinking, Josephine hunched her shoulders and added in a tone barely above a whisper, "Forgive me for repeating myself."

"I apologize, Detective Mueller." This, from von Schmidt. "Madame Fouché-LeBlanc is senile. She tends to retell the same stories."

"And yet—" derision dripped from Mueller's voice "—you allow her at the table, knowing this is her way?"

Von Schmidt visibly winced. "She is not always confused."

As if to contradict this, Josephine lifted her head, glanced around with a wild look in her eyes. Then, catching Mueller's attention, she gave him an unfocused, faintly wobbly frown, as if she were trying to place him but wasn't quite able to make the connection.

Gabrielle's heart leaped to her throat. There was genuine confusion in her grandmother's expression. "I, for one, never tire of hearing your stories, Grandmère. I find them inspiring."

Out of the corner of her eye, she saw von Schmidt's lip curl. "No one asked for your opinion, Madame Dupree."

"I believe," Mueller began, looking at Gabrielle with those eyes of his that could melt icebergs, "we have lost the point of this conversation. Madame Dupree, you say you served most of the 1928 at your anniversary party, yet here we are drinking it now. Explain this to me."

Gabrielle clutched her hands together in her lap, her fingernails digging into her palms. She could point the finger at von Schmidt. He had, after all, "saved" the 1928 from confiscation. No, too risky. He would only find a way to place the blame back on her. Better to continue the lie she'd concocted for his benefit. "The champagne is from my family's private stock."

"Ah." This seemed to satisfy the detective's curiosity. He said nothing more.

Discussion turned to the likelihood of the Americans joining the war and what that would mean for the Third Reich. The meal went on for another hour, and then several minutes past that. At last, von Schmidt released the women from the table. Hélène took the lead. Gabrielle was only too happy to help her grandmother to her feet and follow behind her mother.

Mueller's voice stopped her at the doorway. "Madame Dupree, I have a strong desire to see your wine cellar." He set down his napkin and stood. "You will take me there now."

He knew. Somehow he knew she was lying about the champagne. Or maybe it was von Schmidt he didn't trust. Either way, she had to think of a way to keep him out of her caves. His eyes saw too much, and his mind drew too many accurate conclusions. "It's late, Detective Mueller. My grandmother is tired. I need to escort her to her room and see her settled."

"By all means, tend to her needs."

Gabrielle nearly slumped in relief. He was going to let her go. She was actually feeling pleased she'd maneuvered around his request, perhaps even a little thrilled. But he spoke again. And she knew her troubles were only just beginning.

"You have fifteen minutes to care for your grandmother. Then you will show me where you keep the champagne that should have been sent to Berlin months ago."

Chapter Twenty-Six

JOSEPHINE

Josephine was glad to be sent to her room like a naughty child. She'd pushed von Schmidt nearly past his limit tonight, and in front of a powerful guest who'd also, rightfully so, found her tedious. No woman in her right mind would do such a thing as to encourage both men's irritation. Which, of course, was why she'd done so.

Things were going according to plan. She was thinking clearly, coolly, her mind firmly in the present tense. It would not last long. This illusion of a confused mind was becoming too easy to maintain. Her world was disappearing, the blankness rising, her grasp on reality at risk.

Repeating stories from the past helped ground her. But also made her long for a time that could never be relived.

She was cold.

She needed heat, needed it more than air. It was all she could do not to hurry up the stairs and crawl under a sea of blankets. She had to get rid of her granddaughter first. Gabrielle, after all, had a Gestapo agent to cajole and needed these extra minutes to prepare herself.

Out of habit, as much as need, she reached to the banister for support, something she hadn't needed to do until recently. Her body grew as weak as her mind. She shrugged off Gabrielle's assistance. "I prefer to go up to my room on my own." She said this in an imperial tone, keeping her eyes on the railing beneath her hand.

"You're unsteady."

"Fetch Marta, then."

She might as well have slapped her granddaughter. She disliked hurting the younger woman, but she didn't want another lecture, or another warning. She wanted to be warm. She also wanted to be alone. Sorrow slashed across her heart and there was nothing to do to stanch the bleeding. Her closeness with her granddaughter was yet another casualty of this new and brutal war they fought in the confines of their own home. "Please, Gabrielle."

Her granddaughter surprised her by relenting to the request. "I'll get Marta." Her voice held defeat. "If that's what you want."

"It is what I want." Josephine turned off her mind while she waited for Gabrielle to return with the housekeeper. Marta then accompanied her to her room. As the other woman fussed over her, they spoke of inconsequential things. The weather, the meal itself, nothing of Nazis or Gestapo agents or Waffen-SS units. Her friend's voice brought Josephine comfort over the clamor of the commotion in her head, like a long-forgotten lullaby.

She allowed Marta to help her into bed. The moon was full, a bright, round ball in the sky. "There is too much light in my eyes."

"I'll draw the curtains." Before she crossed to the window, Marta reached to take Josephine's hand, a silent show of support. Josephine was the first to pull away.

And then, the light was gone, and she could think better.

Marta touched her hand again. "*Bonne nuit*, Josephine. *Doux rêves*."

Doux rêves. Sweet dreams. Impossible when a Gestapo agent wanted Gabrielle to show him the caves. Josephine squeezed her eyes shut. "*Bonne nuit*, Marta."

She kept her eyes shut until she heard the door close. She could see nothing but the sliver of moonlight flickering through the gap in the drawn curtains. She heard a small sound and listened. Nothing but the steady rhythm of her own breathing. She threw aside the covers and felt her way through the darkness. She needed to retrieve her journal from its hiding place behind her nightstand. Feeling her way down the wall, her fingers stopped at the baseboard. She quickly worked away the slab of wood, slid the book out, then returned the plank to its original position and climbed into bed.

A terrible silence descended over the room. Josephine could feel her pulse thudding in her ears, in the hollow at her throat. Was the party still going on?

Of course it was. Von Schmidt had Germans to impress.

She lay awake for at least an hour, possibly two, holding her journal tightly against her chest, listening for footsteps in the outer hallway.

Something about today—or was it tonight?—kept nagging at her, right there in her mind, shimmering just out of reach. Something in von Schmidt's behavior. His deference to the Gestapo agent, yes, obviously, but more than that. He'd been unusually nervous, his gaze darting from Detective Mueller to his food and back again. He'd behaved like a man hiding

something. The 1928? No, she decided. Something else had
been nagging at him. And now it nagged at her.

When are you coming home, Josephine?

The question came at her as she stared at the cracked plaster
of the ceiling overhead. It was Antoine's voice, as clear as if he
were sitting on the edge of her bed. His face was not so clear.
No matter, she had his features memorized. Handsome, rug-
ged, muscled from the many hours he spent in his vineyard,
gloriously larger than life. He'd been smart, quietly funny,
a man of integrity who loved the Lord as much as his vines.

Not yet, Antoine. I can't come home yet.

She swung her feet to the floor and climbed out of bed.
Journal in hand, she moved to the window and spread the
curtains apart to let in the moonlight. She caught a movement below—somewhere in the darkness—at the edge of the
vineyard.

There. A silhouette. No, two people. One of them wearing clothes that blended with the night, the other…a woman.
In a gown that glittered in the moonlight, keeping her distance from the man in black. A third figure joined the duo,
a man, sent away almost immediately. The woman reached
out a hand to the door of the wine cellar. Twisted a key in
the lock. Swung open the door. Paused to let the other figure
enter first, then followed.

*Be smart, Gabrielle. Be wise as serpents and as gentle as doves.
The Lord is with you.* Josephine lifted up another prayer for her
granddaughter's safety then moved to her writing desk, her
feet knowing the way better than her mind.

She turned on the light and opened the journal, quickly
scanning the contents. She reviewed her notations. Reading
the entries sharpened her memory but was also a sort of bloodletting, painful and yet necessary. She stopped at something

she'd jotted down the week of von Schmidt's arrival. *Hélène has taken over the German's social calendar.*

Whose idea had that been, hers? Or Hélène's?

She flipped pages, again stopping to read the news of the wine levy. Three million bottles a month was an impossible request. But like the bread and fish that fed the five thousand, the Lord would provide.

Josephine found a running tally of the items she and Marta had hidden from the Germans. With her friend's memory stronger than her own, Marta had placed marks beside the treasures they'd personally squirreled away.

Odd. Only half the list had received a mark. And then, she remembered. The Renoir. The other missing valuables. Von Schmidt was stealing from her family. Statuettes, paintings, silver serving dishes, a Ming vase. Tapping her chin with her forefinger, she forced herself to concentrate, to think.

The sound of approaching footsteps and low conversation had her quickly dropping her hand and shutting off the light. She strained to hear over the drumming of her heartbeat. Two voices, one masculine. One feminine. A man, a woman. Von Schmidt and Hélène. The flirtation turning into something more? Something indecent?

How quickly Josephine wanted to judge the other woman. Yet, deep in her soul, where a woman must be brutally honest, Josephine knew this was her fault. She'd insisted Hélène make herself indispensable to the German.

She put her ear to the door and listened to the muffled conversation. The back-and-forth turned her blood cold. *Your fault,* she reminded herself. The voices faded. She could sense, rather than hear, the two moving across a threshold.

Heart in her throat, she waited for the snick of a lock that would seal her daughter-in-law's fate. When it came, the sound reverberated in Josephine's ears, pounded in her soul. Pushed guilt into her stomach. Tears filled her eyes. Then resolve. Hélène had given her the window of time that she needed.

Josephine opened her door and peeked out. The hallway was empty. She took a few hesitant steps. The gloom concealed her progress. No one saw her descend the stairs or move toward the library. The door was locked.

She had the key, of course she had the key. Von Schmidt had confiscated what he thought were the only two copies. Josephine had kept the third.

Smiling, she stepped into the library, pausing inside the bright shaft of moonlight. The German had dared to set himself up at Antoine's massive desk, which had been hers after her husband's death. Another mistake on von Schmidt's part, assuming Josephine would not wish to work in such a masculine setting. He could not have been more wrong. She'd never cared for frills. She only wanted to be close to her husband. After all these years, she still found Antoine here in this room, with these books, at this desk.

She sat in the chair that still held the mold of her husband's larger frame. For a moment, she let the worn leather wrap her in its sweet embrace. She thought of Antoine. Then, she went to work. She shoved the chair back and knelt down, sent her fingers roaming across the panel beneath the drawer. She felt the latch's release, smiled at her own resourcefulness as she drew out another key, another unknown copy, this one for the desk itself.

Von Schmidt was not so clever.

Josephine opened the locked drawer and quickly rifled through the contents. She discovered a list of names that sent chills through her. She knew these people. Most were friends. Her contempt for von Schmidt could not be stronger. He'd subdivided each person via their nationality and profession, French Jews, foreign Jews, business owners, men in powerful positions, men who made important decisions, then he'd sorted them alphabetically from there.

"You horrible, awful man," she whispered into the dark, still air.

There were other notations by some of the names, as well as dates. She looked over her shoulder, considered, then made her decision. She would share this with Gabrielle. She would trust her granddaughter to know what to do with this information.

Josephine copied the list of names quickly into her journal, her hands steady despite her rising fury. She paused, lost her way for a moment. Her thoughts tried to bleed into one another. No, this was not a time for her mind to play its tricks. Why had she come to Antoine's study? Looking down at the names, she knew this was not the reason.

She searched her journal, discovered her answer three pages later. The missing LeBlanc treasures. She returned to the desk and found what she was looking for without much trouble. Von Schmidt had made a detailed list of the items he'd confiscated from her home. *Her home.*

In a fit of rage, Josephine checked his list against the items in her journal that hadn't received Marta's special mark. A perfect match. But where was he hiding the stolen goods?

This time, she went back to the desk for the answer. She easily located shipping receipts. A particular destination caught her eye. Lisbon, Portugal. A neutral city in a neutral country where German authorities had no jurisdiction. Where a man like Helmut von Schmidt could store his stolen treasures without raising questions from his superiors.

Was it any wonder Josephine felt nothing but disgust for the man?

Chapter Twenty-Seven

GABRIELLE

Gabrielle nearly convinced herself the situation wasn't dire. Detective Mueller seemed perfectly content to keep his inspection contained to the front of the wine cellar. Ten minutes had come and gone, and he'd barely moved past the entryway. There'd been no mention of single-vintage champagnes. Nothing about the 1928.

Still, she shivered. She blamed the visceral reaction on the dense, cold air in this part of the cave and not the way the hard-eyed police detective seemed to be searching for something specific. Clues, perhaps. Clues to what? A crime committed against the Third Reich.

Which one?

She shivered again. Too late, she wished she'd thrown a jacket over her evening gown before leaving the château. Firming her jaw to keep her teeth from chattering, she continued watching Mueller methodically inspect the limestone at his feet, the wall to his immediate left, the ceiling over-head. He glanced down the darkened hallway that stretched deep into the earth. In any other man, she might have found his attention to detail impressive. "How far do these corri-dors extend?"

"Miles."

He snapped his attention to her face.

Something there, in his eyes. Something clever and ruth-less. And…what? What was that sliver of something else she caught in his expression? She shook her head and scrambled to explain. "The ancient Romans dug these tunnels, or what the *Champenois* call *crayères*, to mine the salt and chalk. Then, sometime in the 1600s, I don't know the exact date, local monks figured out these caves provided the perfect tempera-ture and humidity control to store their wine. All these years later, we—" she made a sweeping motion with her hand that included herself "—the modern-day *Champenois* continue in the same tradition as those long-ago men of God."

"You store wine bottles, cases and barrels in here?"

"*Oui*, all three."

He went to the door leading out into the vineyard and pressed his palm flat against the thick wood, pulled away. Pressed again. The wind howled outside, battering a hard fist against the spot where Mueller kept resting his hand. His manner was deceptively bland, as he said, "Your chef created an exquisite meal. I was not expecting such fine cuisine so far from Paris."

And Gabrielle hadn't expected such high praise from some-one wearing a Gestapo uniform. "Marta is not a trained chef," she said cautiously, unsure the point of this discussion. "She is, however, an excellent cook."

"Her talents are worthy of at least one Michelin star."

Again, he surprised her. "I will pass along the compliment."

"See that you do." He moved to the small wooden table where François kept a collection of tools and notebooks, a piece of black coal, an adding machine.

The cloying scent of cigarette smoke clung to him, as it did her, though neither had indulged. The scent came from von Schmidt and his guests. And, of course, her mother.

Gabrielle had just entered the parlor after leaving Grandmère in Marta's care, when Mueller remarked on her mother's brand of cigarettes. "I'm surprised you smoke Lucky Strikes, Madame LeBlanc. American cigarettes are not easy to come by these days, and certainly not in the occupied zone."

"I stocked up before the war."

Although this response seemed to satisfy Mueller's curiosity, it did not lessen his disapproval. "German cigarettes are far superior. In the future, you will remember that."

Hélène had agreed to switch brands immediately.

Now there was no talk of cigarettes. Or fine cuisine. There was only silence as Mueller picked up a notebook and moved to a rack of upturned bottles. Eyes narrowed, he flipped through the pages, stopping, considering, moving on. Gabrielle raised her thumb to her mouth and nibbled on the nail, a habit she'd vanquished in childhood, or so she thought.

Why wasn't he bringing up the 1928?

"What do these numbers and dates refer to?"

She quickly scanned the page. "Each number represents a rack of champagne undergoing its second fermentation. In chronological order, number one is closest to the door, number two next to that, and so on down the line. The corresponding date—" she pointed to one of the line items "—indicates when the bottles were originally placed in the rack."

Moving to the first row, François's notebook still in hand, Mueller continued comparing, checking. His hand rested on the butt of one of the bottles. A full five seconds lapsed before he freed it from its position and studied the contents.

"The second fermentation for that particular wine is nearly complete," she began. Adding, somewhat condescendingly, "As you will notice by its clarity and the large amount of sediment gathered at the neck."

Mueller's mouth formed a tight, flat line. He was very good at showing his irritation in the smallest of ways. "Do not patronize me, Madame Dupree, or assume—" he returned the bottle to its place in the rack "—that because I take my time in the front of your cellar this means I have forgotten why we are here."

She tried not to shudder, even as panic gnawed at her composure with sharp little spider fangs. "Understood."

"Who turns the bottles in the process the French call, *remuage?*"

"That duty falls to the man you sent away just before we entered the cellar. François is in charge of manipulating the bottles, one-eighth of a turn at a time."

"Ah, yes. François, your cellar master. He is very protective of you."

"Loyalty is a valuable asset at Château Fouché-LeBlanc."

"So I have been led to believe." He returned the notebook to the table, an odd smile playing at his lips. "You will show me the champagne now."

Gabrielle's blood froze in her veins. "The...champagne?"

"The 1928. The reason for this late-night excursion into your *crayères.*" His tone was every bit as patronizing as hers had been. "Please, Madame. Lead the way."

She expelled a breath. "Follow me."

Welcoming the extensive walk to the back of the cellar, she took the opportunity to gather her composure. These were her caves, her champagne, her birthright. She knew every crack and crevice. And still, she nearly stumbled down the last flight of stairs.

Mueller did not reach out to steady her.

For that, she was profoundly grateful. She didn't think she could bear his touch.

The final turn loomed. She took it quickly, then guided him to the cases of the 1928. It was a calculated move that put his back to the fake wall she'd built once by herself, and again, months later, with François's assistance.

Saying nothing, Mueller went straight to the crates, forced one open and retrieved a bottle. Cradling it in his hand like a seasoned sommelier, he studied the label closely. "What makes this particular wine special?"

His tone never varied. His eyes never left the bottle in his hand. Was he baiting her? Leading her into a trap? "Herr Detective—"

"I told you how to address me."

She pressed her lips together, began again. "Detective Mueller, most champagnes are a blend of several base wines, as many as a dozen but no fewer than three. The process is like putting together a complicated puzzle that requires a kind of taste memory."

Keep him distracted, she told herself. *Keep his back to the fake wall.* "Sometimes, very rarely, when a harvest is exceptional, we—the people of Champagne—declare a *millésime*, a vintage." She kept her eyes focused on his face, not a single flicker in the direction of the wall behind him. "The 1928 is considered one of the best single vintages of this century."

"When did your grandmother step down as the head of your champagne house?"

The change of subject was so unexpected it took Gabrielle a moment to process the question. "There was no specific stepping down. It was more a gradual letting go. She guided me along, answered my questions, and slowly let me take on more and more of her duties." She took the bottle from him and placed it carefully back in its nest. "Then, one day, I found myself making decisions without consulting her first."

"You make it sound very amicable." He did not seem convinced.

And she remembered her grandmother's plan to make von Schmidt think Gabrielle had snatched control by scheming, rather than Josephine handing it over willingly. "Nothing is ever completely amicable."

"Not even between a grandmother and her beloved granddaughter?"

"Not even then."

He flicked a cool-eyed look in her direction then bent over the stacked crates, taking what appeared to be a silent inventory of the champagne. Abruptly, he straightened, spun on his heel and focused solely on the fake wall.

Gabrielle's breath stalled in her throat. His gaze never faltered. It kept moving and shifting over the many stones.

"I never knew my grandfather," she blurted out. "He died of a ruptured appendix when my father was still a boy."

Momentarily distracted, he paused his inspection. "Your grandmother never remarried?"

"She dedicated the rest of her life to preserving Antoine LeBlanc's legacy. And..." She drew in a fast breath. "If you asked her, she would say she found love twice in her lifetime. First, with my grandfather. Then with the champagne house after his death."

"What about you, Madame Dupree?" The hard, guttural accent somehow softened over her name. "Did you discover a similar devotion after your husband's death?"

"I have followed in my grandmother's footsteps." It was the only answer she would give him. "This is her acclaimed rosé."

She tried to hand him the champagne. He waved her off and focused on the wall once again. There was nothing in his manner to alert her as to what he was thinking, what conclusions he found. Why could she not read this man?

He looked up at the far corner and frowned at a spiderweb. He moved closer, his brow creasing in concentration. He started to speak, then his jaw clamped shut. Clearly, he was putting together a hypothesis as his eyes tracked from spiderweb to spiderweb, stone to stone, left to right, right to left. Left to right.

Then, he glanced at her. His eyebrows lifted. *He knows.* With his face half-covered in shadow, he looked every bit the sinister Gestapo agent about to make an arrest. *It's over.*

Something hot and terrible crawled over her skin. Not fear. Something worse. Something without a name.

Mueller's hand lifted from his side. An inch higher, higher, moving toward her face. Or possibly her jaw, her neck. The world slowed to a crawl. Higher, his hand came up higher. Was he planning to grab her by her throat and squeeze the life out of her?

Gabrielle held perfectly still. For a second her fear turned to defiance. Let him try to hurt her. Let him show his true nature. She lifted her chin a fraction higher. At the moment she thought his hand would reach for her, he spun around and flattened his palm on the fake wall instead. "It's very curious. The construction is stunningly inferior in this portion of the cave."

Her throat cinched and no words came out. Feebly, her own gaze followed his hand as his fingers caressed the stones.

"Very curious, indeed."

The pulsing of her blood grew louder in her ears. She couldn't think, couldn't breathe. The ceiling seemed to lower. The walls pressed in closer. She wished she had a pistol, a knife, a weapon of any kind. It was the thought of a cornered animal with no way out.

She thought of her peace-loving husband, of his gentle nature, so like his father. His father. Max. Gabrielle was supposed to meet Max within the hour. Would he come looking for her if she failed to show? Would he know to come this far back in the cave?

Mueller pushed away from the wall and came toward her again. The sound of his heels on the stone was as loud as a thunderclap. He suddenly had a grip on her wrist, not tight, but with enough pressure to make his point. She nearly cried out, not from pain. From shock.

He'd moved so quickly. She hadn't thought to pull out of his reach. Now he was looming over her from his superior height, looking every bit Hitler's instrument of death, holding her wrist in his large hand. And yet, not hurting her. Why did her mind lock on that thought?

"You will ship all of the remaining bottles of the 1928 to Berlin in the morning. You will also send what is left of the 1919, the 1920 and the 1921."

Gabrielle's mouth worked, but nothing came out. How did he know she'd chosen to serve those specific single vintages at the anniversary party?

"Do you understand this request, Madame Dupree?"

He was so big, so strong, and she was too small, too weak, too soft...

Non, she was not weak. She was not soft. She was a fighter. A warrior. Josephine's granddaughter. She was a LeBlanc. "Yes, Detective Mueller. I understand this request."

Chapter Twenty-Eight

HÉLÈNE

It snowed overnight, a light dusting that would melt by midday. The weather mirrored the condition of Hélène's heart, cold and bleak. How ill-prepared she'd been for war within her own home. How utterly unsuited and naïve to think she could control the battle. That the decision had been hers to make.

The layers of protection she'd placed around her heart had not been enough. She was shattered, a sketch of her former self, left with nothing but shame and dishonor and a heart in pieces. The first night had been the hardest. The following two had proved no easier. A fair trade for her life, and that of her family—her daughters—that was how she rationalized her relationship with von Schmidt in her mind.

Hélène would not allow herself a moment of regret. It was done. No going back.

She fell to her knees and prayed for forgiveness, as she did every morning. How could the Lord forgive her? How could she forgive herself?

Shoving to her feet, she searched for her cigarettes. As she fit one between her lips she thought of her encounter with the Gestapo agent three nights ago. Hélène hadn't expected Detective Mueller's instant suspicion of something so simple as the brand she chose to smoke, purchased from a little shop in Paris because it had been Étienne's favorite.

She didn't even like to smoke. She did so in honor of her husband's memory. Every puff filled the void he'd left in her life and made her think of him. Closing her eyes, she tried to summon up his image. His features wavered in her mind, nearly there, nearly real. But not quite. She barely recalled the hue of his hair, the tenor of his voice. She whipped open her eyes. She would not lose Étienne again. Not again. Hands trembling, she opened a drawer in her dressing table and withdrew the photograph first, then the wristwatch.

It took her only a moment to memorize the beloved oval face, the impossibly green eyes, the thick wavy hair their daughters had inherited from him. She glanced at the watch next. It had stopped again. She'd forgotten to wind it. She reached for the stem, then changed her mind. No. She would let the gears remain dormant in silent tribute to the man she still loved.

She returned the items to their resting place and reminded herself. No regrets. She'd made her choice. She now had a purpose. For as long as Germany occupied France, and von Schmidt occupied the château, she would pander to the enemy and organize his parties.

Seeing to her duty, she spent the rest of the morning, and most of the afternoon, finalizing last-minute preparations for tonight's official welcome of Detective Mueller to the region. The details kept her busy all day, making it impossible to find a spare moment for herself. Now, with plenty of time left to dress for the party, she entered her youngest daughter's bedroom.

Paulette stood at her closet, studying the contents. "Maman, perfect timing. Which gown should I wear tonight? The blue?" She reached in and plucked out a dress the color of a brittle, cloudless sky. "Or—" her hand plunged in again "—the green?"

Hélène considered both options, then pointed to her choice. "The green. It will highlight the golden tints in your hair and make your eyes sparkle."

A self-satisfied smile met this response. "I think so, too."

Hélène didn't linger. She had her own evening gown to choose. Tonight's party would be a difficult test, and only the first of many. Another step deeper into the lie of her own making.

She would not regret, or think of herself, or what her actions did to her soul. She would think only of her daughters. They were alive and would one day—someday—live in a free France. She had to believe that, or she would break. She slipped into her evening gown, one of her most flattering and von Schmidt's favorite. He would notice, and assume she'd dressed for him. She would not correct his assumption.

Mouth grim, she secured the last pin in her hair and studied the result of her efforts in the full-length mirror. Skimming a half inch above the ground, the pale lavender silk, tucked at her waist by an invisible seam, clung to her curves and left just enough to the imagination to be considered elegant rather than tasteless.

She retouched her makeup, adding kohl liner to enhance the almond shape of her eyes. At her writing desk she reviewed the guest list, mostly Germans but a few local *Cham-*

penois. Would they speak to her? Only the ones who'd made similar liaisons as herself.

How many? she wondered. Too many, and she pitied them all, as she pitied herself.

Consulting the clock, she decided she had time to check on the caterer. The kitchen was a hive of activity. Under Monsieur Chardon's careful watch, a sea of hired staff moved with purpose and efficiency, filling silver serving trays with caviar, poached salmon and all forms of French delicacies. Lucien Trevon and his sisters were among the servers.

Hélène nodded in approval.

She entered the main salon and paused a moment to catch her breath. The stillness on the air was disconcerting but would be shattered soon enough. Her heels struck the parquet flooring with ruthless efficiency as she checked the decorations. A few mistakes caught her notice, not enough flowers in one arrangement, too many in another.

The sound of heavy footsteps had her gasping. Her hand went to her throat. "Gabrielle, you startled me."

Dressed to contend with the bitter temperatures in the vineyard, her daughter wore heavy boots and a thick jacket, and held a mug of fragrant coffee between her palms. "I was heading to my room when I thought I heard a noise." She took a sip of the steaming liquid. "You look tired, Maman."

She was tired. Bone tired. But she thought she'd camouflaged the signs with her makeup brush. She went to the closest mirror to check for herself. One glance was enough to send her back upstairs to her dressing table. She headed for the stairwell.

Gabrielle followed her. The entirety of her worry shone in her eyes. Hélène hated seeing her daughter so conflicted. "You have something you wish to say to me?"

"I... Yes. Wait a moment." She placed the mug of coffee

on one of the stairs then pulled Hélène into a fierce embrace. "I hate that you are in so much pain."

She stiffened in her daughter's arms. "Any pain I suffer is my own doing."

"I love you, Maman," Gabrielle whispered. "I love you. I don't say it enough."

Hélène began to cry. She wanted to cling to her daughter a moment longer. Just one more moment. "I love you, too, *ma fille*. I don't say it enough, either."

By uttering the words, she took ownership of her past and present sins, and silently appealed to the Lord for forgiveness. She stepped back and asked the same of her daughter. "Forgive me, Gabrielle. I have not been the best of mothers."

"You have been the best mother you know how to be. And that, Maman, has always been enough."

She didn't deserve such leniency from the one daughter she'd neglected in favor of the other. Hélène cupped Gabrielle's cheek. She knew it was futile to say the words, but she said them anyway. "I should have done better by you. I should have done more."

Gabrielle's hand came up to cover hers. "You did plenty."

They shared a sad smile, then parted ways.

Hélène staggered to her room. She made a moue of distaste at her reflection. She'd vowed not to cry over her fate, and here were tear tracks on her cheeks. She cleared her mind of all thought and began erasing her distress with a calm, steady hand.

The transformation took longer than it should have. By the time she arrived back downstairs, the guests were already arriving. Her heart took an extra hard beat. Too much laughter rang from French lips, a cruel mockery of the young men dying on the battlefields so that they could enjoy this freedom of drinking champagne with their German occupiers.

Von Schmidt caught her eye and motioned her to join him. She answered his call with a slow, steady pace. He was encircled by a group of men of varying ages and sizes. Several were dressed like him. Some were in formal dinner attire. One wore the black uniform of the SS.

She made the short journey across the room to the sound of whispers spoken loud enough for her to hear. So much condemnation, so much indignity to endure.

Humiliation wanted to overwhelm her, wanted to slow her steps and quicken her breath. "Good evening, gentlemen." Her smile was meant for the entire group, and none of them individually, not even von Schmidt.

He seized her arm at the elbow and squeezed harder than was necessary, a silent warning to speak nothing but happy words to their guests. His gaze roamed her face, then lowered over her gown. There was an air of ownership in his manner. And why wouldn't he look at her that way? He did own her. "You're wearing my favorite." Appreciation filled his voice. "I approve."

"I…" She swallowed back the catch in her throat and forged ahead with this unpleasant charade. "I dressed tonight with you in mind."

An audible gasp from a woman off to her left told Hélène she was still being watched. She could not let that knowledge flummox her. She had Nazis to entertain. One of their group, a short little man with small eyes and a receding hairline, openly leered at her. He wore a black Waffen-SS uniform, the iron cross pinned at the center of his shirt collar. He held a high rank. The single oak leaf signified he was a full colonel.

"You have exquisite taste in women, Herr Hauptmann," he said. "Please, introduce us."

"Hélène, this is *Standartenführer* Bauer. He is the regiment leader of the SS unit that is currently billeting in Reims."

She drummed up a smile. "Welcome, Herr *Standartenführer*."

"*Enchanté*, Madame." He took her hand and touched a kiss to her knuckles. A flush crept up her neck. His breath reeked of alcohol and cigarettes and the grip on her hand felt like a vise. She tried to pull away. She couldn't help herself. He repulsed her. But he held fast to her hand, his grip tightening, as if he was used to such a reaction and enjoyed the opportunity to display his dominance over a weaker individual.

Von Schmidt did not come to her rescue. He, too, repulsed her.

Hélène thought matters couldn't get any worse. But then she heard a familiar female tittering from across the room. Her eyes went wide at the sight of Paulette surrounded by a group of male admirers. All of the young men wore Waffen-SS uniforms. A strangled sound slid past Hélène's lips, immediately muffled.

"You will excuse me, gentlemen. I must see to my daughter. She is young and…" Hélène hesitated, trying to find the words that would explain this new terror in her heart. There were none. So, she said again, "She is young."

Chapter Twenty-Nine

GABRIELLE

Gabrielle stood on the edge of the party, calculating when she could make her exit. She had work to do for her father-in-law, for France, for the man who'd been shot out of the sky. Max had been hiding the airman for months and the strain was getting to him. That had been the reason for their meeting three nights ago, to discuss the airman's rescue.

Another hour, she decided. Then she would slip away and help Max transport the young pilot to the railyard where a resistance worker would take him across the border. They'd agreed the party would be the perfect cover to break curfew, especially with so many of the newly stationed SS in attendance. They may never get another opportunity like this.

That meant enduring the chorus of *Heil Hitlers* awhile longer, something that required a spine of steel and a frigid heart. She'd acquired both since France declared war on Germany.

Josephine had already gone up to her bedroom, and that

was a relief to Gabrielle. Nazi occupation was wearing on her grandmother. It was wearing on them all, especially Hélène, who had the most to lose and yet took the greatest personal risks. Gabrielle might disagree with her mother's route, but she understood her reasons. And respected her courage.

The three LeBlanc widows waged their own wars against their captors. Gabrielle, Josephine, Hélène, all of them fought without breaking, without getting caught, and without pulling Paulette into their acts of treason. Gabrielle sighed softly. No one watching her sister now would ever think the world was at war.

How much had changed in so little time, and yet her sister had not changed enough. She was no longer a girl. She was an eighteen-year-old woman and should not be so ignorant of the realities of war. Gabrielle expected more from Paulette. It was time her sister understood parties such as these were not to be enjoyed, but rather endured.

Champagne glasses clinked, while oysters sat in nests of ice, and all manner of gourmet delicacies made the rounds on silver trays. Where had so much plenty come from?

Gabrielle didn't want to know.

The air was rank with cigarette smoke and loud with the sound of laughter. Her mother stood beside von Schmidt, looking serene and perfectly comfortable. It was a lie. Earlier tonight, Gabrielle had seen the despair on her mother's face, and the underlying shame. In that moment, she'd been overwhelmed with love for the woman who had given her life, and had feared if she left the words unsaid she may never find another chance to say them.

Her mother took too many risks. She was at her most charming tonight, bestowing smiles and exchanging witticisms with men in SS uniforms. Men who, if they knew her lineage, would send her to her death without hesitation.

Gabrielle suddenly felt eyes on her. The sensation left her chilled to the marrow. She looked for the source. With a jolt, she realized Detective Mueller had arrived and was now watching her. His face showed no expression. Like her, he stood on the outside of the festivities. A man not happy to be here.

Their eyes met and she wasn't quite sure what she saw there. Suspicion, doubts. Her stomach rolled. Did he suspect what she did for the good of France? Did he know she planned an act of treason this very night?

In that moment, she hated him, and every other Nazi in her home, in her country. *Evil men. Murderers.*

Could Mueller read her hatred? Her fear?

She lowered her gaze. Then thought, no. She would not cower under his stare. She lifted her head. He was still studying her with that utter lack of expression.

Someone said his name, another man in uniform. Mueller's eyes lingered on her a moment longer, then, slowly, he turned his head and their strange bond was broken.

Breathing hard, feeling as if she'd crossed an invisible line, though not sure when or how, she quickly escaped the house. She needed to be in the cold, raw air. She walked for a time. The night was clear, the stars a million sparkling diamonds against the black fabric of the sky.

Headlights approached from the heart of Reims. More Germans arriving to drink LeBlanc champagne. Despite the chill in the air, the big, black, ugly Mercedes bounced down the drive with their tops down to show off their bejeweled passengers, coming to a halt outside the château to deposit their insufferable cargo.

Gabrielle should get back to the party, before she was missed. She retraced her steps along the balustrade. Needing to remember where she came from, what she fought for, she paused and looked out over the vineyard. Several guests milled about her. Most were smiling, laughing, and Gabrielle was struck by how many local Frenchwomen were on the arms of German soldiers.

Selfish, foolish creatures. Their fierce resolve to remain untouched by the war would be their undoing. Or perhaps, she was being uncharitable. Perhaps their reasons were more like her mother's. Gabrielle would never know the truth. It was impossible to see inside another's heart.

The hair on the back of her neck stood on end, alerting her that she was being watched again. A movement in the dark captured her attention, the smudge of a shadow in the form of a man. Detective Mueller had come looking for her.

She'd known he'd follow her, had felt it in her gut, in the kick of antagonism that hit her square in the heart when their eyes met. He peered at her without attempting to come any closer. One shoulder propped against the wall, he just stood there, cloaked in shadow, watching her. A sense of déjà vu rocked her to the core. He'd stared at her like this once before, only a few days ago in the wine cellar. She found the experience just as unnerving now as she had then.

He pushed away from the wall and took a step toward her. Another step. *Another.* She tried not to shrink away from his slow, determined approach. "Madame Dupree."

The way he uttered her name, in that heavy German accent, with such purpose, without inflection, as he would use to relate the current weather, it made her hands tremble. "I sent the champagne to Berlin, as you *requested.*"

"It was not a request." The firm set of his jaw assured her he was not in the mood to pick his way through niceties. This was a party, in his honor. And yet, he was out here baiting her with his considerable height and menacing presence.

"Nevertheless, I followed your orders, as you knew I

would." It was not what she'd meant to say. She knew better than to engage his wrath. Her nerves were showing.

"I tasted your grandmother's rosé just now." He imparted the news as if it were an item he needed to tick off some internal list.

"How did you find it?"

"It was—" a single eyebrow lifted "—magical."

She could hear it then, the pounding of her heart. The fear rushing through her veins. And yet, confronted with the sarcastic reminder of her grandmother's enthusiasm over the blending process, spoken with the finality of a judge rendering a verdict, her defiance wanted to rear. She shoved it behind a bland smile. She'd hoped not to see him tonight. She needed to keep her wits about her for the sake of the stranded British airman. She should not have come outside and drawn Mueller's notice.

He took another step, coming closer, as if he meant to impart a secret. Her skin suddenly recoiled at his nearness. His words, when they came, brought only confusion. "Your grandmother is right to feel pride in her accomplishment."

He spoke of wine while she was planning a daring rescue. Throat thick, she held steady, unmoving, anxious to see how long he would hover over her, how long she could stand his nearness. He kept at a respectable distance.

For the span of three, rib-cracking heartbeats they stared into each other's eyes. Then, he spoke again. "The women in your family have much to be thankful for. You are three generations of widows, alone in this world, and yet have found a way to run a successful champagne empire without the help of your men."

There were threats in that carefully modulated speech, and yet she couldn't isolate a single one. Gabrielle felt her confusion morph into something darker, her desire to escape more powerful, more insistent. Her primitive need to run was almost too much to contain. "We do what we must to survive."

She knew her mistake at once. Mueller's face changed before she finished speaking. Ambivalence drained out and suspicion flooded in. "How far, I wonder, are the women in your family willing to go? What compromises do you make?" He flicked a glance in the general direction of her mother and von Schmidt. "What risks do you take?"

Accusation and distrust filled his smile. No, not a smile. A sinister twist of lips that showed enough teeth to make his point.

"I only meant," she began, letting him see her fear, letting the emotion bleed into each faltering word, "that we are no strangers to hard work."

He didn't respond right away. As the tension stretched between them, solitary church bells marred the night air, the strikes melding with the beat of her heart. He casually looked her over, running his gaze from the top of her head to the tip of her ridiculously female shoes.

Without warning, he seized her wrist and brought her hand within inches of his face. He took his time inspecting her palm, her cracked nails, the various scars. She held perfectly still under his appraisal. He would find no secrets here. The callouses were real. The scars her badges of honor.

He shot a look her way, quick and dazzling, just a flash of approval. And then, his expression was wiped clean and her hand was falling back to her side. "You have the hand of a farmer."

"I *am* a farmer."

His gaze fell on the vineyard. "I suppose you are."

Gabrielle hugged herself and rubbed her arms for warmth. She wanted to escape inside and stand before the fire. But she would not. Nor would she let this man see the inner workings of her mind. Yet every time their eyes connected that was exactly the impression he gave. That he could read her thoughts.

She searched for some semblance of control, a speck, that was all she needed. She nearly had it in her grasp when a high-pitched female giggle jolted her attention to the interior of the château. She didn't need to search long to discover that Paulette was being Paulette. The eighteen-year-old was becoming a terrible flirt. Boys flocked to her, like bees to honey. Lemmings to the cliff. All desperate to win her favor. Something she bestowed a bit too freely. Yet, somehow, she always managed to stay just on the right side of propriety.

For how long?

Gabrielle saw her sister's hand reach out, then rest on the arm of a local boy hired to work the party. Paulette appeared fond of him, but not as much as he was of her. It seemed the only quality the young woman looked for in a suitor was his admiration of her.

Not a very high bar.

"Your sister is in high spirits this evening."

"She enjoys parties."

"I think—" he divided his gaze between Paulette and the local boy, then considered the group of Waffen-SS soldiers that had previously surrounded her "—she is very free with her affections."

A cold, deadening sensation filled Gabrielle's lungs. How did she respond? With the truth. "Paulette is a happy, popular, well-liked young woman."

"Evidently." The absence of any emotion in that single word hit like a punch, the pain was that sharp and unexpected. "You will want to speak with your sister before she brings unnecessary attention to herself. And, by association, the rest of your family."

Gabrielle didn't appreciate the warning, spoken in that

calm, cool tone. It felt like a trap, a way to lure her into believing he was doing her a favor. She didn't think any further than that. She simply began to step away from him, desperate to distance herself from what she heard in his voice. Not a warning, after all. A threat.

"I will speak with my sister right away." Her voice came at her as if from a great distance, sounding tinny in her own ears. "If you will excuse me, Detective."

"By all means." He stepped aside and let her go without another word.

Gabrielle entered the château just as her mother approached Paulette. Good, she thought. This was good. They would join forces.

Together, surely, they would speak sense into the girl.

Chapter Thirty

JOSEPHINE

As German occupation crept on, Josephine's sense of time fragmented into a spattering of unrelated moments. She spent hours examining the contents of her memory, too many times coming away empty. The champagne house continued meeting the impossible quotas set by the *weinführer*, but Josephine left the particulars to her granddaughter and spent more time in her room, or in Marta's company.

This arrangement suited her. She tired easily and rarely ventured out of her bedroom during waking hours. She tried not to wander too much at night, though there were moments when she would find herself in a dark part of the château, confused and frightened, unsure how she'd ended up there.

Some good came from her moments of confusion. Von Schmidt had grown tired of her ramblings. He'd banished her from the evening meal. Tonight, however, he'd demanded her presence. She couldn't think why. Perhaps for no other reason than to throw her off-balance and relax her guard, as deceptive and cunning as the serpent in the garden.

He'd compiled the usual coterie of guests at his table. No Frenchmen, of course. Only Germans, and only men who served his upward mobility within the Third Reich. They brought their well-groomed, heavily jeweled companions. It appalled Josephine to see so many local women taking Nazi lovers. Some did so for survival, others for more selfish reasons. How dare they prefer their comfort over their pride.

Hélène lifted her glass and made a toast in honor of one of the couples at the table, a woman not much older than Paulette and a German officer close to von Schmidt's age. "To your engagement," she said, raising her glass a bit higher. "May you find eternal happiness as husband and wife for many years to come."

Josephine and Gabrielle shared a horrified look. Hélène appeared truly pleased by this abominable union. She also appeared perfectly comfortable in her role as hostess at the right hand of her own German. There was truth and there was deception, Josephine thought. Hélène's relationship with von Schmidt appeared to fall somewhere in between.

Josephine's fault, she knew. She'd encouraged her daughter-in-law to make herself indispensable to their oppressor.

Or had the idea come from Hélène? Josephine couldn't remember which of them had broached the subject first. She needed to remember. She thought, maybe, the distinction was important, a clue as to whether or not Hélène could still be trusted. Or if she'd become...

No assumptions, not yet.

Josephine would check her journal later, when she was certain the rest of the household slept. In the meantime, she had her own role to play. That of a woman with a frail mind. The charade was not so far from the truth.

"I have a desire for duck tonight." As she glanced around

the table, she pretended to slip deeper into a state of confusion. "Perhaps in a lovely orange sauce. Marta does such a fine job with sauces."

"Grandmère," Gabrielle said gently, her hand coming to rest on her forearm. "We already ate the main course. You praised Marta's culinary skills, several times in fact."

Had she? Josephine went quiet, thinking maybe…yes. Her granddaughter was correct. She'd already eaten the fish. Not duck, but a lovely sea bass. *You know this, Josephine.* Taking her glass, she tried to drink, but the water turned acrid in her mouth and she choked on the sip.

Von Schmidt expelled an impatient breath and stared at her through hard, unforgiving eyes. She knew the look. He was preparing to give her a harsh insult.

Hélène forestalled the reprimand. "I believe we can all agree that the sea bass was cooked to perfection. The cherries jubilee will be even better. It is one of your favorites, is it not, Helmut? As it is mine."

He reached out and closed his hand over Hélène's in a gesture that spoke of a shared intimacy that made Josephine heartsick.

"You and I, my dear, are of a similar mind in this, as we are in so many areas." He brought her hand to his lips. "It is always a pleasure to have your exquisite presence at my table."

His table. The swine.

Josephine had to lower her head to hide the snarl of contempt that formed on her lips, but not before she caught Hélène's stricken expression. That look told her much and she thought of an Oscar Wilde quote. *Truth is rarely pure and never simple.* Josephine sighed. She wanted to be anywhere but at this table.

When the dismissal came, she was happy to escape to her room.

Time passed. She didn't know how much. She sat alone,

dressed for bed in a warm robe, the air scarred by the grating of her breath. When had she changed out of her evening gown? Had Marta helped her?

Her feet were cold.

They were always cold. Josephine glanced down. She still wore the shoes that matched her dress. She tapped her toes on the floor, *tap tap tap*, and tried to recall when she'd slipped them back onto her feet. Or had she never taken them off?

She tried to stand. Her ankle twisted, sending sharp pain up her leg. Stupid, stupid shoes. She reached down to remove them. They were too heavy and clumsy in her hands. She dropped them to the floor with a thud and gave them a little kick. That felt good. She kicked them again. Then went on the move, pacing from bed, to window, to dressing table, faster, faster, faster, her mind whirling, her bare feet circling within the same path. She hated this confusion in her head.

A familiar spurt of fear tangled with the first stirrings of anger. Not anger, rage. So much of it. She wanted to howl in frustration. This world, it was too much for her. A sob burst from her throat. *I want to come home, Lord.*

But her blood still pumped. Her failing, traitorous body still coursed with life.

Let me come home. It's time.

There was no response from the Father. No sound but the shuffling of her feet between bed, window, dressing table. Bed, window, dressing table.

Bed, window. Her feet stopped. She shoved aside the heavy blue curtains. Blue? No, that wasn't right. They were supposed to be green with gold brocade. Josephine had chosen the pattern not long after her wedding day. Had someone replaced them?

Had she?

Outside, the dark of night was not so black anymore. The

pearly light of the moon had married with the hazy mist of dawn. She'd been pacing all night. And her journal was in her hand. She didn't remember retrieving it.

She stared out across the vineyard.

Through the fog, she could see a movement, the gauzy sway of something black against the gray. She blinked, squinted, trying to see past the stingy light, determined to separate the foreign from the familiar. Two shadows came together, merging into one big smudge inside the fog. They separated and then joined again. Josephine rubbed her eyes.

A chill of foreboding galloped through her blood as she glanced at the strange, moving images. Neither dark nor light, but a dingy ash. She rubbed at her eyes again, her vision slowly clearing. The details were more visible now. They made more sense.

The two figures, easier to distinguish apart from the fog, came together and separated a third time. She identified the taller, larger form. A man. The shorter, smaller belonged to a woman. Young, old, she couldn't tell. Arms entwined, heads moving together, bodies pressing closer. A lover's embrace.

Josephine gasped, suddenly empty of the ability to breathe. She forced herself to watch, when all she wanted to do was look away. To pretend she wasn't witnessing the ugly truth playing out before her eyes. Her suspicions were realized in a moment of painful clarity.

And then, it was over.

The man stepped back from the woman. She reached to him, but he turned, shoulders set at a proud angle, and walked away, melting deeper into the mist. Even before he disappeared, the woman placed a hand to her heart. Lifted her fingertips to her lips, touched her heart again.

The image froze in Josephine's mind. She stood suspended

in a moment of disbelief, her hand itching to write down what she'd seen. How could she put this terrible reality on the page?

She must.

She did.

When she was through, a breath went out of her in a hard exhalation of ragged sound and air. She was shocked, of course. But part of her experienced only acceptance. Part of her had expected nothing less from her granddaughter.

After all they'd sacrificed, all the risks each of them had taken, part of Josephine couldn't shake the notion that this one, selfish act would result in her family's doom.

Chapter Thirty-One

GABRIELLE

Gabrielle read the journal entry, her eyes racing over the page, anguish covering her heart. All her attempts to talk reason into her sister had been for nothing. Paulette had done as Paulette always did—whatever she wanted.

Until this moment, Gabrielle had convinced herself her sister was nothing more than an outrageous flirt playing with her admirers' affections.

She'd been lying to herself.

Deep down, she'd known a forbidden romance was inevitable. Of course she'd known, because here she sat, receiving the news of her sister's indiscretion without the slightest hint of shock. Anguish, yes. Fury. Alarm. But, no. Not surprise.

Paulette was too impulsive for her own good. Gabrielle read the entry a second time. She had questions. Her grandmother's comments were not very detailed. Looking up from the page, she asked, "Did you recognize the boy?"

Josephine shook her head. "It was foggy. The light was poor, and they were too far away for me to distinguish more than their shapes."

Gabrielle had a moment of desperate hope. "You are sure the woman was Paulette?"

"I know my own granddaughter."

"Of course you do. I didn't mean to imply otherwise." She thought for a moment. Her mind hooked on an image from the party. Paulette's hand resting on that local boy's arm. "He's probably one of her schoolmates. My guess is the boy from the party last week, the server Maman hired." *The boy's life she'd saved.*

It was the most logical explanation, the only one Gabrielle would entertain. Surely, Paulette would not fraternize with the enemy with this level of intimacy. Besides, where would she have met him? As soon as Gabrielle had the thought, another image from the party materialized. Paulette surrounded by German soldiers. One in particular had been especially persistent. A lieutenant with the Waffen-SS. Very good-looking, very attentive to her sister. But not a boy, a man in his twenties. He'd since dined at von Schmidt's table.

Gabrielle hated the ugly suspicion filling her mind. But she had to admit this theory fit every detail, including—especially— the need for secrecy, and the need for Paulette to break curfew. She had to speak with her sister.

The clock told her Paulette was already in bed for the night. Gabrielle could wake her. No, her sister was still a teenager and all that implied. Confronting her in the middle of the night would only result in deflection and angry denials.

Her mother, then. She would go to Hélène with this. Later tonight, or early tomorrow morning. When she was sure the other woman was in her room and Gabrielle herself was back from her own midnight errand. She glanced at the clock again.

If only Josephine had told her about this sooner. Already, time worked against her. She would have to leave soon to meet Max. She passed the journal back to her grandmother and kissed the older woman's cheek. "I'm glad you showed me this."

"The girl must stop this foolishness at once," Josephine said, the manifestation of the family matriarch in her stiff posture. "I'll speak to her myself."

"I think we should leave this to Maman. She has the greatest influence with Paulette." It was the right move, the only move now that Gabrielle considered the situation with a bit more perspective.

"Perhaps you're right. But see that it's done quickly." Josephine closed the journal and secured the leather strap. "I have a bad feeling about this relationship."

Gabrielle did, too.

Later, when she exited the house, mounted her bicycle and blended with the night, she put aside her worry for her sister and focused on the more immediate task before her. Another dangerous mission, her role small but important. The midnight air still held the bite of winter and nipped at her exposed skin with needle-sharp precision.

A hawk swooped low, silent and deadly and practically clipped Gabrielle on the shoulder. She swerved, hit a rut and nearly lost her grip on the handlebars. She righted herself before disaster struck. What was she doing, condemning her sister for taking risks when she herself took more than her share?

Not unlike her sister, she put her family in danger every time she broke curfew. She considered ending her resistance work, then immediately rejected the idea. What Gabrielle did for France was necessary, important.

She kept pedaling.

Tonight, she risked her life a third time for the British airman that still lived in Max's wine cellar. The contact from their network hadn't shown last week. There'd been no explanation. Until yesterday. He'd been arrested for derailing a large shipment of champagne meant for Berlin.

They would try again tonight, with a different plan and different players, except for Max and Gabrielle. Despite the cold stiffening her muscles, she pedaled harder, putting her farther from the safety of her home and deeper into danger. The Waffen-SS encampment came into view. She increased her speed. Soon, the camp was out of sight and she was breathing normally once again.

Max was waiting for her at his usual spot. He didn't look good. His calm, careful façade was nonexistent. Gabrielle scrambled off her bike and let it drop to the frozen ground. "What's wrong, Papa?"

Sadness came into his eyes, and then regret. Or was that fear? "The strain is too much, Gabrielle. I grow weak under the stress. We must have success tonight. We must get this man away from my home."

The desperation was not like Max.

"We will." She let the air out of her lungs in a long sigh. "Our plan is a good one."

They'd decided the railyard was too risky, especially now that an SS unit patrolled the area. A local vine grower authorized to conduct business in the Free Zone had agreed to smuggle the Brit across the border in one of his wine barrels. She didn't ask the man's name, or if he was local, and Max didn't supply this information. Anonymity was always best. "Am I still on watch during the transfer?"

"*Oui.* You will keep an eye on the main road. If you see anything suspicious, you will blow into this whistle three times. Three. No more, no less."

She took the bird whistle he held out. The paint had chipped away from the mouthpiece but, after a careful inspection, it appeared to be in good working order. Just to be certain, she tested the sound with a hard, fast blow and sighed in relief. The whistle would suffice.

It would work. It had to work. For the airman's sake. And her father-in-law's.

"I'll alert you when all is clear with the same signal." Max showed her a second, identical whistle before shoving it in his coat pocket. "Once you hear the three chirps you will know it's safe for you to return to your bed. Do not come back here. Go straight home."

There had to be more she could do. When she said as much, Max refused to entertain the idea. "I already put you at too much risk. Now, go. Godspeed, Gabrielle."

They embraced. She mounted her bicycle and slipped soundlessly into the night just as a delivery truck rumbled down the drive. She did not look in the driver's direction and prayed he didn't look in hers.

The temperatures had dipped since she'd left the château and the air carried the scent of snow. Gabrielle hardly noticed as she pedaled past Max's house, through the courtyard and out onto the road. She swung her bicycle in the direction of the SS encampment, then came to a stop and waited for the signal from Max.

The next twenty minutes progressed without incident. Although she jumped at every sound, every snap of a twig, or click of a cricket, the road remained empty. Gabrielle attributed the lack of activity to the strictly enforced curfew. Her breathing finally found its rhythm when the high-pitched bird whistle rent the night air.

Three shrills. The airman was on his way, tucked inside a wine barrel.

Relief made her knees weak. She would leave for home

now. She *should* leave for home. She could not. Something about Max's behavior disturbed her. Instinct told her he was on the verge of cracking. She would not sleep well until she saw his face one final time.

The man she encountered in the courtyard was not happy to see her. "I told you not to return."

"I wanted to say good-night."

It was a flimsy excuse, but Max only nodded. "The hard part is over, Gabrielle. We did what we could for the boy. The rest is out of our hands."

She knew he was right. She lifted onto her toes and kissed his cheek. "Then I'll say good-night."

"Wait. Now that you are here, I have something to discuss."

"All right."

He placed a hand on her shoulders. "This German living in your home, this wine merchant." He nearly spat the words. "He flaunts his relationship with your mother. Talk of their liaison is all over Reims."

Heat drained from Gabrielle's face. "How bad is the gossip?"

"It's not good. She has few friends left in Reims, and none who will come to her aid if the tide of war shifts."

Gabrielle had known Hélène would be judged for her relationship with von Schmidt. But this? It was worse than she'd expected. Fear for her mother scrambled to the surface. She tried to breathe through the worst of it. No air came into her lungs.

"I also understand Detective Mueller has taken a special interest in you."

The accusation all but slapped her in the face. Her first instinct was to defend herself. But she made her mind slow down, to think logically. She must explain the situation calmly, and with truth. Only truth. "His attention is motivated purely by suspicion. He is a hard man, Papa. He trusts no one. Not the French. Not his fellow Germans. And most definitely not me."

This was her truth, her reality. As a widow, she was easy prey for a man such as Mueller, if her father-in-law was right. He could not be right.

"You are certain his interest in you is nothing more than Nazi suspicion and distrust?"

It was clear Max didn't fully believe her, and now she doubted herself. She forced her wild beating heart to find a steady cadence. "Why do you ask such questions?" She clamped down on the sob bubbling in her throat. "What have you heard that makes you believe petty gossip over my word?"

"You were seen with Mueller on the terrace during a recent party at your château. He had hold of your hand. It is said you did not pull away."

French spying on French. Friends turning on friends. *No one is safe.* Josephine had said this. Her neighbors had made it so. "Detective Mueller approached me that night, this is true." She sounded too defensive and readjusted her tone. "He'd previously discovered I still had a sizable amount of the 1928 in my cellar and told me to send the remaining stock to Berlin. He was assuring himself I'd followed through with his demand. He grasped my hand to make his point."

"Gabrielle." Max met her gaze with less suspicion and more concern. "Do not forget this man is Gestapo. He is a wolf in wolf's clothing. I sense no mercy in him. You must keep your distance."

"I have come to the same conclusion. Do not let your heart be troubled, Papa. I am always careful in his presence."

"That's all I ask." He kissed her on one cheek, then the other. The affection was real, even if his eyes were still flat. "Go home and get some rest."

"I will say the same to you. Get some rest. You seem especially tired tonight."

He gave her a soft smile. "Nothing the end of the war won't cure."

That sounded more like the man who'd been her staunchest ally following Étienne's death. "May that day come soon."

They shared a grim smile. With nothing more to say, she mounted her bicycle and pedaled toward the fog rolling in from the north. At the edge of the vineyard, she glanced over her shoulder. Max remained rooted to the spot, his eyes not with her but fixed on a distant spot beyond the courtyard. Something in his posture, the stance of a defeated man, left her with the impression that she would never see him again.

She raised her hand in farewell. He did not return the gesture. His eyes were on the black Mercedes coming down the drive. She hadn't heard the engine. Max must have. He remained perfectly still, his hands stuffed in his pocket. He didn't try to run. He merely stood in the harsh glare of the headlights, resigned and defiant. Gabrielle instinctually moved toward him. He must have sensed her purpose, because he gave a single shake of his head, as if to say: *stay back.*

Clutching the handlebars, she squeezed hard, so hard her knuckles turned bone white. At the last instant, she would run. But not before. If possible, she would come to Max's rescue. She hovered just inside the fog's milky-white shroud and waited for some signal to act, to retreat, to call out—she didn't know which would be best.

Two men—SS soldiers—climbed out of the vehicle. "Hands up," one of them shouted in German, then repeated the command in French.

Max did as he was told, hands aligned with his head, palms facing the men. A third figure exited the car. He moved at a slow, casual pace, as if he were out for an evening stroll.

Gabrielle struggled to think over the wild drumming of her pulse. She was too far away to make out the man's features. But she knew that slow, predatory gait. She recognized those broad shoulders, that hard, unbending spine. Detective Mueller.

A wolf in wolf's clothing.

A man without mercy.

The wind picked up, battering at her exposed face and hands. She should have worn gloves. It was a ridiculous thought at a time such as this. It seemed impossible, unimaginable that Mueller could be here. That he could know to come to Max's house, tonight, of all nights, at this very moment.

He stopped his approach just outside the halo cast by the headlights.

"Monsieur Dupree," he said in that guttural, broken French that was an abomination to the ears. "You are under arrest. Your vineyard and champagne house have been seized and placed under direct control of Berlin."

Max arrested. His home taken. Gabrielle placed her hand over her mouth. No. She moved closer. *No!* She screamed the word in her head. Over and over and over. No, no, no.

"What is the charge?" Max asked, palms still facing his accuser, his voice sparked with very real panic, his outstretched arms shaking.

"Treason. Sabotage. And several other lesser offenses against the Third Reich. Now, put your hands behind your back. You, there." Mueller motioned to the soldier on this left. "Bind this man's wrists."

Max's eyes were huge as the soldier circled him. He was shaking uncontrollably now, and several tears leaked onto his cheeks.

Gabrielle's own tears fell. She leaned forward, willing her father-in-law to stay strong, to know that she would do what she could to rescue him. If not tonight, tomorrow. She would go to de Vogüe and seek his help. Unless he'd been arrested as well.

Would the Gestapo come for her next?

She choked on her own breath, just a small stammer of sound. A mistake. Mueller's head rotated in her direction. He remained outside the light, but she knew his eyes searched the dark. She melted deeper into the mist that was growing thicker, ever thicker. Not thick enough. For a ghastly second, she thought he saw her.

But he didn't move toward her.

The rushing in her head became a painful throbbing in her throat, in her ears. Seconds passed. She allowed herself a single pull of air, and then held it.

She was still holding her breath when Mueller finally turned away and addressed the soldier at Max's back. "Put him in the car. We will finish the rest of this at the police station."

Chapter Thirty-Two

Hélène looked around her bedroom, shame and despair her familiar companions this morning. It was not yet dawn. She should try to sleep, but she couldn't seem to find the strength to move away from her dressing table. She lacked a reason. So here she sat, wearing last night's dress, feeling the weight of her sin as if it was a living, breathing thing. She hated what she'd become, what he'd turned her into, knowing she'd make the same decision again, if only to keep him away from her daughters.

Paulette. Gabrielle. Each deserved a better mother than the one she'd given them.

A steady ache lingered in her heart as she surveyed her reflection cast in the pale glow of the moon. The woman staring back—her eyes were empty. Nothing there anymore. Nothing but gloom and bitterness, so much bitterness. She could hardly remember the woman she'd been when Étienne was still alive. When hope and faith and love for the Lord had shared equal space in her heart.

She blinked at the stranger in the mirror, a woman stripped of her last scraps of dignity. Everything that had once defined her was gone. No pride left, no self-respect. No purpose in life other than to serve a greedy man's whims. She felt lost, deserted by even her own self.

Where was her purpose now? Where was her reason to navigate through another day? She would find it, as she did every morning. She heaved herself to her feet and ran a hand through her hair. She was tired, so tired of the continual rustling in her soul, a certainty that she'd gone too far and would never find her way back. Death by a thousand little cuts.

Create in me a clean heart, O God.

Why would the Lord help her now?

She thought of ways to end the horror that had become her life. Poison, a pillow over mouth and nose, a bullet. The idea of ending a life—her own—*his*—was an offense so large it threatened to take her to her knees. Could she pull it off? Could she—

The familiar creaking of the door had her going perfectly still. It was the sound of her doom. The herald of another piece of her soul being ripped away. Footsteps, nearly soundless, the door shutting. Her heart skidded into an erratic rhythm. This waking nightmare would not destroy her. She would not let it.

She would face it with poise.

With a million sparks of her shame splintering the remnants of her self-respect, she made the slow turn to face von Schmidt. And nearly collapsed in relief when she saw the woman standing with her back against the door. Not him. Not...*him*.

"Gabrielle." She breathed her daughter's name, no louder than a whisper, as much a prayer of thanks as a question. "What brings you to my room at this hour?"

Nothing good, surely.

"Am I disturbing you?"

The hesitation was new, unexpected. "*Non*, I couldn't sleep."

Gabrielle moved deeper into the room, but her image remained dark and blurry. A shadow within a shadow. Like mother. Like daughter. The young woman was dressed to move around in the night. Whatever risks she'd taken this evening, she'd survived them. Though the hunch of her shoulders indicated an unhappy ending. No matter the outcome, Hélène couldn't—wouldn't—judge her daughter for her choices. She was not that much of a hypocrite.

As she came closer, Hélène saw the changes in the young woman. She used to be well-shaped, leanly muscled and much stronger than her petite frame would suggest. But the war had eaten away the pounds and had robbed her daughter of what had once been her robust, enviable figure. She stopped her approach several feet away, close enough for Hélène to read the anguish on her face. The daughter had come to speak reason into the mother. "Gabrielle—"

"We need to talk about Paulette."

The words pulled her up short. "What about her?"

"She has been sneaking out at night to meet a boy." Darkness fell over Gabrielle's face. Hélène's spirits followed.

She glanced up to the ceiling, not sure why, perhaps to gather her thoughts. "You are sure this isn't a mistake?"

"I'm afraid there is no question. She was seen. Not by me." Or by Helmut, praise God. He would have said something about Paulette skulking around past curfew. Hélène would have known his displeasure in a hard slap to her cheek.

When Gabrielle didn't give up her source, she didn't press. That was their way. Fewer questions, fewer lies to tell. What mattered right now was that Paulette was sneaking out of the château at night.

Hélène searched for her composure, her eyes still on the ceiling. She could feel the pieces of her scattered thoughts slowly converging, rearranging themselves into a single, terrifying question. "Who is the boy?"

"I don't know."

Find out. She could hear the command in her mind. She dipped her head down, feeling something oddly calming move through her. "It was probably Lucien Trevon."

It had to be him. Paulette had been so worried over the boy's arrest. He'd been released the next day because von Schmidt had put in a good word. *Please, God. Let it be the Trevon boy.* "I saw Paulette with Lucien at the party."

She searched her memory, thinking…yes. Yes, that was true. She had seen the two together, once, briefly. Hélène had hired the boy to work in the kitchen. Paulette had sought her friend out early in the night, when Hélène was giving out instructions to the temporary staff. Her daughter had hugged Lucien tight, and told him how happy she was to see him safe.

Had that been the beginning of a deeper romance between the two?

Gabrielle's eyes bore into hers. "You are confident Paulette is meeting this boy from school?"

She could not make that claim. "I will speak with Paulette this morning."

"Thank you, Maman."

"Is there something else bothering you?"

Gabrielle opened her mouth, looked ready to confide something, then clamped it shut again. "We'll speak about it later. Right now, Paulette is your only concern."

Hélène watched her oldest daughter leave the room with one thought in mind. She had her reason to face another day.

By the time she bathed and changed into fresh clothing, the sun had appeared over the horizon. Paulette would still be abed. This conversation could not wait.

To her surprise, she didn't have to wake her daughter. She was already dressed for the day, sitting by the window, a sketchpad in her lap, her hand making quick, furious strokes across the page.

"Paulette." Hélène shut the door behind her with a soft snick. "You're up early."

She kept sketching, a smile playing at the edges of her mouth. "I wanted to catch the morning light."

"What are you drawing?"

When Paulette didn't respond, Hélène moved closer and searched the page for herself. A rush of blood flooded her head. The face of a man, not a boy. The artist in her recognized the quality of the work. It was a masterful rendering, drawn with a heart full of admiration for its subject. The girl was in love.

Hélène wanted to weep.

"Who is this in the picture?" She would keep her voice free of emotion. She could manage that at least. "Is this someone you met at the party? A new friend, perhaps?"

Paulette's hand paused and she looked at Hélène for a brief moment, secrets moving swiftly behind her eyes. This was her daughter's most calculating expression. She had learned to recognize it years ago. "I suppose you could say he's a friend."

Hélène fixed on the image and felt the jolt of recognition all over again. He'd sat at their dinner table, twice, wearing his SS uniform. A young man on the rise, as von Schmidt had said. Friedrich Weber. Entitled. Rude. Twenty-six years old, and already a lieutenant, in line to become a *hauptsturmführer* before his next birthday. The anger and fury she expected to feel wasn't there. Only fear. "What would you call him, Paulette, if not a friend?"

The question made her daughter's mouth twitch, the perfect line of her lips sliding into a small, mysterious smile that she quickly pressed away. "My future. My love. My very heart."

Hélène had thought it bad that Paulette was engaged in a love affair with a local boy. This was so much worse. "You must stop seeing him at once."

"Why would I do that?" Paulette looked genuinely confused. "I love him, Maman. And he loves me."

"It's not a matter of love." Hélène produced the obvious reason why, praying it would be enough. "He is too old for you."

"Papa was six years older than you. What's two more years?"

"My relationship with your father was different." Special. Her deliverance. Étienne had been a good person, the best of men. "This man," Hélène said, and reached for the sketchpad, flapping it in the air. "He is our enemy."

Paulette grabbed for the book, hugged it to her heart. "It's not Friedrich's fault he was born in Germany. He is French in his soul."

Was that the sort of lies he spewed to her daughter?

"He is not French. He is a German soldier. And not just any German soldier. SS."

"Why should I care about that?"

The words were tossed out with careless abandon, but they hit Hélène like a blow. *"Chérie,"* she said. "Darling girl, don't you understand the inappropriateness of this romance? The danger?"

"You have a nerve." Paulette's face went rigid, as impenetrable as a slab of hard oak. "When you also involve yourself with a Nazi."

Her daughter had a point. So, too, did Hélène. "I don't know what you've heard—"

"What I've heard?" She let out an ugly, disgusted laugh.

"It's not what I've heard. It's what I know. I know all about you and von Schmidt. *Everyone* knows."

This accusation was not wholly unexpected. Still, Hélène wanted to defend herself. "There is a difference between a German in a soldier's uniform and one that voluntarily joins the SS." She paused, listening to her daughter's stony silence. Waiting for her to say something, anything. But the young woman's face remained as unforgiving as stone.

"Paulette. The SS is at the very core of Hitler's evil. They do terrible things for their Fatherland. They hunt down people they perceive as enemies of the state and make them disappear. A woman does not have romances with these men. She stays away from them. Do you understand me?"

"I understand you're trying to scare me."

"Good. You should be scared." Now that she had her daughter's attention, Hélène pressed on. "The Nazis have sent tens of thousands of people to labor camps. They are constantly finding more to put on the trains. These prisoners come to terrible ends. They are often tortured, executed, starved or simply worked to death."

No longer stone-faced, Paulette stared at Hélène with large, round eyes. The eyes of a frightened child. "None of that is true. I asked Friedrich. He says these are rumors meant to make Germany look bad in the eyes of the world."

"What I tell you are not rumors. They are truth. And do you know who orchestrates these horrors? The SS. Men like your lieutenant. They target anyone they deem unfit, members of the Resistance, Gypsies, Communists, but mostly—" she held Paulette's eyes "—Jews."

"We are none of those things."

Oh, but they were. Hélène needed to tell her daughter. She had a moment of indecision, but it passed quickly. The time had come to share her secret. "Have you never wondered why my father left for America? Have you never considered the origin of his name? Abraham, son of Isaac and Naomi. My father is Jewish. His father and mother were Jewish. That makes me—"

"Don't say it." Paulette's hands covered her ears. "I won't listen to any more of your lies."

Hélène knelt in front of her daughter.

"I am a Jew, Paulette." She spoke calmly, surprised by the sense of peace that moved through her. Saying the words, proclaiming the truth—*her truth*—wasn't a burden any longer. It was a release.

"You are French, Maman. You were born in Paris. You are a LeBlanc."

"I am also a Jew." The secret she'd spent so many years feeding no longer held her in its grip. She was free. She'd denied her identity for too long. No more. If she was arrested now, she would go to her death knowing who she was. Where she came from.

"It isn't true," Paulette wailed. "It *can't* be true. You attend church. You worship the Christian God. Your hair is blond."

Hélène almost couldn't look at her daughter. Her hysteria was heartbreaking. But she must finish this. She fixed her eyes on the young, frightened face. "The Nazis are getting serious about hunting down Jews in France. You have to know what that means."

"No, I won't think about it."

"Yes, you will."

Paulette shed big, fat tears. Hélène hugged her daughter long and fierce and when she stepped back, she saw that the tears continued falling in fast streams down her cheeks. "Maman? What is to become of us?"

"We are safe for now. Very few people know my secret. None in Reims outside this home. We must keep it that way."

She thought of the list of names von Schmidt had demanded she provide. Surely, others had created similar lists, under equal duress. Her own name could show up on any one of them, if someone thought to look hard enough into her background.

"You cannot tell a soul about this, Paulette. No one can know." Taking her daughter's hands, she said, "You understand now why you must end your affair with this SS soldier, yes?"

"I... Yes."

But would she break all ties with him? Would she forget about the man she sketched with so much love and admiration? Paulette was rarely malleable. And this was her first taste of love. Perhaps, she would prove smarter than Hélène gave her credit for. Perhaps she was no longer a spoiled child.

She looked into her daughter's eyes for some kind of confirmation, a sign that Paulette would do the right thing. She saw only anguish. How she wished for the time, not so long ago, when Paulette was caught up in the thrill of being admired by boys her own age. When that attention was harmless and innocent.

The young woman had a difficult choice to make. If she chose wrongly...

If she thought only of herself...

The girl's own words came back to plague Hélène. *What is to become of us?*

Chapter Thirty-Three

GABRIELLE

After a quick wash and change of clothing, Gabrielle went in search of her mother for the second time in a matter of hours. Apprehension had her feet moving quickly through the darkened corridors. Wind whistled through the cracks in the windowpane, an ominous sound that pushed her faster. Each high-pitched howl diminished her ability to remain calm in the face of so many setbacks, all of them out of her control. *One problem at a time.*

The cold was nearly unbearable in this section of the château. She blew into her cupped palms to warm them, her mind racing as fast as her feet. She silently reviewed the events of the last six hours, bouncing from her sister to Max, from one broken piece of her heart to the next. A forbidden romance... an arrest...a selfish act of a selfish girl...a sacrificial deed of a selfless man...the Gestapo. Guns. Torture.

One problem at a time.

She had to keep telling herself that, or she would go mad. Surely, her mother had spoken to Paulette by now. The thought of her sister engaging in an illicit love affair made Gabrielle's stomach pitch. The glimpses of maturity she'd seen in the girl had not been strong enough to change her character.

She still put her needs ahead of others. Gabrielle should not have been surprised. People like Max risked their lives so that one day the rest of them would be free. And here was Paulette, doing as she pleased, not a single thought to the people she put at risk.

If her mother hadn't talked to the girl, Gabrielle would. From the corner of her eye, she noticed a shadow flickering in the hallway. The form elongated then morphed into the shape of a female. Her mother. Gabrielle started toward her, one—just one—question on her lips.

"Not here." Hélène shook her head then motioned Gabrielle to follow her. Once inside her mother's bedroom, she imparted the distressing news in the hushed tones they always adopted when von Schmidt was still in the house. "It's not a local boy."

She'd expected this, and still her pulse sped up. Needing to know, even as she sensed the truth would enrage her, she asked in a low hiss, "A German soldier?"

"Worse."

What could be worse than a German soldier? *A Gestapo agent.* Mueller's image formed in her mind. No, impossible. Paulette was a child. He was a grown man. There were many such liaisons in Reims, some with even larger age gaps. Yet, strangely, Gabrielle knew the detective was not a man such as those Germans. No, he was not her sister's beau. "Who, then?"

After a brief hesitation, Hélène responded in a voice filled with defeat. "She is meeting an SS officer, a lieutenant. You will know him. He has sat at our table."

"Please tell me it's not the one who demands to be served first, ahead of even von Schmidt."

"That's the one."

Gabrielle couldn't remember his name. She wasn't sure it mattered. The lieutenant was a proud man and loved to proclaim his hatred of Jews. He was an Aryan with a heartless smile and lethal edge that seemed especially vicious because of his youth. "That foolish, thoughtless girl."

"Don't be too hard on your sister. She is young. And in love."

"Love?" Gabrielle could feel her skin burning. "What does that child know of love?"

"Enough to take great risks after curfew." Her mother's voice went hoarse. "I fear he is an accomplished seducer. He's overwhelmed her with pretty lies and false promises."

"You make excuses for her, still. Paulette is equally to blame. She is spoiled and cares only for herself." Years of frustration came pouring out. Hélène had given Paulette whatever she wanted. She'd allowed the girl too much freedom. Her mother had never taught moderation, not when the girl was a child, not when she'd entered her early teen years, not even now when she was on the verge of becoming a woman. "This is your fault. You spoil her and now look what she's done."

"I'm fully aware of my personal culpability."

"You have to fix this. You must make Paulette understand the dangers of this romance."

Face pinched, Hélène sighed. "I handled it already. Your sister knows what she must do. Now, if you will excuse me, I have work to do, and so do you. The champagne is waiting."

As far as dismissals went, it wasn't the most subtle. Just as well, Gabrielle decided as she exited the room and pulled the door shut with a furious click.

The time for subtlety was over.

An hour later, as she stood in her workroom, Gabrielle rubbed at her tired eyes and tried not to think about her sister. Or Max. The grief in her was overwhelming. She desperately wanted to journey into town, to see for herself what had happened to her father-in-law.

It wasn't possible.

She would be required to explain her presence at the jail and, possibly, in her effort to protect Max, could end up exposing her own involvement in any number of criminal acts. No, better to wait for word of Max's arrest to come to her. Then she would venture into Reims.

It wouldn't be long now. News like this traveled quickly.

She put it out of her mind. Driven by a need to lose herself in the art of winemaking, she began testing her blends. She relied on her senses, drew on impressions stored in her memory, determined to create a wine as unique as the soil that produced it. She chose five of her favorite *vin clairs*, sniffing between each pour, letting her nose guide her through the process.

She took a sip, drew back at the taste. Foul, rancid. "Another failure," she mumbled.

Someone entered the room, shut the door. She felt the dark presence before her eyes latched on to the shadow moving over her. "I'm sure you exaggerate, Madame Dupree."

Gabrielle flinched as the deep, rough voice rubbed over her skin, as slick and unwelcome as the scales of a snake. Shock would be the expected response at this intrusion. She gladly gave in to the emotion as she quickly spun around, the beaker firmly clutched in her fist.

First, she gave him surprise. Then, she let him see her irritation. "Detective Mueller." She placed all the ice she could summon into her voice. "I wasn't aware we had a meeting."

"This is not an official visit."

His Gestapo uniform made every visit official.

Had Max given her up? Was that the reason the detective studied her face so closely? Gabrielle wouldn't blame her father-in-law if he'd confessed. It was said everyone broke under torture, eventually, with the right incentive. Imagining Max beaten until he confessed his crimes brought a level of fury she'd never known she could feel.

It would be worse for her. She was a woman. And feared Mueller had been preparing for her arrest since their first encounter on the streets of Reims.

There were moments when a character was tested. Was this her moment? Would she break, or find the strength to stand? Gabrielle watched him watching her and suddenly the air felt different. It smelled different. Nothing felt right.

And Mueller had yet to state his business. She held steady under his silent inspection. A gentleman would stay an appropriate distance from her. The detective proved to be no gentleman. He stood barely two feet away from her. So close she could smell his scent, a mix of bergamot, sandalwood and lime. A Nazi should not smell like a normal man.

He should not look so immaculately dressed in the black uniform of the Gestapo. A perfect fit, and yet, today, she noticed that his shoulders tested the seams of the jacket and the hat he removed from his head was a half-size too small.

She was losing her mind. What did the fit of his uniform matter? Or the size of his hat? She drew in a sudden breath, reaching for a calm she didn't feel. No matter what Mueller did next, she would not break. She would not show weakness. She would accept her fate with the dignity she'd witnessed in Max last night.

"This is where you blend your *vin clairs*?" He reached around her to the table at her back and ran a fingertip along the edge. "I had not thought making champagne required this amount of organization. You seem to have a system to your art."

He wanted to talk about the finer points of champagne

making? An ache took up residence behind her eyes. "I prefer order."

"May I?" The wine was wrested from her fingers before she could protest.

No, her mind screamed. Gabrielle never allowed anyone to taste her failures. "Please. Don't. It's not right."

Her plea came too late. He was already lifting the beaker to his lips and taking a long, slow sip of the golden liquid. "You are correct." He frowned into the glass. "This is a very poor attempt."

The ache behind her eyes became a relentless pounding. Something inside Gabrielle went cold at the way he set the wine on the table beside her, as if it were an offense to his superior palate. That she'd had the same reaction didn't soften the blow of his cold displeasure. With an impatient swat of her hand, she pushed a stubborn strand of hair off her face. "Why are you here, Detective Mueller?"

"I arrested your father-in-law this morning. I thought you should know. Although…" He trailed off, angled his head. "I think this is not news to you."

Her pulse tripped over itself and she was breathing too hard, trying to keep herself under control. "Why would you arrest Max? He's a harmless old man."

"Not so harmless, or so old," Mueller countered. "Maximillian Dupree is an active member of a large network of resistance workers. I am in the process of sorting out the names of his compatriots, male and…female."

She bit her lip hard. "Max is innocent of whatever it is you think he did."

A hint of something came and went in Mueller's eyes, something she couldn't quite define but knew she didn't like. "And yet, he has supplied me with information to make several more arrests."

Gabrielle's skin iced over. Max would not have broken easily, or quickly. There must have been enormous pain involved in his interrogation. She hadn't thought she could feel so helpless. She sought refuge behind her crossed arms. "May I see him? Is that possible?"

Mueller did not answer the question. "How much, I wonder, do you know about your father-in-law's criminal activities?"

Afraid to show her guilt, afraid to accept what she sensed was coming, Gabrielle busied herself straightening the beakers of the *vin clairs* into perfectly precise, ruthlessly neat rows. "I know he is innocent."

"Madame Dupree." Mueller came up behind her. Too close. She had to fight the instinct not to shrivel away from his distinctive scent. Mouth flat, she jerked around to face him and nearly lost her balance. She reached for the table at her back for support.

"I am told…" His gaze found the ribbon of hair that always fell loose by her ear. Slowly, he looked back into her eyes. "…that you visit your father-in-law's home often, sometimes at night after curfew. This is disturbing news."

"He is my family, of course I visit him. We discuss my husband, his son. Sometimes our conversations go long."

"That is your defense?"

She breathed in. Breathed out. The churning in her stomach would explode into panic if she didn't keep it in check. "It's the truth. Will you tell me why you arrested Max?"

"A parachute was found in his wine cellar, hidden inside an abandoned barrel. There were also weapons and ammunition." He said this all so casually. "I must now send my soldiers to search every cellar in the region. Yours will be today. You will want to prepare."

What sort of twisted game was he playing now? "Why… why are you telling me this?"

For a split second, Gabrielle thought she saw a hint of something not altogether dark in his eyes. She wanted to appeal to that sliver of humanity. But, no. That look, it was a trap. A mistake of the light. His way of lulling her into a false sense of security. "How long do I have?"

"Two hours."

He was warning her. But why? The answer came to her in a flash. He wanted to catch her in the act of hiding incriminating evidence.

She didn't know what to think. What to feel. Something strange was creeping into their conversation, something ugly. She tightened her arms around her waist and fumed. This man. This Nazi brute with his games. His terrible tricks. His confusing warnings and hidden threats.

She thought she might cry. She didn't dare.

"Perhaps you didn't hear me." He moved with lightning speed, so fast she hadn't seen him coming. He managed to penetrate the knot of her arms and grip her wrist, his hold firm but not painful. He always moved so quickly, she realized, and liked to grab her wrist to make his point. Yet, he never hurt her. He never crossed that line. His touch, why did she not recoil? Why was she not repulsed? Another of his tricks.

Games within games. Lies inside lies. She had never felt more alone.

"Listen to me, Madame. And listen good. In just two hours," he said, "your wine cellar will be overrun with SS soldiers."

A sob rose in her throat. This was some sort of bad dream. Mueller was… He seemed…

What did he want from her? Oh, but she knew. She *knew.* Shame had her staring at her feet.

"Don't look down. Look at me. Straight at me." He coaxed her to do his will in that low, awful, reptilian baritone that made her skin crawl. At last, she found the revulsion missing from her earlier reaction. "You will prepare for my impend-ing search of your wine cellar. Do I make myself clear?"

She met his gaze with an unwavering stare of her own. Chills crept across her skin and her eyes filled. No, she would not cry for him. Dry eyes were her only defense. "Perfectly."

"*Gut.* Good." He let her go.

She stumbled away from him, moving toward the door, stopping only once her spine ran up against the thick barrier that kept her one step away to freedom. Escape was just on the other side of the slab of wood. She was suddenly hot, so hot she thought she would faint if not for the support at her back. She dropped her gaze. A beam of light shone like a beacon at her feet. She wanted to fall into that light. Max deserved bet-ter from her. "Tell me what will happen to my father-in-law."

Mueller looked at her steadily. In that moment he was very German, very ruthless, every bit a high-ranking official in the Nazi secret police. "Tell me what you know of his activities."

"I know he is innocent of any crime." *Against France.*

"You are a loyal daughter-in-law."

The admiration she heard in the words—it was more than she could take. More than she could stomach. Her husband was dead. Her grandmother was feeble of mind and body. Paulette was cavorting with the enemy. Their mother was a collabo-rator. And now, *now*, Gabrielle had lost Max, too. "Please, I beg you, don't hurt him. He is—"

"It's time for you to stop talking."

She clamped her lips tightly shut.

He nodded his approval. "You may begin preparing for my return."

"*Oui. Bien.* I will go now." Groping behind her, she grasped the doorknob. A hard twist and she was free. Or nearly so. She took a step backward, and then another. The third car-ried her out into the hallway. From there, it was a matter of putting one foot in front of the other, each faster than the last. And then, she was running. Not to the wine cellar. To God.

For the first time since France declared war on Germany, Gabrielle sought refuge in the Lord. Up ahead, she saw the tiny chapel that had stood on LeBlanc land for two centuries. Every member of her family had been baptized inside those stone walls. Gabrielle included. She ran faster. It wasn't until she was inside the building, down on her knees atop the hard stones, hands clasped together beneath her chin, that she allowed herself to lift her eyes to the Cross.

She felt God's presence immediately. She wanted to rest in the sensation.

There wasn't time.

She shut her eyes and prayed for her father-in-law. She prayed for herself, for her family. For an end to this hideous war. And then, circled to the beginning and prayed again for Max.

He'd been so proud of his resistance work. Gabrielle had shared in that pride, thinking the righteousness of their cause protected them from capture. Her conviction had been as pure as the taste of a perfectly blended champagne. Now, she was confused and lost and in need of guidance. She could not do this on her own.

Protect him, Lord. Protect Max.

Protect us all.

The tears came then, rivers of them. One day, Gabrielle vowed, she would find absolution for failing to save her father-in-law. One day.

She allowed herself another five minutes with her God, then she rose and went to prepare for the infestation of SS soldiers on hallowed LeBlanc ground.

Chapter Thirty-Four

JOSEPHINE

Josephine flattened her hand over the book in her lap. The thick creamy pages made a pleasant, fluttery sound as she leafed through the entries, searching, searching. For what? She couldn't remember. The reason was gone. So many lost moments, too many, most of them recorded in this book.

She continued turning the pages. Once she started she couldn't stop. Some unknown, urgent purpose drove her. She'd learned to follow the instinct. This book, it was personal, used by someone who took her words seriously. Was that her? She never thought of herself as a serious writer. She felt a small spark of a thought. It nearly slid away, but she grabbed for it and then...

It rattled clear.

There was something she was supposed to remember. Yes, yes. Something for her granddaughter Gabrielle. A day, a time, an event. It was here, in this book. If only Josephine could recall what she was supposed to be looking for, then she could relay the information.

She would find it.

But not if she rushed.

Dipping her head, she inhaled deeply of the sweet, papery scent. Nothing—her mind was still a blank. Flip, flip, flip. A sense of calm moved through her, down along her spine, deep into her bones. This was her journal, her words. She told her secrets to these pages. When her mind went blank, and her thoughts became tangled, she was able to come here, and revisit forgotten moments from her past. This book was her memory now, both her pain and her comfort. Her refuge. Her truth.

And yet, even here, there were certain things her memory refused to relinquish onto the page. Entire voids of time and events were missing. That left her sad and frustrated.

Why had she not started keeping track of her thoughts sooner? Possibly, the failure was a small mercy. She was only supposed to remember her husband kissing her before heading to tend his vines. Not his collapse—she could not recall that clearly and rarely tried anymore. Had she been in the vineyard with him that day? Beside him, picking the grapes? Or had she been at the château, tending to their small child?

The details would not come, and they weren't in this book. Josephine started to wonder if maybe his death never happened. Maybe it was just a terrible dream, a waking nightmare she couldn't seem to shake. Antoine was alive, working the vines even now. He would walk through the door and—

She was so confused.

Her hand opened and closed over the silky paper beneath her palm. Her journal. She would locate her memory in these pages. She stopped her frantic searching and read.

3 September 1939

France declared war on Germany today. Hélène answered the phone and gave us the news. I decided to cancel the anniversary party, then agreed to postpone instead.

There was more here. But not what she'd come looking for.

22 June 1940

Helmut von Schmidt, the German wine merchant who lies on invoices, has requisitioned my home.

Not that, either.

She kept searching, sometimes going forward, sometimes backward. The tone of the entries seemed to change in the winter of 1941. A page, and then another, and then two more. Each filled with lists and other information Josephine found in von Schmidt's desk. A record of shipments, mostly champagne, to various war zones. She'd added a personal note. *Where the wine goes, so goes the German army.*

Another page listed valuables and personal treasures missing from the château; some had marks next to them, others did not. Josephine couldn't remember why she'd made those strikes on the page. Or why she'd included mention of a shipment to Portugal. She read her personal comment, made in bold, angry strokes. *Von Schmidt is a swine. Something must be done to stop him.*

She found another meticulous record of events and dates. The activities of the resistance. She read quickly through the entries.

—Three of my neighbors were caught palming off inferior blends to the Germans. All three have been thrown in jail, their champagne houses shut down indefinitely.

—Marta and I switched the labels on several single vintages. Josephine's note: *Marta knows which are the real single vintages and which are the fakes.*

—François and Pierre transported a family of Jews in wine barrels across the demarcation line last night. They returned to the Occupied Zone with wine in the same barrels. Josephine's note: *I have very brave men in my employ.*

—Train car derailed carrying large shipment of wine. Josephine's note: *Better the soil drinks our wine than the German dogs taste a single drop.*

—Local man shot for raising a clenched fist as Germans soldiers were staging a parade, another caught and executed for cutting telephone wires. Josephine's note: *None of us are safe.*

—Lucien Trevon arrested for handing out pamphlets for the Free French, released the next day. Josephine's note: *Hélène has made a terrible bargain to save this boy.*

Josephine kept reading, stopping on the page that spoke of Hélène becoming von Schmidt's social secretary, then the hostess for his parties, then something uglier. She'd recorded other dates and times. The Japanese attack on Pearl Harbor in December of 1941. The Americans entering the war at last. Gabrielle slipping out of the house at night. Paulette's clandestine meetings with a boy. Josephine's note: *My home has become a breeding ground for liars and cheats. I include myself in this judgment. We do what we must to survive.*

Next page...

SS conducted an unplanned inspection of our wine cellar. They found nothing. Gabrielle was fully prepared for the search. Josephine's note: *How did my granddaughter know about the raid?*

Next page...
There. At last. The entry she'd come seeking, not for her granddaughter. For herself.

11 May 1942

Capitaine von Schmidt and Hélène are arguing as I write this. I listen at the wall with my ear pressed to the plaster. He accuses her of hiding her jewelry from him. He accuses her of many things. There is more shouting, mostly from him, terrible vows of retribution for her deceit. I hear the breaking of glass, the crack of a fist, von Schmidt's furious exit from the house. Josephine's note the following day: *Hélène's makeup is heavy this morning. It does nothing to conceal her black eye and split lip, or the fury in her eyes. Her anger is nothing compared to mine. Von Schmidt is out of control. Something must be done to stop him.*

Josephine's hand trembled over the page, her resolve robbing her of air.

Yes, she thought. *Something must be done.*

Part Four

Chapter Thirty-Five

GABRIELLE

17 July 1942

Max disappeared two days after he was taken into custody. More arrests were made. Gabrielle was not one of them. She couldn't feel grateful, not until she knew what had become of her father-in-law. Unfortunately, no one in their network had the information. Nor were they looking for answers. They had their own worries.

German occupation was slowly starving the people of Reims. The SS continued their random searches, which extended beyond wine cellars into homes and businesses, often because of tips from local citizens. The Nazis encouraged these betrayals, offering rewards as small as a few extra eggs in a basket, or a piece of rancid meat.

The LeBlanc wine cellar was often the target of these raids. Gabrielle had begun receiving cryptic warnings ahead of time.

Always from an unknown source, usually a telegram with a series of random letters that spelled out no word she knew, not in French, German or English.

The first time she'd received one of the messages, she hadn't understood. The SS soldiers had arrived unexpectedly, and she'd been forced to explain the reason behind an entire rack of mislabeled bottles. Later that night, she'd pored over the telegram with renewed vigor. It hadn't taken her long to understand a warning had been buried in the strange cipher. By morning, she'd cracked the code. When the second telegram arrived, she'd been ready for the raid. The soldiers left with several cases of mediocre champagne, while satisfied with the answers they received to their questions.

Although Detective Mueller accompanied his soldiers, he physically separated himself from the actual plundering. He rarely touched the bottles himself, but always—always—directed his men to the less sought-after blends instead of the truly superior ones.

Today, he took his usual place beside Gabrielle and aligned his shoulders perfectly parallel to hers, with only inches standing between them, as if they were a united front. His solid presence beside her made her feel less alone. It was another one of his lies. Another lure that cost her sleepless nights. After all, he did nothing to stop his men from stealing her champagne.

"Halt," Mueller said when a soldier bent over a case of Josephine's rosé and pulled out one of the bottles to inspect it closer. "Give that to me."

He studied the label, inspected the bottle itself, rotating it around slowly. He released the cork with startling finesse, his head set at an angle so he could listen to the sound the wine made. Gabrielle heard the satisfying sigh of effervescence and wanted to weep over its perfection. Mueller gave her a quick glance. The look, one of approval. Warmth wanted to overwhelm the coldness in her heart. It was a sensation she did not trust. He studied the cork next, testing its feel in his palm, remarking on its color, checking the sides and then the bottom.

The detective knew what he was doing.

He motioned to one of the soldiers. "Glass."

The man dug inside the pouch slung over his shoulder, then handed the detective a champagne coupe. Without glancing at Gabrielle, Mueller poured the rich pink liquid into the glass. He studied the bubbles, sniffed at the wine, took a sip. Several seconds went by before he swallowed.

More seconds passed as he lingered over the afternotes. "This is an inferior blend." The declaration contradicted the appreciation in his eyes. "Germans deserve better than this fizzy dishwater."

She gasped at the insult.

He made a grand show of emptying the rest of the rosé onto the wine cellar's floor. "Leave it for the French. Take that wine instead." He pointed to crates of a blanc de blanc. A remarkably inferior blend, comparatively speaking, to her grandmother's rosé. "All twenty cases."

The men went to work.

Gabrielle shrank back from the activity, arms wrapped around her waist, her mind in a whirl of confusing thoughts. She knew Mueller had just shown her extraordinary favor, but she couldn't comprehend why he'd saved the rosé. What did he hope to gain? His behavior made no sense. Unless...

Was this part of some sort of twisted strategy to lull her into submission?

She knew better than to trust him. It was the uniform. That emblem of Nazi power. Wearing it made him less human. Something to be feared.

She was right to fear him, to distrust him. To hate him,

even. He'd arrested Max, among others, and had made them disappear.

Mueller was still looking at her, and she tried not to look back, but the intense quality of his stare started the blood rising up to her throat, to her cheeks. Miserably confused, she glanced down at her feet. The toes of her work boots were only inches from where he'd dumped the precious rosé. The pink liquid had turned several shades darker as it seeped into the limestone, looking more like blood than wine.

The raid finally came to an end.

Gabrielle was given permission to leave.

She said not one word of farewell to Detective Mueller. They exchanged a final look absent of expression. He nodded and retreated with his soldiers. And, of course, her wine.

Gabrielle returned to the château.

On her way, she glanced over her shoulder, not sure what she hoped to find. There was nothing there. No threat. No promise. No enemy. No ally. No one waiting to arrest her. No one standing to help her carry her burdens. Only empty air stood between her and a wine cellar with fewer bottles of champagne now that Mueller and his men had seized another twenty cases.

She could only assume the wine was being loaded on a train to Berlin, never to be seen again. Not unlike the people Mueller arrested. Her mind wanted to believe he was not what he seemed, that he was somehow better than the uniform he wore. Somehow...more. She could not quite get there. He saved some of her champagne, but still took too many cases. He continued making arrests, and people still disappeared.

She must see things as they really were, not how she hoped them to be. She must be smart, and not be fooled by whatever game he was playing.

Lies within lies. She was suddenly very tired.

I send you forth as sheep in the midst of wolves.

Entering the château, alone, exhausted, she set aside her mangled thoughts and considered the ever-growing problem in her home. Von Schmidt's behavior was becoming more and more erratic. Behind his eyes, Gabrielle could see him thinking, plotting. Making plans. He no longer pretended civility when it was just the LeBlanc women in the house. More often than not, his true nature won over the sophisticated mask he wore around his fellow Germans. He was rude, scathingly dismissive and feral in his displeasure whenever his patience snapped.

Which was too often, and mostly directed at Hélène.

"Gabrielle, come quickly." Her mother beckoned from the small parlor just off the main salon. "There's news from Paris."

Gabrielle hurried into the room. The rest of her family were already gathered around the wireless, every one of them in a state of shock. Von Schmidt was also there, not shocked, instead pleased by the news coming in from Paris. He stood near the fireplace, studying the glowing tip of his cigarette. The small, secretive smile curling his lips meant nothing good.

A German voice spoke through the wireless in heavily accented French. "With the assistance of the French police, 13,000 Jews have been arrested for crimes against the Third Reich. They are being held in the Vélodrome d'Hiver until transportation can be provided..."

The voice droned on. Gabrielle barely heard the details of how the French police had joined forces with the SS to arrest innocent people for alleged crimes.

What crimes? She wondered, knowing she wasn't the only one of her family silently asking this question. Shock and horror showed in the wide, darting eyes of everyone in the room.

All, except von Schmidt. "At last," he said. "At last, the Jews are being punished for their crimes against humanity."

"*Mon Dieu.* I can't bear to hear any more." Paulette, hands over her ears, ran out of the room, sobbing.

What crimes had so many Jews committed? Gabrielle asked herself again, her own hands clenching and unclenching at her sides. Men, women, children, arrested. For what? For being born Jewish? For daring to breathe the same air as Germans?

It was all so unbelievable. Gruesome. Anti-Semitism on a whole new level.

And von Schmidt, the deplorable human being, was happy. "Tell me, Herr Hauptmann," Gabrielle said, unable to hold silent a second longer. "What did 13,000 French citizens do to deserve arrest and deportation?"

"They are not French. They are Jews. They have infested Europe with their tainted blood. They have stolen jobs and dominated businesses where they have no right. It is long past time they were put in their place."

Gabrielle had heard much of this before, at the dinner table in this very home. But never out of von Schmidt's mouth. He'd shown his approval with a nod of his head. A smile, a grunt. "How can you advocate sending innocent people to their deaths?" she asked him. "Many of them children."

"Ridding the world of Jews is an acceptable sacrifice for the good of Germany."

Stunned speechless, Gabrielle watched the hate flicker across his face. The fervor of a true believer shone in his eyes. When had he become so bold with his convictions, so rabid? "You fiend. You are a—"

"Be very careful what you say next, Madame Dupree. You would not wish to be labeled a sympathizer of the Jews."

Hélène flinched. Tears filled Josephine's eyes. Marta openly wept.

Scowling, von Schmidt extinguished his cigarette, immediately lit another and turned his displeasure toward the settee.

"You, there. Old woman." He stabbed his cigarette in Josephine's direction. "Why do you shed tears for the filthy Jews?"

"You want to know why? I will tell you." Josephine stood, her tears falling without remorse, her head tilted at an incensed angle like a wild boar uprooted in the forest.

This would not end well. Gabrielle rushed to her grandmother's side, linked their arms, and pulled her close. "Grandmère, you don't have to answer his question. You don't—"

"Yes, Gabrielle, I do." Josephine's eyes glittered with purpose. "The Jews are God's chosen people. All nations will be blessed through them. All but the Third Reich. The Lord will not bless such evil."

Von Schmidt went very still. "I have to wonder why you defend a race so far removed from your own. What, Madame, drives this loyalty? Or perhaps, I should ask…who?"

Josephine lifted her chin higher. There was no hesitation in her, no fear, only conviction. "I am a Christian, this is no secret. Jewish history is our history. Their pain is our pain."

Von Schmidt drew closer, the look of retribution in his eyes.

"Herr Hauptmann von Schmidt." Gabrielle said his name in an overloud voice. "We're all on edge after the news from Paris. The shock has made us not quite ourselves."

He placed his gaze on her face. "Mark my words, Madame, the Jews will be eradicated from France, as will anyone who comes to their defense. Keep that in mind the next time you want to speak your thoughts aloud. You do not want to find yourselves on the wrong side of history."

Clearly outraged, Josephine started to respond.

He cut her off with a slash of his hand. "Another word out of you and I will be forced to report your sympathies to my superiors."

Gabrielle's skin heated with anger. She wanted to shout at von Schmidt that he and his superiors were the ones on the wrong side of history. That they would one day be forced to answer for their *sympathies*. But she kept silent and continued holding on to her grandmother, silently urging her to stop engaging in further discussion.

"Your silence is sensible. Now. I have a meeting with several wine merchants in Paris tomorrow. You," he said, taking Hélène by the arm, "will accompany me upstairs and pack my bags."

"Yes, Helmut."

Josephine, her arm still entangled with Gabrielle's, waited until the two disappeared before muttering barely above a whisper, "That man, he is out of control. Something must be done to stop him."

Chapter Thirty-Six

HÉLÈNE

Stepping into the room that had once belonged to her daughter, but was now filled with von Schmidt's effects, Hélène shut the door and stared straight ahead. She took a moment to breathe past her nerves. *He doesn't know your secret. He would have turned you in by now.*

This was true, if for no other reason than to forward his own career.

He'd proven that when he'd provided his superiors with the list of local Jewish business owners and their families. Such a calculated move would have brought him great reward, if he'd been the only one to supply the names. Three others in his ranks had produced a similar list.

Now was not the time to dwell on such matters.

Hélène needed to gather her composure and set aside her building fury. It took her a moment, and longer than perhaps it should. When she fastened her gaze on von Schmidt, she found she couldn't lift her eyes higher than his chin.

"You're upset," he said, reaching for her, taking her hand in his, giving it a squeeze. "No, don't deny it. I can see it in the way you avoid looking at me directly."

She forced her gaze higher. A superior grin passed over his lips, then moved into his eyes. Hélène hated that smug expression. "It was difficult watching Josephine contradict you."

"That was unwise of her."

His words made her wince. But she felt, finally, they were speaking candidly. And in their candor she heard his threat. His patience had come to an end. Josephine was in grave danger. Hélène would do what she could to protect her mother-in-law. "You said it yourself. Josephine is old and, most days, confused. She can barely remember the names of her own granddaughters. She is harmless."

It was only half-true.

"You make a salient point. Now let me make mine so there is no misunderstanding." With a quick, swift sweep of his hand, he gripped her arm. "My loyalty is to myself."

This, she knew.

"But also, with the Third Reich."

"Of course." Why would he think it important to make this clarification? "I am aware of your allegiance, Helmut. You welcome Nazi elitists into this home, men who see themselves as superior to others, men like *Standartenführer* Bauer and Lieutenant Weber. And now you are one of them. You talk like them. You think like them. They have corrupted your mind."

She'd spoken too freely. She felt her mistake in the tightening of his fingers on her bicep. It was too late to take back the words. She wasn't sure she would if she could. His grip tightened.

He was hurting her.

"You think it's only me who is like them? You give these men your smiles, your laughter." Mouth grim, he dragged her to the full-length mirror next to the bureau and forced her to face her reflection. "Look at yourself, Hélène. Look at the color of your hair, the blue tint of your eyes." He shook her hard enough to rattle her teeth. "You are one of them, too. One of us."

Hélène tried not to sway on her feet. Her throat was raw with unshed tears. It felt like she'd swallowed a collection of knives. Still, she said to him, "One of us?"

"Yes, us. Aryan. The pure race." His voice was driven, possessed. Evil. What made his words worse was that nothing he said was original. He was parroting what others professed before him. "We are among the privileged elite. Is that not exciting?"

Hélène stared at the face next to hers in the mirror. Side by side, cheeks pressed together, two images of the same coin. But their eyes were not the same. Hers, frightened, appalled. His, glowing with zeal. She'd known Helmut to be a greedy man, but never a fanatic.

When had this transformation happened? Why did she not trust it?

Something bleak and angry rose up from her soul. Her heart began to thump fast and hard. She thought she might be ill, right here, at von Schmidt's feet. She pulled in several tight breaths until the sensation passed, then spoke to their shared reflection. "Privilege at the sacrifice of an entire race of people is not exciting, Helmut. It's monstrous."

"Wanting to purify mankind does not make us monsters. It makes us noble."

"Noble?" She repeated the word, keeping her voice mild, her sentences short, even as her mind raged. "Genocide is not noble. It's the method of animals."

She expected an open-palmed slap to her cheek.

He laughed at her instead, the sound a little wild, and—again—not quite right. "You are wrong, my dear. Animals kill to survive. Nazis kill to purify. You will remember my words. Say it. You will remember what I have said to you this day."

"I will remember." She yanked her arm free and pushed away from him. She wanted nothing more than to be away from this room, this man. She still had to pack his suitcase.

"How long will you be in Paris?" she asked, training her voice to a throaty purr as much to distract him as herself. "One night, two? No longer, I hope."

After a moment, he seemed to come back to himself. The smug, knowing grin was back on his face. This man, she knew. This man, she understood. "Don't tell me you're worried I will replace you."

Her breathing faltered, ever-so-slightly, but she kept her smile bland, even as her mind wished, prayed, begged the Lord that von Schmidt would do just that. That he would cast her aside as nothing more than a piece of overused baggage. "I simply need to know how many changes of clothes to pack."

His gaze stayed on her face, and she knew he was attempting to read her. "I plan to be gone for a few days, at least three, possibly four."

She walked past him. "Will you require a business suit for your meetings, or will your uniform suffice?"

"I will need several suits. As I said, I expect to be gone awhile." His voice wasn't pleasant and, again, she thought something was wrong, something off. His tone was too syrupy, too sweet, the slippery hiss of a snake before a deadly strike.

"Very well." She stood at the threshold of the closet and, lifting onto her toes, retrieved the valise from the shelf above her head. Her movements were stiff and impatient as she filled the case with various articles of clothing and von Schmidt's personal items.

The thought of him leaving for more than a night brought such joy she had to fight to keep it off her face. He could not know how much she wanted him out of her life, not just for the days he would be gone, but forever. *I could make that happen.*

Emotion roared through her. The disquiet she'd been feeling since becoming this man's mistress twisted hard in her stomach, almost painful, and her blood surged with a sudden burst of power. A strange sort of excitement. It was too much feeling, too fast. She felt like screaming. And then, a rush of calm swept through her.

I could make that happen.

She finished packing, shut the case, secured the straps and sent her mind somewhere else. She gave Helmut her full attention. He seemed as preoccupied as she, and it wasn't long before he sent her away. She returned to her room and went to stand before her reflection.

How often had she gazed into this mirror? How many hours dedicated to the application of makeup, the adjustment of her hair, the addition of another layer of camouflage?

She touched her chin, curved her fingertip along her jaw, pulled at the skin at her cheek. She was no longer a girl anymore. She was not an old woman, either. She was trapped somewhere in between. Mature, but not young. Still beautiful. More curse than blessing, that. The lines around her mouth and at the corners of her eyes were minimal considering her age. Blond hair, blue eyes. *You are one of us.*

Not far from the truth, but not how he meant. She'd supplied the list of local Jewish names. Men, women and children who would soon be rounded up and sent to the camps. It didn't matter that she wasn't the only one to do so, or that her list wasn't as extensive as the others. What she'd done, turning on her own kind, it made her a monster. No better than a Nazi.

But maybe, yes maybe, it took a monster to defeat a monster. A plan began formulating in her mind.

She went to the window and looked out. It was the time of day when everything softened. The sun dipped below the horizon. That final burst of light caught in the clouds and lingered in a kaleidoscope of pastel colors. Pink melted into blue into gold into yellow and even purple. It broke her heart to look at that sky so full of God's handiwork, knowing others were locked in a sports arena, or a train car, or a terrible cage, unable to absorb the beauty.

With trembling fingers, she lit a cigarette and considered her options. She sat in front of the mirror again, staring at her face. She stayed there for hours, smoking, thinking. Night fell. The moon rose. And still she sat.

And she stared.

A band of clouds drifted over the moon slowly, slyly, casting her troubled reflection in shadow. Her mind went to dark places, where monsters roamed freely and atonement awaited the brave.

Von Schmidt would be leaving in the morning.

Hélène would be ready, knowing she would never find peace until the man vanished from her life for good.

Chapter Thirty-Seven

GABRIELLE

Von Schmidt's departure was met with wary celebration in the LeBlanc home. He did not return in three days. He did not return in four. A week passed. And then half of another. A surprisingly stoic Detective Mueller showed up twice during the second week, asking rapid-fire questions of each woman, saving the harder ones for Hélène.

She seemed perfectly at ease under the continued questioning, a little too perfectly at ease to Gabrielle's way of thinking. She could not dislodge a chilling suspicion that her mother knew more than she was letting on. Hélène said pleasant, ambiguous things about von Schmidt, but nothing that helped explain his continued absence or ongoing lack of communication.

Mueller arrived for a third visit, no longer stoic. He insisted the entire household meet him in the parlor. "I have a few more questions."

He started with Hélène.

Before he began, she asked, "May I smoke?"

He nodded.

She brought a cigarette to her lips, reached for her lighter. Her eyes stayed on Mueller as she lit the tip and blew out a stream of smoke that gave away the brand. Lucky Strikes. American. She had not switched, as she'd promised. She took another drag.

Mueller's eyes narrowed, but he didn't remark on her impudence. "When did you last see Hauptmann von Schmidt?"

She studied her cigarette as if the answer was written across the paper cylinder. "The seventeenth day of July."

Mueller consulted his notebook. "You are certain it wasn't the sixteenth?"

"It was the seventeenth."

"And that was the last day you saw him? The seventeenth," he said, then added before she could respond, "What was the reason for his trip? How long was he supposed to be gone?"

Unruffled by the barrage, Hélène batted back her answers as fast as he'd fired off the questions. "Yes. The seventeenth. Business. Three, possibly four days. He wasn't clear."

"Why didn't you report him missing when he didn't show up as planned?"

She took a long, slow drag of her cigarette, blew it out just as slowly. "I am not his keeper."

"You are employed as his—" Mueller glanced at the notebook again "—secretary?"

"His social secretary," she corrected, twisting her head and blowing another stream of smoke into the air. So calm. So in control, Gabrielle thought. Even her mother's eyes gave away nothing of her thoughts. "I am mostly a glorified party planner. Helmut tells me the number of guests he plans to entertain, what he wants served at the table, and I accommodate his wishes."

"Helmut? You are on a first-name basis with Hauptmann von Schmidt?"

Hélène crushed out the cigarette, crossed her legs and folded her hands in her lap. "He encourages familiarity."

"You two are close?"

Her eyes blinked once, twice, then went blank. No one looking at her would think she had a deadly secret hidden behind that cool exterior. "He expects me to anticipate his needs. That requires a certain level of familiarity."

"These are not the duties of a glorified party planner."

She shrugged. "I serve as his hostess. I organize his calendar. Ensure that his clothes are properly cleaned and pressed. Basically, I see to his comfort."

"You see to his comfort, nothing more intimate than that?"

"Nothing, no."

Gabrielle was still considering her mother's lie, told without a slice of hesitation, when Mueller darted a look at her. "And you, Madame Dupree. Why did you not report Hauptmann von Schmidt's disappearance?"

"Please understand, Detective Mueller. *Capitaine*...Hauptmann von Schmidt seized our home for his personal lodgings." She could not keep the heavy judgment out of her voice. "He did not ask our permission. He is not our guest. He is not our friend."

Mueller's eyes, a rigid, clear blue, skimmed over her face. "You wished him harm."

"I didn't say that."

"You didn't have to." He fired the next question at Josephine in a precise, cold tempo that grated on the ears. "When was the last time you saw Hauptmann von Schmidt?"

Josephine drew back. "I don't..." A small flutter quivered at her throat and the color in her cheeks completely ebbed away. "I don't know this man, I..." Her words trailed off.

Mueller took a moment to study each of them in careful, meticulous succession. "One of you is lying. I will find out which one." He snapped his notebook shut and rose abruptly. "My men will now search the château."

He headed out of the parlor.

Gabrielle chased after him. "Detective Mueller. Please. I'm sure this isn't necessary."

Paying her no heed, he swung open the front door and motioned for his soldiers to come forward. "Search every room."

"Detective," she said again, a little more desperately. "I'm confident there's a logical explanation for Hauptmann von Schmidt's absence. He'll return soon."

"He won't return. One of you made certain of that." He didn't say *murder*. It was implied.

"Where is your proof?" she demanded.

"In this house. My men will find it."

In that moment, there was nothing of the man she'd met in her wine cellars during the raids. Nothing of the man who'd steered his soldiers away from her most valuable champagnes. Gabrielle had begun to believe...

She'd begun to hope...

Bitter disappointment scorched through her. She'd been played a fool, outmaneuvered by a master manipulator. Unable to look him in the eyes, she stared at the intersection of his collar and the iron cross at his throat. "None of us is lying," she said again, praying it was true.

"So you keep insisting."

"It's the truth." She wondered at her own resolve. Her courage. The women in this home hid their secrets well. They'd each prepared for today's search, knowing it was inevitable. Still, Gabrielle should not feel this calm. Her peace came from God, not herself, not this man she'd begun to think might be more, possibly, than a monster. And thus, as SS soldiers tore through the château, she leaned against a wall and fixed her eyes on the Lord.

The search took two hours. Mueller conferred with his soldiers several times. Then, suddenly, it was over, and he was approaching her again. "We will leave you now." His voice took on a low, enigmatic tone that fell only on her ears. "My return is imminent."

The next morning, a full hour before dawn broke over the vineyard, persistent knocking woke the entire household. Gabrielle, already dressed and sipping coffee in the kitchen, was the first to arrive in the foyer, Marta only a few steps behind. "They're here," the housekeeper hissed. "The Gestapo. They have come to take us away."

"Shhh."

The knocking stopped. Gabrielle and Marta froze, waiting. Neither spoke. What was there to say? The knocking began again, louder, rattling the door on its hinges.

Marta took a step forward.

"No, I'll handle this. You go upstairs. Wake Paulette, then both of you go to my grandmother's room. Do not come out until I tell you. Quickly now." Gabrielle pushed Marta into action. "Quickly!"

The housekeeper threw herself up the stairs. Gabrielle took her time walking to the door, releasing the lock, turning the handle. The glow of headlights hit her in the face. She blinked away the spots and attempted to stare into the heavy fog. Her efforts were rewarded with the image of German soldiers on her doorstep.

She counted two of them, with eyes like flints, immaculately dressed in their SS black. She knew these men. They were the brutes that had arrested Max. Behind them stood Mueller. His face held no expression. When he started forward, the soldiers shifted aside to make a path.

Danger swirled around him, shrouding him as easily as the fog cloaking the morning air. The sweet sound of birdsong contradicted the ugliness of the situation.

Gabrielle struck a pose of impatience. "It's rather early for a social call."

"And yet," he said, his gaze traveling over her muslin shirt, wool trousers and heavy work boots. "I see you were expecting me."

He'd thought to catch her unaware. Even without his cryptic warning, Gabrielle had known he would come at an inconvenient hour. Let him see her resolve. Let him know she understood how his mind worked. "I have always handled the unexpected well."

A flicker of appreciation gathered in his eyes but was gone so quickly she wondered if she'd imagined it. "You will step aside and let us in your home."

Before she could respond, he moved past her, the two soldiers hard on his heels.

She scurried around all three, until she was once again face-to-face with the detective. He stood with his feet splayed, hands linked behind his back. The pose of an arrogant man certain in his convictions. Here to do his duty. This, she sensed, was the real Wolfgang Mueller. A man without qualms.

Rage dominated her thoughts. For one black moment she was tempted to slap that self-righteous look off his face. "What is the reason for this visit?" she asked.

With a smile slightly warped at the edges, he stated his business in guttural, heavily accented French. "I have come to take your mother to the police station."

"You're arresting her?"

"That has yet to be determined."

The ragged edges of her remaining hope splintered into a thousand pieces. The pain was unbearable. She could feel the soldiers watching her. The anticipation was there in their ready stances. They hoped she would do something foolish and they would be forced to stop her.

She could feel the urge to battle, but she'd lost Mueller's attention. His eyes were locked on something behind her. Gabrielle shifted around and gasped at her mother standing calmly at the top of the stairs. She was dressed in a thick robe, her face free of makeup, her hair hanging loosely past her shoulders. She'd never looked so disheveled. And for once, her age showed.

A dozen warnings ran through Gabrielle's mind. *Run, Maman. Run!*

It was too late. Her mother was prepared to accept her fate. Gabrielle saw her conviction, her acceptance of the inevitable.

Mueller walked to the edge of the steps. "Hélène Jobert-LeBlanc, you will come with me. You may do so willingly. Or my men will drag you away."

"I will come willingly." She tightened the belt at her impossibly small waist, the gesture highlighting her weight loss. "But perhaps you will allow me a moment to make myself presentable?"

"You have ten minutes."

She was back down in seven, looking more herself, but just barely, in a simple blue dress that hung on her gaunt frame. She'd pulled her hair in a tidy knot at the nape of her neck and had applied lipstick. "Shall we, Detective?"

Without waiting for his response, she strode out the front door. Head tilted at a regal angle. Marie Antoinette heading to the guillotine.

Gabrielle stared at her mother's rigid back, her heart thumping hard in her throat, fear surging in her mind. She bit her lip to hold back a scream. It was Max all over again. She had to do something, say something. She rushed out into the fog.

Mueller caught her by the arm. The headlights of the Mercedes glinted in his eyes. "I wouldn't advise interfering." His gaze bore into hers. "You will only cause your mother unnecessary grief."

A threat. A warning. They were one and the same with this man. The cold breath of terror filled her. "Why are you taking her away?"

"There has been a development." He didn't explain. "Now turn around, Madame Dupree. Turn around and go back inside."

She refused to move and watched, helplessly, as he climbed in the back seat behind her mother. Gabrielle didn't dare look away, didn't dare, as the Mercedes disappeared into the fog.

Not again. She could not remain passive again. She would beg for her mother's life.

She informed the other women of her plan, then sprinted to the shed behind the champagne house. The car had no petrol. She would have to use the bicycle. She lifted up one quick, fervent prayer and took off in the direction of Reims. The journey was both endless and strangely brief.

Mueller met her at the door of the police station, wearing the face of the Gestapo. "You should not have come here."

She felt unusually weak, and very much aware of the perspiration sliding down her back. "You have to let me see her."

"She is being prepared for questioning."

The Gestapo didn't question, they interrogated. They coerced. They tortured.

Helplessness descended over her as it had in the vineyard during Max's arrest. "Please, let me speak with her. Five minutes, that's all I ask."

"You can do nothing for her now."

It couldn't be true. "There's been some kind of mistake," she said, aware of the frantic nature of her tone. "My mother had nothing to do with Hauptmann von Schmidt's disappearance."

He said nothing.

Gabrielle took a breath and realized she was breathing hard, trying to keep control. "She's innocent of this crime."

Mueller moved quickly, so quickly, she jumped back. "I'm not going to hurt you."

He already had. He'd arrested Max. And now her mother.

"Go home, Gabrielle." The way he said her name sent chills down her spine. Soft, full of kindness, perfectly articulated, his French impeccable in a way it had never been before.

Who was this man?

The Nazi with your mother's life cradled in the palm of his hand. "I can't leave. She is my mother."

He came to stand by her, so close she had to lean back to look into his face. "You must go and let me do my duty."

An intimate staring contest ensued. Gabrielle was the first to look away. Mueller was the first to speak. "Go home."

"I can't."

"This is not a choice." He ushered her outside and left her standing alone on the sidewalk. The first light of dawn broke over the horizon, highlighting the cathedral spires.

She had no power here. All her bravery, all her bluster, was fraudulent at best. She drifted to her bicycle without noticing what she was doing and found herself sitting on the seat.

Her mind kept circling back to one question. Where was von Schmidt? Was he dead? If so, how? Why? Who would want him dead? There were signs of guilt that pointed toward her mother. Toward all of them, really. Where was the body? No body, no crime.

The church bells sounded on the air, prodding her into action.

She pedaled home and used the journey to review the last time she'd seen von Schmidt. They'd been in the parlor. Listening to the wireless. The news from Paris had been devastating. Two days of arrests. 13,000 Jews taken into custody.

Von Schmidt had been overly pleased. He'd argued with Josephine. Or rather, Josephine had argued with him.

He'd threatened reprisal, then insisted Hélène pack his suitcase. She'd gone without protest, looking resigned.

Something in her mother's behavior. In the conversation before von Schmidt left the room. Or was it after? She reviewed every word. A memory struck. Words hissed in Gabrielle's ear. *Something must be done to stop him.*

Which of them had said that? Josephine. Josephine had made the vague threat. No, it was absurd. Unthinkable. She couldn't—wouldn't—believe her grandmother had a hand in von Schmidt's disappearance. Besides, she wasn't the only one that had cause to see him dead.

Josephine. Hélène. Neither of them could have done this... alone... But together? United in their common cause? Gabrielle pumped her feet faster, thinking, praying, *Please, God, let me be wrong.*

Chapter Thirty-Eight

JOSEPHINE

Josephine was in her room, lying on her bed, staring at the cracked plaster above her head, enduring the endless stretch of silence between waking, dressing and Gabrielle's return from the police station.

Worry seared in her throat, but she kept her eyes on the ceiling. Kept trying to piece together the events of the past two weeks. There was something important she was supposed to remember. A moment, a thought, a quiet act of valor.

The answer was in her memory.

Her mind refused to cooperate.

The darkness that had once been only a nagging presence now bled into every thought, every image, sweet and velvety, more comfort than concern. The sound of hushed female voices filled her head. She thought she heard her name. She couldn't find the energy to respond.

The voices changed, becoming more urgent, more agitated.

When she heard the unmistakable sobbing from her grand-daughter, she flew off the bed and fought her way across the room, pushing aside the foggy thoughts crowding her brain. She found Marta hovering over Paulette, who sat on the floor, hunched over, her arms hugging her knees to her chest, her lips flat, tears pouring from her eyes.

Josephine dropped to the floor beside the girl, gathered her into her arms and began stroking her hair. "Here, now, what's all this?"

"Oh, Grandmère." Paulette looked up at her, her eyes pools of anguish, her whole body shaking. "They've taken Maman away. They're going to send her to her death, I just know it. Then, what will become of us?"

In that moment, Josephine felt as though someone had slapped her awake. Everything was clear. The smell of Paulette's freshly washed hair, the scent of soap and shampoo, the chill in the air. The radiator against the wall useless without fuel. The terror in her granddaughter's voice. "Your mother has only been taken in for questioning."

"By the Gestapo," the girl wailed. "They know she's a Jew. It's the only explanation that makes sense."

"The Gestapo is a police unit, Paulette. They investigate crimes. Right now, they believe something has happened to Hauptmann von Schmidt."

That, also, was clear in Josephine's mind.

The German wasn't, as she'd suspected, sitting behind some desk in Paris, smug and well rewarded for his loyalty to the Third Reich.

Where was he, then? Josephine's mind spun with possibilities. An extended vacation he'd failed to report to his superiors, a missed train, a case of the flu. Foul play. Death. That last possibility seemed unlikely. Except, in her gut, she thought it was more than likely. "I'm sure this is all a misunderstanding."

"Do you think Maman did something to Hauptmann von Schmidt?"

"Your mother is not capable of harming another person." Or rather, she hadn't been capable before the enemy moved into their home and demanded she warm his bed. Josephine had witnessed Hélène's transformation. The confident, elegant woman had become tense and watchful, her quiet fury bubbling just below the surface. "She did not hurt the German."

"Will that matter? She's committed other crimes."

"What other crimes?"

Paulette shuddered so hard Josephine felt it in her bones. "She has lied about her name. If the Gestapo discover she falsified her papers. If they find out that she—"

"Hush, now. I mean it. Your mother is a LeBlanc. Our name will keep her safe." Josephine knew that wasn't true.

And so, too, it would seem, did Paulette. "We have to do something, Grandmère. We have to protect her or we will all be doomed."

"Your sister is already working on the problem."

"What can Gabrielle do?"

What, indeed? Once the Gestapo involved itself in a matter, a miscarriage of justice was sure to follow. Josephine was powerless all over again—as powerless as she'd been when Antoine had collapsed in the vineyard. When her beloved son had succumbed to his unseen wounds left from another war.

She wanted to climb into the dark shadows that awaited in her mind. She was not that much of a coward. She called on the Lord, praying for His divine deliverance. "We have to trust your sister will do everything she can to save your mother."

Paulette said nothing, staring at the floor. The tears continued streaming down her cheeks, and her shoulders shook. Josephine looked to Marta. "She needs tea."

"I will see to it at once." The housekeeper closed the door behind her.

"My bones are too old for this floor. Help me up, Paulette."

She watched the girl rise, her skin pale and gray. Then reach out a hand. "I will go to Friedrich. He will help Maman."

Friedrich. Friedrich. That name, Josephine thought as she struggled to her feet, it belonged to a man she knew. A very bad man. "You were supposed to end that romance."

Paulette bit her lip. "I did end it."

The girl was lying. There was not a whisper of doubt in Josephine's mind. She had a glimmer of a response to warn her granddaughter from this course. The argument was so clear. The words were on her tongue. And then, they were gone.

"Don't worry, Grandmère. I know how to save Maman." Paulette aimed her body toward the door, then slipped out of the room.

Josephine let her go, sensing she should stop her. But not sure why.

She needed to think. Organize her thoughts. Someone—a man—a fiend—had gone missing. No, not missing. Another ending. Guilt, it suddenly filled her until she was choking from the sensation. She took the emotion and turned it into resolve. She would remember. She wouldn't let the thought fade. She closed her eyes a moment, let her bottom lip go soft and reached for the memory. Reaching…reaching…

The darkness came quickly, spreading like flame to paper, and she let it swallow her whole. It was easy to bask in the silence that followed. Soothing, pleasant. Infuriating.

She placed her fingertips to her eyes, pressing hard. No use, she thought, dropping her hands. Her mind was blank again. There was a minor scuffle out in the hallway. The furious female voices forced open her eyes. She tilted her head, listening.

Footsteps pounding, coming closer, the door swinging

open, Gabrielle standing on the threshold. "Where is Paulette going in such a hurry?"

"I... Paulette?" Confusion blistered her throat, her mind. "Has the baby gone missing?"

"Oh, Grandmère." Gabrielle's shoulders slumped, then she glanced to the heavens. "Please, Lord. Please, not now."

Josephine heard her granddaughter's frustration, her fear. "The baby? Is she ill?"

"She's fine." Again, the frustration. Now peppered with impatience. Then, a snap of her shoulders. "I need to see your journal."

Darkness and silence, they filled her mind, rolled around in her brain. Darkness and silence. "I don't keep a journal."

"Oh, but you do."

In the next moment, Gabrielle was on her knees, tossing aside the rug that lay in the middle of the room, slipping her hands over the floorboards.

"What are you doing on the floor, dear?"

Her granddaughter didn't answer. She pushed and tugged at a wooden slat. Her fingers were clumsy, slick with sweat, trembling. Her face had gone unnaturally pale, but her eyes burned with determination. At last, she worked one of the planks free. A low, strangled hiss escaped her lips. "It's not here."

Josephine peered into the shallow crevice, seeing nothing but wood shavings and dust. What had her granddaughter hoped to find hidden in the floor?

Gabrielle jumped to her feet. Hands planted on her hips, her eyes darting around the room. She made a choking sound in her throat. "Where did you put it?"

"Put what, dear?" The fog in her mind was growing thicker. She rubbed at her temples. The darkness crept over her thoughts. She wanted to succumb. Oh, how she wanted to take refuge in the blessed nothingness that called.

But Gabrielle was speaking to her, *at* her, asking her questions. One, and then another. The words came at her too fast. Josephine couldn't keep up. She shook her head, forcing aside her confusion. "Does Marta know? Grandmère, does she know where you keep it?"

"Do I know where she keeps what?"

Gabrielle whirled around, the slab of wood still clasped in her hand. "My grandmother's journal. I need to know where she hides it."

The housekeeper swallowed, her nervousness plain as she caught Josephine's eye.

Josephine didn't know what to tell the other woman, except the one thing she knew to be true. "You may trust Gabrielle with my secrets."

Chapter Thirty-Nine

GABRIELLE

Gabrielle caught a familiar wisp of flour and sugar as Marta hastened past her. She watched the older woman approach her grandmother, her own thoughts swirling. Sorrow built, a need to mourn reared, but Gabrielle remained determined to think only of the journal, and finding the truth, not that her grandmother's closest confidante was a woman other than herself. The revelation did not belong in this moment.

Marta paused beside Josephine. "You are sure you want your granddaughter to read your private thoughts?"

Josephine hesitated. "I think, yes. *Oui.*"

"All right." The housekeeper continued to the nightstand, then shoved it aside before lowering to her hands and knees. She removed a section of the baseboard that ran along the floor and retrieved several items from the wall. She handed them, one by one, to Josephine. A diamond bracelet. A rope of pearls. More jewelry. A pair of silk stockings.

The treasures kept coming.

Gabrielle watched her grandmother accept each item, study it, then set it aside on the nightstand. Not a single light of recognition showed on her face. Josephine had retreated to some hidden place in her mind.

A sense of failure crept along Gabrielle's spine. She fought it. Von Schmidt wasn't dead, not by her grandmother's hand. Or her mother's. There was another explanation for his disappearance. There had to be. She would find it.

At last, Marta's hand came away from the wall with the leather-bound journal. Bypassing Josephine, she gave the book to Gabrielle. She opened the cover and began leafing through the pages as her grandmother looked on. Reading Josephine's most intimate thoughts felt wrong, a violation of her privacy. It had to be done.

Gabrielle continued flipping, skimming the pages. She kept searching for…she would know when she found it. There were long, emotional, beautifully worded entries that read almost like poetry. She ignored those—no time, no time—and concentrated on the lists. Then the entries that included dates and times and brief descriptions of events, many pertaining to the current war, some from the previous one.

The entries were as varied and sporadically penned and randomly phrased as Josephine's recent behavior. Gabrielle hadn't expected that. Nor had she expected the very real sense of sorrow fluttering in her stomach as she read what seemed to be the ramblings of a senile old woman. She continued flipping through the entries. The time it took gnawed at her patience.

She stopped at a list of family heirlooms. The hair on the back of her neck quivered. Some of the items had marks by them, others did not. She asked Marta for clarification.

The housekeeper studied the page. "Those—" she pressed

a fingertip to several items with marks next to them "—are the valuables your grandmother and I hid from the Germans."

Another jolt of surprise. No time for shock. "And the ones without the marks?"

"Those are the valuables that have gone missing since Hauptmann von Schmidt arrived."

The swine. She turned to a single entry about a shipment to Portugal. Her mind worked quickly, measuring, calculating, drawing conclusions until certainty filled her. This was it. Proof, or at least the *suggestion* of proof, that von Schmidt hadn't met his doom in this house. He'd run off to a neutral country to sit out the rest of the war at the LeBlancs' expense. It wasn't hard evidence, but perhaps enough to deflect suspicion away from her mother.

It was, quite possibly, even the truth. At the bottom of the page was a personal note. *Von Schmidt is a swine. Something must be done to stop him.*

More proof, pointing away from Hélène. And straight to Josephine. Gabrielle ripped the page from the journal. Confident she had a viable theory to bring to Mueller. But at what cost?

Her hands started to sweat. She had to think, had to protect both women. Her finger moved over Josephine's personal notation, smudging the ink, blurring the incriminating words.

Josephine came up beside Gabrielle. The older woman said nothing, not a single whisper of a word passed her lips. Only a firmness around the mouth showed her mood, a light in the eyes that spoke of quiet resolve. Gabrielle remembered how they'd stood in this same posture. The night before von Schmidt left for Paris. *Something must be done to stop him.*

Her finger moved faster, scrubbing at the page, erasing the evidence against her grandmother. Her throat went dry. It couldn't be true. Grandmère wasn't strong enough of body, or mind. Others were. Others loyal to their family. Gabrielle could think of at least three candidates, four if she included her mother.

Needing to know the truth, she asked Marta to follow her into the hallway. "Did you help my grandmother get rid of von Schmidt?"

"She would not have asked that of me."

"Would she have asked it of my mother?"

"*Non.* Of this I am absolutely certain."

Gabrielle wanted to be as confident as the other woman. Something held her back. She consulted the paper in her hand, then thought back to the page before it. Almost immediately, she remembered the entry, and the personal note beside it. *I have very brave men in my employ.*

Pierre. François. She needed to speak with them both. François first. He would be in the wine cellar. She hurtled toward the back of the house, chased by the roar of blood in her ears and the cold dread that her grandmother had followed through with her threat.

Chapter Forty

HÉLÈNE

They didn't start the interrogation immediately. They left Hélène in a tiny, windowless room, seated before a scarred table in a ladder-back chair, her arms secured at her back. The air smelled of sulfur and human sweat. Each of the four walls were painted a dark, dingy gray. A Nazi flag hung directly in front of her. Taunting her. Reminding her where she was and who held the power.

Hours passed. How many, she didn't know, but long enough that her bladder filled to capacity. She sensed this was some sort of intimidation tactic. By the time her interrogator entered the room, her head was pounding. Her stomach hurt and all she could think about was her need for relief.

Face expressionless, Detective Mueller took his place across from her on the other side of the table. He set a thick file on the scratched surface between them. She felt sick looking at all those papers. "Hélène Jobert-LeBlanc," he said, opening the cover. "Is that your full name?"

"*Oui.*"

"Jobert is your birth name? Your, how do you say it in French? Your *nom de jeune fille?*"

"Yes." She lied with remarkable ease. She'd had decades of practice. "Jobert was my name before I married Étienne LeBlanc."

He made no comment.

Returning his gaze to the dossier, he searched several pages. Hélène shifted uncomfortably in the chair and feigned a haughtiness she did not feel. "Am I being charged with a crime?"

Mueller glanced sharply at her. "We will get to that in good time."

The questions began in earnest then. He asked her when von Schmidt had requisitioned her home. The details of his daily routine. On and on, the same questions over and over. "When did your relationship become intimate?"

He caught her by surprise, though she did her best to conceal her reaction. She pondered the merits of truth over lie. She chose evasion. "I was not aware I was being watched so closely."

"Do you work for the Free French?"

She froze in her chair. "I do not."

"Really?" He flattened his hand on the file. "We have information that someone from your home has been relaying vital information about the destination of champagne shipments from Reims to certain war zones."

Hélène's mind raced, recalling overheard conversations between Helmut and others. None of them were about champagne shipments. "I am at a loss."

"Hauptmann von Schmidt kept detailed records in his desk.

As his secretary, you had access to this information." He did not refer to the file when he said the words. "Are you still claiming it was not you?"

She crossed her legs, fumbling for calm. "It was not me."

"You answer too quickly."

"The truth always comes quickly," she said, unable to contain a hint of defiance in her tone.

He seemed to consider this. "If you didn't pass along the information, someone else in your home did. Perhaps you have a name for me."

Her fear peeled away, exposing her fury. "Are you asking me to betray one of my own family members?"

"I am suggesting you think carefully before you answer my questions. Cooperation with the Free French is an act of treason."

The threat settled over her. She thought she'd been arrested for von Schmidt's murder. That, she could understand. She'd plotted, and planned, and was certain she could make him disappear. Her mistake had been waiting until morning. Von Schmidt had departed the château before dawn, giving her no chance to rid the world of one more Nazi rat.

As if the detective's thoughts tracked in a similar direction, the questioning returned to von Schmidt's disappearance. He stopped only when a knock on the door heralded one of the local French police. "Detective Mueller, sir. Pardon me. We have a situation that needs your immediate attention."

"It cannot wait?"

"*Non.*"

"Very well." He pushed his chair back. "A moment, please," he said to Hélène. Gathering up the file, he stepped toward the doorway.

Before he left, she requested the use of the facilities.

He directed his icy regard over her. Then, to her surprise,

granted her request. He did not, however, uncuff her hands. "When she is finished," he told the guard before he left, "take her to one of the cells."

For a terrifying moment, she could not rise. Her legs were boneless, so that she had to lean on the table to find her balance. After she found blessed relief, and the guard had shoved her into a cell, her hands finally free of their manacles, she thought she heard the heartbreaking sound of soft, pitiful weeping.

She tried to pinpoint the source, but a hard, angry masculine voice dominated all other noises in the building. "I demand you arrest her."

Hélène thought she recognized the furious tone of that voice. It belonged to a man, younger than Detective Mueller. It belonged to—*no, mon Dieu, no.* The voice belonged to the lieutenant Paulette had been sneaking out to meet.

"Arrest her on what charge?" This, from Detective Mueller.

"She is a liar, just like her mother. She..." Hélène couldn't hear the rest of the lieutenant's accusation. Only the weeping, now gut-wrenching sobs that belonged to Hélène's child. Her baby. She would know the sound of Paulette's tears anywhere.

Oh, Paulette, what have you done?

Hélène pressed her hand to her mouth to stifle her own sob. She felt a strange sense of disorientation, like falling endlessly into a void.

"You have proof of this, Lieutenant?"

"She told me herself. And this girl, this child, she is complicit in the lie." The lieutenant's voice held a savage tenor. "She must be punished."

"I am French," Paulette wailed. "My mother is French. We are—"

A loud crack cut her off. Someone had hit her daughter. Hélène went blind with rage.

"I've heard enough. Take her away."

"Please, no. I can explain." Paulette's panicked cries were ignored. "I am French. My father's family is of noble blood."

There was no response to her daughter's claim. Mueller seemed solely interested in praising the lieutenant. "You were right to bring the girl to me. You are an asset to the Third Reich, Lieutenant Weber. I will make certain you receive a commendation. You're dismissed."

The click of heels, then the dreaded "Heil Hitler."

Hélène could feel the sting of tears at the back of her throat. She knew then, with unavoidable certainty, her time was up. Her daughter had gone to her Nazi friend and told him everything. *Oh, Paulette.* All the terrible compromises Hélène had made to hide her identity, all the sinful deeds she'd done to stave off discovery, all the lies she'd told to protect her family. They had been for nothing. Deep down, she'd always known the truth would come out.

She'd thought that when the moment came, she would be ready to face the consequences. And she was. For herself. She would never be ready for her daughter to suffer alongside her.

The guard appeared in the hallway—his hand buried in Paulette's hair as he dragged her along behind him. *My baby. My child.*

The girl stumbled, gripping her jailer's wrist, begging for mercy.

He wrenched open the cell door and tossed Paulette through. She landed at Hélène's feet. She quickly pulled her daughter into her arms, drew her up onto the dirty cot and waited for the girl to catch her breath.

Don't panic, Hélène told herself. *Think clearly. Comfort your child.* "Paulette."

"Maman?" Paulette lifted her head, revealing eyes empty of light. Of hope.

Hélène's anguish was complete. "My dear sweet child," she whispered. "I'm so sorry."

Paulette stared at her with wide, wounded eyes. "This is all my fault," she said. "I should never have gone to Friedrich. He claimed he loved me. He said I could trust him. He lied."

"Hush, now. None of this is your fault." *It is mine.*

"But it is my fault, all of it. I told your secret and now we are both in trouble."

Yes, Paulette had told her secret. A secret Hélène should never have shared with her daughter. But maybe Paulette was still safe. She wasn't, by law, a Jew. "You are guilty only of trusting the wrong man."

Paulette didn't seem to hear her. Her eyes clouded over as more tears tracked down her cheeks. "He promised me we would sort everything out once we got to the police station." She swiped at her eyes, gave a bitter laugh. "He was very kind and understanding. He kept reassuring me all would turn out well. And I believed him."

Oh, Paulette, Hélène thought on a sigh. *How could you have been so naïve?*

"He told that awful Gestapo agent you're a Jew. He held nothing back. He called you terrible names. He called you—" she choked on a sob "—a dirty, filthy Jew. He said I was no better."

It was not the first time Hélène had heard the slur, though not since she was a girl.

"They're going to send you away, aren't they?"

Hélène had no fancy lies to give her daughter. Not a single word of hope. She only had the truth. Stark and painful. "Yes, Paulette. They're going to send me away."

And she couldn't stop it from happening. She didn't mourn for herself, but for her daughters. And for Josephine. They had known the truth and kept it to themselves. That alone was a crime against the Third Reich. Would Gabrielle and Josephine would be arrested next? Hélène had brought ruin to her family. Her greatest fear realized.

The guard, a member of the French police, entered the cell again.

She struggled to stand. But he didn't look at her. He reached for Paulette's arm and yanked her to her feet. Paulette shattered into uncontrollable sobs. "Maman."

Hélène was by her daughter's side in a heartbeat. "No, please." She clawed at the guard's arm. "She is just a girl. She did nothing wrong. It was me. I confess. I—"

"Shut up." He placed his hand over her face and shoved her to the ground. She hit hard, but immediately tried to rise. He kicked her in the stomach. "Stay down."

Again, she ignored the pain and tried to stand. She was too slow. He'd already dragged Paulette out of the cell. The girl was blubbering, begging, pleading, her words incomprehensible.

Her daughter was breaking right before her eyes.

"Please," Hélène begged, lurching forward, reaching for her daughter. "Take me. Not her. It's me you want."

He slammed the door on her pleas. She had a moment of complete and utter despair. *It's over.* Paulette would never withstand interrogation. Hélène wanted to close her eyes, to find a prayer, an image for the future. All she saw was death.

Chapter Forty-One

GABRIELLE

Gabrielle took the familiar route at record speed. Down the twenty-one stone steps, through the vineyard, past the champagne house and onward to the miles of limestone caves cut beneath the chalky earth.

Dusk had fallen over the vineyard. The sky overhead was caught in that otherworldly moment between day and night, where light battled the dark, but in the end, always lost the fight. Suddenly, she remembered that night long ago, when she'd hidden the champagne behind a collection of strategically placed stones. She remembered how François had seen her faulty construction. And again, when Detective Mueller had shown uncommon interest.

It always seemed to come back to the wall, the first of her many lies.

The panic tried to rise, to blunt her edge, to make her weak. Fear was also there, in her throat, on the back of her tongue.

She was at the door now, plowing through. "François," she called out, blinking rapidly to adjust her vision to the low light. "François, are you here?"

No answer.

She continued down the corridors, calling out until she reached the end. She stared at the fake wall. The lone bulb flickered, dimming the light, making it hard to see. Her eyes closed momentarily, while her mind raced. Von Schmidt had wanted LeBlanc champagne. And, it would seem, their valuables, stealing them little by little until he'd amassed a small fortune.

Then, there'd been his sudden and vigorous support of the Nazis' policy to rid the world of Jews. No one hearing him would doubt his loyalty to the Third Reich. But one thing Gabrielle knew for certain. Von Schmidt's loyalty was always to von Schmidt.

Her theory made sense.

She wanted to rush to the police station and present her evidence. She couldn't go to Mueller without the facts. All of them.

Footsteps sounded behind her, penetrating her thoughts. Not François. She knew his gait. Instinct told her to keep silent. She circled around, backpedaling to her left, into the shadows, staying out of sight, pressing deeper into the dark.

Paulette's lieutenant stepped into the circle of dim light. He had a gun in one hand, a torch in the other. He was looking for something—someone. Paulette? Not here. He would have to know not to look for her sister here. Or had this been where they'd met for their trysts?

Then why draw his weapon?

Gabrielle watched him shining the torch along the walls, down the hallway, up to the ceiling. No, he was not here for romance.

She kept silent, absolutely silent. And absolutely, perfectly still. The beam of light slashed at her feet, caught hold, then traveled up her body and shone in her face, momentarily blinding her. "Ah, there you are." His voice held a satisfied edge. "Your man, the cellar master, I think you call him, told me I would find you here."

François would have told this man nothing. He was here because he knew they kept the special champagne in this section of the cave. He'd been among Mueller's soldiers on several of the raids. That meant, like so many before him, the lieutenant was here to rob her family.

"Must you shine your torch at me?" She covered her face with her arm. "I can't think properly with all that light in my eyes."

He lowered the torch.

She lowered her arm.

They stared at one another for a full five seconds, both blinking rapidly. Gabrielle took control of the conversation. "Are you here for the champagne?"

He made a scoffing sound in his throat. "It's not the champagne I want."

"My sister isn't at home right now."

"No, she is not," he said, his gaze furious, his face red. "She has turned out to be quite the disappointment."

Gabrielle didn't like what she heard in his voice. "What have you done to Paulette?"

"She is sitting in a jail cell, where she belongs for telling her lies. And now you will join her there."

Gabrielle stared at the gun pointed at her head. One bullet. It would take only one. To her head, her heart. A quick death. She could scream.

No one would hear.

"I know the truth about your mother. I know she is a Jew." He sounded disgusted, almost petulant, as if this discovery was a personal offense. "And now the Gestapo knows as well."

Ice spread in her lungs. She looked at him through a haze. Her hope was gone, vanished like a mirage already faded from view. Gabrielle knew in her bones that her mother would disappear by morning. She couldn't save her now. Maybe she never could.

She could save the other members of her family. *Not if you are dead. Not if you are arrested.* "I won't leave with you, Lieutenant. I won't let you arrest me."

"You speak as if the decision is yours." He advanced on her, his features distorting in the low, flickering light. "The females in your family are very free with their affections. What do you expect from filthy Jews?"

Gabrielle knocked the gun from his hand, the move swift and surprising. The weapon hit the stone at their feet, a shot fired off, hitting limestone. Only limestone. Praise God.

Eyes bulging with fury, the lieutenant lurched for the gun. She kicked it away, and watched it disappear under a rack of champagne.

"You will regret that." He slapped her, hard. So hard her teeth rattled. Pain bloomed in her cheek and jaw. She thought of nothing but escape and leaped toward freedom.

He caught her quickly, a swift grab of her arm, and spun her to face him, pulling her close, closer. She beat at him with her fists, managed to get in a few good blows, including one to his face. He reared back, and she twisted hard.

His hands slipped. She sprinted to her left, careened into a rack of wine bottles. Several toppled from their nest, the glass shattering at her feet. She lost her balance and reached out for purchase. Nothing there.

Falling. She was falling. She waved her arms. Caught her balance.

He wheeled around and came for her again.

He was faster, stronger, his legs longer, his training superior. He caught her again, drove her to the ground and pinned her beneath him. "I made your sister pay for her lies. Now it's your turn. When I am finished, the Gestapo can have what is left."

He was going to hurt her. She could attempt to plead and reason and beg, but it wouldn't stop him. Nothing would stop him. That was her truth now.

Gabrielle shifted beneath him, trying to get away. But he was so much bigger and stronger than she, and he had violence in his eyes. He slapped her again. Stars exploded behind her eyelids and she found herself begging, after all. "Please, don't do this."

"Shut up." He wrapped his fingers around her throat and squeezed.

Gasping for breath, her lungs on fire, she threw her hand out, connected with cold glass. Not broken, fully intact. Rescue. Salvation. She closed her hand over the bottle. The champagne. Always the champagne. Her purpose. Her life's work.

Her deliverance.

She twisted her wrist and, in a burst of unexpected strength, swung her arm in a wide arc. The crack of bottle to skull was deafening. He slumped forward, landing hard on top of her. His weight was unbearable, suffocating. She pushed and shoved. And then, finally, squirmed out from under him and clambered to her feet.

His body lay still, unmoving, a huge mass on the floor. *Nobody could survive that blow.*

Had she killed him?

Breathing raggedly, she knelt beside the motionless body, sent her fingers running across his throat. His skin was warm beneath her touch. Then, there, a pulse. Thready and slow. Alive. He was alive. She was not a murderer.

She stood, and then looked down at the lieutenant. No, she was not a murderer. But she was in trouble.

Chapter Forty-Two

JOSEPHINE

Josephine couldn't find her journal. It wasn't where it should be. She fitted the baseboard back in place and stood. She frowned, fearing she'd misplaced it. A deadly mistake. She ran her gaze around the perimeter of the room, searching for some small item, a pen, a piece of fabric, anything, that would spark her memory, unwilling to admit, even to herself, that she'd forgotten where she'd put the book. *Badly done, Josephine.* She told the pages secrets, some her own and some that belonged to others.

Anyone could have found it.

She sank onto the bed and glanced around helplessly. As a child she'd spent her nights writing in her journal, filling the pages with her hopes and dreams. When she filled one book, she began a new one, recording details of the future she would have, wondering if her life would be a happy one, or one full of sorrow like her mother's.

The men in her family died young.

But that wasn't what she was supposed to be thinking about. A blackbird landed on the ledge outside her window, edging cautiously along the sill, as birds often did when they were on unfamiliar territory. The creature stared at her through the glass. His small dark eyes blinking at her knowingly, as if he understood she was losing her mind. He could not know such a thing. He could not know.

She went to the window to shoo him away. Below, in the final burst of light from the sun, she saw her granddaughter moving quickly, practically running. The young woman flew across the terrace, disappeared over the balustrade, then reappeared at the very edge of the vineyard. She didn't look right or left, only straight ahead. She was holding something in her hand, Josephine couldn't see what it was. A man in a black Nazi uniform, the crisp red armband with the swastika visible even from this distance, appeared in the vineyard. Moving like a predator.

Josephine had seen this man and this woman come together in the vineyard.

The scene was all wrong.

Wrong man. Wrong woman.

Find the book.

She quickly retreated from the window and began a frantic search, tossing pillows to the floor, blankets, sheets. She tore apart the closet next. Ravaged the drawers. Somewhere along the way she forgot what she was looking for, then remembered— the book with her secrets—and began searching harder.

In the bathroom, she caught sight of her reflection and cried out as she saw the crazed look in the overwrought, unfocused eyes. The sweep of tangled gray hair billowing around her face. So, this was what she'd become.

Grimacing, she returned to the bedroom she'd ransacked herself. It took several slow intakes of air for her to slow the wild beating of her heart. She wanted to turn off her mind, to forget that unhinged woman in the mirror. *You are Josephine Fouché-LeBlanc. You are strong and capable. You are better than this.*

She emptied her mind of the panic, of the blackness creeping in until finally—finally—she was thinking clearly, coolly. With purpose. A name came to her then. Marta. Marta was the keeper of Josephine's memory now. She would know what had become of the journal.

Josephine swung open the door and called out into the abandoned hallway. "Marta, hurry. I need you. Come quick."

At least two seconds passed, then she vaulted toward the stairs, down the first flight, and the second. She couldn't wait for the housekeeper to come to her. Marta met her in the foyer and took her arm. "What is this? Josephine, what is wrong?"

"The book. Marta, I can't find the book."

"You mean your journal. I have it. You gave it to your granddaughter Gabrielle, who then gave it to me."

A pounding filled her head, loud and insistent. A memory flashed. The woman in the vineyard. The man following her. The book. That incessant pounding again. Marta letting her go, turning…

Someone at the door.

Marta moved quickly.

The man in the black Nazi uniform, the crisp red armband with the Nazi swastika, standing on the threshold, holding on to her granddaughter's arm. Again, the scene was all wrong. Different man. Different woman.

Josephine shook her head. The gesture served its purpose, replacing her confusion with clear thinking. "Detective Mueller, I demand to know what you are doing with your hand on my granddaughter."

If he noticed the angry intonation, he didn't react. "I am releasing her into your custody. You will want to keep a close eye on her in the future. She should not be out past curfew."

His words confused Josephine. He'd taken Hélène away with him this morning. But was returning with Paulette. "What of my daughter-in-law?"

"The matter is more complicated with Madame LeBlanc." Without asking permission, he stepped across the threshold, his hand still on Paulette's arm. Only then did Josephine notice her granddaughter's red-rimmed eyes, her puffy cheeks, the subdued posture.

This was not the Paulette she knew. The girl's mouth was drawn, and she seemed incapable of walking on her own, as evidenced by her leaning into Detective Mueller as he guided her into the foyer.

A foul Nazi should not be allowed to touch her granddaughter. Josephine quickly took Paulette's hand. Marta moved to the other side. Together, they half carried, half dragged the girl to a chair.

Eyes void of emotion, Paulette stayed seated, upright and silent. Unresponsive, at first, until Josephine said her name. Then, she began crying. Hot, miserable tears. The girl tried to speak, but her sentences ran together, and she made no sense.

Nothing about this made sense.

Mueller spoke into the confusion. "She was brought to me by her—" he seemed to search for the right word "—friend. The lieutenant wanted her arrested, but she is guilty of no crime. The Nuremberg laws are clear on this. Her mother, on the other hand, is not so fortunate."

"You arrested Hélène? On what charge?" Josephine demanded, then remembered the missing German. "You have news of *Capitaine* von Schmidt?"

"That matter is still under investigation." He seemed to think over his next words. "I have arrested your daughter-in-law for lying about being a Jew and for falsifying her papers accordingly."

He spoke the words simply. Without emotion. Josephine

could only gape. Hélène's secret was out and here this man stood, a representative of the Gestapo, calm and detached as he gave her the news.

Was he waiting for confirmation, a confession of her own?

He would get none of that from Josephine Fouché-LeBlanc.

She was guilty, all of them were guilty. They had committed crimes against the Third Reich, and he knew. Somehow, he knew that they had lied and schemed to protect each other. They would lose everything now. Their champagne house, the château, possibly their lives.

Battling furiously against the pain in her heart, Josephine held the man's stare. There was nothing there, no indication what he would do next.

What was he waiting for? Perhaps he wanted the women together, so he could cart them off as a family and make an example of them for their neighbors.

Then why did he not have an entire battalion with him?

"Where is your other granddaughter?"

She said nothing. Only held his stare.

"Where is Madame Dupree?" he asked again, the first signs of impatience in his voice. "You will tell me where she is," he demanded.

Josephine looked up into his eyes, scowling, and searched through the wreckage of her mind for something she was supposed to remember about her granddaughter. Gabrielle. Moving through the vineyard. The other man following her. "You are not the only German to come seeking her."

The detective stiffened. Something came and went in his eyes. Alarm? Fear? "There's been another?"

"The lieutenant," she said. "Paulette's friend. He followed Gabrielle into the wine cellar."

Mueller was on the move before she finished the thought. "*Mein Gott*. Pray I'm not too late."

Chapter Forty-Three

GABRIELLE

Gabrielle let several minutes pass. Then she crouched down and checked the lieutenant's pulse again. Thready. Weak. But alive. He was still alive.

And still a threat.

He could come around at any minute. Then what would she do? Subdue him again. *Subdue him now.* The gun. She needed to find his gun. She searched beneath the rack of champagne where she'd kicked it, careful to avoid the shards of glass from the broken bottles. There, she saw it. Her hand reached for the weapon. Her fingertips touched the metal. She could end this with a single pull of the trigger. She paused, God's words running through her mind.

Be not overcome of evil, but overcome evil with good.

A variety of emotions followed the thought. Gabrielle had done things in this war of which she never thought herself capable. She'd stolen. She'd lied. She'd risked her life and that of others. She would not commit murder.

Her throat hurt where he'd grabbed her. She touched it. Her head hurt. She touched that, too. Everything hurt. She took shallow, steady breaths. Lieutenant Weber had come to harm her. She'd fought for her life and prevailed. There was no reason for this to go poorly. Unless she panicked. She made herself think about next steps.

Something had to be done with him.

She could not do it alone. Her gaze landed on the wall she and François had rebuilt together. François. It was a lot to ask. The stakes were higher. The risks greater. There was no other way. *We are at war,* she told herself. Survival came at a price to the soul.

The sound of footsteps spun her around.

Too late. Detective Mueller was there, ramrod stiff, a pistol in his hand, pointed at her heart. Gabrielle watched him with a surreal feeling, even now, knowing he was everything she feared in the enemy, hated even, she found herself noting the handsome face, the athletic build, the pale blue gaze. Not hard. Not soft. But steady.

"Let me see your hands." He spoke in perfect French. Then repeated the command again in English with a British accent. The change in his voice was remarkable. Confusing.

Who was this man? It was not the first time her mind had pondered the question.

"Hands up," he said again.

Gabrielle swallowed and did as he commanded, only to find the pistol pointed at her head now. He was going to shoot her.

This place, she thought. *Where the lies began. This is where I will die.*

She thought of the family she had left. Josephine, too old to defend herself. Paulette, too young and naïve and reckless.

Gabrielle must save herself, for them. "I didn't kill the lieutenant," she said in French. Then switched to German. "He's
not dead. You can check for yourself."

Mueller pulled back the hammer of his pistol. The future
came and went with the sound—voices of children she would
never have, sounds she would never hear again. A grape press,
the snick of clippers to a vine. Her grandmother's laughter,
her mother spritzing perfume at her neck, the slow release of
a champagne cork.

Gaze on her face, Mueller took one step, and then another. His eyes had narrowed to tiny slits. A man taking aim.
She tried to scream. It had no sound. Nothing but air forced
through her throat. His finger squeezed the trigger.

The bullet went wide and hit the wall high and to the right
of her head. Her ears rang from the percussion. Bits of stone
rained down, sticking in her hair, peppering her shoulders,
her arms. A rush of terror flooded her brain. And all she could
think was that he'd redirected his aim. The bullet penetrated
the wall mere inches above her head. One shot was all it took
to expose the room where she and François had painstakingly
concealed the greatest of her family's treasure. Proof she'd
committed treason.

Mueller would arrest her now.

But he wasn't looking at her. Or the wall. He holstered his
gun and focused on the lieutenant's prone body. Bending over,
he checked for a pulse, ran his hands over the lolling head, his
fingers coming away with blood. "He's alive."

He stood, wiped his hands on the handkerchief he pulled
from a pocket, then moved to stand before her. She felt tears
on her face. She didn't want to cry. But couldn't seem to stop
herself. She started to shake uncontrollably. "Who are you?"
she asked.

"A friend." The words refused to register. Her mind could

not accept them, or the voice that spoke her language like that of a native.

His fingertips touched her throat, the move almost reverent, though his eyes held great fury. "The lieutenant did this to you?"

She nodded, feeling relief. Regret. Confusion. Fear. "Who are you?" she asked again.

His response was the same as before. This time in English, spoken with the British accent of the peerage. And…his eyes. That pale, pale blue stared back at her free of hate, of cruelty, of things she'd thought were a part of his very nature.

Warmth took up residence in her heart. She wanted to believe this man was more than he seemed. That he was, indeed, a friend. It would be a foolish mistake on her part. And yet, she found herself saying in a voice full of hope, "I don't understand."

"I know, and there is very little time for lengthy explanations." He returned his attention to the prone body, a hiss slipping past his lips.

Not even sure this moment was real, confused by the contradictory emotions rolling around in her heart, her head, Gabrielle felt the need to defend herself. "He attacked me," she said, her voice cracking. "He tried to strangle me and I…" She swallowed. "I stopped him. I didn't plan to kill him. I just. He was on top of me. And I—I didn't kill him. I—"

She wanted to say more, but her tongue felt too thick for her mouth.

"It's all right. You're safe now." The words sounded rough in his throat. "You're safe."

His hand moved to her cheek, his thumb wiping at the tears leaking from her eyes.

She blinked at his show of tenderness. His behavior was at odds with everything she thought she knew about him. She didn't know what to make of the gentle touch as he cupped her chin. The long stare as he pulled his hand away. The lack of derision on his face.

Only sorrow in his features now. Also, strength.

The next thing she knew, she was stepping toward him, wishing to be in his arms, to rest in the knowledge that he was, as he claimed, a friend. Impossible. He was a Nazi. Gestapo.

Or was that the lie? Was Wolfgang Mueller, as she'd suspected, more than he seemed?

Gabrielle didn't know what to think anymore, what to believe, who to trust. The world suddenly went dark, her vision as black as night, and she felt herself swaying, falling. She didn't try to catch herself.

And then, she was in his arms, her face pressed into his neck, his smell of sandalwood, bergamot and lime encircling her. The scent of her enemy. Bringing her comfort. Her tears flowed freely, soaking into his neck, the shirt collar below, while his hand stroked her hair.

Her thoughts were disjointed. Friend or foe? Enemy or ally?

Both, neither, she reveled in the strength of his arms wrapped around her. She could feel the hard lines of his biceps sheltering her in place.

Then, she remembered who he was. The world he represented. His arrival this morning on her doorstep and her mother's arrest, and she shoved out of his embrace. He gave not an ounce of protest. She stared at him, her breath bursting from her chest, horrified at herself, ashamed of her weakness and her betrayal of the husband she'd lost a lifetime ago.

How could she have found even a moment of rest from this man, her enemy. She tasted copper in the back of her throat. The taste of her humiliation.

"You have questions."

She nodded.

"They will have to wait," he said, not unkindly.

She nodded again, grateful for the reprieve. She needed to catch her breath, while her mind reviewed each moment she'd spent in this man's company. The small favors he'd afforded her. The tiny protections. The warnings she'd thought were threats but now understood to be protections.

Who are you?

He spent the next few minutes securing the lieutenant's hands behind his back, rolling him over, then propping him against a wine barrel. As she watched, Gabrielle knew she was witnessing a man proficient in all aspects of police work. She now knew what to ask. "You're really Gestapo?"

He presented a tight, uncomfortable smile, followed by a very small nod. He walked over to the wall, rested his palm beside the gaping hole he'd blown into the stones, peered into the room beyond. "Not what anyone would call quality work, but acceptable to the untrained eye." He spoke in French, the hideous German accent no longer woven through the words. "The spiders are a nice touch."

Gabrielle tried not to show her shock. "You are Gestapo, but—" she paused "—not a Nazi."

As soon as the words left her mouth she knew them to be true.

His words confirmed her suspicions. "I work in the dark to serve the light."

Yes, she thought. Of course. All along, something in her had recognized the good in him.

He looked down at the lieutenant, frowned. "I'll take care of this problem."

Despite her confusion, and the pain in her throat, and what felt like daggers being plunged into her brain, Gabrielle rearranged in her mind everything she knew about this man. She placed past events in a different order. She reframed the facts, the clues that had been there all long, the mixed messages, the warnings, and then, in a brief flash of insight, the British accent.

Her mind worked it all out, and she knew the truth in her heart. "You are a secret agent working for the Allies."

"It is better for you if I don't respond."

"But how is that even possible?"

He turned thoughtful, considering, then gave one short nod as if coming to a decision. "I have been embedded in Germany since before Hitler became Chancellor in 1933. I attended university in Berlin, then worked my way up through the ranks of the police. It was a natural progression to move into a position with the Gestapo."

While she did the math in her brain, calculating his age, and how long he'd been undercover—nearly a decade—he explained that his mother was from German nobility, his father an English code breaker who'd worked for British naval intelligence during the last war.

Mueller had spent most of his summers in Germany with his mother's family, but his loyalties had always been with England. He'd followed in his father's footsteps and joined the intelligence unit of the British army. Hitler rose to power that same year, and Mueller had been tasked with going undercover for an indeterminate amount of time. "There are others like me, in all branches of the German government."

But he'd been assigned to the Gestapo, the most ruthless arm of Hitler's military. If he was found out, Gabrielle shook her head, hardly able to comprehend what the Nazis would do to him.

How lonely his life must be, how utterly isolated he must feel. A decade away from family and friends, with only himself to rely on. No confidante. No helpmate. No partner. How well she understood his burdens. And yet, his sacrifice made hers seem small.

"You must forget what I just told you."

She smiled through her tears, realizing she wasn't crying for herself anymore. Or not only for herself, but also for him, and the uncertainty of his future. "I am very good at keeping secrets from the Germans."

"It is not only the Germans you must avoid." He took her hands. "There are people in the British government who will do whatever it takes to ensure my cover is never blown. You understand what I'm saying?"

She thought, maybe, she did. His trust in her was humbling. She owed him the same. And told him of her resistance work.

"I know. Your father-in-law gave you up."

"Max… He— Oh, Max."

"He told me only after I helped him escape across the border. Before I handed him over to the British, he asked me to watch over you."

"You helped Max escape France?" There was wonder in her voice, relief.

He went on to explain how *Kriminalkommissar* Mueller earned his reputation. People did, indeed, disappear once he took them into custody. But instead of executing them, or sending them to the camps, he'd been providing safe passage across the border.

"You save them all?"

"I do what I can. It is not always enough. Choices have to be made. I fail too often and succeed not enough. So, again, I will say, for your safety, Gabrielle, you must tell no one who I really am."

She understood the stakes. And yet, found herself asking, "What is your real name?"

"You can only know me as Wolfgang Mueller."

She remembered the coded telegrams. He'd been protecting her since his arrival. "Why watch over me?" she asked. "Is it only because Max asked it of you?"

"Have you not guessed?" The tenderness in his eyes was that of a man struggling with a depth of caring. "It hit me the first time I saw you. Your fierceness, your strength of character. You stood on that sidewalk and looked me straight in the eye. You never buckled, never wavered. Not then. Not at the table when your grandmother told the same story three times. Not later that night, in this cave, at this very wall, when I openly questioned its construction."

"I never understood why I couldn't hate you," she admitted. "I wanted to. At times, I think maybe I did. But I couldn't hold on to the emotion for long. I think, perhaps, despite that wretched uniform, I sensed the light in you, some part of me recognized the man you truly are."

He placed her palm flat against his heart, held it there with his own. "Although you have only known me as your enemy, I have admired your courage from the start. I—"

A moan from the lieutenant cut him off midspeech. "You need to go now."

Gabrielle followed the direction of his gaze. "What do you plan to do with him?"

"I am very good at making people disappear." He glanced at the hole in the wall. "I will also fix that."

She asked one more question, this one about her mother. "You will let her go now?"

"I'm afraid matters are not that simple. She is the prime suspect in von Schmidt's disappearance."

"She didn't kill him. I have proof." Gabrielle showed him the page she'd ripped out of Josephine's journal.

His eyes narrowed over the paper. "It's possible von Schmidt ran, but it will take me time to investigate." He turned thoughtful, tapped his fingertips against his thigh. "All right.

Let's say I solve the mystery of his disappearance, and your mother is exonerated. There is still the matter of her falsified papers and her Jewish heritage. The lieutenant may have told others besides me."

Closing her eyes, Gabrielle took a deep gulp of air. "My mother is as good as dead."

"Your mother must disappear, the sooner the better."

Gabrielle knew he was right. She didn't like it, but she knew Hélène would never be safe in France with the Nazis in control. "Will you let me see her one last time?"

He didn't respond, but there was an instant of connection, of understanding between them, before he went, with economy and grace, like a panther, to the spot where he'd propped up the lieutenant. After checking for a pulse, nodding slightly, he secured the man's feet, retied his hands, covered his mouth, then tied him to a wine barrel.

Returning to Gabrielle, he took her arm. "Come with me."

He led her through the labyrinth of corridors, his hold light, barely a suggestion of touch. She didn't realize he was granting her request, not fully, until they left the château, traveled to Reims, and she was standing outside her mother's jail cell with his whispered warning ringing in her ears. "The walls in this building have ears."

He left them alone, his trust in her complete.

Gabrielle would honor that faith and heed his warning. She wrapped her hands around the bars and said, "Maman."

Chapter Forty-Four

HÉLÈNE

Someone was calling her.

She heard it again.

"Maman." Hélène bolted upright.

At the sight of Gabrielle's drawn face, the breath went out of her in a slow, painful exhalation. She felt surprise, shock even, that her daughter stood on the opposite side of the jail cell. She hadn't been arrested, then. And, despite the events earlier in the day, Paulette hadn't been arrested, either.

Both her daughters were safe.

Hélène wanted to sing praise to the Lord, to show her faith in worship. She'd heard Detective Mueller quote the Nuremberg Laws earlier, the ones that condemned Hélène for being a *Mischling* of the first degree who'd attended synagogue with her father. The same laws also pardoned her daughters because of their diluted blood. Part of her knew only bliss—Gabrielle and Paulette were safe—but part of her knew great sadness. Gabrielle was here to say goodbye.

She would accept this unexpected gift. And return it with one of her own, words that should have been said years ago. "You are the daughter I never deserved, but the one who brings me the greatest joy. Live well, *ma fille*. Love hard. And always let the Lord be your guide and your light."

With a grief-stricken cry, Gabrielle reached through the bars and enfolded their hands. It was then that Hélène noticed the scarf around her daughter's neck. It was a nice touch that highlighted her gray-green eyes. Now was not a time to discuss fashion.

They didn't speak of von Schmidt's disappearance. They didn't speak of the labor camps or the fate of a woman with Jewish blood in her veins or why the police station was empty but for a single guard from the French police. They spoke only of the man they both loved. "Your father would be proud of the woman you've become."

"I miss him, still," she whispered, her eyes bright with the tears she fought valiantly to hold at bay. "I will miss you, I think, even more."

Hélène's heart ached at the knowledge that Gabrielle knew her flaws, knew the sins she'd committed, and still gave her no condemnation. She had to bite the inside of her lip then, to stop herself from breaking. "You cannot know how honored I am to call you my daughter and how very much I love you."

"I love you, too, Maman." The voice came at her like a dream, just a little hazy, a little distant. "You will survive this."

She knew she wouldn't. There was no more fight left in her. Sighing softly, she pulled her hands away, reached up to touch her daughter's cheek. "I have one final request."

"Whatever it is," Gabrielle said, "ask. I will do it."

"Send Paulette to Paris, to my friend Mademoiselle Ballard." The obscure yet talented fashion designer had been one of Hélène's closest friends, and far too mercenary to shut down her atelier during the war. "She will employ the girl in her shop and teach her skills that will serve her after the war."

"Why do you protect her still?" Gabrielle asked, a chill in her voice. "When she is the reason you are locked in this cage?"

"It is as much my fault as it is hers. I told her my secret. That was my mistake."

"Why, Maman? Why did you tell her?"

Hélène had asked herself the same question many times today. The answer never changed. "I had hoped she would understand the reason she needed to end her liaison with Lieutenant Weber. She did not break off the affair."

"I'm not surprised."

Unsure how to interpret Gabrielle's tone, Hélène told her how Paulette had turned to her beau. "She thought he loved her enough to help me. She made a terrible mistake trusting him."

Despite her momentary recoiling, and the look of judgment that filled her eyes, Gabrielle merely nodded.

Hélène thought about how broken Paulette had been, sitting beside her in this cell. The remorse in her posture, in her words—they had been real. Would her shame be enough to change a lifetime of selfish regard for no one but herself? "She cannot stay in Reims. Detective Mueller let her go because of her French blood. By definition, she is not a Jew. The laws protect her, both of you, but the lieutenant may press the issue of your complicity in my lies."

Breaking eye contact, Gabrielle lowered her head, took a ragged breath but said nothing.

"You will see to this matter for me?" Hélène asked. "You

will contact my friend and make the arrangements for your sister's departure from Reims?"

"I will."

"*Bien.*" Hélène gave her daughter the details she would need to make the arrangements.

No words were exchanged for several seconds after she finished. Hélène felt Gabrielle's sorrow, saw it in the tears gathering in her eyes. This truly was goodbye.

She knew that now, accepted it.

She'd imagined the end of her life would be harder to face. All she felt was relief. No more lies. She didn't have to run from herself anymore. She reached for her daughter's hands again. "Take comfort in knowing I did what I did to protect you and your sister. For that, I have no regret."

There was no time to say more. The guard came and tried to take Gabrielle away. She refused to let go of Hélène's hands. Hélène held on as well. With a snort of impatience, he snatched at their fingers, prying them apart with brute force.

He dragged Gabrielle away.

"Maman." She reached to Hélène.

Hélène reached to her, seeing the beloved child she'd borne in that tortured, twisted face of grief. The perfect little baby that had slept through the night almost from the start.

And then, the room was empty, her hand still reaching for Gabrielle. The sound of muttered, angry voices mingled with her own heavy breathing.

Alone now, she let out a choked sound, half gasp, half cry. There would be no escape, no salvation for her body, only her soul. Her legs gave way, and she fell to the cot, landing with a thud. She tipped to her side. There was a shuffle of fabric as she shifted and laid down her head. She tried to heave herself up, but her body wouldn't cooperate. Her teeth chattered.

She lay there for hours, praying for mercy until the fat full moon was high in the sky.

The voices sounded again, closer this time. Her name. Spoken in guttural German. Then, "You will come with me, now."

She looked into the eyes of Detective Mueller. Thin blue slits filled with purpose. He led her outside, to the back of the building. Cold air slapped her face, an angry, icy draft.

It is finished.

Chapter Forty-Five

GABRIELLE

By the time Gabrielle was dragged away from her mother and shoved into the main portion of the police station, Mueller was gone. Since he'd driven her to town, she was forced to walk home in the dark. Because it was past curfew, she kept to the shadows. She arrived at the château with sore feet, a heavy heart and a desperate need to be alone. How ironic, when once she'd thought of her loneliness as a curse.

Not tonight. She wanted solitude to grieve and to mourn and to pray for her mother's flight across the border. She also wanted to review everything she'd learned about the man who called himself Wolfgang Mueller. He also called himself a friend.

Gabrielle had never been one for blind faith.

Which was why she veered off to the wine cellar instead of going straight to the château. She moved quickly through the corridors, blinking past the gloom. At the fake wall, she stopped, frozen, her breath ragged in her throat. Weber was gone. His weapon had been removed. The hole in the wall was patched, the glass and debris swept away. But, most telling of all, the wine barrel Mueller had tied the lieutenant to was missing. All she had to do was think back over her own resistance work to understand what had happened to the SS officer.

She turned to go, then stopped. There, atop another wine barrel, was the page from Josephine's journal, folded, with a new message penned in bold, masculine strokes. Deep inside her head, she heard Mueller's unaccented French say the words as she read them. *I brake the jaws of the wicked, and plucked the spoil out of his teeth. Job 29:17*

Warmth overtook her limbs and the remaining scraps of doubt fell away. Wolfgang Mueller was, indeed, a friend. A man she could trust. Gabrielle was not alone. And no one could ever know the truth.

With surprisingly steady hands, she tucked the paper in her pocket, promising herself she would read it again in her room. But first, she had one final stop. One final goodbye to say. The journey required considerable stealth. As she made her way to her family's private cemetery, tears threatened. She blinked them back. *Not yet,* she told herself. *Do not cry yet.*

At Benoit's grave, she pressed her forehead to the headstone and, finally, unashamedly, let the tears flow. "I love you, Benoit. I will always love you. You were the boy of my childhood, the husband of my youth and the very essence of the woman I am today. You will be with me, always." She placed a hand over her heart. "I will never forget you. But it's time. I must let you go."

The wind picked up, brushing across her wet cheeks. "Goodbye, Benoit." Peace filled the ache in her soul. "Goodbye, my love. Goodbye."

She hardly remembered returning home or entering the

château. She desperately wanted solitude, more now than before, but was forced to set it aside when a weeping Paulette met her in the kitchen. The girl looked positively stricken. "They know Maman's secret," she wailed. "And it's all my fault."

Gabrielle was in no mood to placate an overwrought Paulette. She was silent a moment, a ball of rage and disappointment rolling in her stomach. She didn't want to look at her sister and remember what she'd done to their mother. It took every ounce of fortitude not to grab the girl by the shoulders and shake her for her recklessness. "I know about Maman."

This brought on more tears and Paulette's weeping turned into big, gulping sobs. "I thought I could help her. I didn't mean to make things worse. You have to believe me, Gabrielle. I didn't mean to—"

"You never mean to, Paulette. That's the problem. You only think of yourself." Her voice was filled with years of resentment. Here her sister stood, mere hours after nearly destroying their mother, seeking absolution. Even knowing all was not lost, Gabrielle couldn't drum up the strength to ease her sister's guilt.

In that moment, she didn't know who she pitied more. Paulette, for her carelessness, or herself for her inability to follow the Lord's command and forgive the girl.

"You have to do something to fix this, Gabrielle. You have to save Maman from the camps."

Now she turns to me. The thought came with much resentment. This was her moment of truth. The moment when she placed her trust in a stranger over her own sister. "It's too late, Paulette. Nothing can be done. Maman is gone."

In that, at least, she told the truth.

"No!" Paulette fell to her knees, her guilt spewing from her eyes in genuine, gut-wrenching tears.

Gabrielle's own heart broke. Her anger and bitterness instantly dissolved, and she joined her sister on the floor. She took the girl into her arms and rocked her, letting her cry. Letting her mourn their mother. And, yes, letting her absorb the guilt of her actions.

The girl shook violently between sobs.

"I'm sorry, Paulette. I'm so very sorry." Gabrielle meant every word. "Hush, now."

"It's all my fault," she repeated. "How do I live with this shame? How?"

Gabrielle was crying, too, the sobs coming up through her chest. It was a day for tears and regrets. She pressed her wet cheek to the crown of Paulette's head. She could alleviate her sister's pain. All it would take was a few words. She didn't even have to use names. She could claim the resistance took their mother away. And reveal her own secret work for France.

The words were moving through her throat, coming to the tip of her tongue. She swallowed them back. Paulette could not be trusted. She'd proven that today. No amount of remorse could change what she'd done.

In later years, Gabrielle knew, when the war was over and she told family and friends about this decision to keep her sister in ignorance, she would have to face the shock and horror etched on their faces. She could save herself that heartache. It would be a simple matter of saying, *Maman is safe.*

She couldn't do it. She'd given her word to a man whose bravery humbled her. Whose life depended on her loyalty. A man who worked in the dark to serve the light.

There were other words she could give her sister, words that might help ease her guilt. But Gabrielle didn't say those, either. She simply held on to Paulette and let her cry.

Part Five

Part Two

Chapter Forty-Six

GABRIELLE

Paulette left for Paris a few months after Hélène disappeared. Gabrielle had wanted to send her away sooner, but a few tangles needed unraveling, the most problematic being Mademoiselle Ballard's initial reluctance. It had taken several conversations and a book of Paulette's sketches to convince the woman to agree. The rest of the details fell into place from there. Then, on a rainy afternoon in November of 1942, Gabrielle escorted her sister to the train station.

Their parting was stilted. There was no more sobbing on Paulette's part. No conversation from either of them. Nothing but the wind striking their faces, the hot steam pouring out of the locomotive's engine, and the grinding of gears as the train pulled to a stop.

Gabrielle offered no words of advice to her sister as they stood huddled together under the shelter of her umbrella. Paulette didn't ask for any.

"You will let me know once you arrive at Mademoiselle's apartment?"

From beneath her hat, Paulette's eyes slipped past her, brushed over the train, then slid back. "I'll get word to you, yes."

There was nothing more to say. The girl needed to leave. She'd made terrible choices, and had nearly ruined them all, and now their mother was gone. Gabrielle needed to forgive Paulette. She knew this in her heart, as sure as her Christian faith dictated. She also knew, as she stared at the bent head and hunched shoulders, that sending her sister to Paris was the best solution for their family.

And still, saying goodbye was not as easy as she'd expected. Surely, she could give Paulette some small word of hope. She opened her mouth to tell her sister that everything would be all right, that the war would be over soon, then immediately came to her senses. Lives were still at stake and Paulette must face the consequences of her actions. That was the underlying truth that had brought them to this train platform and the reality that Gabrielle had to say goodbye to another family member.

She reached for Paulette, not sure if she meant to pat her arm or tug her into a fierce hug. The blast of a high-pitched train whistle had her stepping back and doing neither. "Take care of yourself, sister."

Paulette stared at her hands and said nothing. In the ensuing silence, a porter took her bag, reviewed her ticket, then sent her to the proper section of the train. When she mounted the steps, Gabrielle lifted her hand in farewell. A pointless gesture. Paulette didn't spare a single glance backward.

Gabrielle left the train platform, her breath puffing before her, rain splattering at her feet, the tension of the past few weeks unspooling in her stomach. Back at the château, another coded telegram was waiting for her, the first in over a month.

Mueller wanted her to meet him in the wine cellar at midnight.

The air was eerily quiet as she entered the caves five minutes early and shut the door behind her. She moved through the corridors at a sedate pace, the racks of champagne standing like silent sentinels poised and ready to be called into service.

There was little sound beyond the strike of her heels to the limestone, the drip, drip, dripping of water from a small fracture in the ceiling. The crackling of electricity through frayed wires. Gabrielle tried to picture her ancestors making this same trek through the labyrinth of hallways. But her mind wouldn't conjure up the images, Instead, it brought her to the night she'd taken her first step in her personal battle against the Nazis.

At first, she'd waged war for the future of the champagne house and preservation of her family's legacy. Her actions had been driven by the memory of the ones they'd lost and her love for the women in her home as well as the people they employed. With the German invasion, Gabrielle's battle had become simpler, and yet somehow weightier, bigger than herself, than the champagne house, than even France. A single life saved was reward enough.

Now, another purpose, a new calling, an alliance with a man who wore the enemy's uniform. He'd taken the name Wolfgang. *Der wolf.* Fitting, after all. She'd thought him a predator. But no, he was the other kind of wolf. A protector. The alpha male, willing to sacrifice himself for the survival of his pack.

Gabrielle came to the end of the wine cellar and stopped when she saw the lone figure leaning against the makeshift wall. Something moved in her chest, and she suddenly felt light-headed, the quick jolt of pleasure as unexpected as the fast beating of her heart.

She forced her feet to stay in motion, each step accomplished without conscious thought. She watched him watch her, his look soft and full of masculine appreciation. She didn't ask how he'd gotten past the locked door at the cave's entrance. Some secrets didn't need solving. "I received your message."

"I tried to stay away," he said, still lounging against the wall, looking deceptively casual. "For your safety, as well as your family's."

"I'm pleased you lost the battle."

There were no more words between them for several long seconds, their individual breathing punctuation to an otherwise profound silence.

"It's impossible," he said, and not for the first time in this hallowed space. "This." He waved a hand between them. "Us." Another wave, then he was no longer leaning, but standing tall and coming away from the wall. "It cannot be. It will not happen."

She swallowed, aching for what they couldn't have. "No, it will not. It cannot."

"Another lifetime. Perhaps then," he said, leaning forward, close enough now for her to inhale the scent of sandalwood and leather. "Or perhaps in a different world, at a different time in history, it would have been conceivable."

The ground shifted beneath her feet. She felt cold to her center and there was a strange twist in her stomach. "But not now," she said, finishing his thought for him.

He nodded and his face changed, as if he had pulled away a mask, leaving his features bare of the subterfuge and lies that kept him alive. This was a man, who had a heart for a woman. To know and accept that she was that woman, that she brought out his truth, it slayed her.

She'd been prepared never to find love again.

She had not been prepared for him.

Nothing stood between them now, nothing but a foot of

air. And a war. And a duty to a higher calling. Silent promises passed between them, none of which they would say aloud. It was enough for Gabrielle to know what might have been.

He was talking again and shifting the tone of their conversation. Whatever moment had passed between them was gone. "Von Schmidt was located in Portugal this morning."

"He ran off, after all." She tried not to show how furious she was at this news. Her mother had been suspected in a murder that had never taken place.

"The man was not so cunning, or so smart. He did not try very hard to cover his tracks. The arrogant mistake has sealed his fate."

The arrogant mistake. Yes, she could believe it of the man who'd seized her home and made demands on her family, the greatest of her mother.

"He is currently en route to Berlin, where he will be tried for treason."

"He lives to face trial, while my mother has been forced to disappear." Her bitterness bounced off the chalky walls. *Had Mueller waited to arrest her mother...*

The thought had no easy conclusion. Regardless of what they knew now, von Schmidt had been a high-ranking official in the Wehrmacht. His disappearance would have required retribution. Had Mueller not arrested her mother, someone else in the Gestapo would have. Paulette would have gone to her lover. The sequence of events would have been the same, with one exception. Had anyone other than Mueller arrested her mother, Hélène would have been sent to her death.

Gabrielle could see God's hand in this. His providence. "Will you tell me what happened to my mother?"

He hesitated but for a second. "She is safe."

"Can you tell me where she is?"

"The details are better left unspoken."

Gabrielle let out a shaky breath, accepting the need for her to stay in ignorance. This man risked much for her and her family. Humbled, and more than a little awed, she allowed herself to think of a time when they could meet again, without the war between them. Then shut the possibility deep within her heart. "What happens next?"

He gazed at her without expression, though she felt strong resolve in him. "I have been called back to Berlin, to oversee von Schmidt's arraignment and trial." There was a hardness in his voice that reminded her too much of his alter ego. "I leave at daybreak."

"So soon?" She recognized the feeling of loss in her chest. She was no stranger to the sensation. Another man taken from her by war.

"My stellar police work has caught the attention of Heinrich Himmler himself. He is eager to meet me." His tone held a trace of bitterness, but was replaced with resolve. "I will soon be deeply embedded at the very seat of Nazi power."

Detective Wolfgang Mueller would be feet away from one of Hitler's most trusted accomplices, perhaps even the führer himself. Because of her. And the journal entry she'd given him. A boon for the Allies, but also very, very dangerous.

"I am here to say good—"

"*Non*, do not say the word." Reaching up, she touched his lips, lingered less than a second, then dropped her hand. "This is not an end. It is simply a pause. One day, this war will be over, and we will meet again."

"I'll find a way back to you," he vowed.

"However long it takes, I will be here, waiting." The words were as true as her feelings. So strong. So quickly changed. No, not changed, revealed. Illuminated.

Uncovered.

They stood silent, staring hard, breathing harder. Gabrielle could not find tears for this parting. Her sorrow wedged too deep for weeping. She hardly knew this man, and yet, in her heart, she accepted that he was her greatest ally in the war. They would live separate lives, for the good of others, connected only through memory and the silent promises neither dared to speak aloud, even in this private, intimate moment.

"Stay alive," she said.

And then, they were in each other's arms and his head was lowering to hers and what had seemed complicated seconds before was suddenly very, very simple. Separate, but together. The kiss lasted no longer than three beats of her heart. He set her away from him but kept his hands on her waist, and his gaze locked with hers. "I will pray for you."

"We will pray for each other. I want to lift you up by name." She cupped the sculpted lines of his cheek. "Will you trust me enough to leave that small piece of yourself in my care?"

He took her hand, pressed a kiss to her palm. "My name is Richard. Richard Doyle."

So very British, she thought, so perfectly suited to the man standing before her with such tenderness in his eyes.

Again, sorrow and hope shared equal space in her heart. She touched his lips and then pressed a kiss to where her fingertips had been. "I will pray for you," she said. "Richard."

Chapter Forty-Seven

GABRIELLE

The war waged on. The people of Champagne slowly starved under their Nazi oppressors. Gabrielle became responsible for finding provisions, both for her family and, when possible, for the resistance.

Not long after Richard left for Berlin, she received word via a series of coded messages that her mother had arrived in America and was living with her father in New York. Paulette stayed in Paris, while Gabrielle took full control of Château Fouché-LeBlanc.

The *weinführer*'s quotas continued putting a strain on resources. Working on Sundays became a way of life. The sacrifice of the Sabbath did not mean she didn't seek solace from God. Gabrielle spent many evenings in the LeBlanc chapel, alone and in prayer, her thoughts often straying to the man who'd saved her father-in-law and mother. Sometimes, she even opened her heart to possibilities of a future after the war. Hope, it would seem, was not dead in her heart.

Josephine spent most days in Marta's company. Gabrielle understood, but it still hurt to know her once-close relationship with her grandmother was forever changed. At least Grandmère was alive, and Gabrielle counted that as one of her most precious blessings.

On a bright morning in August, with the 1944 harvest looming, she took the familiar trek through the château, outside onto the terrace, down the stone steps. At the edge of the vineyard, she stopped and paused.

The vines strained against the wires that held their trunks steady and their grapes from skimming along the ground. Their bushy canopies were nearly black in the predawn light, a series of round, shadowy figures poised in the lapse between night and day.

A pair of birds whistled to one another. Their trills and gurgles combined to make a happy, harmonious melody. Gabrielle took the sound as a good omen. As she headed into the vineyard, the church bells began marking the top of the hour, seven strikes of clapper to bowl joined in perfect sync with the seven pings of her heart.

She didn't hear her name at first. "Gabrielle." Marta all but ran toward her, tears streaming down her face. "You must come back to the château. There is news from Paris."

"Has something happened to Paulette?"

"Non, *non.* Your sister is well, as far as I know. It's happening. The liberation of Paris. A full assault. The resistance has joined the battle and is working directly with the American and British forces." Marta reached for Gabrielle's hands. "This is it. The end of our suffering. The Germans will finally be thrown out of France."

The news only got better. Josephine, Gabrielle and Marta

congregated in the parlor to listen to General de Gaulle's triumphant speech. "…Paris liberated! Liberated by itself, liberated by its people with the help of the French armies, with the support and the help of all France, of the France that fights, of the only France, of the real France, of the eternal France!"

"It's over," Gabrielle whispered.

As de Gaulle continued his speech, she thought briefly of Richard Doyle, then set the memory of him aside and moved to sit beside Josephine. She took the frail, weathered hand. "Paris is free, Grandmère."

The eyes that turned to her were clouded with tears. "Reims will be next."

It took another fifteen days for her grandmother's words to come true. Reims wasn't liberated until the eighth day of September.

A week later, Paulette arrived home. Gabrielle greeted her at the door. Their reunion was no happier than their farewell.

The years had not been kind to her sister. Though the girl, now a woman, still held a strong resemblance to their mother, Paulette looked harder in the eyes, rail thin in the body, and her gaunt face was still filled with that heartbreaking mixture of guilt and grief.

Gabrielle suffered her own combination of guilt and grief. She'd done this to her sister, turned her into a shell of her former self. She would tell Paulette the truth now. All of it. As she'd told Josephine the day after Paris was liberated.

Over a meager serving of watery soup and moldy bread, Paulette spoke of their mother with immense sorrow. Not wishing to upset Josephine, Gabrielle waited until after the meal to make her confession. She found Paulette on the terrace, absently looking out over the vineyard, smoking a cigarette that smelled the same as their mother's brand. A tribute, perhaps, to the woman she thought lost to her forever. The scent gave Gabrielle a vague queasy feeling.

"You've taken up smoking," she said to ease them both into the difficult conversation.

"I took it up not long after I arrived in Paris." She studied the glowing tip. "I don't particularly enjoy it."

"Yet you smoke anyway."

Paulette shrugged, the gesture reminiscent of their mother at her most carefree. "War will do that to a person. It will make you turn to small vices to get through another day."

The bitterness was new, as was the rough, indifferent air that could not be faked. Gone was the passion for life that had once defined her sister. There was nothing of the selfish, flirtatious girl left. *And it is partly my fault.*

No, Gabrielle realized, this conversation would not be easy. "I have something to tell you about Maman."

Before she lost her nerve, she told her story. She held nothing back, no detail, no vital piece of information. She started with von Schmidt's disappearance. Their mother's arrest, Lieutenant Weber coming upon her in the wine cellar, his attempt to strangle her, the champagne bottle she'd cracked over his head to halt his assault. Then, Detective Mueller's arrival on the scene, his revelations and his vow to escort Hélène safely across the border.

Paulette took a step back, the sound of her gasp as loud as a slap.

"Why are you telling me these lies?" she demanded, a catch in her voice. All of a sudden, she looked every bit the young ingénue she'd once been, a mosaic of hope and fear in her eyes.

"They aren't lies, Paulette. Maman is alive and living in New York."

"Alive. In New York. All this time." As if needing a moment to process what she'd just heard, Paulette glanced out over the moonlit vineyard. She attempted to take a pull from her cigarette. But her hands shook violently, and she couldn't fit the end between her lips. After three failed attempts, she gave up. "You knew, all along, you knew the truth. You knew Maman was safe. And you kept it from me?"

"*Oui.*"

"When I came home from the police station, devastated and blaming myself, you knew. On the train platform the day I went to Paris, you knew."

"I knew."

Paulette hurled herself across the space between them, her hands flaying, scratching at her face, connecting only once before Gabrielle caught her wrists and yanked away from the curled fingernails digging at the empty air. "Calm yourself."

The words only made her sister battle harder. She was no match for Gabrielle. She had the benefit of two inches and five extra pounds on the girl.

"You let me go to Paris thinking Maman was dead. You knew I blamed myself. And you said nothing."

Gabrielle's reply was harsh, forced out between her clenched teeth. "You'd already made too many mistakes for me to trust you with the truth."

"You blame this on me? You made the choice to lie, yet somehow it is my fault." Paulette wrenched her hands free. "I have never hated you more than I do at this moment. I will never forgive you, Gabrielle. Never."

She didn't blame her sister for her hate, or her lack of forgiveness. She could only hope in time, Paulette would find it in her heart to understand why she'd withheld the truth from her. "When Maman comes home—"

"Home?" Paulette's laugh was full of wretched anger. "She can never come home. She was a collaborator. Do you know what that means? Do you know what they are doing to women like her in Paris?"

Gabrielle blinked, too stunned by her sister's rage to give a response.

"They shave their heads and take them through the streets to be pelted with garbage and hurled with insults. Then they arrest them for treason and then they… *Non*," she snarled, her face draining of color. "Maman can never return to France."

"What is all this shouting?" Josephine came to stand between the sisters. She glanced from Paulette's furious expression to Gabrielle. "This is no way to welcome your sister home."

"She is not my sister." Paulette glared at the older woman. "This is not my home."

"You are a LeBlanc," Josephine said firmly, in the voice of the family matriarch. "You are the last of us. The champagne house, the vineyard, this château—they will all be yours someday."

"This is not my home," Paulette said again, and her expression went brutally hard.

Gabrielle reached for her. "Paulette—"

"Do not touch me." She took a step back, then turned her wrath onto Josephine. "You can keep your champagne house and your precious vineyard. You can keep your legacy. I don't want it. May it die with you and may that day come soon."

Gabrielle gasped at the venom in her sister's tone. "You don't mean that, Paulette."

"I am not the liar here. That honor is all yours."

She had no defense. "I'm sorry, Paulette."

"I'm not. I will go back to Paris. *Non*, I will go to New York. To Maman." She headed to the château, then whirled around to face Gabrielle. "I choose exile over this vineyard.

This house. Over you. And even you." She stabbed a finger at Josephine. "You have always loved Gabrielle best."

Head high, eyes dry, Paulette left the terrace. Gabrielle and Josephine stood frozen in the aftermath of her storm.

"She is angry and in shock," Josephine said softly. "She will forgive us in time."

"I don't think she will, Grandmère." A clock chimed the top of the hour. "I fear we have lost her forever."

"Do not give up hope. Time is a great healer."

By silent agreement, they turned to look out over the vineyard and the legacy they'd built that Paulette had so callously dismissed. The moon cast its silvery light over the windblown vines. The champagne house loomed large in the distance.

Gabrielle could not find her joy. The LeBlanc women had survived the war, but at great cost. "We are alive," she said, desperate to take comfort in that truth. "We prevailed."

"Was there any doubt?" Josephine patted her arm. "A thousand German soldiers are not equal to one LeBlanc woman."

Struggling for control, Gabrielle let out a breath. "We are the last of our family. We will rise from the ashes of this war and create fine champagne, the best the world has ever tasted."

Josephine's eyes closed, as if working through a moment of pain, then she nodded. "*Oui*, Gabrielle. With the sovereign Lord as our guide, we will do all that, and more."

All that, and more. So much more. They would rebuild, with the champagne Gabrielle had hidden on a dark, rainy night on the eve of war.

Chapter Forty-Eight

GABRIELLE

7 May 1945

Gabrielle entered the château, her spirits still high after rejoicing in the streets of Reims with her fellow *Champenois*. The war was officially over. After five long years of Nazi occupation, the end had taken less than ten minutes. With a sweep of pens to paper, top-ranking officials from the Allied and German forces signed the surrender documents in the Reims school building where the American General Dwight Eisenhower had set up his temporary "war room."

How fitting that the enemy was forced to surrender in a city where they'd caused such pain and death, not only during the current war but also the one before. Gabrielle was still thinking about poetic justice when Marta peered around the corner. "You look happy, *chère*."

"It's been a good day."

Marta's smile came fast and true. "A very good day." She turned to go, then paused.

"Was there something else?" Gabrielle asked.

"A letter, from New York. It arrived while you were gone. Your grandmother is reading it now. You will want to hear the news, I think."

There were countless questions on her tongue, but the housekeeper was no longer standing in the doorway. A clock chimed from somewhere in the house, startling Gabrielle into motion. She stepped into the kitchen. And froze.

Her grandmother sat at the scarred table in the center of the room, head bent over a single sheet of paper. She'd seen her in this same posture nearly six years ago. The war had ravaged her, body and mind and soul, and she looked every bit a woman in her eighties. Gabrielle cleared her throat. "Marta tells me we received a letter from New York. Is it from Maman?"

Faded blue eyes rolled up to meet hers. "Ah, *ma chère*, come. Sit. And I will read what your mother has to say."

The letter itself was short, not more than a page and a half. It started with a salutation, and a brief summary of Hélène's life in New York. "We had a lovely spring," Josephine read. "There was much celebration when news arrived of Germany's imminent surrender." She paused, her forehead creased by a frown as if trying to make sense of the scene. "Paulette is more herself these days. She sleeps better now and is only plagued with the occasional nightmare."

Josephine sighed, the sound heavy and full of sadness. Marta sat beside her and patted her arm. "It is to be expected. The girl had a rough time during the war."

"I weep for her."

"We all do."

Feeling her own tears welling, Gabrielle carefully took the

letter from her grandmother and, after scanning the page, finished reading the rest. "The skills Paulette learned in Paris have put me in mind of an idea. We plan to open our own little boutique in Manhattan next autumn. With my sense of style and her creativity, we just might make a go of it."

I pray you succeed, Maman.

She'd nearly made it to the end of the letter when the sound of pounding on the front door cut her off. All three women jumped at the noise. Marta started to rise. Gabrielle said, "Let me."

It was an odd hour for visitors, even considering the joyful events of the day. Allied forces were everywhere and…

Something like hope moved through her. Her hands shook as she freed the lock then reached for the handle. The door creaked on its hinges and seemed to want to stick as she tugged. Two men stood on her doorstep, a British soldier. And…

"Papa!" Gabrielle yanked her father-in-law into her arms. He was older, and thinner, and much smaller in the shoulders, but he was alive. "Oh, Papa, you made it home." The words hitched in her throat. "Are you well? Let me have a look at you."

She stepped back and smiled into the dear, dear face. Max sighed, a slow lifting and lowering of his shoulders, then opened his arms as if to let her have a nice, long look at him.

So many emotions poured through her—shock, happiness, relief. "I feared we would never see each other again. But here you are."

"It's good to see you, *ma fille*."

"I have so much I want to ask. How have you been? *Where* have you been?" Once the words started tumbling out of her mouth, she couldn't stop them. "How did you get home?"

"There will be plenty of time for answers. But first, there is someone I wish for you to meet. The man who saved my life." He motioned to his companion. "Gabrielle, meet my friend from the British army."

The soldier stepped forward. "*Bon soir*, Gabrielle."

It required several seconds to place the man in the uniform of the British army. Then, he took off his hat and the wind tousled his hair and she knew him in an instant. Her lungs stopped working. Her heart quit beating. "Richard," she said, deaf but for the roar in her ears.

His vitality hadn't dimmed. He looked solid and real and alive. He'd survived the war and she couldn't stop staring. He seemed plagued with the same affliction.

Max cleared his throat. "I wonder, Gabrielle, if perhaps your grandmother is at home?"

Eyes still on Richard, she nodded. "You'll find her in the kitchen with Marta."

"I know the way." Max shuffled past her, pausing only a second to kiss her cheek and whisper, "He's a good man, as fine as my Benoit, and certainly as brave."

Her father-in-law's words were tantamount to a blessing.

How often she'd played this reunion in her mind, and still, she couldn't stop staring.

Richard broke the silence first. "May I come in?"

"I… Yes. Please. Come in. Come. Come."

He moved across the threshold, looking nothing like the Gestapo agent he'd once been and everything like the brave man Max claimed.

Gabrielle shut the door behind him, wondering if he'd been at the signing, not sure that it mattered. All that truly mattered was that he was alive. And looking well. There was much to say. But for now, all she wanted to do was take him in with her eyes. The broad shoulders, and the blue-blue eyes that had presented themselves in her dreams many nights since his departure.

With no more pretense, deception or war between them the mood should have been light. The air seemed to pulse with tension.

"This is one of the reasons I came." He indicated the bottle he held in his hand.

The glass was streaked with dust and caked with mud in several places, but Gabrielle easily read the label. "The 1928 I sent to Berlin."

"I recovered every case. Apparently, Hitler was not much of a champagne connoisseur. He seized the wine out of greed." He placed the bottle in his palm, his gaze narrowing over the label. "I only brought this one bottle with me. The others will be delivered later in the week, along with the rest of your champagne, and the thousands of cases stolen from your neighbors."

"It's a blessing you found even one bottle. Thank you." The words didn't seem enough.

"I'm afraid the news I come bearing isn't all good."

She waited.

"By the time von Schmidt was captured, he'd already sold most of the valuables he stole from your family. I have the list of missing items and have begun making inquiries. I will recover what I can, but it's a tangle. It may take years."

"What are a few years?" She surprised herself with the certainty in her voice. "When I am so very good at waiting."

He looked at her for a long moment, and she watched the wariness drain from his features. Then his face broke into a smile. "And I'm very good at keeping my promises."

She took the bottle from him, set it on a nearby table, then placed her hand on his heart. "Welcome back, Richard."

He wrapped her in his arms. Promises were made. Promises they would have a lifetime to keep. And then they kissed. Long and deep and when they pulled apart they both acknowledged that the spark of attraction was stronger now than when they'd last met.

"I think it's time my grandmother met my friend Richard Doyle." She reclaimed the champagne bottle, took his arm and led him through the château.

It was Josephine's idea to open the champagne. Gabrielle found the glasses. Richard pulled the cork and poured the liquid. A brilliant, bubbling gold. They toasted to the future.

Outside, church bells rang. The high-pitched peals rolled through the village, across the vineyard, summoning workers home, families to their dinner tables and, inside the château on the hill, they called Gabrielle and Richard out into the night.

With the vineyard as his backdrop, moon and stars overhead, Richard took her hands. He pressed his lips to her right palm, then her left, then pulled away to gaze into her eyes. "I love you, Gabrielle. I felt the stirrings of it the first time I saw you. It only grew stronger from there."

She drew her hands free of his, gathering her thoughts. She would prefer never to think of their original meeting. But it would stand between them if they didn't speak of it now. "I wish I could say the same. It would not be true. Wolfgang Mueller was a chilling, fearsome man. I was terrified the first time we met."

"A calculated move on my part, and one of the many regrets I carry with me from the war. I can only offer you a contrite heart, and say I am sorry for the pain I caused you."

Absolution came easy to her lips. "I forgave you the night you told me your real name."

A look of uncertainty moved in his eyes. That moment of naked vulnerability touched her in ways mere words could never have done. "Tonight," she said, "we begin anew. No more façades. No more deception between us. No more lies, only truth and honesty."

"And the knowledge that together, we are better. Together—" he smiled, and oh, what a smile it was "—we are stronger."

"Together," she said, understanding his heart as if it were her own, "we are one."

She slid into his arms then. Once there, she knew only conviction. This man was her future. She would live out the rest of her days with him by her side. "This is when you're supposed to kiss me, Richard."

"Gladly." As his head came down to hers, Gabrielle lifted onto her toes, welcoming him into her life, on this, the first of many nights they would spend under the moon and stars, on the edge of the vineyard her family had tended for two hundred years. And, God willing, would tend for many— many—more to come.

★ ★ ★ ★ ★